Kiss *by* Kiss

MISSES OF MELBOURNE

BOOK 2

VICKI MILLIKEN

Bonnie May Books

Published in Australia by
Bonnie May Books

ABN 23 005 104 640
PO Box 937
Williamstown
MELBOURNE VICTORIA 3016
AUSTRALIA

vicki@vickimilliken.com
www.vickimilliken.com

First published in Australia 2021

National Library of Australia Cataloguing in Publication entry

A catalogue record for this book is available from the National Library of Australia

ISBN: 978-0-6487850-0-2 (paperback)
ISBN: 978-0-6487850-2-6 (epub)

Cover photography by Kolupaev (1920s style woman)
Cover layout and design by Pascal Han-Kwan
Layout and typesetting by Sophie White Design
Printed by Ingram Spark

For Courtney

CHAPTER 1

Friday 7 August 1925

On the surface, it was a typical Friday night. Couples rotating anticlockwise around the dancefloor, with hues of colour interspersed with the sombre tones of black and white. The band's tempo flowed freely – a jazz foxtrot. Sprays of wattle – feathery clumps of golden-yellow flowers – adorned the floor-to-ceiling columns and a lavish application of streamers decorated the gallery, punctuated with balloons in muted shades of blues and greens. But there was nothing typical about this Friday night.

Daniel Sinclair blamed his best mate. Alex had fallen for Daniel's sister, Eliza, and proposed less than twenty-four hours ago. *Where was the traitor?* No sign of him on the dancefloor. For years, they'd enjoyed the pleasures and freedoms of a bachelor lifestyle. The end had come quickly and without warning. Daniel sighed. He couldn't even contemplate bachelor shenanigans without his wingman.

So, where did that leave him? A fleeting image of his girlfriend tugged at his conscience. *Evelyn!* Was her absence the reason tonight's atmosphere held the appeal of flat champagne? Or was it the aftermath of the unparalleled enthusiasm of the past fortnight, when Birmingham's Danse Palais had played host to a program of nightly entertainments welcoming ten thousand American officers and sailors to Melbourne's shores? Like every good party, it had ended. The city had farewelled the fleet yesterday evening, amidst tears and cheers – depending on your sex.

Shunning the heady floral scents and the familiar scene of movement and colour, Daniel escaped onto one of the many balconies that studded the venue and took a fortifying breath of the crisp night air.

A flicker of movement caught his eye. The silhouette of tangled limbs on the neighbouring balcony. *Good for them.* At the sound of a low guttural growl, Daniel took one last look, intending to withdraw and allow the amorous couple their privacy. The woman arched her neck, and her swain began worshipping the length, low and slow. Her features, captured by a prism of light, caused him to draw breath. Her eyes widened in recognition as they locked with Daniel's. *Bec!*

His feet were moving before he gave thought to his actions. A boisterous group in the corner of the lounge area momentarily curtailed his speed. Ignoring the hearty jostling, he pushed firmly past them and crossed to the entrance of the adjacent balcony. When he dived through the curtain veil, Rebecca – Bec – Cross stood alone, arms crossed.

Daniel eyed the sprig of crushed wattle bloom secured to her dress. It was rising and falling in time with her short, shallow breaths. 'Are you all right?'

'Why wouldn't I be?'

'You —'

'What?'

'Looked like you needed ... extricating.' He'd been about to say *saving*, but this was Bec. *Miss Independent.*

Her sculpted brows rose in disbelief. 'I didn't and don't need your help.'

Daniel anchored his hands on his hips and stepped towards her. No one got under his skin like this woman. 'Truly, Bec? He was all over you. From where I was standing, you were being attacked by ... *an octopus.*'

'Argh! That's offensive. I'll never look at him the same way.'

'Good. I'm glad,' Daniel shot back, stretching his six-foot-one frame and levelling her with the sort of glare that shrivelled men – working men. But not Bec. She glared right back, her grey eyes smoking, the tip of her turned-up nose pointing towards him in defiance. 'What if you'd been caught?'

She leaned forward, rocking onto the balls of her feet. 'We were caught, thanks to you.'

Daniel took another step towards her, unsure how to handle her casual bravado.

'Your sense of timing needs work. Perhaps Jim could give you some pointers.'

Jim? Pointers?

Bec's gaze dropped to his lips before returning to his eyes. A haughty eyebrow raised the stakes.

Acting on pure impulse, his lips sought hers. He'd teach her a lesson.

Bec appeared to hesitate, as if assessing her choices and his intent. The tip of his tongue swept the seam that sealed her top and bottom lips together. She closed the distance, opening her mouth and laying siege to the inside of his mouth.

It was the type of kiss best described as an argument ... without words. Urgent, intense, electrifying. It was as if Bec was stuck on one speed.

His body hurtled into overdrive. But before he could settle into a rhythm, Bec was bracing her palms against his shoulders and putting distance between them.

Grazing his bottom lip with her teeth, she nipped it sharply, levelling him with a gaze cast from steel. 'I can take care of myself. I am not *your* responsibility, and you are not *my* protector.'

Daniel watched her whirl and sweep back through the curtains towards the ballroom. Snatches of the jazz melody 'It Had to Be You' mocked him, before the folds of dark-crimson velour cloistered him. Turning, he gripped the balcony railing, the stone cold beneath his fingers. *What on earth had possessed him to kiss Bec?* A groan escaped his throat. He felt ill-equipped to answer that at this moment.

Bec! Opinionated, sassy, and with such a smart mouth. A kissable mouth, as he'd discovered. She'd fired a quiver of arrows from those Cupid's-bow lips, and he'd been a willing target. An excellent markswoman. Daniel ran the tip of his tongue across his bottom lip. *Was that an indent?* When had she learned to do that? Had Jim taught her? Did it drive him crazy like it did Daniel?

Daniel groaned again, running his fingers through his sleek black hair. *Why Bec?* Her views contradicted everything he believed and were a source of persistent annoyance. Not quite the bane of his life, but close. And her intrigues were none of his business ... except ... she was his sister's best friend, and therefore fell under his protection. Not that she ever appreciated his efforts.

Daniel shook his head. So, to protect her, he'd kissed her – after remonstrating her behaviour with the American. *That made no sense.* Nothing was making sense, not his behaviour or hers. Bec wasn't a practised flirt – she had too much heart. *Of course she'd ever admit it.* Over the years, he'd observed her playfulness – although never with him – and boldness. Yes, that was the facet most on display with him.

So, why the flirtation with the American? He wasn't the man for her. Daniel couldn't have said how he knew that. He just did. The man who married Bec would need to be a titan, and there was no certainty that someone of that calibre even existed.

But why had she kissed him? And kiss him she had, he assured himself. She had been as invested as he. But her staying power needed some work – the kiss was over before it had even properly begun. Next time ... *My God! What was he thinking? There wouldn't be a next time.*

Daniel consulted his watch. Eleven o'clock. It had been a disturbing week, his mate's engagement to his sister only half of it. His application for promotion was not looking promising and his boss was acting oddly – never a good sign. Adjusting his collar and tie, Daniel made a snap decision to hunt down Alex. He needed a drink, and that was something best done in company. Surely his mate could leave Eliza's side for half an hour. Afterwards? Well, he'd let the night unfold and see where it took him.

Momentarily dazzled, Bec slowed her footsteps and focused on controlling her breathing. Her hasty retreat had catapulted her into the bright lights of one of the many lounge areas laid out across the Danse Palais. Aware of several curious glances, she coaxed her lips into an upward arc and her fingers to uncurl.

A quick survey revealed that the Birminghams – Mr and Mrs – were engaged on the far side of the dancefloor. Petting was frowned upon and could have patrons removed from the venue if they were discovered. And Bec had taken part in two bouts this evening. *A record.*

What on earth had possessed her to kiss Daniel? He was arrogant and held far too many opinions. Their kiss had certainly put a stop to hearing any more of those – at least for tonight. A young man approached her, an invitation on his lips, and she realised her smile must have turned triumphant. Or perhaps her indiscretions were written on her face. With a shake of her head, Bec escaped the lounge, skirting the edge of the dancefloor, her heels tapping on the polished timber.

The kiss with Daniel weighed heavy in her thoughts. Deciding to be honest with herself, Bec acknowledged that she'd wanted to kiss him, to be kissed by him from the moment Eliza had introduced them four years ago. At the time, the immediacy of the thought had shaken her. As had his attitude. He'd been too sure of himself. Although, whether this was something she'd detected during their initial conversation or judged from his reputation with women, she couldn't say for sure. In any case, she'd categorised him as dangerous – both to her equilibrium and her feminist ideals – and dismissed him. He was a player. *And she was not one to be played.* So, she became, in his eyes, his sister's annoying best friend. It was something she took pains to cultivate. It wasn't hard; Daniel's arrogance would try the patience of a saint.

She and he were completely unsuited. Daniel thought a woman's place was as a wife and child bearer, and as such she should be grateful for the protection of her husband. And his many girlfriends seemed to agree with him. Simpering ninnies, the lot of them.

Bec wasn't against marriage – she hoped to marry before she abandoned her twenties – but she wanted one that recognised her as an equal partner. And apart from her parents', she'd seen little evidence of marriage being anything other than a sacrifice of independence for respectability or social status. *A pity Daniel was so darned good-looking, and now she knew ... a divine kisser.*

A change of tempo announced the start of Birmingham's progressive dance set. Not wishing to be partnered, she increased her pace, not stopping until she reached the steps that led to the gallery overlooking the dancefloor. A few minutes of respite was what she needed.

Why tonight? She wouldn't deny it hadn't been enjoyable, quenching her thirst after years of restraint. Bec giggled. She was turning this into an episode of biblical proportions. It was one brief kiss. And while he may have started it, she'd finished it. Bec smirked. *Not the usual reaction he got, she'd bet.*

At the top of the stairs, she turned left, drifting through the rows until she found the perfect seat from which to see but not to be seen.

Eliza was not in sight. Bec didn't know whether to be grateful or aggrieved. She'd come tonight at her friend's request. Alex Heaton, a 1920s poster boy for masculinity, had proposed to Eliza the night before in his suite at the Federal hotel. Although, it hadn't been the only event to occur there if Eliza's glow and Alex's smirk were anything to go by.

Bec had arrived at the hotel a few minutes after Daniel had stormed into the foyer, demanding to speak with Alex. The duty manager had made discreet enquiries by telephone before connecting them to Alex's room. Upon learning that his sister and best friend were unable to join them for another half an hour, Daniel had become incensed, requiring Bec to intervene. Corralling Daniel in a private sitting room, with the kind assistance of the manager, she'd been vastly entertained firstly by an outburst of anger, followed by pacing and later by a show of manly back slapping and hugs on hearing the news of the couple's engagement.

Where was she? Another scan of the dancefloor failed to locate her. Alex was missing, too. Bec pursed her lips, her thoughts turning gloomy. She was thrilled for her best friend. Hell, she'd masterminded the whole thing. But already Eliza was less available, Alex proving opportunistic in securing an unfair allocation of her friend's time and energies. *And after only twenty-four hours.*

Bec sat and leaned her chin atop her hands on the gallery rail, idly counting the number of men sporting patches of thinning hair below. She sighed. *Was this what Friday nights were to become?* Dancing the night away with balding men; feigning interest in social trifles, upcoming balls and dances; anticipating spring fabrics and fashions? All without the shared confidences of a best friend? *The future looked dull.* She hated that a substantial dose of self-pity had replaced her jaunty self-confidence. Even counting her blessings –

she was a working woman, exercising her independence and freedom, unfettered by tradition or convention – failed to spark her mood.

Bec raised her gaze to the other side of the horseshoe-shaped gallery. Her latest admirer, Jim Johnson, saluted her before returning to his conversation. He was one of the American naval officers who had captivated Melbourne over the last fortnight. From their first introduction at the Lord Mayor's Ball to welcome the officers of the fleet, they'd slipped into an easy, light-hearted flirtation. This was despite him being the target of Bec's accounts of the dangers of drop bears and the use of boomerangs to round up small children.

Jim had remained behind when the fleet sailed, at the direction of the admiral, to assist the American Consulate in dealing with the men who had missed their ships. Only a warrant officer could arrest Americans on foreign soil, although Jim had confided that he hoped it didn't come to that. Twelve of the missing twenty-two had self-reported and were leaving tomorrow night – setting sail on the Destroyer *Chase*. He was committed to locating the remaining ten, as desertion from the United States Navy carried serious implications.

They'd sure had some fun – he was very tasty, easy on the eye and a good, if somewhat *enthusiastic*, kisser. Still, comparing his expertise to an eight-armed mollusc seemed a tad exaggerated. *And how would Daniel know, anyway? Maybe that's how Evelyn kissed.*

Bec giggled again and then brightened. Jim was here until the end of the month – another three weeks – and despite her assertion to Daniel that she'd never be able to look at him again, she was planning on doing more than that. Jim was a safe and attractive diversion. She didn't intend to come to a marriage ignorant of the art of kissing and petting – at least above the waist. She was twenty-five, and a woman's education needed to be comprehensive in this day and age.

A rustle of fabric snapped her out of her reverie, and Eliza slid into the seat beside her. 'No need to ask what you've been doing,' said Bec with a grin, taking in Eliza's flushed face and swollen lips.

Eliza ignored her observation. 'Why are you hiding up here?'

'I had an unfortunate encounter with your brother, and I'm cooling my temper before re-entering the throng.'

'Ah, yes, I heard part of your exchange while Alex and I were ... star gazing.'

Bec swallowed. 'Um ... how much did you hear?'

'Enough,' said Eliza, bumping her shoulder. 'An argument without words. A *highly* effective technique.'

Bec pretended to study the orchestra. They appeared to hover, silhouetted against a night sky studded with stars, no doubt the result of some clever lighting. 'It was a mistake. I don't know what came over either of us.'

'Hmm.'

'We don't even like each other.'

'Hmm.'

'He's not my type.'

'Hmm.'

'Good, I'm glad we've cleared that up,' said Bec, turning to face her friend and forcing herself to make eye contact.

Eliza nodded. 'You're unsettled. Having successfully stage-managed my engagement, you're at a loose end. Daniel was simply ... let's call it collateral, in the wrong place at the wrong time. And your reaction resulted from his inability to reserve his opinion.'

Bec smiled. *Yes, that summed things up nicely.*

'I think you need a new project.'

When had Eliza become so intuitive? That was exactly what was missing. Problems demanding solutions, friends and causes in need were her speciality. 'Any ideas?'

'No. But it needs to be something you can sink your teeth into.'

Bec suppressed a chuckle, ignoring her friend's quizzical look and allowing her gaze to rest on the dancing tableau below. She guessed Eliza didn't mean Daniel's bottom lip.

As if she'd called him by name, he appeared on the dancefloor below. A head of patent-leather hair tilted to catch the conversation of the woman he was partnering in a waltz. Her autumn-coloured tresses swept back, revealing an animated face. *He usually prefers brunettes.* Surprised she even knew that, Bec pulled her thoughts into order. Had she been unconsciously cataloguing his preferences all these years?

Well, remember this, she scolded her subconscious, *his lips come as part of a package, one you've never been tempted to buy into before.* Their differences were too great to be papered over by one kiss. *'Humph!'* Bec ignored Eliza's surprised expression. It would take many more than one.

CHAPTER 2

Monday 10 August 1925

Bec smiled as the YWCA's Melbourne headquarters came into view. It was a handsome building of red brick, ribbed with horizontal bands of cream trim. The morning sun, less sleepy in late winter, gilded the tip of the steeple on the corner tower. Energy percolated through Bec's veins. The organisation represented a haven for friendship, community and a path to self-determination for many women and girls – including her.

Passing through the entrance, Bec navigated around four young women in an animated discussion, unaware they were taking up the width of the corridor, and narrowly missed a delivery man and his trolley teetering with fresh fruit and vegetables destined for the kitchens.

In contrast, the office she shared with her boss, Elsie Timms, the Employment and Vocational Secretary, was calm. Files lay where she'd left them on Friday afternoon, stacked on her desk, patiently awaiting her attention.

Bec loved her work, matching those seeking jobs with positions. Every placement instilled a sense that she was making a real difference in the lives of the women and their situations. Although, it still irked her that many looked upon their employment as a stopgap between school and married life, and they didn't make the most of protecting or advancing their opportunities.

Elsie encouraged her to measure progress by the number that didn't. Bec grudgingly acknowledged that these were increasing – she herself had no intention of surrendering her position after marriage. She just wished it would happen faster.

Elsie eddied through the door mid-morning, her enthusiasm so palpable, Bec was surprised her wheat-coloured locks were not standing on end.

'I have news.'

Mondays always meant news. The department heads met first thing to plan out their week and review operations, projects and finances.

'I nominated you for our Great Debate.' Bec's confusion must have shown as Elsie explained, 'As one of the speakers. It'll be the jewel in this year's fundraising campaign.'

'Ah ... thank you,' Bec hedged. She'd never felt comfortable in front of an audience – school concerts had been particularly unnerving. She'd been lucky that she was tall and always dispatched to the back row of any performance. But this time, there'd be no hiding. Already her pulse was drumming from the mere thought of taking centrestage.

'Are you up for it?' Elsie asked from her now seated position, sandwiched between two vertical filing cabinets.

Had Elsie sensed her reluctance? Her face was probably a billboard of mixed emotions. 'Of course! Why wouldn't I be?'

'Those of a more conservative bent might consider the topic contentious.'

Daniel's face popped into Bec's mind.

Elsie tapped the end of her pencil against her lips. 'You may be subject to criticism. Not everyone understands that debating is just another form of theatre.'

Bec faced Elsie's keen regard without flinching, hands braced on her knees. 'I don't care. It'll be exciting.' The last she'd added more to convince herself than Elsie. She straightened her spine. 'What's the topic?'

'It's a mouthful,' said Elsie, reaching around for a piece of paper under her blotter to read, '... *the emotional, intellectual and physical demands of the role of tram conductor are not conducive to the employment of women.*'

Bec forgot her hesitation. Committing to a public debate on the scope of work from which women could choose felt right. It was nonsensical that the Melbourne and Metropolitan Tramways Board restricted women from being employed as conductors. The bus companies had no such qualms. She could do this. She *would* do this.

Bec rummaged around her desk, emerging triumphant, a dog-eared newspaper clipping clutched in her hand. 'Humph. Have you read that article in *The Age*? Of our role in the Great War? I quote, "... *there was scarcely a masculine job that feminine brains and hands could not and did not accomplish with skill inferior to none* ..." and that, from the American Ambassador in London – a man!'

'Yes, dear. You don't need to convince me. But the

views you express, as part of the debate, will reflect on our organisation, so you may need to temper your expression. I haven't seen the final list, but I imagine it will contain several strong personalities ... not unlike yourself.'

Was Elsie criticising her? Bec's gaze skittered to the delicate fronds of the potted fern beside her and counted to ten. She watched as dust mites danced among the green leaflets, energised by the sunlight filtering through the window.

Her forthright views and ideas on workplace success for women were well known by her colleagues at the Y, and by family and friends. Elsie had joked after she'd interviewed an applicant once that Bec's zeal had probably driven the young woman to return home and devote herself to perfecting household duties, the opposite of what she'd intended. Ever since, she'd tried to temper her enthusiasm ... when she remembered.

From the corner of her eye, Bec saw Elsie rise and close the door that linked their office with the main corridor. Silence replaced the daytime hum of voices and activity.

Bec was vocal about removing the barriers that narrowed the employment choices for women, be they single, married or widowed. Society still held an expectation that women would step aside and return to domestic duties, or be content aspiring to marriage as their highest goal. It made her blood boil. *Fifty, fifty-one* ... counting to ten was overrated.

Elsie came to stand in front of her. 'Breathe, dear. You look like you're about to explode.'

Bec took a noisy breath and met Elsie's gaze. 'While I don't want you to reconsider my appointment, why me? There must be so many other more experienced public speakers with less ... explosive dispositions.'

'Vocational guidance isn't just for our girls. We need to develop our staff, too.'

Bec nodded. The diversity of roles and opportunities was one reason she'd applied for a position with the organisation. The other, that the Y would not expect her to resign when she married.

'Your efforts in expanding the Thrift Club savings scheme have been well recognised. An increase in two thousand pounds on last year was quite a feat.'

Bec felt heat warming her cheeks. *God, she never blushed!* She loved fixing problems – other people's problems. And the Thrift Club, which was an initiative to encourage working women to develop a savings habit, had just needed a little focus.

'We think you would stand to gain a lot from the experience ...' At this point Elsie hesitated, repositioning her glasses, '... and expand your personal outlook by considering others' points of view.'

Opening her mouth to speak, Bec thought better of it and closed it again, sending her boss and friend a polite smile. She was excited about being given the opportunity, although it was weighing as a type of punishment for her forthright manner. She was open to other opinions – it just made life easier if they were consistent with hers. No one – apart from Daniel – ever challenged her directly. She'd assumed that was because they agreed with her.

'Now don't go all strange on me. I'm one of your strongest advocates,' said the older woman, laying a consoling hand on Bec's shoulder. 'You're smart, passionate and resolute in the campaigns you undertake. And the Y is richer for that.'

But ...? Bec steeled herself. There had to be a but.

'Sometimes, persuasion and flattery are a better means of winning people to your side than an outright intellectual skirmish.'

Bec smiled. Elsie's advice echoed her grandmother's growing up. *Temper your temper!* Despite being a supporter of the suffrage movement, Adelaide Carey had held tight to the view that in relations with men and women alike, overt blue-stocking-type behaviour did you no favours. She hadn't gone so far as suggesting it would make Bec unmarriageable, but the implication had been clear.

'But aren't debates supposed to be fiery affairs?'

'Yes, but in a theatrical sense. A bit of heat, spice, a dollop of cream and a dusting of flour.'

Bec screwed up her nose. That sounded like a recipe for a gut ache.

'Jenny has taken over the organising and is available to help with research. I'm sure you've guessed we're taking the negative argument.'

'Jenny? I thought she was leaving for America?'

'She is, but her travel has been delayed. Her husband won't be in Alabama until November, and he wants to be there to make the introduction to his family.'

Bec thought back to the whirlwind of the last fortnight. A coup for Australian and American relations – political and personal. Jenny, who until recently had managed the Melbourne headquarters, had lost her heart to an American sailor. They'd married before he'd sailed.

'That's great news.' This time Bec's smile was wide, and she could feel her sense of humour returning. 'She'll be on hand to help curb my impetuous reasoning.'

'All right, now that's settled, let's get back to work. Have you had any thoughts about suitable positions for those young ladies we met last week?'

CHAPTER 3

Later that evening, Eliza linked her arm through Bec's as they made their way through the foyer, waving goodnight to Hannah, who ruled reception. 'It seems like ages since we've had a good chat.'

'I know. I'm not used to having to compete for your time.'

Until Eliza's engagement, Bec and her best friend had been inseparable. They worked together – well, in the same building; Eliza tutored dance, singing and drawing – travelled together to and from the city by train most days and enjoyed the same pursuits – mostly dancing. Although, unlike Eliza, who partnered professionals in exhibitions and entered the occasional competition, Bec's interest in dancing was for flirting and fun.

Eliza sent her a rueful smile. 'Alex has been a little possessive, I admit. And before you say anything, I take full responsibility for allowing it to happen. But he can be very persuasive ...'

They joined the flow of foot traffic towards the city's main railway station.

Bec rolled her eyes. 'You're not going to turn into one of those women at the beck and call of her husband, are you?'

Eliza grinned, squeezing Bec's arm. 'No. But I am going to enjoy the benefits of an attentive fiancé.'

Bec felt like a grump. She offered her friend what she hoped was an apologetic smile.

'But, enough about me. You hinted earlier that you have a new project. Any chance it involves Daniel?'

'What?' Bec tripped on an irregular section of the footpath, and if not for Eliza's arm, would have fallen.

'After Friday night's kiss, I thought you might see him in a new light. He'd make a great project – a long-term one – and we'd be sisters-in-law.'

Her heart, already pulsing from the near fall, sped up. 'Eliza. As much as I'd love that, I mean us being sisters-in-law, Daniel is a project for someone else. I clearly remember saying he's not my type. We're not each other's type.'

Why did Eliza have to bring up her indiscretion? She'd confined the memory to some hidden recess, and now thanks to her friend, it was back, storming and stomping through her mind – not dissimilar to the man himself.

'But he —'

'Already has a girlfriend.'

Eliza pulled a face.

'You'll learn to like her.'

'No, I won't. She's always bleating about something and hanging off Daniel like a barnacle. She's due back this Saturday – it's a pity she couldn't have stayed in Sydney permanently.'

'Amen.'

'But, back to your project —'

'Oompff!' Bec had been scanning the clocks as they approached the wide stone steps that marked the entrance to the station. A newsboy, sights set elsewhere, had barrelled into her.

'Sorry.' Scooping up the newspapers strewn around her, he was off without even a backward glance.

'Are you all right?' Trousered legs and an outstretched arm appeared in front of her.

'I think so.' Bec nodded to the man, clambering to her feet, unaided.

A pair of concerned, startling blue eyes regarded her. 'Damn nuisance they are, these boys – pardon my language. The government needs to do something. The metropolitan dailies, too. Street urchins, all of them.'

Bec nodded again. Eliza was brushing the dust from the back of her coat.

Bushy black brows drew together. 'Too rambunctious for their own good. No respect for anyone, not even a lady. I'll call the police.' He was looking around, his brown felt hat held high in the air.

Bec had no intention of becoming an obstruction or a news item. 'No need. It was my fault. I wasn't paying attention.' She didn't doubt the man's chivalry, but she wasn't injured, and these children were no doubt helping to put food on their families' tables.

But either the man hadn't heard her over the sound of the lads as they advertised their wares or thought he knew best. Bec watched him battle his way upstream through the evening's pedestrian deluge to the traffic policeman.

'Come on.' Bec grabbed Eliza's hand and set them in motion. She hoped the man didn't think her ungrateful when he found that they'd disappeared, but she didn't need his help.

They made it to the platform in time, squeezing into the back corner of the last carriage. Bec turned her shoulder to a disgruntled businessman who obviously thought his briefcase more deserving of a seat than she did, and faced Eliza.

Her friend's green eyes studied her from beneath a blunt fringe. 'Apart from a pair of ruined stockings, how do you feel?'

Bec examined her legs, ignoring the *tut-tut* of the man beside her, and moaned when she caught sight of the large hole in the medium-weight silk. 'Embarrassed more than anything else.'

'Are you ready to tell me your news?'

Bec drummed her fingers where they rested in her lap. 'The Y has scheduled a debate as part of its fundraising program. Elsie has nominated me as part of the team.'

'That's fantastic,' said Eliza, giving Bec's arm a squeeze.

'I know. I'm excited.'

'Although, I would have preferred it if your project included Daniel.'

'*Eliza!*'

Her friend threw up her hands to ward off Bec's censure. 'I'm sorry. What's the topic?'

'That women aren't fit for the role of tram conductor.'

Eliza screwed up her nose. 'Who chose that?'

Bec's eyebrows shot up.

'Well, it's not a terribly glamourous role, is it?'

Bec grinned. 'Nothing that a splash of lipstick wouldn't fix.'

'Or a short skirt.'

At North Williamstown station, they alighted and walked

arm in arm the short distance to Eliza's house.

'No doubt your news will spark some lively conversation over dinner.'

'And give Daniel indigestion.' The tiny nugget of uneasiness that had formed at the thought of seeing him for the first time since their kiss vanished. Bec was back on familiar ground. Daniel's views on women's role in the workforce were as well known as hers. Females as tram conductors? He'd probably turn apoplectic.

A voice rumbled over Bec's shoulder, 'Why would you want to do that?'

'Daniel!' Bec spun around, resisting the urge to cool her cheeks with the palms of her hands. 'You know, eavesdropping is a deplorable habit.'

'But ignorance could make me sick.'

'It was a private conversation. And an unlikely occurrence given your cast-iron stomach.' Bec met his glare with a nonchalant shrug and walked on.

Sweeping through the front gate and under the old elm tree that guarded the entrance, they clattered across the verandah and through the front door. Bec savoured the warmth after the draughty train carriage. As Daniel strode towards the kitchen, she took her time to hang her coat and scarf.

'Um, Eliza, do you think I'm too opinionated?' She'd been tossing Elsie's comment back and forth in her mind all afternoon.

Her friend stopped mid-step and swung around. 'Why do you ask? Is this about the debate?'

'Elsie hinted that at times I ... well ... that I may get carried away.'

Eliza's green eyes flared. 'You're bold and passionate, of course you have opinions.'

'Too many of them?'

'Bec, you're a champion of women's equality. And I, for one, love you just the way you are. You'll do great.'

It wasn't a yes or a no, but it was enough. 'Thank you. You're a good friend. I needed to hear that.'

'Eliza tells me you've been selected for some debate, dear,' said Mrs Sinclair, pushing her knife and fork together into a six o'clock position.

Five sets of eyes turned in Bec's direction. Some, like Mr Sinclair's, were interested, others like Daniel's were openly mocking. Bec was amazed to have secured Alex's interest at all, given he'd been making eyes at Eliza all evening. Since announcing their engagement, he'd become openly besotted.

'Yes. Representing the YWCA. Advocating for the employment of females as tram conductors.'

'Why would women want to do that, dear?' asked Mrs Sinclair. 'Such a dangerous occupation.'

'It's more concerning that those who do, can't apply because the Tramways Board refuses to employ them.'

Daniel threw his serviette down onto the table. 'That's because it's too physically demanding for women.'

'Piffle!' returned Bec, glaring at him.

'It does seem to require quite a bit of strength, dear, don't you think? All that jolting and swaying, the unexpected braking,' said Mrs Sinclair, frowning.

Daniel nodded. 'And injuries are not uncommon. Worse

than crossing the road and being hit by a car.'

Bec's irritation ratcheted up another notch. Had he heard about the incident earlier this evening? Had he seen her sprawled on the ground? *And not rushed to help?* She would have refused, but he should have offered. 'What's crossing the road got to do with this?'

'I was simply trying to make a point.'

A stupid point, in her opinion. But at least it seemed he hadn't witnessed her embarrassment.

Mr Sinclair, no doubt used to harnessing fractious councillors, intervened to steer the conversation into safer waters. 'Who's on your team?'

'Activists and agitators, most likely.'

Bec ignored Daniel, stopping short of turning her back on him. He really was insufferable. 'Ida McAuley, one of the voices from the Victorian Women's Council. Our third team member is still being recruited.'

'I'd expect the Tramways Board would have an interest in fielding a representative for the affirmative, especially the chief engineer, huh Alex?' mused Mr Sinclair.

'For sure ol' Strickland would be involved somehow,' agreed Alex. 'And the Tramways Employees' Association. Interesting timing, given the current unemployment numbers and the log of claims served by the union.'

'It's not a political debate,' said Bec.

'It sounds political,' declared Daniel. 'An attempt to stir public sentiment.'

Bec rolled her eyes. 'Nonsense. It's part of our annual fundraising.'

'For public entertainment and speaker advancement,' said Mr Sinclair.

Bec nodded, carefully threading peas onto the tines of her fork. 'That's right. An exhibition of passion, eloquence and high-quality argument.'

'No doubt it'll be a spectacle for sure,' said Daniel.

Bec filled her mouth with her fork, narrowing her eyes.

Eliza frowned at her brother before turning to Bec. 'Your participation, of course, is dependent on surviving the inaugural Icebreaker Challenge this Sunday.'

'I do think manning a cake stall would have been warmer,' said Mrs Sinclair.

'But not half as much fun,' defended Bec, fork poised. The challenge was an initiative of hers to add a bit of buzz to the fundraising drive. The program had become staid, the idea a way of attracting the participation of a younger age group. Eliza had stared at her as if she'd lost her mind on being told the news of their entrance into the event, suggesting that hypothermia wasn't out of the question. She could see the headlines, she'd told her, '*View confirmed – Beauty and Brains do not co-exist!*'

'This Sunday?' groaned Daniel.

'Yes,' said Bec, carefully aligning her utensils. Best not to have anything in her hands. Daniel's tone was not encouraging.

'I —'

Was he goading her intentionally? She cut him off. 'You and Alex volunteered to scrutineer the lap counts. You can't back out now.'

Daniel frowned and opened his mouth to speak, but Bec was not prepared to entertain his excuses. He probably planned to spend all Saturday evening with Evelyn – welcoming her home. 'Bring her along, it doesn't start until ten.'

'Who?'

'Your girlfriend.' Bec smiled, unfazed by the scowl Daniel directed her way.

'That won't be necessary. I'll be there.'

CHAPTER 4

'So, you're set on this, then, are you?' asked Daniel.

Bec jammed her gloved hands deep into the pockets of her coat. 'Do you mean the debate? Or your appearance on Sunday?'

'I'll be there Sunday. I take my commitments seriously. I'm talking about the debate.'

'Yes.' She wriggled her fingers. The blood never seemed to reach her extremities in winter and they were perpetually cold.

Daniel was walking her home, as he did every Monday evening. Eliza would ordinarily accompany them, but she'd stayed behind to wish Alex goodnight. Bec wouldn't be surprised if they were still locked in one another's arms by the time Daniel returned. Mrs Sinclair had relaxed some of her rules regarding Eliza's behaviour since her engagement, and Alex wasn't short of initiative. Bec missed her friend and envied her new relationship. The way Alex gazed at her when he thought no one was looking ...

'Do you even know what a tram conductor does?'

Bec was jolted from her musings. Daniel had obviously been stewing about the debate while her thoughts had drifted in other directions.

'I —'

'And under what conditions?'

'Well —'

'The early mornings, the late nights, in all weather?'

'Damn you. At least let me answer before bombarding me with another question!'

Daniel withdrew into silence – a grumpy one from the set of his mouth.

'I'd be lying if I said I had in-depth knowledge, but I'm not stupid. I have ridden on trams *and* I read the newspapers,' said Bec, trying to temper the frustration in her tone Daniel had ignited.

'It's not the same.'

'And I'll do research. Jenny Sherman is going to give me a hand.'

'The blind leading the blind,' scoffed Daniel with a wave of his hand.

'Well, what would you suggest?'

'Talk to a conductor. Next time you're on a tram, watch what they do, how they're treated. Don't just daydream out the window. Immerse yourself. You don't want to appear ignorant.'

'*Ignorant?* Diplomacy never was your ... *Argh!*'

Bec had been concentrating so hard on maintaining her temper, she'd stopped watching where she was walking. Williamstown's footpaths were notorious – hazardous in daylight, perilous at night. She was normally as sure-footed as a mountain goat – learned from painful experience –

but tonight had come unstuck on a pothole the size of her mother's Sunday roast.

'Got you.' Daniel locked his arms around her shoulders and pulled her tightly to his side.

His quick reflexes had saved her from falling. Twice in one day would be a record. 'Thanks. I know the route between our houses like the back of my hand.' She was babbling. He still had his arms locked around her. 'You'd think I'd be able to navigate it blindfolded by now.' His mouth moved closer, and her heart launched into a syncopated rhythm.

'Of course, you can't save yourself with your hands stuck in those pockets.'

Bec's head whipped back, and she pushed away from him. Whatever feeling had stolen upon her vanished. God, he should have been a preacher's son. *Worse, he was right.*

'Come on,' he said, taking possession of her gloved fingers.

'I —'

'Yes, I know, you're very capable,' he said before she could voice her protest. 'But these footpaths have become treacherous after the last rain. Let's call a truce for the rest of tonight, huh? At least until I see you safely home.'

She was relieved that Daniel seemed disinclined to talk. It gave her an opportunity to ponder the puzzle of her awareness of him. It had been there from the start. Within minutes of their introduction, she'd sensed an attraction – a *mutual* attraction. She'd hidden hers behind a feisty façade, reasoning it was because he would seek to curb – maybe even repress – her modern ideals. But a small part of her – a very tiny part – had feared her capitulation more. He could be persuasive; she'd watched the reaction of countless women over the years to his lopsided smile and the deep timbre of his voice. Evelyn hadn't put up any resistance.

She should never have kissed him! There had been sparks. Not the sort that had become a habit between them, where if he said something was black, she argued it was white. The sort ignited by chemistry. Until then, she would have sworn she was hardened to his charm, and it was disturbing to think her resolve had crumbled at the first testing ... or in this case, the first tasting.

'All right?'

Bec started. 'What?'

'You squeezed my hand.'

'I did?' Her mind and mouth were not communicating. She couldn't tell him what had snared her thoughts. At that moment, she became aware of the mechanical concerto of motorbikes headed towards the back beach – impromptu night racing, if the papers were to be believed.

She nodded. 'I did. Sorry. I was lost in thought. The motorbikes startled me.'

An eyebrow raised to half-mast was the only sign that he thought her behaviour odd. Thankfully, like her, he was no longer in a combative mood, and they continued in silence.

Bec attempted to ignore the toasty warmth generated by Daniel's hand and return to her thoughts. *A hopeless exercise.* With his fingers loosely curled around hers, the gesture was casual yet intimate. Had her hand always fitted in his so well? Wouldn't she have noticed? She'd danced with Daniel hundreds of times.

At the sight of her parents' front gate, Bec rescued her hand as if it had been in danger of fusing with his. A quick glance found his profile untroubled. *Thank God!* She couldn't explain why her awareness of him had resurfaced so strongly.

'Safe and sound,' said Daniel, unlocking the latch and propelling her through.

His palm branded the space above the hollow at the base of her spine. *This man and heat were inseparable!* She fought to keep her tone relaxed. 'Thanks.'

'And, Bec ...'

'Yes?'

'I wanted to apologise for my behaviour on Friday evening. It won't happen again.'

'Right ... good. Apology accepted. Goodnight.'

'Goodnight, Bec.'

She hurried up the path, conscious of his gaze, if the warmth travelling down her spine was any indication. She didn't dare turn around and quickly let herself into the house.

Leaning back against the door, she stripped off her gloves and took a deep breath. *Right ... good!* That was the best she could come up with? She should have been stronger. *Don't give it another thought, I haven't.* Except she had.

Why? Was it the kiss? Her reaction? His reaction? Or her lack of finesse in extricating herself? Bec shook her head. It was the intensity of her response – and his reaction to that intensity – that continued to trouble her. She'd been on the verge of surrendering, her common sense absconding once their lips had locked. Bec pressed a palm between her breasts. Thankfully, a tugging feeling in her chest had alerted her that her mind had stopped functioning. She'd panicked and called an abrupt halt before things could escalate.

'That you, love?' called her mother. 'We're in the living room.'

'Coming.'

She didn't know why, but Daniel's apology annoyed her. Was he sorry he'd kissed her? Disappointed? *She'd show him!* Then just as quickly she thought, *God! No, I won't.* This wasn't a competition. She had to stop these mental gymnastics. His apology had drawn a line under what was a cursory encounter. In Daniel's world, it was probably little more than an automatic action, employed to any available set of female lips. She was making too much of it.

Jim was the only person she was interested in locking lips with, and they'd arranged to meet tomorrow night. Bec savoured a tingle of anticipation before slipping her gloves into the pocket of her coat and hurrying down the hallway to greet her parents.

CHAPTER 5

Tuesday 11 August 1925

Jim shepherded Bec from the ballroom to the farthest end of the terrace, away from the light spilling from the windows and any keen eyes.

'Any luck with your missing sailors?'

He looped his arms around her waist. 'Are you tryin' to get rid of me?'

'Why would I want to do that? I am the envy of every girl in Melbourne,' quipped Bec.

'Every girl?'

'You have no idea of the number of broken hearts across the city since the fleet sailed. You could probably have the pick of any woman you liked,' she said, leaning back to admire the way his navy-blue jacket hugged his torso.

'Really?'

'Really.' She fiddled with a gold button level with her chin. 'But I have no idea why I just told you that.'

'Lucky I'm not interested in all those other women, then,' he teased, adjusting his position against the fluted railing and gathering her closer. 'What if I told you I'd been asked to extend my stay for another month beyond this one, to tidy up a few loose ends?'

Her eyes met his. 'I'd say it'd have to remain our little secret.'

'Back home, secrets are sealed with a kiss.'

His wink suggested otherwise, but Bec enjoyed the banter. 'I'm always interested in learning new customs —'

'There you are!' drawled a familiar voice from behind her.

Bec groaned. *Was he stalking her?* Fired by a spark of pique, she leaned forward and kissed Jim firmly on his lips, whispering, 'Later,' before turning slowly to face Daniel.

'Here I am.' She considered spreading her arms wide in a theatrical gesture but compelled herself to hold them loosely at her sides.

Daniel narrowed his eyes. No doubt he'd hoped his observations on Friday night had tempered her *enthusiasm* where the American was concerned. He should have known better. And why her idle dalliance should even interest him, she didn't know. His interruption puzzled her.

'Jim,' Daniel acknowledged Bec's date before returning his gaze to her. 'Eliza, Jenny and I are heading home and wondered if you wanted a lift.'

'How thoughtful.' Bec hoped her expression and tone conveyed that she was aware of his true intention to thwart her flirtation and that she wouldn't stand for his intrusion.

She felt Jim lengthen his torso behind her, no doubt levelling Daniel with a look of his own. 'I'll see my girl home. No need to trouble yourself.'

'It's no bother. There's room for one more,' Daniel replied politely – too politely.

Bec frowned. 'On the train?'

'No. Colin Upton's Studebaker.'

'A bit out of his way, isn't it?' Bec was sure Colin didn't live west of the city.

'Oh, you know Colin, always looking to show off his pride and joy.'

Bec hesitated.

'It has a heater. Very welcome on a winter's night like this,' Daniel added.

She released a heavy sigh. 'Can you give us a moment?'

'Sure, I'll just wait over here.'

'*Daniel.*'

He grinned. 'Just inside the door, then.'

He's deliberately provoking me. Bec relaxed her features before turning to face Jim. 'Sorry about that. Now, where were we?'

Jim pulled her closer. 'I was preparing to further your cultural education, I believe.'

'It'll have to be the abridged version, I'm afraid. I'm a sucker for a heater,' said Bec, looping her arms around his neck and tilting her head to accommodate his lips.

He tasted of smoky caramel and a touch of rum. *Now, this was how a kiss was meant to be*, she thought. *No challenging for control, no chemical fireworks, just a simple exploration of mutual desire.* She pressed closer as Jim skimmed his palms up the side of her ribcage. So what if there was no fanfare?

Bec moaned low in her throat – an expression of both pleasure and frustration. It was no use. She couldn't enjoy Jim's attentions knowing that Daniel was standing ten feet away, no doubt popping his head in and out of the door to monitor their progress.

Skating her hands between their bodies, Bec withdrew.

At Jim's questioning look, she smiled ruefully. 'You know who has somewhat dampened my appetite.'

'We call 'em *fire extinguishers* back home.'

'That's clever. We use the term *alarm clock*. Same difference, I guess.'

'Come on, then, let me escort you in. I'll be out of town for the next few days. There have been sightings of some of the missing men up Ballarat way. Will I see you on Saturday?'

Bec looped her hand into his proffered elbow. 'I'll look forward to it.'

'Believe me, honey, the pleasure will be all mine.'

Bec had tucked herself into one corner of the back seat, behind the driver. If pressed, she would have admitted that an early night appealed. The mood at Birmingham's had seemed flat. She wasn't sure whether it reflected the hearts of most of the female population or her lack of sleep during the last fortnight. But she didn't appreciate Daniel's orchestration of her departure. She didn't need a self-appointed big brother. She'd managed to get to this age successfully without one. Daniel's meddling was unnecessary and unappreciated.

As unlikely as it seemed, she was missing Evelyn's presence – just not the woman herself. At least with her around, Daniel's whereabouts were certain. He could be found tethered to her side – the woman's slavish admiration meant she twined herself around him at every opportunity. Sometimes Bec wondered if Evelyn even knew how to stand on her own two feet. She didn't know what irritated her more, that Daniel's tastes extended to such a spineless specimen of womanhood, or that Evelyn lacked mettle, apparently content to live in Daniel's shadow. Not that it was any of her business.

A squeeze of her hand drew her attention from the inky blackness outside the window to her best friend's concerned face. Bec gave her a quick smile and returned the pressure. They'd been friends too long not to know when one of them was upset.

Colin, on the other hand, despite bouncing from pothole to pothole, was keeping up a ready stream of conversation. He drove as he danced, Bec decided – haphazardly but cheerfully.

Jenny supported him, being in fine spirits, having received a letter from her husband that morning. He must have written and posted it before they'd sailed, Bec mused, as the ships had arrived in New Zealand only yesterday according to *The Argus*.

Daniel faced forward, alert for any piles of brickbats and rock that the heavy steam rollers, whose efforts were the only thing keeping the road passable, had missed. The Studebaker's headlights struggled to pierce the squally conditions.

'Now, what was that you were telling us before about some debate?' Colin asked.

Bec blinked. Debate?

Daniel turned his head to the side window and mumbled, 'It's not important.'

'No, no. Awfully interesting. Something about women as tram conductors and —'

Her pique forgotten, Bec sat up straight and leaned forward. 'Do tell, Daniel.'

She watched him run a hand around the back of his neck, before adjusting his position and turning forty-five degrees towards Colin. With one side of his face in shadow and the other cast in the half-light from the dashboard, he reminded her of the ghost from *Phantom of the Opera*. She stifled a giggle, doubting he would thank her for the comparison to the star of a gothic horror novel.

'I've been asked to join the debate on why the role of tram conductor is unsuited to females.'

Unbothered by the gasps of surprise from the back seat, Colin nodded. 'Makes sense with your engineering knowhow and experience. Let the science do the talking. Who are you representing?'

'The State Government.'

'Should be a straightforward debate, I imagine. Beggin' your pardon, girls, but the trams are no place for females. Some passengers get rough, especially after a few drinks, and I wouldn't want to see any girl or woman hurt,' said Colin.

Bec couldn't believe what she was hearing. 'Humph! I suppose you think we should chain ourselves to a kitchen chair, too.'

'Well, females have a certain knack in that department.'

His tone sounded as if he was serious. Bec exploded. 'And that's why —'

'Who's on your team?' interrupted Eliza, tapping Daniel on the shoulder.

Bec flung herself back against the seat and crossed her arms to stop them from reaching for Colin's neck. He wasn't worth it, and she didn't fancy walking home.

Daniel appeared to hesitate. 'Well, I only know of one other.'

'And?' prompted Jenny, her voice hinting at Bec's own impatience.

Daniel's reluctance surprised her. She expected him to wax lyrical of the expertise and eloquence of his team. With her trifling experience, she'd be no match for Daniel or his peers. Speaking was in his genes – his father was a local councillor and his grandfather, too. She could only hope that the skill of her team members surpassed hers. Victory would have been sweet, but now she just wanted to make sure they weren't embarrassed in defeat. *A tall order.*

'Um ...'

'Goodness, Daniel, it's not like you to be at a loss for words,' said Eliza.

'Bec.' The name ricocheted around the interior of the car. 'We're officially teammates. I'm strengthening the side of the negative.'

Colin was stunned into silence as hoots of laughter exploded from the back seat.

'You and Bec on the same team. That's priceless,' crowed Eliza.

'Karma!' Jenny giggled.

Bec's good humour had returned. Fate and the weight of its fickle pendulum had swung her way. 'We'll make a feminist of you yet.'

Daniel shook his head, turning to face the front. 'Never in this lifetime.'

Snapping off her bedside light, Bec lay on her side, hands tucked under her chin, and ran over the events of the evening. It was something she did most nights before surrendering to sleep.

Daniel's response to her feminist statement niggled at her. It begged the question, why would he agree to argue a point of view that he strongly opposed? And why would the state furnish a representative for the affirmative? And why Daniel? Bec yawned. It just didn't make sense.

CHAPTER 6

Wednesday 12 August 1925

'Ah, I've missed this,' confessed Daniel, sitting with his ankle resting on his opposite knee, whisky tumbler dangling from his fingers.

'Me? Our catch-ups? Whisky? Escaping the world?' Alex grinned.

'Everything. Life hasn't been the same since you got *handcuffed.*'

Alex quirked an eyebrow.

'I know, it's been less than a week, but it feels like a lifetime. I can't tell you the last time I saw sunrise ... or even wanted to. Birmingham's has become monotonous of late – same people, same conversations. And I haven't had a decent drink with proper conversation since ... well ... since the last time you and I sat here!' Daniel waved an expansive hand, encompassing the alcove in the lounge of the Federal hotel, where they had often, over the years, retreated for a quiet drink.

'You are out of sorts, old man.'

Daniel saluted him with a sip from his drink. 'Whereas you look ... content.'

Alex ignored his observation. 'Is Evelyn part of the tapestry of monotony you've described?'

Daniel swirled the amber liquid around his glass, savouring the complex scent of alcohol enriched with hints of vanilla and toffee. 'Possibly. I'm questioning whether I need to move on.'

'The plot thickens. What's really going on?'

'My promotion is what's going on.' Daniel ran his fingers through his hair. 'I told you Chalmers – my boss – is considering whether to challenge the public service's rule of seniority and recommend me for promotion.'

Alex nodded, leaning forward.

'It's a big deal, never been done before. I've only been in the department twelve months.'

'But you've done more in that time than others.'

It was true. Daniel had overseen several important projects, proving himself the equal of many of his superiors. 'It doesn't count.'

At the lift of Alex's brow, Daniel qualified, 'Obviously it counts, but years of service hold sway. The condition can't be simply brushed aside.'

'So, what are your choices?'

Daniel moved to the edge of his chair. 'Well, I learned his support has strings.'

Alex's eyebrows shot up. 'What sort of strings?'

'First, I have to show I can successfully navigate an argument against my natural point of view.'

Alex slapped his thigh. 'The debate.'

Daniel nodded. 'Yep. And he stressed the word *successfully*, so no half-measured effort will be accepted.'

'I wondered why you'd put your hand up. It's had me

puzzled since you mentioned it yesterday evening.'

'Believe me, if I could get out of it I would.'

'Anything else?'

'Chalmers has assigned that dolt, Theo Blake, to the debate, as well.'

'The same guy that argued *against* electrifying the tram network?'

'The very one. He's lobbying for the same promotion and we're in competition for Chalmers' support. But get this, he's joining the affirmative side.'

'That's not cricket!'

'Bloody insulting is what it is. I deserve that promotion. Blake's never around for the hard work. And now Chalmers is giving him the easy ride.'

'Are you sure it's worth it? This promotion?'

'It's more money to afford being able to move out. And it's the stepping stone I need to shift into politics. I'm more than ready.'

They lapsed into silence before Daniel thumped his glass onto the small table between them. 'Wait till you hear the clincher. He couched it conversationally, so I don't know how serious he was – my boss, that is.'

'Go on.'

Daniel mimicked the singsong Welsh accent of Louis Chalmers. 'I not gonna lie to you, son, oratory and administration skills can only take a man so far. Have you considered the advantages of a wife?' Daniel picked up his glass and took a long swallow. 'Someone who will make it her career to further yours.'

Alex let out a low whistle. 'What did you say?'

'What could I say? Not even my oratory skills are ready

for *that* debate. I escaped with an excuse about a brief I needed to prepare.' Daniel drained his glass. 'You're the first person I've told.'

'*God!* Do you even want to get married?'

Daniel laughed. 'This from you? *Mr Smitten.*'

'I had a choice. Marriage wasn't served up as a condition of my employment.'

'I don't know. I guess if I found the right woman.'

'Humph! Not Evelyn, then.'

'Not Evelyn.'

Alex tossed back his whisky and called for two more. 'How long have you got?'

'What?'

'You know, to decide on a wife.'

Daniel shrugged. 'I don't know. I wasn't in the mood to discuss timelines. I got the hell outta there.'

'Do you reckon Chalmers gave the same advice to Blake?'

'Maybe. By all accounts, he's as good as engaged to some country girl. He travels up to see her most weekends.'

'You don't have to do it. There are bachelor public servants, even lord mayors. Maybe it's a test to see if you can be pushed around.'

Daniel brightened. Perhaps, although Louis Chalmers wasn't a man with a well-developed sense of humour. 'So, you think I should ignore his advice, then?'

'Don't ignore it. You don't want to give Blake an even greater advantage. Or to appear unreasonable.' Alex leaned forward. 'I know, say you're not averse to marriage, but you don't want to rush it. After all, marriage is like a lottery.'

Daniel saluted Alex with his fresh glass. 'And lotteries are illegal, right?'

'That's right.'

'How did you know?'

'With Eliza?'

'Yeah.'

'It's inexplicable how it happened. One minute she was just like every other girl, the next she was the one I wanted to hitch myself to for life.'

Alex's experience sounded to Daniel a lot like a lottery – all luck and no skill.

'What about Bec?'

'*Bec?* You may have noticed our views on marriage aren't well aligned. The polar opposite of one another.'

'Is that why you kissed her? At Birmingham's.' Alex held up his hand. 'Don't even think of denying it. Eliza and I heard everything. I thought I might need to call the fire brigade.'

What to say. He couldn't come up with any rationale for why they'd ended up locked together. Apart from one. 'All right, all right. Physically, there might be an attraction.'

Alex almost choked on his whisky. '*Might?*'

'That's all I'm admitting to.'

'Marriages have started with less, mate. Your future wife could be right under your nose.'

CHAPTER 7

Thursday 13 August 1925

A perfunctory knock on the door heralded an explosion of women into the office Bec shared with Elsie.

Eliza led the charge, flourishing a paper. 'The art class finished the debate poster. Their best yet.' It seemed she'd brought the entire class of seven, no, eight, with Jenny's animated face bringing up the rear. They gathered eagerly around Bec's desk, and Eliza placed the artwork atop the papers Bec had been working on.

Against a white background, a twenty-something man wearing a two-piece suit stood in front of a framed carnival mirror, the type that curved first one way and then another, distorting the reflection.

The mirrored surface transformed the man into that of a tram conductress, attired in a jacket and skirt. Long legs extended from the bottom of the skirt and the man's chest had broadened attractively. The woman sported a come-hither smile. *THE GREAT DEBATE* was lettered in scarlet capitals at the bottom using simple geometric shapes. Below that the date – 10 September – venue and ticket price.

'Well, what do you think?' Jenny demanded, hands clasped to her chest.

'It looks great – such a clever idea. I love it.'

'She hasn't realised,' said Eliza. 'Look closer.'

Bec again studied the illustration, even turning it over. But apart from stains of colour bleeding through the paper, she wasn't sure what she was missing.

'It's you!' Ten voices rang out.

'So it is,' said Elsie over Bec's shoulder. 'And a remarkable likeness it is too.'

Bec held it at arm's length. Now that she looked, really looked, she had to agree.

'Our very own poster girl,' teased Jenny, winking.

'And the man,' Eliza clapped her hands, 'is Daniel. Although you can't see his face, his hairline gives it away.'

Bec grinned. The debate was turning out much more fun than she had anticipated. First Daniel's appointment to their team and now this – he would be annoyed. Of course, his likeness wasn't as telltale as hers, but that stubborn chin – even in profile – and the small heart-shaped birthmark above his collar were unmistakable to those who knew him.

Elsie squeezed her shoulder before addressing Jenny. 'What's the plan for the poster?'

'Newspapers, our own magazine, of course, bulletin boards and as many shop windows as we can manage.'

Elsie's tone became businesslike. 'I'd like as much exposure as possible. I'm meeting with the finance committee tomorrow to propose half the profit from ticket sales is used for the accountancy course Bec has been advocating for.'

Spinning around in her chair, Bec gazed at the woman she regarded as her mentor. 'Truly?'

'Strike while the iron's hot, I say. Everything's in place – tutor, course material, candidates and a willing employer. We just need funding. This poster will be a winner. The proceeds, a fitting reward for your hard work.'

Bec was speechless. She hadn't thought she'd ever see this project come to fruition. The Y had funded domestic training for women last year, but had considered the idea of accounting too progressive. There wasn't an employment avenue for the girls once they'd completed their training. There was no unsatisfied demand for female accountants, only factory and shop workers and domestic servants. Undeterred, and despite countless knockbacks, Bec had finally found a firm willing to participate.

'I'll take an armful and recruit Dad to drum up support through the business community in Williamstown,' said Bec, finally.

'I'll organise a rush print order. We'll take them this evening straight after work,' said Eliza.

Despite the crowded office, Elsie had started to pace. 'And maybe your young man,' she pointed to Eliza, 'can convince the Tramways Board to post them in the trams for maximum exposure.'

Eliza clapped her hands. 'I'll call his office this afternoon.'

The energy bouncing around the room amazed Bec. Funding! She wouldn't get ahead of herself. The committee could still say no. Or maybe no one would turn up to watch the debate. Or only a few people. She couldn't let that happen, even if she had to carry a sandwich board through the streets to promote the event herself. This debate and her nomination were becoming the best thing that had happened in ages.

As she and Eliza burst through the entrance, setting the door's cheery bell ringing, Bec sobered at the sight of the customer occupying the middle chair in her father's barbershop – *William Tailor*.

Her father turned from briskly brushing remnants of hair from the man's nape with a smile. 'Now, what brings two pretty young ladies to my shop at this hour?'

Before Bec could forewarn her, Eliza enthused, 'We've come to promote our Great Debate fundraiser.'

'And what are you waving around there, then, young Eliza?' her father asked, passing a cane to his customer before stepping forward to drop a kiss on the foreheads of both women.

'A poster for your front window.'

'Well, looky here. That's my Bec ... isn't it?'

'Yes. Clever, huh?'

Bec watched Tailor senior lever himself to his feet and shuffle over to tower behind her father. Even leaning on a cane, his height was imposing. He eyed her, Eliza, and finally the poster over her father's shoulder.

'Humph!' William Tailor's moue tightened in disapproval as his gaze returned to rake over her.

Bec felt fire enter her cheeks but refused to cower under his scrutiny. He was worse than any naysayer. His censure of the modern female bordered on bullying. Since she was thirteen years old, he'd appeared to devote himself to deriding the development of her independent thoughts and views. If he had but known, his scorn – and behaviour – had only strengthened them. He was a man who had loomed, frequently and persistently, large in her teenage years. He wasn't as agile these days, what with his cane and all, but she did her best to avoid him, anyway.

'And who's the young fella?' asked her father, ignoring his customer's scorn.

Eliza giggled. 'It's Daniel.'

As if noticing her stillness, her father raised a brow. 'Well, what do you think, love?'

Squaring her shoulders, Bec smiled. 'I love it. We're hoping you can convince some of the other businesses to display a copy in their windows.'

'Not mine. I'll not be encouraging any hoydenish debate. Ungodly it is.'

Bec watched her father's lips twitch. 'You're allowed your opinions, Bill, but I can see nothing our good Lord would trouble himself with in this poster.'

'I'll —'

'*I'll* be delighted to showcase it and I know others will too.'

'Emasculating the poor man in that way.'

'It's art, Mr Tailor. And it's for a good cause,' said Bec.

The old man thumped his cane on the timber floor. 'Sinful is what it is, young woman. Although I don't know why, I'd think you would know better. Teddy, good evening to you.'

It's Edward, Bec wanted to scream, taking a hurried step backwards to prevent her toes falling foul of William Tailor's cane as he stomped towards the door. *Teddy* sounded so belittling.

Her father, though, seemed to pay the moniker scant attention as he ushered the man through the door. Closing it, he drew the blind.

'And good riddance,' said Bec, rolling her shoulders. Age had not lessened her reaction to the man.

'Old grump,' said Eliza.

'He's that and more. A reminder to all of us of the importance of striving for an open mind.'

'Speaking of open minds, let's discover Daniel's reaction. Do you have time, Bec?'

'Dad?'

'Just make sure you're home by seven.'

Eliza rolled up a poster and tucked it under her arm. 'Come on, then, let's hurry.'

'Surprise!' Eliza reached over Daniel's shoulder and unfurled the poster onto the table in front of him.

Bec secured the corners with the salt and pepper shakers and glanced at Daniel. His expression was hard to read, but his body was tensed as if expecting a punch to be thrown.

'What's this, then?' asked Mrs Sinclair, wiping her hands on her apron and crossing to where Daniel sat. 'Pass me my glasses please, love, behind you.'

Eliza swept up the wire spectacles, bouncing on her toes. 'It's advertising for the debate. My art class finished it today.'

Adjusting the frames on her nose, Mrs Sinclair leaned forward, finally breaking the silence. 'That's Bec!'

'Uh-huh!'

'And ...' She tilted her head, examining the picture.

Bec realised she was holding her breath and steadied herself against the back of a chair.

'Daniel?'

'Yes! Isn't it clever? Daniel? You've been awfully quiet. What do you think?'

Daniel swivelled to look at his sister, his tone barely controlled. 'You call sacrificing my masculinity ... *clever*?'

'Oh pooh! It's art.'

'You've turned me into *a woman*!'

'For a good cause,' said Bec. 'Half the money raised will go to educating girls as accountants.'

Daniel turned sharply towards her. 'That makes me feel much better.'

Bec nodded, undeterred by his sarcastic tone. 'I thought so. Nothing like supporting the progress of women to bring a warm glow to your insides.'

'That might be how you choose to spend your time, but not me! And what's with including the damn mark on my neck?'

Mrs Sinclair cuffed her son lightly across the back of his head. 'Daniel, watch your language, please.'

'Sorry.'

Eliza fiddled with her coat sleeve. 'It was the only photograph of you I had. By the time I saw it, it was too late.'

'It's not so obvious, dear,' said Mrs Sinclair, returning to dinner preparations.

'It's a *heart*. Can't you extend my hairline or something?'

'It's not so easy —'

'And it's too late. Copies have been printed and distributed.' Bec crossed her fingers behind her back. They needed to keep expenses to a minimum. 'Anyway, no one believes you even have a heart.' Intercepting a quelling look from Mrs Sinclair, Bec coughed. 'A heart blemish, I mean.'

Daniel scowled.

'That's right. Who knows you have it, besides family?' Eliza brightened.

'School friends. My university mates. Evelyn ...'

Half the women at Birmingham's, Bec suspected.

Daniel groaned, 'Alex.'

'*And me!*' Bec chuckled.

Daniel appealed to the ceiling, perhaps even offering a prayer, before running his hands through his hair.

Eliza grinned. 'You see? Hardly anyone.'

Daniel shoved his chair back, narrowly missing his sister, and stormed off.

'I guess this isn't the time to warn him he may come face to face with a poster on his way to work in the morning.' Bec tried for a casual tone, but couldn't disguise her impish glee. She'd never seen Daniel so upset. 'Who knows, he may be besieged with a swathe of new admirers. And then he'll thank you.'

'His temper won't last long,' Eliza said. 'It never does.'

CHAPTER 8

Saturday 15 August 1925

'Guess who?'

Daniel's eyes were covered from behind, a playful kiss delivered to his nape and a warm body pressed against his. He fought the desire to cough as a bouquet of fragrance engulfed him.

'Alex?' He heard a strangled sound from his friend's throat standing at his side and imagined a face to match. He grinned.

'Darling, did you *come out* while I've been away? It's only been a week,' Evelyn's voice murmured into the shell of his ear, barely audible over the music's crescendo.

Had she recognised his likeness in the poster stuck up in the foyer? It was enough that his best mate had thrown around a couple of off-colour comments. He wasn't indulging his girlfriend's gibes.

'*Evelyn!* Welcome home,' he said, turning around to greet her with a wide smile. Claiming her hand, he linked it into the crook of his elbow. 'How was your trip?'

Disappointment flickered across Evelyn's face before she assumed a sultry pout, her full bottom lip pink and petulant. She'd been expecting a more effusive greeting – a kiss, guessed

Daniel. But he had never felt obliged to ape convention. A kiss would have felt disingenuous. To be fair, however, she'd done nothing to deserve bruised feelings, either. Daniel squeezed her fingers to reassure her of his attention.

'It would have been tedious but for the company of my good friend, Queenie.' Arching a stencilled brow, Evelyn slanted a triumphant look in Alex and Eliza's direction. 'Who I convinced to return. She'll stay until the end of spring.'

Daniel groaned inwardly. *Not this again.* Emasculation gibes would be easier to deflect than avenging darts. Evelyn still had not forgiven Alex for ending his relationship with Queenie. Initially, her anger had extended to Daniel when he'd refused to denounce his friend or his actions. But she'd eventually calmed down.

Queenie Nolan had appeared in Melbourne from Sydney a little over six months ago. A true femme fatale, who had taken one look at Alex and set out to seduce him. Although it was against their code to interfere in each other's relationships, Daniel had cautioned his friend, fearing he'd fallen hard. But Alex had assured him they weren't exclusive, and his heart was uninvolved.

When Alex had ended the affair to pursue Eliza, Evelyn had been convinced that Queenie was inconsolable. Anyone who'd spent time with the woman would find that laughable. But Daniel could well imagine Queenie had been annoyed. They had made a striking couple and there weren't many single men of Alex's calibre since the end of the Great War.

A glance across at his friend showed a countenance as cool as an ice-cream in a vacuum flask. The only sign of tension was the play of his thumb across the stone in Eliza's engagement ring as he stood, his hand linked with hers.

Eliza's face was pink, but she maintained a polite smile. This would be her first encounter with her fiancé's ex-girlfriend since they announced their engagement.

Bec's feelings were written across her face in jagged font. She was protective of her best friend and by extension Alex. Admirable, Daniel admitted, but not always convenient.

Eyes wide, Bec asked, 'Not enough distraction in Sydney?'

Even Jim looked sideways at hearing her tone. Bec was not a fan of Evelyn's. Daniel recalled soliciting her advice on his relationship a couple of weeks ago. God knows what he'd been thinking. In her matter-of-fact voice, she'd suggested that Evelyn sounded like a lot of trouble and to dump her. He'd been angry at her cavalier opinion. He'd been taught women were the gentler sex, but obviously someone had forgotten to tell Bec.

'She wanted to be with friends. And my parents were happy to welcome her.'

'Hmm —'

'Derek Fisher whisked her onto the dancefloor as soon as he saw us arrive,' Evelyn interrupted. 'There they are,' she said, wriggling her pink-tipped fingers in an impression of a wave towards the couple as they danced past.

'Don't they make a cute couple?' said Bec, smiling.

Evelyn narrowed her eyes in Bec's direction, clearly doubting her sincerity.

At the imperceptible shake of Daniel's head, Bec withdrew into silence. Evelyn was no match for Bec's pointed witticisms and Daniel was not interested in refereeing a spat or placating an aggrieved girlfriend. Especially one who, since the conversation with his boss, no longer suited Daniel's ambitions.

Life had become a collection of puzzle pieces that no longer fitted together. Daniel was damned if he could make sense of things – it was driving his engineering brain mad. Puzzles were something he excelled at. He understood the design principles – the devil-may-care life he'd enjoyed since his university days was over, so too his casual conquests, Evelyn amongst these. But how did he fill the gaps?

At a change in tempo, Alex excused himself and Eliza for a waltz. Bec wound her arm through Jim's, but before they could make their excuses, Queenie arrived with Derek.

'Darling,' welcomed Evelyn. 'I was just telling everyone the good news.'

Remembering his manners, Daniel smiled at Queenie. The woman was bewitching, from the top of her golden-blonde hair to the tips of her manicured nails. Her conversation both entertaining and cutting. Her manner intriguing. Daniel sensed she had few genuine friends. Men wanted to bed her and women to put as much distance between their men and Queenie as possible. All except Evelyn. He wasn't sure if that was a reflection of her confidence in his fidelity or the degree of his disinterest in the blonde bombshell.

'I am thrilled to be back,' she purred. 'Derek was just telling me the latest news.'

Derek arched a brow and inclined his head regally, as if he'd been knighted.

Daniel fought with himself to stop from rolling his eyes. *Dolt!*

'And who do we have here?' enquired Queenie, her steady gaze raking Jim up and down.

'Warrant Officer Jim Johnson. I believe we were introduced at the Lord Mayor's Ball.'

'Did you forget to go home?'

Jim grinned. 'No, ma'am. I'm tidying up some affairs.'

'Your own, or ...?' Queenie directed a meaningful look Bec's way.

'A gentleman never tells.'

Daniel narrowed his gaze, taking notice of the hand now possessing Bec's waist. Had he misjudged things? *Was there more to their relationship than a penchant for kissing and brash comments?* They'd known each other for less than three weeks. Although, more than a handful of girls during the fleet visit had got themselves engaged or married to a Yank in less time.

'Well, I hope that we'll see you often, Warrant Officer Johnson. The female population of Melbourne and Sydney are much the poorer since the fleet left our shores,' said Queenie with a speculative smile.

Wow, she's good, thought Daniel. Jim couldn't fail to interpret her interest – unless he was an idiot! *And Bec couldn't abide idiots.* Yet Daniel watched in amazement as the man offered a casual smile and thanked her for the compliment as if Queenie were a favourite aunt.

Was the Yank that sure of Bec's affections? Did her kisses raid Jim's sensibilities, like they had Daniel's? It would take a seasoned man to resist such fervour. Queenie wouldn't stand a chance with Jim – Bec was worth ten of her. Daniel shook himself mentally – his thoughts were headed in an unexpected and puzzling direction.

He'd known Bec for years. They'd met here at Birmingham's. He remembered being instantly attracted ... and tongue tied. She'd been sassy even back then. Her wide grey eyes had beckoned him, even as her dimple had hinted her amusement at his predicament. He couldn't remember their conversation – it had been brief – but he'd been left feeling as if she'd slammed a door in his face, having been swiftly weighed up, categorised and dismissed.

Jim inclined his head in acknowledgement. 'Now, ladies, gents, if you'll excuse us. The band is playing our favourite song.'

And with that parting comment, Daniel watched Jim manoeuvre Bec onto the crowded dancefloor, into his arms, and effortlessly pick up the rhythm. *A favourite song? After three weeks?*

'There's something about a man in uniform,' sighed Queenie, fanning her face. 'Let's mingle, Derek dear.' Planting air kisses to the side of Evelyn's face and waving fingers in Daniel's direction, she sashayed off on Derek's arm.

'And then there were two,' cooed Evelyn, slanting him a look from beneath her lashes and brushing her breast against his bicep – an invitation he wouldn't have hesitated to accept a week ago.

Daniel hoped his face didn't mirror his jumbled thoughts. In the space of a week – *less* – their relationship had been recast. At least in his mind; Evelyn was playing catch-up. The timing was unfortunate. In the past two, maybe three months, their friends had started referring to them as a couple. Evelyn's insistence that he meet her parents had supported this. Daniel had reasoned it didn't mean anything as the introductions were made at a party – he was one of seventy other guests and had spent less than five minutes in their company. She still hadn't met his. He'd resisted countless hints. Had his subconscious been privy to decisions he was only now becoming aware of?

They needed to get out of here. 'I'm glad you've returned. We have a lot to catch up on.'

Evelyn's face transformed. The uncertainty that had haunted her brown eyes, no doubt a response to his tepid welcome, disappeared. 'I missed you, too.'

Her words failed to kindle his usual enthusiasm. He was glad she'd returned; he just hadn't missed her. 'Let's go for a drink.'

He'd start with his version of his recruitment for the debate and the poster – that would lay the groundwork for future discussions – and end with his commitment to the Icebreaker Challenge tomorrow. For once, he was glad of an excuse to end the evening in his own bed. A sorry situation indeed.

CHAPTER 9

Sunday 16 August 1925

Bec dipped her toe into the water and shivered. How had she ever thought this was a good idea?

'What's the temperature like?' asked Eliza.

'Warmer than the air.'

'That's very reassuring. What is it today – a whole fifty-seven degrees?'

'Less wind chill, make it fifty,' said Bec, sliding her foot back into her rubber boot. 'Thankfully, the waters are calm. Yesterday, it was whipped up as if by a giant eggbeater. I swear, icebergs were washing up on the shore!'

'Daniel tells me coldness is a state of mind.'

'Good, then let him jump in,' said Bec.

'Or maybe my fiancé, that might cool his ardour where Queenie is concerned.'

'Eliza, Alex has eyes only for you. Any chasing being done is by Queenie. Although, I think she may have set her sights on Jim after their reacquaintance last night.'

'Humph! I want to believe you. But he looked as guilty as all get out when I came upon them in the garden at Birmingham's. With her back in town, maybe he's reconsidering his choice.'

'I refuse to believe it. You don't see his face when you're not watching him. He's got it bad. And bad for you alone.'

'Chilly, isn't it?'

Bec swivelled to face Daniel, her gaze sweeping over him. He didn't look like he'd partied all night or dragged himself from a warm bed – and there was no sign of Evelyn. The edginess she'd awoken with dissipated, replaced with a feeling of ... relief? Satisfaction? Whatever it was, she didn't want to examine it too closely. She was simply pleased that he'd actually shown up. 'Apparently, it's all in the mind.'

'Therefore, it would stand to reason that you, brother dearest, must feel a trifle overdressed.'

Daniel grinned, buttoning the top of his overcoat and stomping his feet. 'Well, that's what they used to tell us in our first year at the Tramways Board, before we'd head out for site inspections. We'd experience all of Melbourne's four seasons – frost, sunshine reminiscent of a mild summer morning, then the sky would become leaden with rain, blinding hail and a keen wind, and that was all before lunchtime.'

'You always were better at ignoring the elements than anyone else,' said Alex, wrapping his arm around Eliza's waist and kissing the side of her temple in welcome.

Bec was pleased to see her friend lean into him. She was convinced that Alex had no interest in his previous girlfriend, apart from protecting Eliza from her sharp tongue. Queenie could be quite a cat.

Daniel frowned as he inspected Bec's garb – cloche, scarf, heavy woollen coat and galoshes. 'Are you planning on swimming in those?'

Bec struck a pose. 'Too much, you think?'

Daniel shrugged. 'Not if you're in a race to the bottom of the pool.'

Funny man.

'Can I have all participants and their scrutineers to the starter's area,' yelled a voice over the small crowd. The event had attracted around forty people – all through word of mouth as advertising pennies were in short supply. Bec's initiative had only scraped into this year's program with Elsie's support.

'That's us, let's go,' said Bec, grabbing her friend's arm and gesturing to Daniel and Alex to follow.

'Bossy female,' grumbled Daniel.

Bec ignored him, propelling Eliza along the weather-beaten timber to where a young man, from the Williamstown Swimming Club, began to talk through the rules of the challenge to the fifteen young women assembled.

'The stroke is the front crawl – Australian or American. The goal is to complete as many laps as you can in thirty minutes. If you run into trouble, try to make it to the side of the pool or tread water. A bell will sound at the end of the allotted time. Any questions so far?'

There was silence apart from Eliza's chattering teeth. Bec wrapped an arm around her shoulders.

'Your assigned number is the order in which you'll line up along the seaward side of the baths. Leave your outer garments behind your starting position. Grab a towel from over there. Shortly, Mrs Jenny Sherman will deliver a few words of welcome. Any questions?'

'Will we receive our official lap tally today?' asked a girl to Bec's right, sporting a bright-pink bathing cap.

'Yes. Grab them from me before you leave.'

Bec had drawn number fifteen, which suited her as she'd be able to use the timber pylons as a guide to swim straight. Eliza was swimming in position one.

'Can all the scrutineers identify yourselves, please?'

Daniel, Alex and three other men raised their hands.

'You'll be presiding over three swimmers each. Your job is to keep count of the number of laps completed by each swimmer, on the blackboards at the back. Use tally marks and group them into fives. Any questions? No? We're starting in ten minutes.'

Bec looked around at the mix of expressions on the other swimmers. Some, spurred by youthful exuberance, were already stripping off their outer layers. Others, like her, were leaving the divesting to the last possible moment. Bec jigged up and down. She loved winter – the muted light on a freezing cold morning, toasty fireplaces and soup – but hated being cold.

She reminded herself of the generous support of her sponsors. She had secured one shilling per lap from Mr and Mrs Birmingham and five of her father's barbershop customers. Jim had handed over a one-pound donation regardless of the number of laps she swam. She'd rewarded his generosity with a long, smoochy kiss – which reminded her that he said he'd be here. *Where was he?*

Bec's father had offered two pounds if she'd withdraw. But she was confident he'd pay out regardless. He knew once she set her mind to something, she'd see it through. Thirty minutes of physical discomfort for a great cause. *Brrr! Best get it over with.*

'Having second thoughts?' drawled Daniel.

'Aren't you supposed to be organising your chalk or something?'

'Five minutes,' came the call.

Daniel smirked, folding his arms. 'I hope you haven't dragged me out here under false pretences.'

Galvanised into action, Bec shed her cloche, scarf, galoshes, coat and draped a towel around her neck. An appreciative whistle sounded from behind her. She swung around to find Jim, standing at the front of the onlookers, hands on hips, looking his fill.

'Good morning to you, too,' returned Bec playfully. 'What time do you call this?'

Unconscious of the stern looks and *tut-tuts* of disapproval, he took a step forward before being blocked by Daniel and Alex.

'Last call.'

Bec blew him a kiss, scooped up her clothes and hurried to her position.

❧

'A bit of a conservative crowd, mate,' said Alex, slapping Jim on the shoulder. 'Might want to tone it down. I can't even get away with that in public with my fiancée,' he added before moving in the direction of the start line.

'Stay here and stay out of trouble,' advised Daniel, turning on his heel and following Alex.

The sight of Bec drew Daniel like a magnet. Unable to look away, he watched as she dropped her clothes in the far corner of the boardwalk, and then tugged a bathing cap over her wavy mahogany hair.

Who knew she had mile-long sculpted legs hidden under those skirts she wore? How had he never noticed? He who prided himself on being a connoisseur of the female form. Daniel couldn't blame Jim for his reaction. The shorts of Bec's swimsuit did nothing to hide her lightly tanned limbs. Cut high, they skimmed the tops of her thighs. And the top seemed to plunge from the neck, front and back. He started loosening the buttons of his coat as he hurried to take his position – the day was warmer than he'd expected.

'Welcome, everyone. Thanks for braving the elements for the YWCA's inaugural Icebreaker Challenge,' hollered Jenny Sherman from the side of the pool.

Daniel pretended an interest in the coloured chalk sticks in his palm as he watched Bec from the corner of his eye. *God!* She was going to catch her death in such a skimpy outfit.

'Each of the girls here today has been sponsored at a set rate per lap by some very generous donors – no doubt some of you are here today. They will swim as many laps as they can in thirty minutes to raise as much money as possible for our annual fundraiser. It's not too late to donate if you haven't done so. Please seek me out. Without further ado, I'll hand you over to our starter, Henry.'

Bec took position fifteen. Daniel stared. Those woollen shorts hugged her bottom like a second skin. And those legs – weapons of seduction.

Henry raised his arm where he stood at the side of the pool, halfway down. 'Take your marks. Ready ... Set ... Go.'

At the sound of the bell, Bec was the first to hit the water, her dark-blue cap surfacing and powering away. Her lead quickly extended to a body length, which Daniel credited to needing to warm up all that exposed skin.

How was he going to forget the sight of her in that costume? It must be new; she hadn't looked like that last season. Unless he needed his eyes checked. Were those little buttons on the side of her shorts for show or ease of extracting the body wearing them? Daniel shook himself, remembering he had a job to do. Scanning the pool across positions thirteen to fifteen, he started tallying.

When the final bell sounded, Bec was at the other end of the pool. Daniel grabbed her towel and discarded clothes and joined Alex. He watched her turn and breaststroke back to the starting position, where Eliza was waiting, treading water.

'It's over,' Eliza gasped. 'Thank goodness. I thought I was going to have to pull out – I got a cramp about fifteen laps in and had to dog paddle for a bit.' She giggled. 'I thought Alex …' she shot her fiancé, standing above her, a smile, 'was going to jump in and save me.'

Bec gave her a crooked smile. 'Thank you for being such a sport. I promise next year we'll volunteer for something warmer.'

'Well done, both of you,' congratulated Daniel.

Bec adjusted her costume and scaled the ladder behind Eliza, who was enveloped in a towel by Alex and whisked into a hug, no doubt under the pretence of getting her warm and dry.

'Are they regulation length?' Daniel asked, holding Bec's towel while eyeing her bathers – and the woman within them.

Looking up, she ignored his question, working to unbuckle the chin strap of her bathing cap before peeling it off. As she shook her hair free, he anticipated her lunge for the towel and held it just out of reach.

'Well, are they?'

'Who appointed you the bather police,' she hissed.

'I thought not,' he said, ignoring her outburst and meeting her glare with one of his own.

'Do you want me to catch my death?'

He relented.

Snatching the towel from him, she wrapped it around her body, before making a grab for the rest of her clothes draped over his arm.

'Good job,' said Jim, appearing behind Daniel. 'You were really motoring up and down that pool.'

Daniel watched Bec's expression transform. 'Thanks for coming,' she said warmly. *Too warmly*. 'Not a great spectating event, I'm afraid.'

Jim chuckled. 'Unless of course you count the time spectatin' at the start and the finish when you gals are out of the water.'

Daniel bit back a growl. It was hypocritical to censure the Yank for something he agreed with. But it was one thing to think something and quite a different matter to voice it. Especially in mixed company. And was that a blush? Bec *never* blushed. Was she embarrassed or was she enjoying the American's boldness?

'Gather around,' yelled Henry. 'We'll be quick, as I'm sure these girls would like to get changed.'

The competitors huddled together in various stages of dress. Some in towels, toga style like Bec, others with coats draped around their shoulders or with scarves. Spectators stood in a row behind, acting as a windbreak, backs to the sea. Jim had positioned himself directly behind Bec, his upper body pressing forward. Daniel shuffled through the crowd to stand beside him and keep an eye on proprieties, although he doubted Bec would thank him.

Jenny stepped up onto a box. 'Congratulations, girls. Your efforts this morning ... simply fantastic ... and the monies raised will enable the association to continue its great work in the interests of the health, education and happiness of young women.'

This was met with loud cheering and clapping.

'A special mention to Bec Cross who managed thirty laps – one a minute. She must have got in some sneaky training earlier in the season.'

'That's my girl,' yelled Jim amid general laughter.

Daniel clenched his hands into tight fists and crossed his arms. It was either that or deliver a punch, and he hadn't hit anyone since prep school. Nor could he have said why he had the urge to do so. Jim's familiarity just grated.

'Thanks again, everyone. Please join us for a cuppa and scones at the Sands Café over yonder,' said Jenny, before stepping down.

Daniel watched Bec hover, uncharacteristically uncertain. From the goosebumps appearing on her shoulders, he thought her choice should be obvious. 'What's the matter?'

'We need our official lap records so we can collect our sponsorship monies.'

'I'll take care of it. Go and get some clothes on.' *For both our sakes.*

'Thanks.'

Blowing a kiss Jim's way, she collected Eliza and hurried off. *God, those legs ...*

When Bec emerged from the dressing shed, Daniel awaited her. Alone. Leaning against the timber railing, hands in the pockets of his woollen overcoat, he looked the epitome of casual elegance.

As she got closer, his eyes told a different story – they were blazing – the colour of amber rather than their normal hazel. He wasn't still worked up over her bathing suit, was he? Last summer, she'd counted a dozen girls in similar garb.

'Where's everyone gone?' she asked, striving for a relaxed tone.

'I told Alex and Eliza we'd meet them at the café.'

'And Jim?'

'Ah, Jim. He had to make sure two of his fugitives boarded a local steamer for Sydney. He said he'd see you later.'

Bec's spirits flagged. Had he forgotten he'd been coming home to meet her parents? It hadn't been a formal invitation, but they'd talked about him dropping in after the event. 'All right. Let's go.'

Daniel held out a piece of paper. 'Your record of laps. You set an impressive tally.'

'Thanks,' said Bec, extending her hand.

'Impressive enough that I've decided to sponsor your effort.'

'Thank you. That's great.'

'Is that all?'

She tugged the record from his resisting fingers and scanned it. 'What do you mean? Do you want a medal?'

Daniel's jaw set stubbornly. 'What did Jim receive for *his* donation?'

Bec's thoughts replayed their negotiation – the memory spread warmth to her extremities. *How did Daniel know about that?*

'Nothing —'

'That's not what your face tells me.'

'It's none of your business. He was *very* generous.'

'Four pounds.'

'What? That's —'

'*Excessively* generous.'

Bec cleared her throat and put her hands on her hips. 'What are you playing at, Daniel?'

He shrugged, his gaze dropping to her lips.

She didn't pretend to misunderstand. Did he think she needed the practice? After last time? The nerve of the man. She'd teach him.

Sucking in a deep breath, she stepped forward and took his jaw between her hands. She approved of the smooth texture of his skin and the smell of citrus that teased her nostrils. Intending to deliver a single powerful salute to his lips, she was unprepared when he placed his hands over hers, trapping them. He'd ambushed her. *This was payback.*

Tilting his head to perfect the angle, he assumed control. Unlike last time, when she had determined when to call a halt to things, this time he'd relegated her to the passenger seat. With no map and unclear as to the destination, Bec held on, both to him and to her senses – just.

It wasn't the intensity. Unlike last time, his lips were feather light, touching and teasing. His tongue almost on a leisurely stroll, connecting and pleasuring. When his hands left hers to cup her nape, burying beneath the weight of her hair, she forgot to protest, instead moving her own to fist into the lapels of his coat. He kneaded knots she hadn't been aware of until now, dissolving tension. Time became irrelevant. Bec groaned.

It was only when she felt an icy blast from the onshore wind that she realised they were slowly drawing apart. She sensed reluctance – and not just on her part. Bec willed her fingers, still tangled in the material of his coat, to let go.

He leaned back as if unsure whether she entertained thoughts of slapping him. *She should! Shouldn't she?* Except that would require energy, and she needed any lingering reserves to support her legs.

Bec risked a glance at his face. The smug expression he wore gave her the resolve to shake the gooey feeling that had overtaken her body. This was why she always kept her head – to avoid situations like this. Along with her resolve, her memory returned. She'd groaned, for heaven's sake. How mortifying.

Levelling Daniel with a fiery gaze, fuelled as much by embarrassment as anything else, she growled, 'Satisfied?'

'Are you humouring me?'

Humour had nothing to do with it, but it was better that he believed that than discover how unsettled she felt. She shrugged. 'Now we're even.'

'Even?'

'After last time. This time I'll apologise. It won't happen again.'

Daniel stared at her. 'Right ...'

Awkward! Her gaze held his. 'Four pounds, remember.'

His eyes narrowed and his voice sounded choked, as if being forced through a metal grater. 'I remember.'

It wasn't often that Bec considered a retreat from their skirmishes as her best option. Kissing Daniel a second time had been a miscalculation. His reaction was puzzling. And her reaction to his reaction left her flat. She'd bested him, hadn't she? But there was no warm glow of triumph. On the other hand, the Y was four pounds richer. And there were warm scones awaiting her.

'Come on. I'm famished.'

Daniel nodded.

She hoped his loss of voice wasn't permanent. They had a debate to win.

CHAPTER 10

Monday 17 August 1925

Daniel trudged up the steps leading to the YWCA's Russell Street headquarters. He almost expected to see a noose hanging from the edifice. His assignment to the debate, and his boss's fixation that he was not to treat his involvement as a distraction or a waste of time, still grated. Women were unsuited to this role and one debate was not long enough to list all the reasons why. Yet here he was, meeting with Bec and Jenny to sketch out the arguments for the opposing position. Martyring his opinions at the altar of promotion.

And, it seemed, his entire department had an interest. Someone had managed to get their hands on one of the damn posters and stuck it above his and Theo's desk. Money had changed hands – they were even money favourites. Daniel was determined that would change. His ego, *hell*, his whole self-image, was now wrapped up in this.

He didn't think anyone had recognised him, and he hoped it stayed that way. But more than one of his colleagues had commented on Bec's attractiveness, and the improved appeal of public transport if she were employed. All he saw was her faintly mocking expression, her eyes seeming to follow him around the room.

Stepping across the threshold, a veritable hive of activity besieged him. Young women carrying suitcases, dressed in travelling attire, eyes wide, their faces bright with hope. Others studying noticeboards, some clutching pamphlets and maps or ensconced in chairs reading newspapers. A constant pulse of conversation threaded through the mayhem.

Alex had warned him about the demeanour of horn-rimmed Hannah, the receptionist. He had some sympathy. From what he could see and hear from his position in the queue, she secured the frontline and needed the skill of a military general to do so.

'Thought I'd save you from spending too much time in this madness,' said Bec, emerging from the whirlpool and claiming him.

'Is it always like this?'

'Pretty much. It's quieter earlier in the day. Come on.'

The noise subsided to a low hum as they gained the inner recesses.

'That's better, I could hardly hear myself think.'

Bec's expression could have been lifted from the poster. He supposed he sounded like a grouser.

'All right with you if we take the stairs? It's only a couple of flights.'

Was she calling into question his fitness? Daniel motioned for her to lead on, looking around with interest. From the signage, he learned that the building also housed a main hall for displays, lectures, concerts, lesson rooms and an employment office. He could smell freshly baked bread from the cafeteria, no doubt, and realised he'd missed lunch – again.

Bec was babbling. 'We're using the Connibere room for our meeting. It was named after a wealthy patron. Eliza uses it for her student lessons, but she's ensconced in the staff room reviewing curriculum.'

Daniel glanced at her profile, realising she was unsettled. She kept touching her hair and her cheeks were pink. Was she remembering their kiss yesterday? Perhaps he wasn't the only one to lose his balance. Their second kiss had left him more unsatisfied than the first. He'd been sure their first had been an aberration – after all, he was no rookie. But it hadn't been. And then she'd brushed it off as if indulging a wilful child. *'Satisfied?'* That had stung! Her apology and reminder of the four-pound donation had dispatched his ego for the remainder of the morning.

'Good afternoon, Daniel.' Jenny was setting up chairs and a table. 'Thanks for joining us. How are you feeling about the debate?'

Daniel smiled in greeting, hesitating as he crafted his response. 'Uneasy would best sum things up.'

'But not unobliging, I hope?'

'No, Jenny. I'm here to learn and share my knowledge. Of course I have misgivings, as you know, or at least Bec will have shared with you. But I'm sure we'll work through those.'

'Actually, we think they can be turned to our advantage,' said Bec.

Daniel raised his eyebrows.

'Well, you're the only one on our team who doesn't agree that women would make terrific tram conductors. So, you can help identify a wider range of points for us to prepare rebuttals for.'

'Clever, huh? It's like having an enemy in the camp – who

is on our side,' enthused Jenny.

Daniel contemplated the excited faces before him. 'Yes, I can see how that might work ... that's *damn* clever!'

'Bec's idea. She's a mixture of beauty *and* brains!'

Bec gave an embarrassed laugh, and Daniel's attention was drawn to her mouth and its generous lower lip. He couldn't seem to help but remember the taste of those lips – the hint of salt from the sea baths; the feel of them misted with moisture – and the sensation was tattooed on his memory as if he'd experienced it all in slow motion. And he remembered, just before he took control of the moment, feeling nervous, his mind going blank. *Ridiculous!* That hadn't happened since he was in his late teens.

'Right, where do you want to start?' asked Daniel, pulling his thoughts back to the purpose of the meeting.

'The debate topic refers to the emotional, intellectual and physical demands of the job, so we thought we should make a list of what they are,' said Bec.

'So that we understand them better,' added Jenny.

'And use that information to strengthen our arguments,' said Bec.

It was like watching a tennis match. Daniel focused on Bec. 'Of course, there may be legitimate reasons against which it will be difficult to argue.'

'Like what?'

Daniel's gaze followed Bec's hands as they moved to her hips, resting below a narrow black leather belt cinching her waist. In concert, his thoughts recalled a similar pose yesterday, in far less clothing, awakening parts of his anatomy that had no business being front and centre.

'Well ...' He dragged his thoughts once again back to the

conversation. 'There are over twenty different configurations of trams, and they all require different levels of physicality and agility.'

'I know there are age, height and weight requirements. There's no suggestion of waiving those for women – we don't want special concessions.'

'It's more than that, Bec. Conductors are regularly manhandled – a kick, an elbow, a hot breath down their neck – all while weaving from one end of the tram to the other.'

'Sounds like a typical night at Birmingham's to me,' quipped Bec.

Jenny giggled.

Daniel shook his head. 'And then —'

'That's enough, you two. You're supposed to be on the same side, *remember*? And ...' Jenny held up her hand as Bec went to interrupt. 'The idea was to use this time to capture Daniel's points, not refute them. I must leave here at five. It's four now – we have an hour.'

Bec threw herself into the nearest chair. 'I'll scribe.'

Daniel, placating himself that she looked a little chastened, took a deep breath and sat down opposite her. 'Let's start with the physical ...'

Bec compartmentalised her emotions – a trick her grandmother had taught her when she was ten years old. Her one and only ever tantrum. Her parents had been horrified; Grandmother Adelaide had been unfazed.

Bec concentrated on capturing each point, clarifying and questioning as needed – her personal opinions locked away, her mind having imagined the turning of the key for good measure. Jenny was a paragon of calm and reasonableness. One day, Bec hoped to emulate her.

The hour whizzed by, Bec scribbling furiously. She was forced to admit that Daniel had a wealth of knowledge – *and opinions* – and a formidable ability to articulate both. That boded well for the debate. It was why she enjoyed sparring with him. Her thinking was sharper, more ... energised. *Completely different to when he kissed her, then her thinking became slower* ... Bec pushed that thought into its box and slammed the lid shut – a good reason to avoid a reoccurrence.

At five o'clock, Jenny stood up. 'I've got to run. Do you think the two of you can finish this without bloodshed? Another ten, maybe fifteen minutes of work.'

'We'll be fine,' said Bec. 'But to be sure, take all the sharp instruments with you.'

Jenny grinned. 'Let's reconvene ... tomorrow? Does that suit? Good. Ida, our third member, should be available, too. Can you make four copies of those notes, please, Bec?'

And without waiting for a response, she rushed out the door.

'She's like Australia's very own George Washington, isn't she?' remarked Daniel.

'America won't know what's hit it when she arrives!'

Daniel smirked. 'Where were we? Emotional demands ... we covered general themes of tact, an even temperament, resolve ...'

'And I noted down a requirement for the role not to take comments personally,' added Bec, rereading her notes.

'Uh-huh. And include deference.'

Bec flinched. 'Deference?'

Daniel looked quizzically at her. 'Are you all right?'

Her gut tightened. 'What do you mean by deference? Obedience, submission ... *surrender?*'

'No. I meant that the role needs courtesy and politeness.'

Bec's fingers loosened their grip on the pen, and she focused on adding the words to the list. When she looked up, Daniel was still watching her. 'I'm fine.' Dropping her gaze, she pretended to study the list. 'Anything else?'

'Bec. Has someone hurt you? Jim —'

Her eyes met his. 'Don't be ridiculous. Jim is more attentive and thoughtful than some of our own ... It was something that came up in the staff room. Just another example of ... you know ... the inequality between the sexes.'

Her gaze slid away. She could tell Daniel wasn't convinced, but her overreaction was not something she wanted to discuss. That one word had unlocked a churning discord of memories from her teens.

A change in subject seemed the best approach. Looking up from her doodling, she addressed his chin. 'I've been thinking that we should adopt Jenny's advice.'

'Which piece?'

'The one about being on the same team.'

'Is that a white flag I'm seeing unfurl?' asked Daniel with a lift of his brow.

'Not forever. Think of it more as a need to ... I don't know ...' She waved her hands in the air like a magician. 'Parley rather than parry.'

'A temporary lull in hostilities, then?'

'Yes. Just for the next few weeks.'

'But what happens if one of us forgets?'

Bec shrugged. She supposed if one of them did lambast

the other, a weak apology would be issued and they'd move on. Trust Daniel to make this more complex than it needed to be. Did he want her to draw him a picture?

Daniel leaned forward. 'How about, for a bit of fun, the one who slips up pays a forfeit?'

Bec was suspicious of the glint in his eye. 'A forfeit? What type of forfeit?'

'Ah, that's the fun bit. The injured party gets to decide.'

'What type have you designed before?'

'Well, it was a while ago ... Alex and I used to play this at university.'

A peek into Daniel's past. 'And?'

'Cold showers, midnight runs, that sort of thing.'

Bec pulled a face, shuddering. 'I'm not signing up for that.'

'It doesn't appeal to me, either. Let's agree that the forfeit can't be a physical hardship.'

Bec calculated the machinations. 'Or a financial one,' she added.

'All right, let's summarise the rule as the forfeit cannot cause harm or hardship.'

It seemed too simple, and Daniel was looking too pleased with himself, while trying not to. But she was competitive by nature, and so the idea had appeal. Of course, in her mind, she'd be handing out all the penalties, dispensing them like charms.

'It's a deal,' agreed Bec. Elsie would be proud of her. She'd kept her opinions to herself – mostly. *Tick!* And negotiated to her and Daniel's mutual satisfaction, a fun way to minimise future skirmishes. *Double tick!*

CHAPTER 11

Tuesday 18 August 1925

'May I introduce Miss Ida McAuley from the Victorian Women's Council,' said Jenny with a broad smile as she ushered a tall, angular young woman into the room. 'The last member of our team.'

'Hello, Ida, I'm Rebecca Cross, but everyone calls me Bec.'

'Daniel Sinclair. Pleased to meet you, Miss McAuley.'

'An emancipated man! On our team. How fabulous,' enthused Miss McAuley, her sharp, inquisitive nose twitching. 'Please call me Ida. I'm sorry that I couldn't make the meeting yesterday. Our organisation is evolving and there were things that just could not be deferred. But I'm sure you made great progress, which I'm looking forward to hearing about.'

'Well —' began Jenny, only to be cut off.

'I still can't believe it. Mr Sinclair, you are a beacon to other men,' said Ida, pressing her hands to her bosom. 'Have you always supported women's rights?'

Bec smothered a giggle. She and Jenny might as well slip out for a drink – Ida only had eyes for Daniel. She couldn't wait to hear him explain his passion and commitment to the cause.

'Well —' Daniel began, but Ida McAuley was off again. Bec couldn't decide whether the woman liked to hear her own voice, or simply had to share every thought that popped into her head.

'I read that our male suffragists often experience much worse treatment than ourselves – jeers, whistles and other pernicious insults and assaults. It is a credit to you. And the poster —'

'Miss McAuley, if you would kindly pause for a moment,' interrupted Daniel, planting his feet shoulder-width apart.

The effect was immediate, and Bec savoured the silence. Daniel and his tone held a natural air of command. He was impressive in a distracting sort of way. She'd spent more time thinking about him – *and his kisses* – in the last ten days than she had for the entire time she'd known him.

'I come to the debate, not as an ardent supporter of the labour-reform movement, but as a student of the topic. I hope that my involvement can be an influential factor, a small boost to our success in winning.' He paused, examining his cuffs before locking eyes with the earnest woman. 'Because, Miss McAuley, I am a very sore loser.'

'Well, I thank you for your candour, Mr Sinclair.'

'Yes, thank you, Daniel, for clearing that up.' Bec pressed a page of notes into his hand, eyeing him thoughtfully. He had a silver tongue when he was motivated to use it. 'Now, Miss McAuley – Ida – let's catch you up on our progress. Daniel has been ...' She paused.

'Instrumental?' suggested Jenny.

'Yes, instrumental in helping outline the key points that

our rebuttals will need to address. Here is a copy of the notes from Monday's session, categorised under "Emotional", "Intellectual" and "Physical". If there are points that you think have been missed, please call those to Jenny's or my attention and I'll revise the list.'

Ida removed her cloche and patted her waved hair – no doubt the result of expert hands and a heated iron. Seating herself, back ramrod straight, in the closest chair, she pulled out a small pair of round metal frames and studied the document.

Silence reigned for the second time that evening. Bec watched the woman's eyes skim the pages with a practised air.

'An excellent list, Rebecca.'

Bec cringed. She only ever heard her full name when she was in trouble, but guessed Ida didn't mean any insult.

'Yes, well done, Rebecca,' said Daniel, returning her mock glare with a playful smile. 'Your secretarial skills are almost flawless. One small spelling mistake on the last page —'

'Where?'

'The plural of terminus is termini.'

She hoped the look she shot him conveyed what her polite 'Thank you' couldn't. She circled the word with brisk strokes. 'The next decision is to allocate the speaking order and divvy up the list of points between us to draft our arguments and counter-arguments.'

At this news, Ida primped the hair at the base of her neck and smiled. 'Well, I was always considered a strong lead for the debates at university. So, if no one minds, I'd like to take the first-speaker position.'

'No argument from me,' replied Bec. 'Daniel?'

'I'm sure we're extremely fortunate to have such an experienced debater as our lead speaker.'

Bec resisted the urge to roll her eyes as a girlish giggle – at odds with the woman's thirty-something years – escaped Ida. *God, when he turned on the charm, no one was immune. Except me. Well, mostly.*

'Can I suggest Daniel take the final-speaker position,' said Jenny. 'He would leave a strong impression as the only male on the team.'

Bec nodded. 'That's a great idea. His rebuttal skills are probably the most honed, so it would make sense to use him in that role.'

'*Hello!* I'm standing three feet away. Does this conscript have any say?'

'How about "*Yes*"?' returned Bec, secretly pleased at the annoyance in his tone. 'It'll save time.'

'Of course, Mr Sinclair, if you think you'd perform better in the second-speaker position, you must say so,' said Ida. 'I'm sure Jenny and Rebecca aren't trying to coerce you. But I happen to think they're right.'

Was this the persuasion Elsie spoke of? It sounded like mollycoddling. Pasting a smile on her face, Bec turned to look at him. 'Of course not. I just think we should play to our strengths. You're an obvious choice,' she said, working to temper any remnants of dismissiveness from her tone. *God! This flattery business was exhausting. Even when laced with sincerity.*

Daniel nodded, as if just reaching the same conclusion. He agreed with Bec and Jenny's thinking. It was more the way they'd gone about it that had annoyed him. He was used to making the decisions, issuing them, not having them flung at him and around him. Unless by his boss ... But Bec and Jenny weren't in that position.

'Good, that's settled, then. Bec will assume the role of second speaker,' said Jenny. 'This also has a strong rebuttal responsibility.'

'Lucky she's a natural,' quipped Daniel. Bec froze, and he realised he'd fallen into his usual habit of baiting her. *God, what was wrong with him?* He offered what he hoped was a placating smile, but from the look on Bec's face, he must be out of practice.

Before returning to the general conversation, she poked her tongue out at him. Daniel disguised a guffaw at Miss McAuley's look of bewilderment, no doubt ignorant to the undercurrents, and watched colour flood Bec's cheeks.

Jenny's no-nonsense tone cut through. 'And it's the role that will present half of the team's arguments.'

'So, how does the debate work? How do we divide the arguments between speakers one and two?' asked Bec.

'Ida will ensure the definition of the topic outlined by the other team aligns with our definition, and challenge if necessary. She'll then introduce who is presenting what argument. Daniel, as third speaker, can only summarise all the points, not present new ones, and of course rebut.'

'Clear so far,' said Bec.

'I'd suggest Ida take the points identified against emotional and intellectual, and you take those aligned with physical. That way the split is roughly equal. What do you think, Ida?'

'Well summarised. Yes, I think that is the most sensible course. Of course, I may need some help with my preparation.'

Daniel ignored the silent appeal Ida sent him, grateful when Jenny offered the woman her support.

'That's where I come in. I can assist with that.'

'And I'll help Bec with her preparation,' Daniel said quickly, in case Ida objected. 'Give her the experience of my ... well-honed skills.'

'Great. And between Daniel and me, we can ensure the arguments remain consistent,' said Jenny with a small clap. 'Let's meet here on Saturday afternoon to check progress. Now, I must leave. Can I see you out, Ida? Bec, if it's all right can you do a quick tidy-up?'

Jenny's directness and speed again amazed Daniel. Within five minutes, she'd cleared the room and left him and Bec standing awkwardly beside one another. But not for long.

'So, I'm a natural, am I? What happened to our agreement?'

Daniel cocked his head. 'You're right. I'm sorry. I guess old habits aren't always easy to break.'

'Is that it? *Sorry?* Isn't this what our forfeit system was designed to moderate?'

'Yes.' He watched, transfixed, as Bec tapped her fingernail against her bottom lip. Could it be she was thinking of the same sort of penalty that had sprung to his mind? If so, it wouldn't be a hardship! It would relieve some of the frustration he'd woken up with this morning. Their second kiss, like their first, had ended too soon. Here was an opportunity to fix that ...

'Tomorrow, I intend to do some research to rectify my ... what did you call it last week ... *ignorance*? Since you're such an expert, you can accompany me to make sure I'm paying attention to the right things and not daydreaming out the window.'

'So, we're —'

'Catching a tram. Will two-thirty in the afternoon suit? Yes? Great, I'll see you then.' And with that Bec swivelled on her heel and headed out the door.

Daniel groaned. Not only were her kisses too short, but she lacked imagination. He could think of a dozen ways to use her forfeit ... and riding trams was not one of them.

Then again, she'd said she wanted him along to make sure she was paying attention to the right things. Did that include their burgeoning attraction? It was showing no signs of abating for him, and he was confident she wasn't unaffected, despite her sassy demeanour. He had enough experience with women to recognise the signs. Daniel smiled. Bec just needed some direction. What if Alex was right and his future wife was right under his nose?

CHAPTER 12

Wednesday 19 August 1925

Was it her imagination that Daniel had seemed disappointed in her choice of penalty? For a moment, his lips had parted, and he'd leaned forward as if expecting ... *a kiss*? No, she was being fanciful. Anyway, it wouldn't have solved anything. They kissed as they squabbled, with lips and tongues – all the while wrestling one another for an advantage. And this she knew after two. She laughed.

'What's so funny?' asked a voice close to her ear.

Bec jumped – or at least her mind skittered sideways – engrossed in her thoughts. 'Daniel!'

'Was it a naughty thought?'

'What?'

'Your thought. Was it naughty? You've gone as red as a tomato, and I can count on one hand the number of times I've seen you blush.'

'It was ... none of your business. And it's unflattering to be compared to a piece of fruit.'

'Would you prefer a peach?'

'I'd prefer we got going,' said Bec, charging down the steps to street level.

'*Deflection*. I'm even more intrigued,' he called to her from the top of the stairs, as she ignored him and turned north towards Collins Street and hopefully a waiting tram.

Bec was enjoying their repartee but had no intention of conducting it outside the door of her employer. Too many curious eyes.

Daniel appeared beside her and settled into his stride. 'You left something behind.'

'What?'

'Me!'

'More like a someone than a something. *Try* to keep up. Damn, we just missed it,' she swore as a cable car trundled across the intersection in front of them and headed down the fashionable boulevard, towards the city centre.

'Such language, Miss Cross,' said Daniel.

Bec shrugged off his mock scolding and the *tut-tut* of a stylish gentleman who had overheard her comment. 'Well, I've only got an hour.'

Daniel touched her arm and gestured that they move to the side so as not to impede the path of pedestrians, many of whom appeared hassled from the day's activities. 'Does it matter which tram we catch?'

'Not for our first excursion.'

'Does that mean you're intending to regularly abscond with my person?'

'Just your mind, but I suppose it can't come on its own.'

'No, you'll need my body.'

Bec busied herself with looking up the street. Their wordplay was entering dangerous territory. She wasn't equipped to manage a flirtatious Daniel. A combative one, yes, but he was in an unusual mood this afternoon. Sliding a glance his way, she was relieved he didn't appear to expect a response, his attention directed over her head.

'Here's one. Come on,' said Daniel, grabbing her hand and weaving across the intersection, dodging cars, lorries and other pedestrians.

The man has a death wish. Her thought was confirmed by his next statement.

'We can catch it when it stops over there or jump on as it lumbers past us up the hill.'

Bec shot him a look of disbelief.

'Guess we'll wait.'

As the tram shuddered to a halt at the designated stop, Bec negotiated the steps to the trailer car and took a seat at the front, nearest the window, facing forward. Travelling backwards made her feel queasy.

'Fares, please!' shouted the conductor as he moved through the carriage.

Daniel flashed a card, which satisfied the man of their right for free passage.

'A present from my boss,' he said, in answer to her lifted brow. 'The perks of working for the state's Public Works.'

'I will have to go out with you more often.'

'That could be arranged.'

Her breath hitched. Daniel's tone wasn't the light-hearted response she'd expected. He looked ... thoughtful, his eyes searching her face. She became aware of his thigh pressed against hers. Perhaps it was due to the width of the seats, which were somewhat on the small side, at least for those of an athletic physique, like Daniel.

'We could go on tram dates,' she blurted out. God, she

sounded like a ninny. She was turning into ... *Evelyn!* This was his effect on other females. *Not her!*

A raised voice to their left averted what could have become an embarrassing conversation. 'I gave you two-and-six, and you only gave me one-and-eleven change.'

'Pardon me, madam, you gave me a two-shilling piece,' the conductor replied calmly to a woman dressed in a fur-trimmed coat with a matching hat and muff.

'I did nothing of the kind.'

'Sorry to contradict you, madam, but you gave me a two-shilling piece. It was a bent one.'

'What impudence! I'm going to take your number and report you. A bent one indeed. You'll be sorry you were rude to me,' she sniffed, averting her gaze out the window to dismiss the man.

Bec frowned. Why would the woman cheat her fare? She looked well to do.

'That's not uncommon,' murmured Daniel.

'Maybe he was mistaken.' Although she wondered, as she noted the look of resignation etched into the conductor's face as he continued his progress down the tram.

'Not that way, sir!' Picking up his pace, the conductor hurried forward to redirect an elderly gentleman intent on exiting on the wrong side of the tram. If not for the quick action of the attendant, an oncoming motorcycle would have hit the man. Bec watched, battling to remain in her seat, as the man tipped his hat towards the conductor and continued on unsteady legs, narrowly avoiding a second collision before gaining the safety of the footpath.

'Near give me heart failure, some of those elderly,' remarked the conductor to Bec, on noticing her concern. A loud sniff from the woman on the other side of the carriage suggested she doubted he possessed a heart.

The conductor shrugged and turned away, vaulting across the awkward break separating their car and the lead carriage without a second glance. Bec leaned forward. The road flashed by underneath, the cable along which the tram was pulled, taut with the strain.

'The car is dragged along at the speed of the cable.'

'Mmm.' Bec gave Daniel's monologue scant regard. It was the sense of theatre that had her transfixed. The floor of the carriages acted as the stage. Those boarding and alighting, choosing either to perform a short comic sketch or drama – such as the well-dressed woman and old man earlier – or sit contentedly as members of the audience, watching. The conductor was the jack-of-all-trades – stagehand, leading man, front of house, stage manager. 'Fares, please.' And banker.

'Mind the curve,' the stentorian voice of the gripman yelled.

Bec was pressed against Daniel as they rounded the corner. Almost immediately, she fought to straighten, angling her body away from him.

'Centripetal force.'

'What?'

'The force that draws you to the centre when we traverse a corner. Or maybe you thought it was me.' Daniel stretched his arm along the seat back behind her.

Bec rested her elbows on her knees, feigning interest in the operation of the cable-grip mechanism and brakes that gave the iconic cars their name. The gripman wasn't half bad, either. She appreciated not only his skill to maintain momentum while navigating the antiquated mechanisms, but the man's flexed biceps and forearms, his thighs straining within his serge pants.

'You're supposed to be watching the conductor,' said Daniel. 'Not ogling man mountain over there.'

'You have to agree he's impressive.'

'If you like the strong and silent type.'

Bec's gaze flicked towards Daniel's face. 'Who doesn't?'

'A taciturn man would not suit you.'

'So now you're an expert on suitable matches.'

'You'd be reduced to a permanent state of irritation.'

Bec crossed her arms and narrowed her gaze. 'You mean like now?'

'An overly opinionated one would also be quite a trial.'

'Yes, I have experience of that —'

Without warning, the cable car shuddered, and a torrent of abuse escaped from the gripman. She watched the conductor's arms flail before gripping an iron stanchion. Standing on the footboard of the front carriage, he'd narrowly missed being knocked backwards between the two tram cars. The driver of a lorry, who'd sought to cross in front of them, matched the gripman for indignation.

Daniel had thrown out his free arm to protect Bec from hitting her head on the edge of the window, cocooning them.

'I'm all right,' she said.

'I just need a minute ... to catch my breath.'

Dipping her head, she searched his face. 'Are you hurt?'

'A little winded, that's all.'

He didn't sound winded – he wasn't wheezing. And he didn't look winded – he wasn't clutching his stomach, although his arms were still enveloping her. 'I'll call the conductor.'

Daniel hesitated before slowly straightening. 'No need to trouble him, I'm starting to feel better.'

Bec arched a brow. 'I thought you might be.'

As the tram continued its travels, Daniel ran his fingers through his hair in frustration. Bec was such a vexing female – difficult to disconcert, a montage of snappy responses and dry humour. Did she ever let her guard down?

What would it take for her to see him in a different light? Not as her best friend's brother, nor as an adversary. Bec was the answer to his problem. He was almost sure of it. She was single, attractive, intelligent, and he had no doubt about their physical compatibility. With her, relinquishing his bachelor status didn't seem like such a sacrifice.

But could she ever be satisfied with marriage, motherhood and supporting his career? Daniel gazed out onto the rain-drenched street – the sudden change in the weather seeming to provide a much-needed dose of reality. Not as relations stood between them.

Could he change her mind? Wear her down? Chipping away at her resolve could take years. Chalmers hadn't given him a timeframe, but he wasn't a patient man. Something they held in common.

'How would we organise to interview a conductor?'

Daniel reluctantly shut the door on his deliberations. 'I'm sorry. I was miles away. What was that?'

'I'd like to interview a tram conductor.'

'Why would you want to do that?'

'Well, it was your idea, if you remember. You told me to

talk to a conductor. But on the job, he doesn't have time to answer my questions.'

Daniel's mind kicked into action. 'Hmm ...' From his days at the Tramways Board, he'd met many conductors. 'I may be able to arrange that.'

Bec's face lit up, her dimple drawing his eye to the corner of her mouth. 'Really?'

'I have my contacts, and if all else fails, I have a best mate that works for the tramways.'

'Of course, Alex!'

'There may be a small fee ...'

As quickly as it had lit up, Bec's face clouded with doubt, her lips drawing into a moue.

'All favours come with costs, Bec.'

He tried for a reassuring smile, but it only deepened the furrow that had appeared between her eyes.

'I don't think they put away any funds for that sort of thing and I can't afford to pay him.'

'I'll sort something. I'm sure we can come to an arrangement.'

Was that suspicion deepening her frown? Daniel averted his gaze. She'd handed him an opportunity. He'd play to his strengths – granting favours and gaining forfeits, wearing her down, kiss by kiss. Perhaps he could win her without saying a word. A novel approach that held a great deal of appeal, at least for him. What was a trammie interview worth? Two, maybe three kisses?

CHAPTER 13

Daniel bounded up the stairs to Birmingham's, a date and time for the coveted trammie interview in hand. His excursion with Bec earlier in the day had lent purpose to the rest of his afternoon and early evening. He'd arrived early to catch Bec before the social dancing began.

Surrendering his coat, hat and umbrella to Harry at the cloakroom, Daniel paid the entrance fee and paused inside the door leading from the foyer to the hall, to take stock. A handful of couples stood, conversing on the floor below where he stood; small groups were scattered about, chatting as they changed their shoes, ready for the evening.

In the middle of the floor, under the only lit chandelier, Eliza was conducting a group class. From the large numbers, and the cat-like tread being practised by the females, Daniel concluded she was teaching the French Tango, the latest craze from London and the Continent. His sister was one of the first to champion the dance to Mr and Mrs Birmingham after reading a newspaper article lamenting the lack of teaching venues.

The match-up of men and women was almost equal thanks to the recruitment of Mr and Mrs B – she danced a competent male lead. Even Alex was in attendance, a sure sign that his friend was smitten. Daniel grinned. Attending group class had always been at the bottom of their list of engagements since it attracted the more serious, painfully shy females. Bec was the exception. She always supported Eliza's classes.

Spying her on the outskirts of the group – one of two women without partners – he made a snap decision to join and reacquaint himself with the tango. Four simple steps and lots of body contact. What would be her reaction? Time to find out.

'My dance, I believe.'

Daniel took advantage of the befuddled look on Bec's face – she'd clearly been concentrating – to wrap his right arm around her and grasp her other hand in his.

'It's a close hold, I believe. Like the Argentinean dance. Place your left hand around my shoulders and across the base of my neck. You're a tall girl, you can easily reach.'

'But I'm just learning,' protested Bec. 'I need to see my feet.'

'They're still at the end of your legs —'

'And their position in relation to the floor.'

'I'll lead. Concentrate on me. The floor isn't going anywhere.'

'Humph!'

Daniel was thankful that Eliza had insisted on teaching him the dance one night after dinner. It was straightforward – three steps were variations on a walk, and the fourth resembled the reverse turn of the waltz. After less than an hour, he'd been tangoing like a professional. Of course, dancing with his sister hadn't provided the same sense of intimacy as dancing with Bec. Or the same challenge. Her movements were choppy, and she'd forgotten the basic rule of dancing – the man leads.

'Relax. You're like a coiled spring. Walk as if you're on hot bricks, don't slide your feet – that's foxtrot.'

'Bossy.'

Daniel bit back a chuckle. He was loving this new dance, especially the hold. Bec was tucked close into his right side, their heads inches apart.

'Keep your knees loose and slightly bent.'

He watched her teeth sink into her bottom lip, her eyes glued to his chest. Breathing in the rich oriental perfume she favoured only heightened his awareness, permeating his thoughts. It was impertinent, with just the right hint of spice. A lot like the woman herself. *God! He was becoming fanciful.* It was her thoughts that he wanted to pervade, to tie in knots. There was no place in his plan for her to become indispensable to his.

How could she relax, wrapped around him? Nor did Bec trust herself to surrender, as a good follower should to their partner's lead. Daniel was good, his movements stealth-like. Not as good as Mr B, but the older man didn't muss up her insides like Daniel.

Bec dropped her chin and focused on the top button of his shirt. It was less distracting than imagining the body underneath. But no matter how hard she tried, she couldn't ignore the temptations it presented – the ones unrelated to the dance. The impulse for her fingers to explore the skin at his nape and dip below the collar of his shirt. The compulsion for her hips to ... *Best not to go there*. Walk, turn, promenade. *Concentrate!*

'Focus on following the turns of my body.' He urged her closer. 'And stop thinking so much.'

No! That was not a smart idea. Dances like the tango blurred the lines between what was real and what was not, and dancefloors were full of artifice. Compliments were unreliable, and a hand placed low on your back could as easily be a sign of a tiring partner as an ardent one. She'd learned her lesson at twenty-one, devastated when she'd discovered the fellow was after an introduction to a friend, and not interested in her at all.

Some part of her needed to stay in control. The broad expanse of Daniel's torso wasn't to be trusted beyond leading her through the dance. She resisted its efforts to defy the steely command she held over her logical self. The melody wasn't helping, the tune twisting through her mind, tantalisingly subtle, languorous. *We argue*, she reminded herself. *We don't like one another. We're incompatible!* This became her mantra for the rest of the dance.

Eliza's voice signalled the end of her torture. 'That's it for this evening. Thank you, everyone for coming, and to Mr and Mrs B for jumping in and helping.'

Bec sprang away from Daniel – she didn't want him thinking she had any designs on his person – and automatically joined in the short applause.

'Don't forget, tonight's dancing starts in half an hour,' Mr B boomed, his voice intended to broadcast to more patrons than just Eliza's teaching class.

'Thanks, Daniel, that turned out a lot easier than I first thought.' Bec glanced quickly at him before returning her gaze forward. She didn't trust herself to make eye contact in case her awareness of him was evident on her face.

'All due to Eliza,' Daniel admitted. 'Mum, Dad and I were her first victims – I mean students – before she started public lessons.'

Bec laughed. 'A captive audience.'

As people drifted away, it surprised her to see Eliza and Alex deep in conversation. From the angle of her friend's chin, Bec sensed something was wrong. She started moving and Daniel followed her.

Alex's frustrated voice reached them. 'We need to talk about this.'

'No, Alex. I don't want to talk about it. Maybe you've realised that she's the one you want, after all,' said Eliza in a hurt and angry tone, before turning on her heel and sweeping past Bec and Daniel.

Alex looked up and directed an exasperated glance at Daniel. 'Eliza might be late home tonight. We've got some things to sort out.'

Daniel nodded.

'I wish Queenie had stayed in Sydney. She's a bloody pest,' he confided, before storming off after his fiancée.

A hand on her arm stopped Bec's flight after the couple.

'Where do you think you're going?' Daniel asked.

'To help. Eliza will listen to me.'

'*Nooo*, my little archangel. Alex would not appreciate your interference,' he said, pulling her gently but firmly back to his side.

'How do you know?'

'Trust me. I know Alex.'

'I'm her best friend.'

'And Alex is soon to be her husband.'

'What do you mean by that?' asked Bec, shaking off his hand.

'Um … what do you think I mean?'

Daniel appeared perplexed at her lightning change in manner and his confusion only served to annoy her even more. 'Becoming a wife doesn't mean that Eliza has to lose her freedom to decide her friends, to seek their counsel and to be supported by them.'

'I never said —'

But she was on a roll. Turning to face him, her back to the doors of the Palais, where eager patrons were filing through, she added, 'And it doesn't mean she has to descend into drudgery, lose her independence, fit only to bear and raise children, balance the family budget and not set foot out of the house.'

Daniel's face flushed crimson.

Chest heaving, Bec realised she'd forgotten to draw breath. 'She has choices.'

'Anything else?' Daniel asked in a quiet voice. He'd crossed his arms, and despite the deep creases at the corners of his eyes, he didn't look angry.

Bec's temper fizzled, spluttering like an exhausted firecracker, and her hands, which had risen to her hips, fell to her sides. 'No.'

Daniel glanced over her head. 'Good. As while I'd like nothing more than to continue our … *conversation*, if only to explain my comment and understand yours, we've got company.'

CHAPTER 14

Daniel wished he could have given Bec more notice of the arrival of her friend Jim – his mind rejected the term 'boyfriend' – with Queenie and Evelyn on each arm. Hell, he wished he'd had more notice, given the tirade that Bec had just launched. This wasn't one of their usual squabbles. *Did she truly hate marriage and motherhood that much?* he wondered.

'Well, doesn't this look cosy,' remarked Queenie, untangling herself from Jim, but not before skating her fingers down his arm. 'I hope we're not interrupting anything important?'

Daniel donned his social mask; a bored Queenie was a dangerous one. He wondered if she had designs on Jim. 'Important, but not urgent,' he hedged.

Evelyn moved to his side, linking her arm through his. 'You're early. Eager to see me?'

His smile was automatic but non-committal. His attention was drawn to Jim's greeting of Bec – a kiss to her cheek, his finger brushing an errant curl from her forehead. Daniel's gut tightened as Bec winked at the officer. Casual but intimate gestures. *Did they mean anything?*

'We saw Alex and Eliza leaving. Is everything all right?' asked Queenie in a casual tone that belied the flinty expression in her eyes.

'Why wouldn't it be?' countered Bec.

'She looked like she'd been crying, that's all,' Evelyn announced smugly with a pointed look at Bec.

'It's impolite to speculate —'

'And not the way I was hoping we'd spend our evening,' Daniel interrupted Bec, to prevent a war of words erupting between the two women.

Evelyn simpered and snuggled closer, chastened. Bec narrowed her eyes and glared at him.

Jim squeezed her hand and waited until he had her attention before addressing the small group. 'Well, if y'all excuse us, my girl and I are off to supper and a movie. The one made of our visit. The boys on the *Oklahoma* took a copy with them and I hear it's a bit of a comedy.'

Daniel raised an eyebrow. 'Really?'

'Well, not all of it, there's the formal bit to satisfy Washington, but there are a lot of anecdotal stories from the boys' time on shore.'

Queenie pouted, her voice husky. 'Will you be back?'

Jim flashed Bec a look and grinned. 'No, ma'am. We have other plans.'

With his gut now rock hard, Daniel's imagination lurched down a wild and riotous path, primed by the words '*we have other plans*'. Did these go beyond the freedoms Bec had defended so vigorously earlier?

Seeing them together tonight meant feigning indifference to Bec's relationship with Jim had become impossible. For the American, Bec was a casual flirtation. *Wasn't she?* For him, she was his potential partner in life and one of the keys to his promotion. The least manageable, as it was turning out.

Separating Bec from Jim had become a priority. Perhaps, given Queenie's interest in Jim, she could become an unwitting collaborator, although he didn't fancy joining forces with the woman. And Jim was not a man who was interested in being wrapped around Queenie's finger.

'Well, enjoy. I hope the film turns out to be as entertaining as you expect and your mates haven't set you up to watch a dry government documentary,' said Daniel.

Jim grinned. 'Wouldn't put it past 'em, now you mention it.'

'Before I forget, Bec, I've arranged for that interview you wanted with the tram conductor,' said Daniel.

'Great, that was quick.' She turned to Jim. 'Research for the debate.'

Daniel crossed his big toes inside his patent leather shoes. 'One small wrinkle. He's only available on Friday evening.'

'*This* Friday evening? What time?'

'Six-thirty.'

'He couldn't make any other time?'

'Is there a problem?'

Bec turned a crestfallen look Jim's way. 'We had theatre plans,' she confessed.

'It wasn't easy to organise someone in the timeframe.' He sensed Bec was wavering, but she was still undecided. 'Of course, we can conclude our preparations without talking to him.'

'Honey, if this is important, I can always try to book new tickets,' said Jim.

Bec kissed his cheek. 'Thank you. I'm sorry. The interview was my idea, but I didn't expect it to be on a Friday or take up an entire evening.'

Daniel battled to stop a smile from crossing his face. He hadn't been entirely honest or dishonest. Sydney – Syd – Turnbull, was a trammie of long acquaintance. He had been hard to track down. Syd hadn't been at his usual hotel after work – Daniel had visited two others before finding him ensconced in a back bar. He was the only person who had agreed to the interview. But then, Daniel hadn't sought anyone else. The day and time were of Syd's choosing.

'How long will it take?' asked Bec.

'We'll need at least an hour, maybe an hour and a half.' He'd stretch it to three hours, if it meant keeping Bec from her theatre date.

'And Jenny and Ida are available?'

'Still waiting to hear.' *Damn, he'd better get onto asking them.*

Bec sighed. 'All right.'

'See you on Friday, then,' said Daniel. 'Thanks for being such a good sport, Jim.'

From the quirk of Jim's right eyebrow, Daniel doubted he'd fooled him, but the American gave him a casual salute.

As Jim and Bec turned to leave, Queenie's silky tone detained them. 'If you have trouble changing those tickets, I'm free on Friday night.'

Bec's eyes widened at Queenie's forwardness, but her smile didn't falter.

'That's mighty nice of you. Thank you,' said Jim.

'Yes, Queenie and I could go together, since Daniel will also be tied up,' said Evelyn.

Daniel smothered a chuckle into his fist. The look Queenie

sent Evelyn suggested that was far from the arrangement she had in mind. But one look at Evelyn sobered him. He likened her smile to a sad clown's. Guilt niggled at him. *Why couldn't she be the one?*

Desperate to start her own home, she was attractive, amenable and her views aligned with his. Well, as close as he could tell. They'd never ventured down the path of discussing marriage or children. Daniel fought down a shudder. Evelyn was perfect ... for someone else.

CHAPTER 15

Friday 21 August 1925

'Ladies, meet Sydney Turnbull. Tram conductor extraordinaire. Thirty-five years in service to the public. He started back when the tramways were drawn by horses,' said Daniel, giving the man beside him a slap on the shoulder.

Ida moved forward to vigorously pump the trammie's arm in a handshake that any man would have been proud of. 'Welcome, Mr Turnbull.'

Removing his peak cap, the old man patted his thinning hair and smiled. 'Call me Syd.'

'Syd, I'm Bec, and this is Jenny. Thank you for taking time out to speak with us. I'm sure you'd have much preferred to head on home.'

Tucking his cap under his arm, Syd's sky-blue eyes twinkled from a face chiselled, no doubt, from years of sun, wind and frosty mornings. He looked familiar.

'Danny boy twisted my arm. Told me three pretty ladies wanted to talk to me. I don't get an invitation like that every day.'

Bec smiled at the trammie's nickname for Daniel. It hinted

at a close bond, and a side of Daniel she hadn't experienced. She watched the interplay between the two men as Daniel groaned, and Syd gave him a wink and an elbow to his ribs.

'Said there might be a coupla egg sandwiches and a piece of cake, too,' he said hopefully.

'Fresh from our cafeteria downstairs. Please help yourself,' invited Jenny, pointing to the table on which food, plates and paper serviettes were arranged. 'You too, Daniel.'

Bec took her seat and was unaccountably pleased when Daniel chose the chair beside hers. He looked relaxed, his forehead smooth, and his boyish features in evidence. Settling himself, he repositioned the angle of the seat, his leg brushing hers.

'Sorry.'

His eyes didn't match his apology and Bec's heartbeat performed a slow-motion belly flop as his gaze lingered fractionally longer than politeness demanded.

At Jenny's urging, Syd seated himself, a full plate balanced on one knee. He directed a raised eyebrow at Bec. 'You're the young lady from the poster, aren't you?'

Bec nodded, steeling herself for his reaction. The pendulum of responses she received swung between humour and horror. In Williamstown, she'd found one poster defaced. Someone had gone to a lot of trouble to stencil, with indelible paint, *'The home – a woman's true calling'*.

'Even prettier in person. What say you, Danny?'

Daniel rested his chin on his fist and pretended to study her. 'As pretty as a peach.'

Bec rolled her eyes. Daniel and his fruit comparisons.

'Independent too. You were knocked over by a newsboy on Monday night, if I'm not much mistaken.'

Bec peered at Syd. Of course. The same set of bushy black brows. But this time, his eyes held a hint of reproach. 'I'm sorry I rushed off. I didn't want to make a fuss.'

Shaking his head, Syd's voice registered his disappointment. 'Not a fuss, lassie, but a stand. Sometimes you've got to make a stand. The boys have become a nuisance. They even jump on and off the trams while in motion – knocked a woman off her seat last week and she almost ended up under the tram. Reporting it was the right thing to do.'

Bec shifted in her chair as four pairs of eyes scrutinised her. She suspected the warmth in her cheeks implied to her onlookers she was somehow at fault here. *But she wasn't!*

'You didn't say anything?' Daniel accused.

'I wasn't hurt,' Bec insisted. 'I should have been looking where I was going.'

'Humph!' Daniel and Syd shared a look.

Bec ignored Daniel, keeping her eyes fixed on Syd. 'I meant to thank you for your kindness.'

'Any gentleman would have done the same.'

Daniel crossed his arms. 'You're too independent for your own good.'

Bec gasped. *How dare he.* That comment would cost him dearly. It was one thing to voice an opinion privately, but quite another to do it publicly. It appeared Syd thought so, too.

The trammie frowned at Daniel. 'As the *lady* says, she wasn't hurt.'

Daniel shrugged. 'Maybe —'

Bec forced her voice through gritted teeth. '*Maybe* we can return to the topic at hand.'

Syd nodded, turning to Ida and waving his hand in invitation. 'What would you like to know?'

Ida shifted her gaze from Bec to the trammie. 'Well, Mr Turnbull, is there any reason why a woman couldn't do your job?'

Ida was nothing if not forthright. Even Bec wouldn't have opened with that question. But the trammie didn't seem to have taken offence, appearing to give the question much thought as he devoured the last morsel of his sandwich and wiped the tips of his fingers – stained green, most probably from the daily handling of copper coins – carefully on the crinkly paper of his serviette. 'Well now, there ain't no true reason why a woman couldn't do what I do. If she has no objections to starting or finishing work when most folks are asleep in bed or spending the day as if expecting battle – equipped with up to twenty odd blocks of tickets, timetable, bundy clock key and waybill.'

Ida smiled. 'No objections so far.'

Syd paused, rubbing his chin. 'Of course, I don't know why a smart girl would want to encourage varicose veins, stand for long periods on a vibrating vehicle, expose herself to passengers with infectious diseases and court digestive troubles from irregular meal hours. But, there's no reason why she couldn't,' he concluded, tucking into another sandwich.

A cunning diplomat, our Syd. From the expression on Ida's face, she agreed with Bec's assessment.

'Smart girls are always ready to turn their hand to a new challenge,' Bec countered.

'Anyone, male or female, who could teach the travelling public some manners would be welcome in my book. Perhaps starting with basic hygiene. Twice today I was presented with tickets by men after using them as toothpicks.'

Jenny nearly choked on her sandwich. 'Ewwww! That's disgusting.'

'Yes, young lady —'

Bec interrupted. 'But not a reason that a woman couldn't do the job.'

The trammie studied her for what seemed like minutes before moving his head in an imperceptible shake. The concession had Bec wanting to pump her fist.

'What about the social aspect?' prompted Daniel. 'Do you find yourself sharing a yarn ... a joke.'

Bec bit back a retort. Daniel's question sounded rehearsed, and the casual smile he sent her all but confirmed her suspicions. Men were devious creatures – age was irrelevant.

'Well, Danny boy, to the traveller, we're just a servant of the public, without face or feelings, there to be provoked, abused, scammed with foreign coins and sometimes spat at. And during it all, we're expected to show tact, forbearance and courtesy no matter the aggravation. Not much time for sharing stories. Any more of those sandwiches, by chance? Your cafeteria does a bang-up job.'

Jenny passed across the remaining two.

'Sounds a lot like the qualities exhibited by women all day and every day,' remarked Ida, pursing her lips together as if expecting an argument.

'No doubt. My wife tells me all the time how hard it is to keep her patience with me, but she manages somehow. Married thirty years this December and hardly a cross word in all that time. A barrel full of forbearance on both sides, I'd say.'

'What about knowledge? How much does a conductor need to know, and how long does it take to learn?' asked Bec.

'Well, there's the routine stuff – rules, regulations, stops, fares and sections – that's covered at the training school, which all conductors attend. Not everyone has a good memory for them sorts of things, though. But there's a formula.'

'Similar to memorising recipes and lists.'

'I wouldn't know about that, young Bec. If you say so ... For major changes, like the new electric cars, we'll spend a half-day or so getting educated. Smaller changes are posted as daily operations updates on the bulletin board. We're expected to check those before the start of shift —'

'You'd learn a lot on the job, though, wouldn't you?' interrupted Bec.

'I was just gettin' to that, lassie. At first, you're buddied up with a seasoned trammie. They show you the ropes, tolerate your mistakes and guide your temper. Some say you can train a conductor in forty hours, but I've known a couple that forty years wouldn't have been long enough. They're now in management.' Syd chuckled. 'No disrespect intended, Danny.'

'None taken.'

Truly, perhaps they could team up as a vaudeville act, Bec thought. 'And what about fitness levels?' asked Bec, eyeing Syd's stout figure.

'Don't let appearances be deceiving, little lady. Beneath this uniform hides a physique strong enough to lift perambulators, youngsters, avalanches of drapery parcels, bicycles and inebriates, and other pests on and off the tram.'

Bec's eyebrows shot up.

'And agile enough to swing along the footboards from one stanchion to the other or weave my way through the narrow gangway, juggling tickets and change in a cash bag that would probably weigh half as much as you.'

Bec thought he was confusing himself with Tarzan, dressed in heavy serge garb and a peaked cap. His conspiratorial wink in her direction suggested he could also read minds.

'Well, if there's nothin' else, I'll be getting home to my wife and a warm hearth,' said Syd, checking his timepiece. 'I'll just make the seven-twenty coming up Flinders Street.'

'Thanks, Syd. I'm sure I speak for all of us when I say we appreciate your time after a long day,' said Daniel.

'Anything for you, Danny boy. Thanks for the refreshment, ladies. Mind if I take those pieces of ginger cake with me to share with the missus?'

CHAPTER 16

'Well, that was most informative,' declared Ida, polishing her glasses.

'Theatrical,' said Bec. 'There was no doubt he was *making sport* of the idea of women as conductors.'

'You mean, despite his demurral that *there ain't no true reason why a woman couldn't do what I do*,' mimicked Jenny.

Ida nodded. 'I think the man spoke with a *forked tongue*. But he was entertaining.'

Daniel had enjoyed the theatre, too, although he wasn't about to admit that in present company. Syd's approach had inspired him – he'd successfully made his point without going head to head. *Was it a tactic he could employ with Bec?* He'd certainly been out of line with his comment about her independence. But she could have been hurt.

'No doubt our debate opponents will be much more plainspoken. Do we know who they are?' asked Ida.

'The State Government's Public Works and the Employees' Union each have put up representatives,' said Daniel.

Bec's head swung around. 'You mean besides you?'

'Yes. A colleague of mine, Theo Blake.'

'Having a bet each way, are they? The state wins no matter what.'

'Something like that.' Daniel kept his tone non-committal. 'And a new organisation, the Women's Protection League, which champions marriage and motherhood as a woman's highest achievement.'

Bec's eyes changed from accusing to appalled. 'You jest. I've never heard of them.'

Ida removed her spectacles. 'I'm afraid it's no joke, Rebecca. Born out of the misdirected efforts of an ex-British army officer, he's attracted a small following.'

'Here, in Melbourne?'

'Ignorance knows no boundaries. He claims to be voicing the aspirations of the average woman, on her behalf. Clearly, he saw combat and took a hit to the head,' Ida said dismissively. 'Utter nonsense. To date, we've treated the organisation and their outpourings with silence. No doubt this representative will inspire a wave of feminine wrath, regardless of the debate's outcome.'

'Will we need to consider police presence?' asked Jenny, worrying her lower lip.

'I doubt he'll incite violence, dear – simply a misdirected soul,' soothed Ida, gathering up her handbag, coat and cloche. 'Thank you, Mr – Daniel, for organising Mr Turnbull. Lovely to see you again, Rebecca. Jenny, let's make tracks.'

'We're going to the lantern lecture downstairs, Divining Greek Sculpture,' explained Jenny. 'Do you want to join us?'

'No! Thank you,' said Daniel and Bec at the same time.

'Wonderful sculptors, the Greeks. Their work is the

embodiment of physical strength and prowess,' Ida said reverently, her eyes glazing over.

'And a celebration of nudity.' Jenny giggled. 'If you change your mind, we're in the main hall. Goodnight.'

As the two women hurried out the door, Daniel studied Bec, who had turned her attention to clearing the remnants of the evening's collation. She held herself stiffly. 'Are you sure you're not tempted?'

'I prefer a less vicarious experience.'

Daniel's pulse quickened. *Me too.* Although, he doubted she'd intended her comment as an invitation – there was no artifice apparent in her profile, and her movements were businesslike. In her current mood, she'd probably try to tidy him into a corner – his presence analogous to a piece of furniture.

'So, what are your plans for the rest of the evening?'

She turned to face him, her arms crossed. 'My independent mind hasn't decided.'

'It was rude of me to say what I did, I'm sorry.'

'Sorry that you voiced it, or sorry that you made it sound as if I was ungrateful and badly behaved.'

'Um ... both.'

'Humph! But that's what you think, isn't it?'

Daniel examined the barbell links adorning his white shirt cuffs as he casually strolled to stand before her. 'Yes ... and no.'

'So, which is it?'

His gaze returned to meet hers. 'Yes, I think you're too independent ... *at times*. No, I don't think you're ungrateful and badly behaved.'

'I'll take that as a compliment.'

Attempting to keep his tone even, he asked, 'Would it

have been so hard for you to have accepted Syd's help?'

'I didn't think. It happened so quickly. And I was *unhurt*.'

Bec was a spitfire. Perhaps it was time to take the heat out of their conversation. He had other plans. 'His gentlemanly instincts may never recover.'

'Don't be ridiculous!'

Daniel persisted. 'He's a sensitive soul, taught to protect and serve.'

Bec stabbed her finger into his chest. 'Do not use this as an opportunity to peddle your nineteenth-century views.'

'I'm just pointing out that what you saw was a reflex action.' Daniel captured her finger before she could withdraw it. 'Faced with an attractive young woman in need of assistance. Common sense and common courtesy.'

She snatched her finger back as if scalded. 'I'll keep that in mind. Now, if you've finished sermonising —'

'I have. Do you fancy a drink?'

Her eyes narrowed.

'It is Friday evening.' Daniel checked his watch. 'And it's a bit early to go home.'

She nodded, her mouth drifting into a hint of a smile. 'Sure. I'll grab my coat. By the way, thanks for organising Syd. Do we owe him anything?'

'I sorted it.'

'So, we're in your debt.'

He tapped her on the nose. 'Just you.'

'Me!' Her eyes widened.

'Uh-huh. Just you. And as an independent woman, I know you'll want to settle up quickly.'

'I'll shout drinks.'

'Small change. Syd was expensive,' said Daniel, wondering

if she could hear the acceleration of his heartbeat.

'What are my choices?' Bec addressed his mouth, the expression in her eyes hidden from him by feathered lashes. Only the return of her dimple suggested she was a willing participant in his game.

Daniel knew he was taking a gamble – but at this point he had nothing to lose. 'Allow me to demonstrate.'

Cupping Bec's face, he angled her head.

As her gaze flicked upwards, his eyes were met with pools of molten silver. Daniel dived in, closing the distance between them. He doubted a drowning man could have made his intentions clearer as their lips met. She seemed to understand, opening her mouth and tangling her tongue with his without hesitation.

He sensed in her a mix of excitement and nervousness. Encouraged by a low moan, he explored the underside of her jaw ... the side of her neck. The hint of vanilla on her skin evoked memories of sweet treats and rewards. He gathered her closer – if that were possible. Her body seemed to touch his ... everywhere. Exploring the curve of her spine, he teased each vertebra, feeling her relax, bone by bone.

She arched against him, and he dipped a hand lower, dallying with the globes of her pert behind. Just when he was confident he held the upper hand in their tactile battle, she surprised him by plunging her fingers into his hair to anchor him to her, and grinding her hips onto his burgeoning erection. Daniel groaned, muffling the sound against her neck.

And then she was bracing her palms against his chest, putting distance between them – like the first time. *What the hell!*

Daniel's kisses had overwhelmed her sensibilities, but a sixth sense had registered the sound of footsteps echoing up the stairs. They were about to have company – and this was not the way Bec wanted to be discovered. What had started as a light-hearted diversion had turned heated. The intensity of her response wasn't something she could explain to herself, let alone someone happening upon them.

She felt his resistance. It was as if his chest had turned to concrete and his arms to iron bands. 'Someone's coming,' she hissed.

When her best friend burst into the room, Bec was cradling an empty sandwich platter and Daniel was leaning against the window casement, hands jammed in his pockets.

'Jenny said I might find you both here. I thought we could meet Alex for a drink ...' Eliza's head swivelled from one to the other. 'Is everything all right?'

'Of course. We were just cleaning up before heading off for a drink ourselves,' replied Bec, busying herself with nothing in particular.

'Your timing's perfect as usual, sis.'

Bec frowned. Was Daniel suggesting that he was glad Eliza had arrived? She hadn't meant to be so forward, but his mouth, his hands ... She had to move. Maybe he was turned off by her response – preferring less physicality. It was a first for her, but he probably thought her shameless ...

Eliza opened her mouth, closed it, and then opened it again. 'I'm not so sure, my timing's been a bit off lately, and I feel like I've ...' she tilted her head, '... interrupted something.'

Daniel pushed off the casement. 'Bec and I do have unfinished business —'

'Arguments and counter-arguments for the debate,' Bec interjected with a nod.

She found herself at the end of a pointed glance. 'A conversation from Wednesday that needs further clarification.'

'I thought I'd made myself clear.'

Daniel ignored her interruption, folding his arms. 'And some honing of her technique.'

Heat rushed to her face. *The cheek of the man.* 'Debating technique. He means the honing of my *debating* technique.'

'That too.'

Bec almost stamped her foot.

'I feel like I'm watching a ping-pong match,' said Eliza. 'There's the spectacle above the table, but the real action is happening underneath.'

'Well, this girl is taking her bat and heading home,' announced Bec, sending a glare in Daniel's direction.

'What about our drink?' wailed Eliza. 'Just stay for one.'

An evening spent parrying Daniel's nuanced comments didn't appeal, but her friend sounded genuinely put out. 'One quick drink.'

CHAPTER 17

Ensconced in an armchair in the lounge of the Federal, whisky in hand, Daniel fielded questions from his best mate, although not in words. They were implied by the lift of a brow, the widening of an eye, the tilt of his head. And the most annoying? Flashes of a smirk. He returned each with a flinty stare.

It appeared Bec had shrugged off any misgivings she'd felt earlier tonight. Encouraged by Eliza and Alex, she was recounting her impression of the conversation with Syd, her grey eyes luminous.

'I confess I hadn't expected that a tram conductor needed to have agility and stamina,' said Bec, waving her glass of champagne in the air. 'Syd made it sound as if he trained with Wirth's Circus!'

Daniel chuckled. Bec's mood was contagious. 'I thought the same thing. I had a picture of him swinging from stanchion to stanchion, collecting fares with one hand, lifting perambulators in the other, and performing other feats showing his skill, strength and daring.'

'All he needed was one of their trained seals or —'

'That pony with pants on,' interjected Daniel, imitating a neigh for effect.

'Perfect! The drawcard of the Saturday matinee.' Bec laughed before becoming aware that Eliza and Alex were staring at her. *At them.* 'What?'

They looked at one another, communicating in the way of nearly married couples, before Eliza shrugged. 'You and Daniel agreed on something. Alex and I were savouring the moment.'

'We've agreed on things before,' protested Bec.

'Hmm ... not this year,' teased Eliza, giving Bec's hand a quick squeeze.

'That's all in the past,' explained Daniel. 'Now that we're on the same team, we're practising arguing less.' He ignored the smirk that hovered on Alex's lips.

'That's right, we don't want the opposition thinking we don't get on,' said Bec.

'But what will we do for entertainment?' complained Alex, making a face that matched his tone.

'Things are in a bad way if you're relying on us as a diversion,' quipped Daniel. 'Do you need a few tips?'

'I've received no complaints on that front,' said Alex with an arched look at Eliza. 'Best keep them. I'm sensing your need is greater than mine.'

Daniel pasted a smile on his lips and avoided the curious looks from Bec and his sister. Having made his point, Alex drew the women's attention away from his mate with a question about Birmingham's upcoming Balloon Gala. Had they bought tickets? When Bec indicated a disinclination to attend, Eliza flew into full persuasion mode.

Daniel's attention drifted in and out of the conversation. It hadn't been so long ago that he'd been dispensing advice to Alex in his quest for Eliza's affection. Now it was he who was feeling uncertain ... unsure of the best way to convince Bec of his suitability.

He knew that for her, he was an unwise choice, but he was determined, albeit disheartened, by the challenge that presented. His immediate hurdle was unravelling the accusations she'd flung at him about a married woman's role. He needed to understand the emotion behind that torrent of words – they'd been delivered as if a dam had burst.

'Another?' Alex was holding up his glass.

'No. I'm heading home,' Daniel said, draining his glass.

Alex examined his watch. 'At *nine-thirty*?'

Daniel ignored him, rising to his feet. He was tired.

'I might stay awhile,' said Eliza, studying the stem of her wineglass.

Daniel pierced Alex with a look. Until his sister married, she was still his responsibility.

'I'll make sure she gets home ... *before* midnight.'

Daniel nodded.

'I'll come with you,' said Bec, draining her flute and rising gracefully to her feet.

Well, maybe he wasn't that tired, he thought, suddenly more upbeat. He'd have to walk her home from the station. The night was still young.

'Goodnight,' said Bec, shrugging into her fur-collared coat and securing the oversized button at her hip, before leaning over to give Eliza a quick hug.

Daniel loved the effect of the coat's marine-blue colour on her eyes. It softened the steel grey and gave them depth and mystery. He could get lost in Bec's eyes. They were her best feature outside her sharp wit and intelligence. How had he enjoyed the monotony of his previous liaisons? He must have been sleepwalking!

Bec played her part during the trip to Williamstown, keeping up a steady stream of diverting conversation and laughing at Daniel's quips. But their kiss post-Syd – which was how she chose to characterise it – hung between them. Or at least, that's how it felt to her. She owed him an apology for her forwardness. After all, Daniel was used to Evelyn's submissiveness. Her initiative probably repulsed him. She explicitly remembered *gyrating like a buckjumper*. Her face flamed at the memory of her abandon, and she turned her face to the carriage window. And then there was her outburst at Birmingham's mid-week. The opinions she'd thrown at him needed an explanation ... or an additional apology.

Daniel insisted on walking her home and remained on the train until the station after his. Williamstown was very much a workingman's suburb, with around forty hotels, and not all of these respected the six pm closing time. It wasn't unusual to encounter a man three sheets to the wind, late on a Friday evening. Daniel's presence gave her a sense of security. Her independence didn't stretch to stupidity.

Emerging from the subway at Williamstown's Beach station, Bec decided there was no time like the present to cleanse her conscience.

'Um ... I probably owe you an apology. Two, in fact.'

'I'm listening. Let's go this way.'

Bec hesitated. *This way* meant the long way. She didn't think they'd need more than the ten minutes it normally took from the station to her home. She'd blurt out a quick explanation, finish it just as they arrived at her front gate, wish him goodnight, rush inside and close the door. But knowing Daniel, he probably had questions. Or worse, opinions to offer.

She turned her steps in the direction of the bay and swallowed the lump that had lodged in her throat. 'I overreacted at Birmingham's and I'm sorry. Especially for the bit about a female's descent into drudgery after marriage.'

'Apology accepted.'

Bec released the breath she'd been holding and sucked in a lungful of salt air. *That hadn't been so bad.* Less than ten seconds. Time for apology number two.

'But I don't understand what triggered it.'

Bec rolled her eyes, glad of the darkness. *Never count your chickens.* 'As I said, I overreacted.'

'But all I said were words to the effect that Alex would soon be Eliza's husband.'

Damn Daniel and his questions! Bec sighed.

'Bec?'

'And I understood that to mean that as her husband, you thought he had the right to control her interests and to restrict her circle of friends.'

'I can't see Eliza allowing that, can you?'

'No,' mumbled Bec, shoving her hands deep into the pockets of her coat. 'Although, he's done a good job of monopolising her time so far.' Bec caught her lip with her teeth. She probably sounded like the green-eyed monster. 'I know, I know ... they're in love. That's not my point.'

'Which is?'

Was that amusement threading his tone? Bec gritted her teeth. 'That society expects women to narrow their focus when they get married. To be content to absorb themselves in the workings of the home and the raising of children.'

'Society —'

'Expects home duties to be the pinnacle of our success. We weren't tied to the kitchen during the war. Women got on with things. Things that men never thought we were capable of. Is it any wonder we feel as if we're going backwards now that the war is over?'

'But —'

'In fact, you yourself have expressed views that the women's movement threatens marriage and motherhood. You've openly said that you couldn't see yourself marrying a feminist.' *God, why hadn't she stopped at 'no'.*

'I have ...' Daniel hesitated, as if expecting another barrage of words, but Bec had decided she'd probably said enough. 'The chivalrous role of provider and protector appeals to me. Appeals to my masculinity. I can't deny it.'

'That probably accounts for the type of women you attract,' Bec said mechanically.

'Ouch!'

'Sorry, that was rude of me.' It seemed Daniel wasn't the only one given to plain speaking.

'Mmm.'

'I mean, it's none of my business. I'm sure Evelyn will make a devoted wife and mother, swooning at the merest hint of a threat from life's vices, temptations and coarse influences. You'll be able to play knight errant to your heart's content.'

'Double ouch! I'm sure Evelyn will be relieved she has your vote of confidence. And I'll be sure to keep my sword sharpened for every eventuality.'

They'd reached The Esplanade, the street that fronted Williamstown's foreshore. A westward direction led to the dance hall, where on Saturday afternoons and evenings Claude Hall's orchestra would attract crowds from nearby suburbs. Tonight, its doors were closed and it stood silent. In contrast, Bec was positively loquacious.

They turned eastward.

'Look, it isn't that I don't want to get married and have children. But I'm educated. Not university educated like you, but still smart, and I love what I do at the YWCA.' Bec stopped and faced him. 'I make a difference, damn it, and I don't want to give any of that up.'

'So, a husband and children wouldn't be enough for you.'

Bec shook her head, marvelling at Daniel's ability to maintain a reasoned tone, despite her earlier gibe about his choice of girlfriend. 'No.'

She turned her face seaward, breathing deeply.

'What if —'

Her head swung around, hands finding her hips. 'Would you be satisfied being a husband and father and nothing else?' But even as she asked the question, Bec was regretting the argument. It wasn't the way she wanted to end the evening. So much for a quick apology and acceptance. Maybe she wasn't that smart, after all.

CHAPTER 18

Daniel felt as if Bec had ripped out a rug from under him. *Well, of course he wouldn't!* But that wasn't the way of things. He couldn't bear children. That was a woman's role. Biologically determined. There was nothing he could do to change it. And the bond created meant it made sense for most of the nurturing and raising of those children to fall to the mother. Dammit, Bec wasn't even trying to be reasonable. It didn't mean children and marriage weren't important. It wasn't either or … Except, he grudgingly acknowledged that for women it did become an either-or choice.

Daniel sighed. Bec's question had struck a discordant chord. He'd worked hard to get to where he was. And he aspired to move into politics. He knew he wouldn't be prepared to abandon his ambition for marriage and children. Thank goodness he wasn't expected to. Yet the continuation of humanity required children, and that necessitated marriage.

'I thought not.' Interpreting his silence as assent, Bec turned and resumed walking.

Daniel groaned. The set of her shoulders said it all. This was too much to think about late on a Friday night. *She made his head hurt.* And now she was just walking off without him. He lengthened his stride to catch up with her.

'My own parents have the closest thing to a non-traditional marriage,' she said as he reached her. 'Mum fits in her veterinary work when she can – although she had to forgo her practice when I was born – and Dad helps around the house. When I was younger, he and I would spend entire mornings or afternoons together if Mum was called out.'

Daniel thought back to his own parents. In contrast, his mum had given up her job as a seamstress when he was born. He'd never asked her if she missed it. She'd seemed content splitting her time between supporting her husband in his role as councillor, balancing the family budget and raising him and his sister. Now that he and Eliza were grown up, she played tennis twice a week and volunteered at St Andrew's Presbyterian Church. She seemed happy enough. He'd spent more time with his father, kicking a football, doing chores – like mowing the lawn – or debating matters of worth. Manly things.

Daniel studied Bec's profile. There was a tension about her features. Something still didn't make sense. Had her outburst simply been a rant against society's expectations, or was there something deeper? Was she trying to divert him with provocative questions and comments? It wouldn't be the first time.

He touched her arm. 'Ahem. Returning to your … overreaction. Your words, not mine.'

'Mmm.'

'I accept I was the trigger, but I wasn't the cause.'

'Of course, you never are,' she quipped.

Deflection! Daniel was not to be deterred. 'The passion that you delivered your views with, that had been building for … months, maybe years, if I'm not mistaken.'

Bec was silent, and Daniel wondered whether she was going to ignore him or brush off his question with another smart comment. Her chin dipped, and when she spoke her voice was muted. Daniel had to tilt his head towards her to hear over the sound of the north wind.

'After my grandmother died, when Mum would get called out to assist the local vet, Dad would bundle me up and I'd spend the time at his barbershop. I'd sit cross-legged in a chair in front of the fire reading, lavender from the brilliantine teasing my nose. Sometimes I'd sweep the floor of offcut hair, listening to the hum of male conversation.'

Bec paused, and Daniel caught her smiling to herself. These were happy memories. What did they have to do with her outburst?

'When I was around thirteen years old, I was at the shop, studying – algebra from memory. I'd grown a lot taller that spring – a growth spurt, Mum said. The cotton dress I was wearing was probably an inch or three shorter, and slightly tighter than the season before.'

Bec dragged a wayward curl behind her ear. 'Dad ducked next door for change. He was gone only a matter of minutes. One of the shop's regular customers, a businessman, was waiting to be shaved. I remember him joking with the man in the chair beside him that as a prospective wife and mother, he didn't know why I was wasting time with mathematics. I should, he said, be practising the skills I'd really need. And the look he directed at me … that first time.' Bec shuddered, her eyes staring straight ahead. 'It made me feel dirty. His gaze crawling up my legs, my hips, my breasts. It was as if he was undressing me.'

Anger tightened Daniel's throat; he couldn't trust himself to speak. It made his skin crawl. No woman, let alone a teenager, should be subjected to that type of innuendo.

'That night, I went home and scrubbed myself clean. I spent so much time in the bathroom, Dad chided me for wasting water.'

Daniel wanted to fold Bec in his arms but doubted from her clenched fists she'd welcome the gesture. Had thirteen-year-old Bec been as sassy as she was at twenty-five? Or was this a shell she'd developed and nurtured?

'I'd see him and his wife in the street. Dressed as a gentleman, tipping his hat to passers-by, cane in hand, while she navigated the muddy footpath, left to struggle on her own with a perambulator and a boy of about seven years old. As they passed, I'd hear him swearing at her under his breath, to keep up.' Her tone turned fierce. 'I swore I would *never* be caught in a marriage like that.'

Daniel hesitated before broaching the questions swirling in his mind. 'You said the first time. Were there other times?'

Bec bit her lip. 'Mostly, I learned to avoid him.'

More deflection. He guessed her efforts were not always successful. 'Did he ever touch you? Physically?'

'No.'

'*Thank God!* The man was an ass. I want to hurt him for how he behaved. How he made you feel.' His words seemed inadequate. He watched her impatiently brush a tear from her cheek and secured her hand. Bec started at his touch.

'I don't want to lose you in a pothole, like Monday,' he

said, tucking it into the crook of his arm.

Bec sent him a watery smile, and Daniel wondered if he imagined that she'd leaned into him a little. They walked on in silence, past the reserve bordered by the Botanic Gardens, with its avenue of palms, immaculate gravel paths and ornamental lake. At Giffard Street, they turned north. Bec's parents owned a property opposite the Gardens.

'Does this man have a name?'

'I'd rather not say.' He felt her gaze on him. 'You're not to do anything with the confidence I've shared, Daniel. It was a long time ago.'

Daniel disagreed. There was more to this story, but now was not the time to delve further. He squeezed her hand. 'I'll take it to my grave.' But before he did, he'd make his own enquiries. Williamstown was a big old country town at heart and people talked.

'Thank you.'

Time to tackle her second apology. 'At the risk of prompting more unhappy memories, what was the other thing you wanted to apologise for?'

She shook her head. 'It's not important.'

'Bec, you're not the type of woman who announces the need to apologise and then decides it isn't important.'

She sighed. 'All right. I wanted to apologise for my behaviour earlier in the evening.'

'What behaviour?'

'*God*, do I have to spell it out? My ... *enthusiasm* after Syd's interview.'

Daniel brought them to a halt outside her parents' house and fought to keep her hand as she tried to turn away. He was trying to make sense of what she was saying. 'You're apologising for ... *kissing me?*'

'We both know I did more than that,' she mumbled, trying to free herself, no doubt to escape to the other side of the gate.

Daniel's mind was racing, sifting through images of lips, tongues and hands before the memory of her grinding her hips on his manhood rushed to the fore. She was apologising for *that?*

'I doubt Evelyn —'

He didn't want to hear about Evelyn. He wanted to kiss this woman senseless. To tell her she had nothing to apologise for. He backed her against the gate, watching her eyes widen into pools of grey.

'If you apologise, then I must apologise,' he kissed the point of her nose, 'for this.' He closed the gap between their bodies, pressing his arousal against her and bending to swirl his tongue around the shell of her ear. 'And this.' He lapped and nipped the side of her neck.

The sound of a tuneless whistle concentrated the threads of his control. Probably someone returning from one of the many hotels. He drew back. Bec's eyes were unfocused, and he couldn't resist kissing the tip of her nose again.

'Your apology is not accepted. Now go while I still have the strength to allow you to.'

CHAPTER 19

Saturday 22 August 1925

Daniel had woken up to a mix of emotions. Bec's confidences triggered all the behaviours in him she claimed to despise. He wanted to protect her from men like her father's customer, to punish them and wipe away her fear; to provide for her, to lavish gifts on her. To argue, tease, torment and challenge her before making up – swiving each other senseless. Based on her kisses, he doubted she'd object to the last. But he also knew that regardless of how compatible they were physically, that would never be enough for her.

Bec was a conundrum! She wasn't against marriage, and he wanted to marry her. Of that he was certain. And not just because of his promotion, although it fitted nicely with his plans. She wasn't against children, and he wanted children. But she couldn't expect him to sacrifice his career to raise them. And anyway, Bec's wages weren't the equal of his. Daniel squeezed his eyes shut. Did she want love? Daniel wasn't sure his feelings stretched that far. He knew she was the only one he could even think of tying himself to. Was that love? It didn't sound like the stuff of poets and musicians.

'Argh!' What he needed to do was to go for a run. Clear his head. He was overthinking this.

He headed to the local cricket ground. Ten laps reduced him to a sweaty figure of masculinity, with mud-caked legs and shoes – the sports ground was in a frightful condition – but with questions still raging.

Was Bec feeling raw after her disclosures last night? Did Eliza know about the events that had scarred her friend? Did her parents? Or was he the first person she'd unburdened herself to? And what did he do with the information without breaking her trust? Was her experience with this man the reason for her views on marriage and motherhood? Or had her views already existed, the experience serving to strengthen them?

Daniel walked on, enjoying the solitude. It seemed the unsettled weather had kept people indoors, and the blinds on most houses were yet to be drawn.

Bec's question about choices and expectations was disconcerting. *Would you be satisfied being a husband and father and nothing else?* He didn't have any solution other than the one that had served his parents' marriage best. He had political ambitions and Sate Parliament was no place for children to be running the corridors. Maybe if he had his own business, as her father did, they could have found a workable solution.

Turning into Giffard Street – it seemed his feet had carried him there automatically – he was spared from colliding with a man in a three-piece suit by the gentleman's quick thinking and long arms.

'Must be some trouble from the look on your face, Daniel.'

Daniel looked up into the same grey eyes that had

haunted his sleep. Except these were laughing. 'Mr Cross! I'm sorry, I was miles away.'

'Girl trouble?'

Had Bec said something to her parent? 'Um ...'

'It's usually the only thing, besides money, that causes that look. You don't have money troubles do you, Daniel?'

'Um, no, sir.'

'Thought not. A girl, then. Or maybe more than one, heh? A good-looking man like yourself?'

Daniel grinned. 'Just the one. Although, she's more trouble than a handful,' he said, before realising whom he was talking about, and to whom.

'My Rachel was like that ...' The man's countenance reflected an abiding regard for his wife.

Runs in the family, then!

'Led me a merry dance. Her mother, Adelaide, drummed into her from an early age the importance of being independent. She got herself first-class honours at the Veterinary College, set herself up in practice and she didn't want a bar of anything I proposed. Too restrictive, she told me.' He chuckled, slapping Daniel on the shoulder. 'She liked my kisses well enough, though.'

Daniel cleared his throat. 'What did you do, sir?'

'Do? I didn't *do* anything. I was patient and persistent. That's not to say I wasn't above clearing the decks of her other admirers, but I did it quietly. She was mine. I just waited until she realised it, too. Twenty-eight years married, Daniel. Never been happier. Drop around tomorrow for lunch. I'll ask Rachel to set an extra plate. Good to talk to you.'

Daniel watched his prospective father-in-law turn the corner, his stride as jaunty as his speech was lively.

Any doubts he'd entertained as to whether Bec was *the one*, disappeared. The story would become the stuff of folklore. Passed down to their children and their children's children. He just needed Bec to acknowledge that she needed saving and play the willing heroine.

'Your mother told me I'd find you here,' whispered Eliza, seating herself opposite Bec and shooting a polite smile into the irritated face of a woman at the other end of the table.

'It's a reading room, not a conversation room.' The woman's sibilant whisper earned her several annoyed shushes from other members.

Bec hid a grin and motioned with her head for Eliza to join her in one of the empty meeting rooms.

Once the door clicked shut, Eliza slapped her cloche onto the small round table. 'I pay my two shillings six every quarter, just like she does, the old crow!'

'Did someone get out of the wrong side of bed this morning, mmm?'

'I've just suffered through question time from my parents as to the hours I'm keeping with Alex.' Eliza folded her arms. 'I may be a little ... defensive.'

Bec shot her friend a consoling look. 'The number of hours or the lateness of the hours?'

'Both,' Eliza admitted. 'I've agreed to a one am curfew on Friday and Saturday nights, and nine pm the other nights.'

'What about educational lantern lectures that don't finish until after nine?' Bec teased.

'I think that's what prompted the discussion. I'd been

attending too many, and when pressed, I was a bit light on the educational detail.'

Bec laughed at Eliza's attempt at cherubic innocence.

'What brings you here?' asked Eliza.

'I'm doing research for the debate.' Bec stabbed the air with an index finger. 'Do you know that women in Chile have been employed as tram conductors for decades?'

Eliza shook her head.

'It was first tried when all the able-bodied men were recruited into the army for some war Chile and Peru were waging, and they continued it. And in New Zealand, there's been a woman in the role of tramway general manager since the end of last century.'

'Will you use that in the debate?'

'That Australia is lagging the rest of the world in common sense?' She shrugged. 'Possibly. I haven't assembled all my research yet. When I do, Daniel's going to help me craft my arguments.'

'Daniel, huh? What happened to Jenny?'

Bec shuffled her notes. 'She's helping Ida. And he offered.'

'Hmm.'

'Take that look off your face. He has a way with words. There's nothing more to it than that!'

Bec may as well have been talking to herself.

'You seem to be getting on better with one another,' her friend ventured.

'Eliza ...' Bec warned.

'I can't help it. I want you to be as happy as I am.'

Bec frowned. 'A husband doesn't guarantee happiness.'

'True. That's where love comes in.'

'Another slippery slope.'

'*Bec!* Are you saying you don't believe in love?'

What she couldn't believe was how their conversation had taken such a turn. 'I accept that there is such a thing, and I'm cautiously optimistic about its magical alchemy.'

Eliza leaned forward. 'Just promise me you won't let your head close your heart to the opportunity. The best chemical reactions don't happen in a vacuum.'

Bec scrunched her nose. Now her friend was a chemist – she couldn't even master baking. 'Let's not quarrel. Returning to your brother, he and I have called a truce and are working on respecting each other's opinions. *Daniel has a lot of those.* But ...' Bec held up both hands as Eliza went to speak. 'There is no romantic intention on *either* side.'

'Is my brother such a bad catch?'

Eliza was like a dog with a bone – one of those tenacious terrier types. Bec sifted through the responses that sprang to mind. *Yes*, she realised, would be untruthful. *No*, would strengthen Eliza's fledgling matchmaking attempts.

'For someone, he'll make a great husband. Someone else, that is.' A sense of déjà vu swept over Bec. She and Eliza had been over this before. 'I'll be *happy* if Daniel and I get to the other side of the debate with a better appreciation of each other's point of view.'

'Hmm.' Eliza shrugged. 'If that's your goal, there's an opportunity to practise your appreciation tonight. Alex has secured four tickets for the musical *Wildflower* at Theatre Royal. Please say you're free. It's ever so popular. There's talk that the Melbourne season will outdo Sydney's six-month run.'

Bec rolled her shoulders. Her friend's well-intentioned but misdirected meddling was embarrassing.

Eliza leaned forward, tapping her nails on the table's surface. 'Please ...'

'All right, but only this once. *Do not* organise further dates with Daniel. Orchestrating match-ups is not your forte!' said Bec with mock severity.

'I promise! Just this time.'

CHAPTER 20

Daniel squirmed in his seat. Could things get any worse? His sister taking it upon herself to run his social life! He risked a glance at Bec's profile. She was studying the seat in front of her. He couldn't imagine she was happy about this, either. He hoped she didn't think the theatre was his idea. While he still wasn't sure of his *actual* plan to secure her hand, teaming up with his sister was never part of *any* plan. It was only one step better than asking his mother for help.

As if sensing his unease, Bec mumbled, 'I just want you to know, I had nothing to do with this.'

Bec's admission amplified his feelings of inadequacy. He was finding it hard to remember the time when his popularity with the ladies was unquestioned. 'Me either!'

The tightening of her jaw and the elevation of her chin suggested he'd delivered that statement with more vehemence than he'd intended. *Great!* Eliza's interference now necessitated he make an apology. He was going to kill his sister at the first opportunity. 'Sorry, that didn't come out the way I intended.'

Bec turned her face and speared him with a glance. In the glare of the pre-performance lighting, her eyes were as colourless as hailstones. Daniel shivered. 'Let's agree that my little sister has meddled where she needn't.' Had her face relaxed ... a little? It was hard to tell. 'But on the bright side, I've been keen to see this show ... and sitting beside you is no hardship.'

Daniel watched Bec's eyes narrow. *Terrific! Nothing better than telling a woman – let alone your future wife – she was no hardship.* Ensuring that his sister, seated on the other side of Bec, was distracted, he reached for Bec's hand. After a short tussle he secured it, unsurprised at its coolness.

He squeezed her fingers. 'Have I told you how exquisite you look in that gown?' He was sure a modiste would exclaim over the detail of the sequins and beading – black with sprays of pink flowers. But it was the way the dress shimmied and swayed as she walked that had captivated him. And the hint of her stocking-covered thigh from the concealed side slit had won the approval of other parts of his anatomy.

Bec's lips twitched, as if sensing he was on the back foot. And then the house lights of the theatre were lowered, and he was blind to her thoughts. He only knew that when he dispensed with the armrest, resting her captured hand on his thigh, she didn't withdraw it.

Bec forced herself to relax, conscious of the warmth of Daniel's palm and their tangled fingers. Should she be holding hands with her best friend's brother? They weren't the rules in her and Eliza's circle of friends. Maybe in

Daniel's circle. He was popular with the ladies. Little wonder, given the way he'd confidently captured her hand and delivered his perfectly timed compliment on her gown. He was probably a master at persuasion, too. She would do well to remember that over the coming weeks.

A guff of laughter from a man behind her returned her to the stage and the scene playing out. *Wildflower* was the musical she and Jim had planned to see last night, followed by a light supper with champagne, maybe some dancing. She wondered if he'd changed the tickets, in which case she'd almost certainly see the production again.

She pursed her lips. Or had he taken up Queenie's overture? *How did she feel about that possibility?* A little put out to be sure – the thought of being so easily exchangeable dented her ego. Although at least it was Queenie, not Evelyn – any man would be happy to have Queenie on his arm. *Were her feelings hurt?* No. She and Jim understood there were no hearts to be broken in their relationship.

'This could have been written about you,' whispered Daniel in her ear, snapping her from her contemplation. She sensed his regard but pretended a focus she wasn't feeling on the stage. Undeterred, he continued, 'Vivacious, quick-tempered at the slightest provocation ...'

Bec delivered her elbow unerringly to Daniel's ribs. Another upside of seats without armrests.

'Ow!'

'Inclined to retribution.'

A soft chuckle sent a shiver coursing down her spine. This was the Daniel whose company she was discovering she enjoyed. Less combative, fun even, with a lively sense of humour.

Bec turned her attention to the stage. The plot was entertaining, if somewhat predictable, and the comedy smart. The casting, dialogue and music first-rate. It was easy to see why the production had played to sellout audiences since commencing on the first of August.

The brightening of the overhead lights and an increase in the volume of conversation announced intermission.

Bec's hand was returned to her lap. She wondered if Daniel had been aware of the leisurely circles he'd painted with his thumb across her knuckles.

Eliza's excited voice captured her attention. 'Are you enjoying it?'

'I am.'

'Bec and I were discussing how much in common she and the heroine, Nina, have,' said Daniel. 'What do you think?'

Alex grinned. 'I'm not entering that discussion.'

Eliza looked pained.

'Harsh, don't you think?' asked Bec, adding to her friend's distress. Eliza had obviously harboured such high hopes for this outing and was aggrieved that her brother seemed intent on spoiling his prospects. But Eliza had meddled, and she needed to be discouraged. If that meant uniting with Daniel, then so be it.

'Let's wait for the second and third acts. Bec ... I mean Nina, could still redeem herself,' offered Daniel with a casual shrug and a glint in his eye.

Bec hid a smile as Eliza's concerned expression deepened.

As the lights dimmed for the second act, he cheekily whispered, 'We can all live in hope, anyway.'

Unerringly, Daniel once again secured her fingers, his thumb playing across the indent on her middle finger, from where she held her pen too tight. She tried to ignore the swirling sensations that his touch evoked, redirecting her attention to the stage scenery depicting the stunning Italian landscape. But it was no use.

Bec shifted restlessly in her seat and Daniel's hand tightened fractionally. She glanced across at him. Dark circles of heat gazed back at her – and not in anger or exasperation, the usual emotions she aroused in Daniel. She swallowed and felt that same heat travel down her throat.

With anyone else, Bec would have delivered a quip, conjured up a casual smile. But Daniel's intensity unsettled her. *Had her grandmother been wrong?* Could physical attraction be enough to base a relationship on?

Wrenching her attention back to the stage, Bec scrambled to return to the story unfolding. It seemed Nina had successfully kept her composure – perhaps Bec should have paid more attention to how – and overcome the schemes and provocations of those whose interests were served by her losing her temper. She was in the process of securing her man and her fortune.

The cast returned for five curtain calls – all to a standing ovation – and flowers littered the stage. Bec had been one of the first to jump to her feet, ignoring Daniel's quiet chuckle. The thought that he might enjoy discomposing her niggled.

When the curtain fell for the final time, Bec and Eliza resumed their seats, mutually agreeing to delay exiting until most of the crowd had departed. They lapsed into a discussion on the costuming and performance by the lead actress. Daniel and Alex remained standing, conversing in low tones over their heads.

'Who was your favourite tonight?' asked Eliza, her head

swivelling between the two men.

'Jenny,' they agreed unanimously.

Bec laughed as Eliza consulted her program.

'The donkey?' she exclaimed.

'She was magnificent. The way she strutted onto the stage, wearing that charming little straw boater over her ears,' said Daniel.

'Stole the show,' agreed Alex. 'Couldn't take my eyes off her.'

'You two are ridiculous,' said Eliza, shaking her head.

'Let's go,' suggested Daniel. 'If we hurry, we can meet her in the foyer.'

'And grab an autograph,' said Alex, catching Eliza's hand and tugging her playfully towards the exit.

'I wonder if Jenny has an understudy,' Bec mused to Daniel over her shoulder as she followed Eliza. His demeanour had returned to its urbane familiarity, his eyes no longer smouldering.

'Maybe.' He chuckled. 'It'd be a cushy job, understudy to a donkey.'

Surprisingly, Jenny made a brief appearance, her hind quarters positioned to deter any temperamental outburst towards her adoring fans.

Eliza insisted on an autograph – a horseshoe-shaped stamp – and had it dedicated to Alex and Daniel.

Laughing, they spilled onto the pavement. The temperature difference from the confines of the theatre had each thrusting arms into coats and turning up collars against the night air.

'Will we stop in at Birmingham's?' asked Daniel. Receiving consensus, they set off on foot for the Collins Street Danse Palais.

'How are your debate preparations proceeding, Bec?' asked Alex as they waited to cross the road.

'Slowly. I'm not feeling confident I understand the role enough or that the arguments are as strong as they need to be,' she admitted. 'My research has uncovered several countries that employ females in roles as varied as superintendent and conductor. I'd really like the opportunity to experience a day or two in the role of a conductor and —'

'No!' Daniel was shaking his head emphatically. 'Out of the question. It's too dangerous.'

Bec stared at him. *Where was the man from the theatre? The one who'd tempted her to ignore her grandmother's advice?*

'You heard Syd recount the challenges he experiences.' Bec noted that Daniel's right eye had started to tic. Eliza had once told her she thought he'd outgrown it – but not around Bec. 'You saw the behaviour of the public when we rode together. Why would you put yourself in danger?'

'Daniel, my funding is dependent on our team's success.'

Eliza clapped her hands. 'So you got it? The funding allocation for the new training course?'

'Yes.'

'That's fantastic!'

Eliza nearly bowled her over as she pulled Bec in for a hug.

'On the condition that our team wins the debate.'

'Seems like there's a lot riding on the outcome of this debate,' said Alex.

Bec didn't know about anyone else. She only knew what it meant to her. 'I'm glad you understand. If there's any possibility ...?'

'No!' repeated Daniel.

Bec ignored him. '*Alex?*'

'I don't know, Bec ...'

They turned onto Collins Street, the lights from Birmingham's illuminating the footpath a little further on.

'I will not live my life wrapped in cotton wool.' She wasn't sure whom she was talking to at this point – herself, Daniel, or anyone who would listen.

When she heard 'You tell him, love,' from a woman walking past in the opposite direction, it lifted her confidence.

'And anyway, I think some challenges could be engineered out,' she said, turning to Daniel.

He refused to make eye contact, staring straight ahead. 'Humph! Like what?'

'Like having one entrance and one exit. Like a bus. That would stop the conductor having to hang off the footboard when the tram was overflowing and battling his way through passengers from one end to the other.'

'But that's not something that could be changed tomorrow, and it would increase loading times. The public would never accept it. They think it takes too long now to get where they're going.'

'They do it in Chile,' Bec said doggedly. 'And what's more, the number of male passengers has increased ... and the number of receipts. If the tramways want to become profitable, then women conductors may be the way to go.'

'You want to turn it into a dating opportunity?' Daniel sounded incredulous.

'There's no talking to you in this mood,' said Bec, observing the mulish set of mouth. 'I give up.'

After a tense silence that lasted to the entrance of the Danse Palais, she turned to Alex. 'If there are any favours you can pull with the Tramways Board to get me out on a tram for a day, I'd be forever grateful.'

Undeterred by Daniel's growl and Eliza's troubled gaze, she swept up the steps and into the foyer.

CHAPTER 21

'We'll join you later,' said Daniel to Bec and Eliza, after they'd deposited their coats and the men had paid the entrance fee.

'Oh no you don't, Daniel Sinclair,' declared Bec. 'I will not give you the opportunity to harangue Alex and deter him from helping *our* debate preparations.'

Daniel was not used to being challenged socially. He quirked an eyebrow, raising his chin a fraction. The *look* always worked on Evelyn. He may as well have saved the effort. Bec wasn't backing down. If anything, she stood taller.

'I'd like to dance. With you. If you don't mind.'

The woman was infuriating. He battled with himself as to whether to refuse her invitation, before silently extending his arm. Bec slipped her hand into the crook of his elbow.

'Excuse us.' Nodding to Alex and Eliza, he ignored his mate's grin and marched Bec to the dancefloor, joining the throng circulating to the strains of a waltz.

Daniel purposefully held Bec closer than propriety demanded. But his hope of provoking a response failed. She didn't demur, keeping her face schooled in a polite smile and her body relaxed. The awareness that had been building between them at the theatre was gone. Her eyes, the most startling feature of her face for their size, were no longer flirting with him. Had they ever? Perhaps he'd imagined it – Bec wasn't as experienced as her sharp tongue suggested.

For his part, he'd wanted to devour her. He still did, but out of frustration, not desire. *Did she care nothing for his experience in these matters?* As a graduate engineer, he'd witnessed a conductor crushed under the wheels of a tram carriage. The man's injuries meant he had never worked again. For a woman, those injuries could have been life threatening.

By the time the tempo changed to the rhythm of a tango, Daniel's temper had cooled to a low simmer. As Bec stepped back, he forestalled her departure. '*My* dance, I believe.'

She hesitated.

'Don't even think about abandoning me in the middle of the floor.'

Their gazes warred. Wordlessly, she assumed the closed position – her left hand resting on his nape, her body tucked into his side.

Any sense of triumph he experienced at her acquiescence was short-lived. The restraint Bec had displayed the last time they'd tangoed had been firmly shelved. Anger had unleashed a siren. She flowed, undaunted by the intimate connection, flawlessly following his lead. Her body curled and uncurled, pausing for a beat, before fluidly moving into the next step. Sparks of awareness relighted, licking at his self-control.

He rested their locked hands low against his hip, and his cheek against hers, and remembered to breathe. Later, Daniel couldn't have said what patterns they'd danced. It had been the most unique feeling of two bodies moving as one.

As the echo of the last strains of music died away, Daniel untangled their bodies but kept Bec secured to his side. He wished he was anywhere other than in the middle of a ballroom, under the scrutiny of lights and speculative eyes. Bec too seemed reluctant to lose the connection that had overtaken their earlier hostilities, her eyes wide as she leaned against him.

'And now it's everyone's favourite, the Monte Carlo,' boomed Mr Birmingham from the stage beside Art Bobbie, the orchestra band leader, effectively shattering the web of intimacy they'd spun.

Daniel groaned as a cheer erupted from the crowd and braced for the anticipated jostling as couples scattered to assume their places – the women in the middle, the men to the outside.

'Come on,' coaxed Eliza, appearing beside them and tugging Bec from Daniel's arms. 'You can't stand locked together for a Monte Carlo.'

Daniel would have preferred they sit out the dance. He wanted to savour this chemistry – or whatever it was – between them. But Bec succumbed to her friend's urgings, joining the circle of women, and leaving him little option but to move and join Alex. Her face was inscrutable. Who knew what she was thinking. Perhaps the allure was all one-sided.

'Sort things out, did you?' smirked Alex, clapping him on the shoulder.

'Put a sock in it,' retorted Daniel.

Alex's laughter followed him as the men walked in an anticlockwise direction, eyeing the women walking clockwise. The music stopped, and he found himself face to face with Evelyn, who would be his partner for the next bracket.

'I didn't see you arrive,' she murmured, moving into his arms for a foxtrot.

'We were a little late. Did I miss anything?'

'Only me, I hope,' Evelyn returned with a coquettish tilt to her lips.

It's just a game, Daniel reminded himself. *Play your part.* But he wasn't in the mood. The benevolent smile that he bestowed, the best he could manage, was met with a flash of disappointment before it was quickly disguised.

'You said *we*,' she continued brightly.

'Bec, Alex, Eliza and I. Alex secured tickets for the theatre, and we made up a party.'

'Oh.'

'It was a last-minute thing,' he lied, knowing full well the tickets must have been bought weeks ago. Although to his defence, he hadn't been aware of their existence until earlier today.

The music ended and Daniel thanked Evelyn, promising to meet afterwards, before returning to his place in the outer circle. There was an upside to the Monte Carlo format – the brackets were short, and each one delivered a new partner.

As the circles rotated in opposition to one another, Daniel unconsciously sought out Bec. She was easy to spot amidst the myriad of coloured gowns festooning the other women. Her black gown glistened under the glare of the chandeliers, her svelte form producing whirlpools of light that were mesmerising.

Frustratingly, her eye contact was brief, a glance and a

half at most before she would focus on the person in front or behind him. One time she smiled, her dimple flashing, and his heart quickened, only to discover Jim ahead of him in the circle. *He was becoming obsessed ... and short of confidence!*

When Mr B announced the final progressive, Daniel began calculating his chances of securing Bec for supper. He wasn't sure what he was going to say, but he had to show her how crazy and dangerous her idea was.

He admonished his circle to speed up as they approached one another. But the music showed no sign of stopping, and he silently urged the inner circle to slow down. Daniel shortened his stride and heard the man behind him swear as he was forced to check his own step.

Stop now! he shouted silently.

They'd drawn shoulder to shoulder. Just as he'd resigned himself to an unfair fate, the music stopped, and he dived for Bec, neatly moving between her and the man behind him. An awkward confusion reigned for several seconds.

'Sorry, mate,' he apologised with a polite inclination of his head, as the man claimed the young woman who should have been Daniel's partner.

'That was rude,' admonished Bec as they moved out of hearing range.

'It was necessary,' he countered, his arm boldly encircling her waist.

Bec narrowed her gaze, coming to a halt and stepping out of his hold. 'I haven't changed my mind, so save your breath.'

'If —'

'You can't tell me what I can and can't do.'

'I —'

'And don't use your long-standing friendship with Alex to

sabotage my request.'

'I —'

'You would, don't deny it.'

He pressed a finger across her lips. 'You talk a lot sometimes,' he chided.

'Well —'

He added another finger. 'I won't interfere with your request to Alex.'

It was like watching a flower unfurl, kissed by the first rays of the sun. He removed his fingers.

'Really?'

'But I won't champion it, Bec. I stand by my position that the role is too dangerous.'

Bec's smile froze as she appeared to consider his words. 'But, if I can somehow get approval, you won't try to stop me.'

'No.'

'Not a word I hear often,' drawled Queenie, appearing beside Bec, her arm resting possessively in the crook of Jim's elbow.

Couples were streaming from the floor to supper, surging around Bec and Daniel as they stood, like two stones in a stream.

The corner of Jim's mouth twisted before he smoothly disentangled himself from Queenie and leaned forward to buss Bec's cheek. 'Evenin', darlin'.'

Bec's lips stretched into a smile. Daniel wished he hadn't suggested they go dancing. He should have guessed Jim would be here.

'What's going on?' asked Evelyn, Derek Fisher in tow.

'Daniel was refuting ... or perhaps refusing Bec,' Queenie said archly.

Bec flushed. 'Pfff. What you overheard was us agreeing to disagree.'

'If you say so,' said Queenie, examining her nails.

Daniel's diplomacy was tested. Although why he was defending their exchange, he couldn't say. He could have used Queenie's inferences to his advantage, but he'd never embarrass Bec publicly. 'Bec is campaigning Alex to request permission from the Tramways Board to play conductor for a day, and I —'

Derek's head snapped up from a contemplation of his shoes. 'That goes against the natural order of things, it does.'

'I'm doing research for a debate,' snapped Bec.

Daniel could have sworn Bec had to bite her tongue from adding *you dolt* from the way she clenched her jaw.

Daniel nodded. 'And I don't agree with her approach.'

Queenie sighed. 'Not so interesting, after all. Is anyone else hungry? All this talk has whetted my appetite,' she purred.

And not just for food, thought Daniel, if the looks she was shooting the American were any indication.

'Darlin'?'

Bec nodded.

She looked relaxed and assured beside the officer, unperturbed by Queenie's attempts to engage her admirer. Once again, Daniel wondered at the nature of Bec's relationship with Jim.

Coming here had been a mistake. Whatever progress he'd made at the theatre had been lost. Their relationship wasn't one suited to incremental shifts – that could take years. He didn't have that long or that much patience. It needed to be disrupted entirely. Only then could they build something new. And he couldn't pursue Bec surrounded by the familiar, or an audience – especially this one. *The question was how.*

'Your menfolk are awfully traditional,' said Jim. He and Bec had escaped to the solitude of the gallery overlooking the dancefloor. 'I thought 'Bama, where I'm from, was the most conservative place on earth.'

'Don't mind Derek,' said Bec.

'I'm not just talkin' of Derek.'

Jim was alluding to Daniel. Bec ignored the subtle invitation. 'Are you telling me I've found myself a man who appreciates a woman's capabilities?'

'I've always been a student of female capabilities.'

Jim's deep baritone voice was hypnotising. But unlike another male of her acquaintance, she had no difficulty meeting the appreciation shining from his eyes.

'A paragon of female emancipation?'

'It all depends on the female.'

Bec wished Jim was *the one*. He ticked a lot of boxes. He was old-fashioned in the things that mattered – common courtesies such as protecting her in crowds and taking the road side of the footpath; he respected her independence; and he didn't confuse her heart. With Jim, she enjoyed the occasional butterfly, but kept her sense of equilibrium.

'I wish you were staying longer.' *Did she?* It wasn't what she'd intended to say. It had just slipped out.

'Do you?' He tapped the pout that she fashioned with a finger. 'Aww, honey, I'm enjoying our time together. And I'd snap you up in a heartbeat if I thought that's what you wanted, but I'm gettin' the feeling I'm steppin' on someone else's toes.'

Bec's denial was automatic. 'You aren't.'

Jim captured the hand she'd laid on his forearm. 'Darlin', I'm not blind. Daniel has become awful attentive.'

So, they were going to discuss the man, after all. 'Not in the way you mean —'

'Takin' you to the theatre, organisin' the interview last night. I'm sensin' I'm bein' warned off.'

'What? Alex organised the theatre tickets. Neither Daniel nor I knew anything about them until earlier today. And as for last night, there were four of us, five counting the trammie.'

'Mmm.'

'If it wasn't for the debate, I wouldn't be spending any time with him at all.' Bec felt colour storm her cheeks. *Or kissing or sharing other intimacies.*

'Are you free tomorrow afternoon?'

'Yes ... no,' she moaned. 'Dad's invited someone for lunch, and I'm to make sure I'm home. What were you planning?'

'Wirth's Circus, the matinee session.'

Bec groaned.

'It's all right, honey. It was late notice. I took a gamble you'd be free. We'll go another time. I'll find someone for tomorrow.'

Bec followed his gaze across the dancefloor to the doors leading out to Birmingham's gardens. Tonight, closed in deference to the chilly evening temperature, they created the perfect frame for the bewitching curves of Queenie Nolan. Like moths to a flame, Evelyn, Daniel and a few others stood in a horseshoe around her.

Bec studied Jim's profile. 'I'm sure you will,' she said. She and Daniel weren't the only ones on a better footing.

Something in her tone must have alerted him because his eyes travelled back to her. 'You're still my best girl.'

But not his *only* girl. Another thing she could lay the blame for at Daniel's feet.

CHAPTER 22

'Daniel? As in Daniel Sinclair?' Bec asked.

Her father looked bewildered at the strength of her tone. 'Yes, love. Is that a problem?'

'Why is Daniel Sinclair coming to lunch?' she countered. *Was everyone colluding to throw the two of them together?*

'I bumped into him yesterday morning, and he looked a little down. Female trouble, I think,' he confided with a wink. 'Thought we'd do the neighbourly thing and cheer him up.'

'Pfff! The only trouble he has is his taste in girlfriends. His current one is a vine – the climbing, trailing type.'

'Rebecca!' her mother rebuked softly, although Bec thought she caught the hint of a smile before she turned away.

'Couldn't you have just taken him for a beer?'

'I suppose I could've.' Her father scratched his chin. 'But I didn't,' he said in a voice she'd learned over the years meant, 'And that's the end of it!'

'Don't you like Daniel, dear? I know your views haven't always aligned, but I thought things had improved since he'd joined the debate.'

'Yes, Mum, I like him well enough. And we've toned down our differences.'

'So, what's the problem?' asked her father.

The man has kissed me three times – but who's counting – his tango leaves me feeling restless, and in my dreams, I imagine we have fewer clothes on than a ballroom demands.

Bec shook herself, leaned over and dropped a kiss on her father's forehead. 'No problem. I'm just … surprised,' she said, trying for a light, unconcerned tone.

From the look her parents exchanged, she doubted she'd been successful. She tried another tack. 'Jim bought tickets for Wirth's matinee today. Not only couldn't I join him, but he's probably taking Queenie in my place.' *Thanks to Daniel.*

Her father looked a little more contrite. 'Oh, love, I'm sorry. We'll organise to have Jim over for lunch soon. It's about time your mother and I met him.'

A knock sounded at the door.

Bec nodded before pushing her chair away from the table. 'I'll get it.'

She reappeared, trailed by Daniel, who'd arrived with flowers for her mother and a firm handshake for her father.

'You can tell a lot about a man's character from his grip,' said her father, clapping Daniel on the shoulder. 'Glad you're not one of those thrifty, economical types.'

Daniel grinned. 'I know the sort. Miserly. Then there's the damp-fish kind. I don't know which is worse.'

'Maybe women should start shaking hands. It would save a lot of time and needless conversation if we could determine someone's character so quickly,' said Bec.

'I wouldn't suggest it. It's a grubby custom,' said her

mother. 'I'll show you a palm under a microscope one day, and you can decide. But let's not talk about that just before lunch.'

'So, what would we replace the handshake with?' Bec asked.

'A bump,' said her father, demonstrating his technique and earning him an elbow to his ribs from his wife.

'A touch of noses like the New Zealanders,' said Daniel.

Bec laughed. 'Or a salute, like a sailor.'

'Or a kiss,' rejoined Daniel.

'Another unhygienic custom,' Bec quipped dismissively.

'Only if performed indiscriminately,' said Daniel.

Bec was annoyed to feel heat rising to her cheeks. *Did he have to say that looking at her mouth?*

'I'm partial to a targeted kiss myself,' agreed her father, eyeing his wife.

Flowers in hand, Bec's mother pushed her husband in the direction of the kitchen. 'All this nonsense won't get lunch served. Take a seat, Daniel.'

Bec shook her head and followed her parents. The affection between them was unmistakable. As a child, she'd often come across them in an embrace. When she'd ask what they were doing, her father would joke, *'Just checking your mother's temperature.'* It was a relief when her grandmother explained the act of kissing. For a while there, she'd been concerned that her mother was dying.

Daniel jumped to his feet as Bec set a tureen of curried vegetable soup onto the table. When he started ladling it into four bowls, she stopped in her tracks. He never helped at home. Usually, she and Eliza scurried around, assisting Mrs Sinclair while he, Alex and Mr Sinclair sat talking. Clearly, he was more capable than he let on.

Her stillness caught his attention. 'What's wrong?'

'I'm standing in awe of your domestic prowess.'

'For ladling soup?'

'Or your initiative to make a good impression.'

'You wound me.'

'*Pfff!* It won't work, you know.'

Her father appeared with the roast, and Bec retreated to stand behind her chair. Daniel quirked a brow and circled around the table towards her. Anticipating his intent, she grabbed the back of her chair, but he was there before her.

'Allow me.'

As he seated her, his fingers brushed her nape. Bec steeled herself against the tide of goosebumps rushing down her arms, glad that she'd chosen to wear long sleeves.

Her mother joined them, and Daniel slid into the seat opposite Bec. She dropped her head in anticipation of grace. She was finding his proximity disturbing. It seemed minutes passed before her father's voice washed over her.

'For what we are about to receive, please Lord, make us thankful. Amen.'

'Amen.' Bec opened her eyes but kept her gaze on her soup.

'Bread?'

Looking up, she scowled at the teasing glint in Daniel's eye. Murmuring her thanks, she once again lowered her gaze to her plate.

'Butter?'

She gritted her teeth. 'Thank you.' The man had the temerity to smile at her. *Correction.* It wasn't just his proximity, the man himself was disturbing. A pest. A disturbing pest!

'I hear you and our Bec have joined forces on a debate,' said Bec's father.

'Yes, sir. It's being co-sponsored by the state as a way of promoting conversation about new opportunities. I don't think the time is right politically or socially in Victoria to move on the idea of female conductors, but those in power are aware that women fill the role in other countries such as Chile —'

'You know about that?' interrupted Bec. 'I only read about that yesterday.'

'Yes. And that even since late last century, New Zealand has had a female tramway general manager ... and I think London has a superintendent who oversees conductors.'

'Sounds like you might be on the same team, but you're not doing a good job of sharing your information,' observed Bec's father, shaking his head.

'Well, I only found out yesterday, as I just said,' protested Bec, thinking her father's rebuke unfair – at least towards her. 'How long have you known?' she groused, pointing her spoon at Daniel. Splashes of yellow dotted her placemat.

'Rebecca!'

Bec lowered her spoon, eyeing the closest soup splotch. Truly unfair; she was fielding arrows from all sides. 'Sorry,' she mumbled.

'Since this morning.' Daniel grinned. He seemed to enjoy her discomfort, not at all perturbed by her father's reproach. 'Eliza enlightened me.'

'That's only because I told her yesterday when she tracked me down at the library.'

'Another mystery solved!' joked Bec's father. 'Now, if we can just discover who's been stealing your mother's baking.'

'That's no mystery, my dear,' said Bec's mother.

Her father had the good grace to look sheepish, although he quickly recovered to ask, 'So, if you're not a fan of the topic, why did you join?'

'Yes, that's puzzled me, too, ever since you announced it,' said Bec.

'Would you believe to satisfy my boss's warped sense of humour?'

Her father gave Daniel what Bec would describe as a considering look. She'd been on the receiving end of many of these during her late teens. Typically, it meant, *I'm not buying it!* He wiped his mouth with a serviette, laying his other hand on the table. 'From what I read, Chalmers is not what I'd call a humorous man. He strikes me as unfailingly decent, but a hard taskmaster.'

Daniel's smile didn't reach his eyes. 'His support of my promotion depends on the success of my participation.'

'So, you're trading your ideals to climb the ladder?'

'I'm not trading anything, Bec.'

'But by success, you mean he expects you to win.'

'Yes.'

'And your promotion is important to you.'

'Yes.'

Bec dusted her hands together. 'Well, by my definition, that means you'll do whatever it takes.'

Daniel shifted in his seat but didn't lower his gaze.

Bec raised her chin. *They were going to stare each other down now, were they?*

'So, what is your view of the topic, Daniel, if you think the political and social landscape is not ready for females in the role?' asked Bec's mother.

Bec glared at him. *Yes, Daniel, let's hear your view.* She couldn't wait for her mother's response when he expressed his expectation of a woman's role not extending past the front door!

Daniel quirked an eyebrow in her direction before addressing her mother. 'Well, if you'd asked me two weeks ago, I'd have said, unequivocally, that I was against it, and that a woman's role was in the home, as wife and mother.'

Bec turned her head in anticipation of a response, but her mother was calmly sipping her soup.

Daniel kept talking. 'But now, I'm conflicted. I don't think anyone can deny the biological role women play in birthing and raising children —'

'Or men,' remarked Bec. 'It takes two.'

'Little doubt she's your daughter!' her father teased his wife, who hid her smile behind a discreet cough.

'Or men,' agreed Daniel. 'But raising children takes time and energy. It would be difficult to work as well.'

Bec scowled. *Hypocrite! You're sugar-coating things for my parents.*

'But not every woman can have children,' said Bec's mother. 'Or wants to, or finds someone to marry.'

Bec's brows rose. *What do you say to that?*

'That's true. And in that case, it would be more fulfilling, I assume, for a woman to work than depend on the charity of others for her existence.'

'Of course, marriage doesn't mean a woman loses her independence,' said Bec's father. 'My Rachel, and her mother – bless her departed soul – are, and were, as independent as they come.'

'You make me sound like something out of the Wild West,'

her mother said, sending him an aggrieved look.

Bec pushed her soup bowl away and crossed her arms. This wasn't how the conversation was meant to go. Daniel was skirting around the issue of women as tram conductors. Time to get the topic back on track. And for her mother to deliver a set-down!

'But what about women in the role of tram conductors, Daniel? What's your view on that?' asked Bec, keeping her voice deceptively calm.

'I'm conflicted about that, too.'

Bec snorted. *No, you're not!* She glared at him. *God, he should run for politics.*

Daniel sighed and met her glare with one of his own. 'I think the conductor's role on the cable trams is hard work. Physically, mentally and emotionally. And I don't think a tram is a suitable work environment for females.'

That's more like the Daniel I know! 'And he's supposed to be on our side of the debate,' scoffed Bec, swivelling her head between her parents.

Daniel accepted a portion of roast beef from her mother before replying. 'Bec, every week I read in the newspapers of conductors being injured, assaulted, sometimes killed. Just doing their job. And then there's all the time they spend defending themselves against often petty complaints. I'm sorry, but I was raised to protect females and so it goes against the grain to promote the idea of women in that type of role.'

'I see your point, Daniel,' said her mother. 'But sometimes, females bring a different perspective on things. A different way of handling situations that eliminate the experiences you're familiar with.'

Daniel nodded thoughtfully.

Bec's mother continued. 'I can't speak to the physical hazards, that sounds like an engineering problem, but I've seen many a hostility placated by a fresh approach and a soothing tone. Even in the animal world.'

Daniel finished his mouthful of food. 'I hadn't considered that.'

Why are you being so reasonable? Bec wanted to rage at him.

'It is true that the new electric trams will eliminate some of the dangers trammies experience today.' Daniel scooped up a forkful of peas before eyeing Bec. 'We should ride one so you can see the difference in operation.'

Bec looked at him, stupefied. At this moment, she'd do anything to get away from him. She wasn't looking for opportunities to spend more time together.

'Bec?' her father prompted.

Great, now her parents thought she was being rude. 'Sure,' she said, after forcing a sip of water down her constricted throat.

CHAPTER 23

'Dessert anyone?' asked her mother.

'I'll get it,' offered Bec, driving her chair out with such force she only just stopped it from toppling over.

'The roly-poly should be right to come out of the oven, Bec. And the custard is on the stovetop.'

'I'll help,' said Daniel, pushing back his chair. 'That was a terrific meal, Mrs Cross.'

Daniel could tell that Bec was upset by the rigid set of her shoulders and her non-committal responses during the rest of the meal. He thought he'd been considered and rational in the way he'd presented his views. Why was she so angry? He didn't have to wait long to find out.

'Why are you being so reasonable?' she hissed when he joined her in the kitchen. Unlike his own parents' house, Bec's sported a separate kitchen and dining room, although it wasn't so far away that you couldn't hold a conversation between the rooms if needed.

'*That's* why you're mad? Because I'm not ranting and raving?' he asked in disbelief. *Was he ever going to understand this woman?*

'It's not the only reason. But it ranks highest at this moment. Why else?'

A laugh exploded from his throat. 'With you? I'm never sure.'

Hands on hips, Bec leaned towards him. 'Are you saying *I'm* unreasonable?'

'Bec, I'm not having this conversation here and now. Your parents don't deserve to hear us thrash out our differences across dessert. And anyway, what happened to our truce?'

She threw up her hands. '*You* became rational! That wasn't part of the deal.'

Daniel shook his head. *Bec wasn't making any sense. At least to him.*

'I'll take that,' he said, relieving her of the roly-poly and turning on his heel before she could start a lecture about how she could manage without his help. Plum jam, his favourite.

'Everything all right?' asked Bec's father when he reappeared. He was sitting alone, sleeves rolled up to his elbows, forearms resting on the table.

'Apparently, I'm being too reasonable,' blurted Daniel, before he could stop himself.

The older man guffawed before nodding sagely. 'Runs in the family. Patience and persistence are the key. She's worth it, you know, although I admit to being a tad biased.'

'How ...?'

'I didn't, until now.'

'I'd ask that you don't —'

'My lips are sealed,' Bec's father assured him, before raising his voice. 'Is there any chance of custard to go with this jam roll?'

Bec appeared with the lost jug of custard, her mother bustling in behind. Daniel wondered whether her parents had divided and conquered. Bec appeared calmer, a tentative smile hovering across her lips.

Talk turned to local news – the recovery of the seaplane from the bay that was lost off the USS *Pennsylvania* after suffering engine trouble; the collision of two interstate passenger steamers off the lighthouse; and the upcoming council elections. Was Daniel's father feeling confident about retaining his seat?

Daniel's offer to clean up was graciously declined. 'Edward needs the practice. His dishwashing skills have been absent of late,' teased his wife.

'Go for a walk, enjoy the break in the rain. Bec needs a bit of cheering up after missing the Wirth's matinee this afternoon,' encouraged her father.

Daniel raised his eyebrows.

'Jim bought tickets. *But I was needed here.*'

Daniel quietly toasted her father's planning and Jim's lack of it.

They turned seaward after farewelling Bec's parents and then towards the cast-iron gates of the Botanic Gardens. As Bec moved to shove her hands into the pockets of her jacket – a habit of hers, he'd noticed – Daniel secured her right hand, linking their fingers.

'Can I assume that you're upset because you wanted to see fireworks at lunch?'

'You don't believe in beating around the bush, do you?'

'In your case, it saves me second-guessing myself, and often getting things wrong.'

He was rewarded with a twist of her lips – not quite a

smile, but close. It wasn't until they'd meandered past garden beds amassed with daffodils and jonquils, and were strolling down the avenue of palms, that she spoke.

'It's possible,' she admitted finally, eyes facing forward, 'that I'd hoped you would benefit from a dressing-down from my mother.'

Daniel glanced across at her profile, but it remained guarded. 'I don't think anything she could deliver would compare with that of her daughter's,' he teased.

A stray wind gust swept down the gravel path and Bec seemed to burrow further into her coat. 'I owe you an apology,' she said stoically. 'I was thoughtless ... and I defaulted on our truce ...'

Daniel wanted to punch the air. There were multiple penalties to be had if he played his cards right. 'You did, didn't you?' He paused, allowing the statement to settle between them. 'Maybe more than once.'

'Once.'

'You attempted to splatter me with hot soup —'

'Missed by a mile.'

'Appeared ungracious when I extended an invitation to ride an electric tram.'

'What?'

'And here's me, having been so ... *reasonable* and all. Your penalty will need to be considerable.'

Bec tugged her fingers from his grasp, shaking her head. 'You were rude to me in front of Syd. Our forfeits cancel one another out.'

'You're too late. A forfeit has to be claimed within twenty-four hours.'

'That wasn't in the rules.'

'It's always been in the rules. Since university days.'

'But I —'

'Well, now you know.' Daniel was warming to the plan that was forming in his mind, and nothing Bec could say was going to deter him. 'Maybe your penalty needs to last a whole week.' What was one of her father's pieces of advice? *Clear the decks of her other admirers. But do it quietly.*

'You're entitled to one penalty, Daniel.'

'Tomorrow night, you'll allow me to walk you home after dinner.'

Bec shrugged. 'You do that now.'

'Alone.'

'I doubt Eliza will object to spending more time with her fiancé. But no funny business.'

'You're in no position to qualify my penalties. Tuesday, we'll take that trip on the electric tram together. Wednesday night, we'll refine your debate arguments.'

'That'll further our research,' she reasoned. 'No hardship there.'

'Thursday, we'll go dancing.'

'As normal —'

'At the new ballroom at Newport.' *No chance of running into Jim there.*

'It might be nice to meet new people.'

'Friday, we'll go to the theatre.'

'That's my entire week,' she wailed.

'Not quite. Saturday, we'll go and see the ice dancing at the Glaciarium.'

'You're being ridiculous. Why do you want to use your forfeit to monopolise my time?'

Daniel directed their footsteps along the path that led past the ornamental pond ringed with palms and succulents. It was one of his favourite places to visit, especially when, like today, no one had ventured far from their luncheon table or warm hearth.

'You and I share an attraction.'

Bec stopped. Her eyes widened fractionally, but she met his gaze squarely. 'No amount of physical attraction can outweigh entrenched and differing views or overlook annoying character traits.'

That wasn't Daniel's recent experience. If his view of Bec's imperfect self was undergoing a metamorphosis, so could hers. 'It's amazing what can happen with the right motivation.'

'Is this another one of Louis Chalmers' conditions?'

God, where had that come from? He never should have linked the debate and his promotion at lunch. Or had Alex let something slip to Eliza? He didn't think so. Eliza would have bailed him up. 'Are you suggesting my boss is mandating who I go out with?'

'What's one more discarded principle on the stairway to promotion?'

'*Bec!*'

She shrugged. 'Our priority has to be winning the debate. Nothing can interfere with that. Both of us have things to lose. And I've worked too hard to let this chance slip away.'

'You're talking to a dab hand at juggling priorities.'

His attempt at humour had fallen flat, if the frown on Bec's forehead was any indication. 'All right. Tomorrow ... we'll start getting better acquainted,' she said.

'Actually, today is the start of the week.'

'And I've forgone my date with Jim to spend it with you.

So, today's penalty is settled.'

Daniel's stomach tightened at the sound of the officer's name. He still didn't know whether Bec's heart was involved. 'That was at your father's request. It doesn't count.'

'Is that another rule that you haven't disclosed? And anyway, you benefited.'

He pretended to consider her argument. 'Indirectly, that's true, I suppose. But forfeits are of a more direct nature. The loser, that's you, compensates the other party, that's me, personally.'

Eyebrows elevated, Bec scoffed. 'And these are the rules you and Alex used to play by?'

'Oh yes. Ours were of a more challenging nature, of course. You won't even need to raise a sweat,' he assured her as they crossed the lawn towards one of the many trees dotting the gardens. *Well, that wasn't strictly true.* Turning to face her, he persuaded her forward until their bodies were almost touching.

She quirked an eyebrow, as if questioning his intentions. In response, he cupped the back of her head and lowered his lips to hers. He'd noticed she had a smidgeon of plum jam in the very corner of her mouth, which was his first foray, lapping at it with his tongue until all evidence had been removed.

She giggled. 'What are you doing?'

'Enjoying leftovers,' he murmured, nibbling her lower lip.

'That tickles.'

'Are you ticklish, Bec? I don't think I knew that about you,' he said, exploring the underneath of her jawline and the pulse at the side of her neck. She tasted of citrus and honey.

'Very!'

'Not here,' he said, swirling his tongue around her earlobe before dipping to the hollow behind.

'No,' she agreed, using both hands to anchor herself against him.

Daniel smiled, leaning back on the trunk of the tree, enjoying the sense of her full body weight touching him. He skated one hand to the base of her spine to help support her. *Maybe not ticklish, but sensitive, certainly.*

'Here?'

'No,' she moaned, arching her neck to give him better access.

Returning to her mouth, Daniel kept his kisses light – butterfly weight – and coasted his palms to the top of her hips, her waist, and slightly flexed his thumbs. 'Here?'

She quivered.

'I can't hear you,' he tormented, squeezing a little harder.

'Yes, damn you,' she said, working to pull away from him.

'Then I'll just hold you,' he said, kissing her mouth before dropping his chin onto the top of her head and wrapping his arms around her.

She was just the right armful. Tall, slender, long-limbed and incredibly responsive. And this time they hadn't fought ... each other ... or for control. Patience and persistence – useful advice from her father. But he thought he could handle things where Bec was concerned from here. Seduction was a skill he'd been honing for years.

CHAPTER 24

The young man raised his gaze from the sheaf of papers in front of him and looked at her over the top of his steel-rimmed glasses. 'Would you mind not doing that? It's distracting.'

Everything, it seemed, was distracting to this earnest, pompous secretary. The rustle her skirts made as she crossed and uncrossed her legs; her sighs marking the passage of each quarter-hour she sat here; and now the tapping of her heel.

'Will Mr Chalmers be much longer?' asked Bec.

'Hard to say.' His gaze returned to his papers. 'Not so long, had you an appointment.'

Bec bit back a retort. She doubted too many females were given audiences in Louis Chalmers' diary. Working on the premise that ministers, as elected officials, were accessible to the public, she'd arrived unannounced but determined. After two hours, her resolve had only strengthened. Spending the day as a trammie was important. It didn't matter how much she read about the role, or watched the men performing their duties. It wasn't enough. She learned through hands-on experience. Alex could only champion her request so far, and she still didn't trust that Daniel hadn't talked him out of supporting her.

The clock above the secretary struck three o'clock. She was meeting Daniel in an hour at the other end of the city for her introduction to the newer electric trams. She couldn't abandon her post – Elsie's generosity wouldn't extend to another afternoon away from the office.

Her thoughts circled back to Daniel. In the space of four days, something had shifted in their relationship. But she couldn't put her finger on what. Confiding the distress experienced as a thirteen-year-old was something she hadn't shared with anyone. It had both surprised and troubled her how easily it had slipped out and that he'd listened, respecting her request that he not rush off on his white charger to avenge her. At lunch on Sunday, he'd been articulate, thoughtful and ... *reasonable!* Her parents had later expressed how much they'd enjoyed having him join them. She'd conceded his views seemed to express a genuine moderation.

In the gardens he'd been *reasonable* – there was that word again – even after she'd admitted her hopes for him to be flayed by her mother. His demands had been *unreasonable*, but his kisses had been playful, not combative at all.

Last night, honouring her, *'we agreed, no funny business'*, he'd kissed her forehead and given her a gentle push through the gate. Inwardly, she'd fumed – hadn't he been even a little tempted to ignore her declaration? Refusing to turn around, she'd slipped inside the house, closing the front door with an emphatic click.

'Anderson, do you know when ...?'

'No,' said the secretary, sending a pointed look Bec's way.

'Bec!'

'Hello, Daniel.'

'You know her?'

'Um ... yes. Why?'

'Maybe you can convince her to go home.'

Daniel raised an eyebrow and moved to the seat beside her. 'What are you doing here?'

'Waiting to see Mr Chalmers.'

Daniel shook his head, as if waking from sleep. '*Why?*'

'To ask him to support my request to become a tram conductor for the day.'

'*Bec!*'

The door opened ahead of three men in navy-blue worsted suits, hats in hand. 'Thank you, Mr Chalmers,' the shorter of the three said, shaking hands. 'We look forward to the government's support.'

Both Daniel and Secretary Anderson had risen to their feet as the men took their leave. Seizing advantage of the distraction, Bec headed for the minister, hand outstretched.

'Mr Chalmers, Bec Cross.'

Using a manoeuvre she'd seen at a protest, Bec clasped his hand and sidestepped through the doorway into the office beyond.

'*Bec!*'

Really, Daniel's overuse of her name, in that choked tone of his, was grating.

'Sinclair? What's this about?'

'A misunderstanding, sir.'

Serious but curious brown eyes turned to regard her from

beneath white, bushy eyebrows that matched the colour and texture of his hair. 'What say you, Miss Cross?'

Bec's chin rose. 'I'm here to request a favour, sir. There is no misunderstanding on my part.'

Louis Chalmers broadened his stance and stroked his chin. 'Well, best get on with it. I'm a busy man.'

'It's concerning preparation for the debate on the suitability of females as tram conductors.'

'I'm familiar with the topic.' He nodded towards Daniel. 'Young Sinclair here, too.'

'Yes, we're on the same team.'

'Are you now?' The man pinched his bottom lip between thumb and finger.

'I'm requesting permission to spend the day as a conductor as part of my research.'

'Why?'

'*Why?*' Bec parroted.

'Yes. Why should I invest my manpower and resources in your request?'

'Um ... well, because ... it'll help us win.'

He raised a brow.

Bec folded her arms. 'We have to win ... it's important.'

'What Bec is trying to say —'

'Oh, I think I understand what she's trying to say.' Louis Chalmers speared Daniel with a look. 'I'm familiar with success. Do you support this request, Sinclair?'

'I ...'

Bec held her breath, willing him to back her.

'Well, spit it out.'

'As you know, sir, there's a lot riding on this debate. So ... yes.'

'Humph.' Louis Chalmers flicked back his coat sleeve and checked his watch. 'I'll think about it, Miss Cross. Give Anderson your name and direction and I'll make sure you have my answer by the end of the week. Good day to you.'

Bec's departure from his office was as abrupt as her arrival. In less time than it had taken him to deliver his verdict, she was standing before the secretary, and he had shut the panelled door firmly behind her.

She rolled her shoulders, loosening the tension she hadn't realised she'd been holding until now.

'Your direction, Miss Cross?'

'YWCA headquarters, Russell Street.'

'Of course.'

'Why *of course*?'

The infuriating man shrugged and busied himself with his pen. She eyed the ink bottle sitting within reach of her fingers.

'Let's go.'

Bec turned to find Daniel holding the external door open. As if reading her thoughts, he gave an infinitesimal shake of his head. She hoped he knew how much energy it cost her to walk away as she grabbed her coat and swept past him.

'Are all your colleagues like him?'

'No. Some are worse.' He marched them towards the main staircase.

'I think the interview with your Mr Chalmers went quite well.'

'You do.'

A quick glance revealed a stony mask. 'Yes. Don't you?'

'I'm usually more prepared for my interviews.'

'Yes, well, um ... I realise my appearance must have come

as a surprise.'

Daniel paced down the stairs beside her. If he'd been a light bulb, he would have been blazing by now, such was the intensity of emotion emanating from him.

'I don't know why. It's just the sort of harebrained excursion you'd set off on.'

'Well, how else was I going to secure permission?'

'Not by pulling a stunt like that.'

Bec negotiated the last step to the polished parquet floor before turning to face him, ignoring the *tut-tut* of disapproval from the group negotiating the stairs behind her. She glared. All four men shifted to the side and around them.

Bec leaned in to Daniel. 'Perhaps I should remind you we're on the same team and success for one, means success for all.'

'That's the most screwed-up piece of logic I've heard,' Daniel hissed, steering her to the vestibule's side wall. 'My boss is not the type who likes surprises. You didn't even have an argument prepared. Did you think he was simply going to take one look at you and agree to anything you asked?'

Bec hated that Daniel was right. She hadn't thought through the reasons why agreeing to this would be in the minister's best interests. She'd just assumed that because she thought it was a good idea, he would too. 'All right, perhaps my approach was a little flawed.'

'*A little?*'

'Thank you for supporting me.'

Daniel shook his head. 'Can I remind you that I have a promotion riding on this debate? And making me look ridiculous in front of my boss does not help my cause.'

Bec sobered. In her determination to get her way, she'd

forgotten Daniel's stake in this for all her evangelising on shared success. 'Sorry, I didn't think.'

'No, you didn't.'

'But I also have an important initiative dependent on this and he didn't reject our idea outright.'

'Your idea, remember.'

'You'll want to be a part of it when he sends word of his agreement.'

'Honestly, Bec, you don't have a clue how decisions are made around here.'

'Oh, I imagine there is a great deal of pontification and verbose claims of knowledge.' *Was that steam escaping from his nostrils?* 'You need a woman. She'd cut through all that nonsense. You'd have had time for lunch.'

Daniel gave her a surprised look. 'How did you know I missed lunch?'

'A tram makes less noise than your stomach,' she dismissed. 'Is it a regular thing?'

'I'm afraid so, especially lately. New legislation introduced last year to regulate motor omnibus traffic – buses – has opened up a war of words about privileges and penalties and a fight for private profit over public enterprise. The bus lines, Tramways Board and the government have all waded in. The delegation leaving Chalmers' office was from the bus owners.'

'I remember reading that one line had gone into liquidation – sixteen female bus conductors retrenched. Isn't it interesting that private enterprise doesn't have an issue employing female conductors?'

'That's because they don't get paid the same. I thought you were an advocate for equal pay.'

'I am, but you're being deliberately obtuse,' Bec returned with equanimity. 'If the tramways were privately run, the gender barrier would disappear and then we could fight the pay gap. As it is, we can't get to first base.'

Daniel groaned. 'You're doing it again. Taking the conversation off on a tangent.'

She noticed the dark shadows beneath his lashes and reminded herself that he hadn't eaten. Was it fair for her to wage a skirmish when her opposition was in such a state? 'Just concede I might have a point.'

He hesitated.

No doubt he was weighing up what he'd lose by such an admission.

'You may have a point.'

She sent him a pert smile. 'So, are we still going on our excursion this afternoon?'

'Under the circumstances? No. Thanks to you, I must now prepare for the likelihood that *my support* of your request will be added to the agenda of the meeting I have with Chalmers late this afternoon.'

'Oh. What will you say?'

Daniel appeared to search her face as if the answer was written on her forehead ... painted across her lips. She knew the moment he'd decided. The corners of his mouth tilted ever so slightly upwards, and his eyes lost that unfocused look.

'I'm going to link your initiative to Chalmers' criteria for my promotion and show how his support can guarantee that success.'

'I don't know what that means. It sounds awfully complicated.'

'It's all about the intrigue, Bec – he'll love it. If I play my cards right, your visit this afternoon may have gifted me an opportunity, after all.'

Bec studied him. It was as if he was lit from within. Her gut was telling her something wasn't quite right – she was missing a critical piece of the puzzle. But she didn't have time for more questions – Daniel seemed eager to begin his preparations.

'Will we meet later?' he asked, helping her into her coat.

'No. I'm meeting Jim tonight.'

His hands settled heavily on her shoulders, and he spun her around. 'Jim?'

'Yes. We'd made no plans for tonight. Your forfeit extended only to the tram excursion.' She shrugged his hands away. 'And you've defaulted on that.'

His jaw tightened. 'Tomorrow night, then.'

'Yes.' She turned and walked towards the exit. Stopping, she retraced her steps. 'You may be a master of intrigue and opportunism, but don't forget the importance of trust and delivering what you say you will.' And with that, she pivoted on her heel, confident her afternoon had not been wasted despite Daniel's misgivings.

CHAPTER 25

Wednesday 26 August 1925

Alex slammed his beer back on the bar. 'She did what?'

Daniel raised his glass. 'Walked right up and introduced herself.'

'Why didn't you stop her?'

'I didn't think flooring Bec with a diving tackle, while spectacular, would help my promotion.'

'Too many witnesses?'

'Funny man.'

'What was Chalmers' reaction?'

'Ever the politician. Took it in his stride. Asked me my opinion.'

'Which was?'

Daniel drained his glass. 'What could I say? She'd already admitted we knew each other. I would have looked stupid ... stupider if I'd disagreed.'

Alex shook his head. 'She's a handful. Are you sure she's the one?'

'Bec was your idea, remember? And I never told you she was the one.'

Alex slapped Daniel on the shoulder and called for two more beers. 'It's what you haven't told me. Has Chalmers said anything since?'

Daniel hesitated. 'He asked me how well I knew her.'

Alex's eyebrows rose.

'I told him we had an understanding.' His best friend's eyes grew wide. He finished with a rush. 'And that granting the request would guarantee the success of my suit.'

'What?'

'I didn't lie. An understanding could be many things and success can be measured in many ways.'

'Listen to yourself.' Alex ticked off Daniel's indiscretions on his fingers. 'You've misrepresented your relationship to your boss. Behind Bec's back. All for a promotion?'

'Think of it as a prediction. I just need more time to convince her.'

'And what if she hears of her engagement?' Alex ran his hand through his hair. 'Please tell me that is what you're proposing. Not some pretend courtship.'

'She won't. Unless you tell Eliza. And yes, I'm serious about marriage.'

'Details of your deception won't pass my lips.'

'Thank —'

'But if you hurt her ... sully her name ... I will step in. Best mate or not.'

Daniel nodded. 'Understood. But it won't come to that.'

'So, your manipulation of the truth had the desired effect? Chalmers agreed?'

Daniel winced. 'He's taken it under consideration. I expect I'll know tomorrow.'

'And when are you seeing Bec again?'

'Tonight. I'm helping her with her debate arguments.'

'Mmm. Think about what I've said. The stakes – your personal stakes, not your professional ones – don't get much higher than this. Don't screw up.'

'I won't.' He saluted Alex. 'Thanks for the beer ... and the advice.' Had he gone too far? First Bec's caution of the importance of trust and now Alex's reservations. Daniel squared his shoulders as he headed out onto the pavement. This was no time to start doubting himself.

'Found this dashing fellow out the front and thought I'd invite him in.'

Bec's father ushered Daniel into the kitchen, where Bec was emptying the sink, and her mother wiping the last of the cutlery. 'You're too late to help with the dishes, but perhaps you and Bec can make tea before you start.'

'Dad!'

'Edward!'

Bec and her mother admonished simultaneously.

Daniel grinned. 'Be happy to. How do you take it?'

'Strong, with three sugars.'

'Two,' Bec's mother corrected. 'He's trying to cut down.'

'We'll be in the living room. Rachel takes hers black without sugar. Says she doesn't need any sweetening.' He rolled his eyes before collecting his wife and towing her out of the kitchen. 'One of those shortbreads wouldn't go astray – to make up for that missing teaspoon of sugar.'

Silence descended, and Bec stood awkwardly – inexplicably unsure of where to look or what to do with her hands.

'Let's start again, shall we?' Daniel gave her a lopsided grin and captured her hand, tangling their fingers. 'Hello.'

'Hello.'

He tilted his head and studied her. 'You look … out of sorts.'

'I'm feeling better … now.' Bec dropped her chin. 'I mean …'

'I'm glad.' He squeezed her fingers before his tone became businesslike. 'All right, point me at these shortbreads.'

Daniel found himself humming. He was ridiculously pleased to see Bec. All afternoon he'd reminded himself that his reward for suffering through Theo Blake's seemingly limitless qualification of Daniel's project updates, and their boss's endless discussion and deliberation, lay only a few hours away.

To hear that she may be glad to see him, too, did things to his insides that no self-respecting man would admit to. Although, as his head reminded him, he could never be sure of Bec's true meaning. Maybe she just meant she felt better having eaten dinner, or that now he'd arrived, they could get started.

Bec's voice halted his mental calisthenics as she returned from delivering her parents' tea and shortbread. 'Did you convince your boss to support our request?'

He ignored her use of the word 'our'. 'I think so. He didn't say much, but I could tell he was pleased. He tugged his right earlobe twice.'

'Maybe it was itching.'

Daniel shrugged dismissively. 'We'll just have to wait and see.' He didn't want Bec asking questions about what he'd said or how he'd handled the discussion. Alex's accusation of Daniel's distortion of the truth had returned to weigh on his mind. Until today, he would have regarded his integrity above reproach. *Damn it, he still did.* But had he crossed a line? The question would not be silenced.

'Mmm. So, where do you want to begin?'

Daniel considered the question, and the questioner. Beginnings presented a multitude of possibilities. But Bec looked serious, and it was apparent their ideas of a starting point were not aligned. He held out hope for the end of their evening – her responses were less ambiguous when he took her in his arms.

'Daniel?'

'Um ... let's review the progress of your arguments to date,' he said, reaching for the copy of notes she'd laid in front of him.

His practised eyes sped through the pages – making a few annotations in the margins – deliberately averting them from Bec's curious eyes, knowing it would annoy her. Irritation he had an antidote for – less so indifference.

Bec's voice interrupted him. 'Is it ethical for us to tweak our understanding of the topic?'

He neatened the papers in front of him and laid down his pen. 'Go on.'

'First, we're not arguing that all women have what it takes to be tram conductors. The same as not all men have the requisite physical form, demeanour or education.'

'So, you want to narrow the argument to suitable women?'

'Yes.'

Daniel watched the smile spread from her lips to her eyes.

'And second, acknowledging that while physically, the design of the existing fleet may not be conducive to female participation —'

'That the new W-Class design could be,' he concluded.

'Yes!'

'That's clever. I don't know if it's in the rules, but it certainly makes it more difficult for the other side to argue a black-and-white case.'

'And it incorporates and reflects the advances being made in technology,' Bec added, leaning forward. 'Integrating what we've observed through our research.'

'I thought you confined all your observations to me,' Daniel teased.

Bec fidgeted with an oversized button on her cable-knit sweater, and Daniel smiled as a raspberry-coloured tint surged into her cheeks. He delighted in disproving Bec's insistence that she never blushed.

'I —'

'It's mighty quiet out here. I thought debates were lively, noisy affairs.' Bec's father heralded his approach up the hallway.

'We're considering tactics,' Daniel said, giving Bec a conspiring wink.

Bec turned to her father. 'Are there any rules around the interpretation of a debate's topic?'

'Rachel?'

'The responsibility falls to the first speaker of the affirmative team,' Bec's mother said, appearing behind her husband and pulling out a chair.

'Which isn't us,' Daniel confirmed, tapping the end of his pencil against his lips.

'But the first speaker for the negative can challenge the interpretation, providing they can prove to the adjudicator that their definition is the more reasonable.'

Bec's father rested his hands on the back of his wife's chair. 'I've seen skilled debaters use the subtleties of language to sway the tone of the debate from the initial explanation.' Lowering his head, he continued close to his wife's ear, 'I prefer that to an all-out challenge.' The quelling look she delivered over her shoulder raised a chuckle.

'We'll consult with Jenny and Ida on the best approach,' Bec said.

'You —'

'No, Daniel. We, not I. You're an integral part of the team. And you know how fond of you Ida is.'

'A fan?'

'She thinks Daniel is a gift from heaven, Dad. A male helping the feminist cause! At our first meeting, I thought she was going to canonise him!'

Her mother laughed. 'Don't you have to be dead to be canonised?'

'At least one member of the team appreciates me, dead or alive,' Daniel said with an exaggerated sigh.

Bec crossed her arms. 'Thankfully, you have me to keep your feet planted firmly on the ground.'

Daniel studied her across the table. *Could he get the two women to switch roles?*

'That was always my job,' said Bec's father. 'All those other blokes whispering sweet nothings in your mother's ear. She would have been carried away but for me.'

'I could have been living in a castle —'

'Draughty old things.'

'Or in a country mansion —'

'Isolated, with no one to talk to but sheep.'

Bec's mother hooted with laughter.

'Yep, good thing I was around,' said Bec's father, squeezing the top of his wife's shoulders.

Daniel enjoyed the quirkiness of Bec's parents' exchanges. They were clearly enamoured with one another, even after all these years, if the frequent touches and shared glances were anything to go by. He didn't doubt that his own parents were still in love – he'd caught his father with his arms around his mother only last week – but their affection was more measured, less ... in the moment.

'I might take my leave,' Daniel announced, looking at his watch. 'Early start tomorrow.'

'Don't let Edward scare you off,' Bec's mother said.

Daniel raised his eyebrow towards Bec. 'We've probably gone as far as we can tonight.'

'Yes,' Bec agreed. 'I'll incorporate the notes you made and tee up a meeting with Ida and Jenny.'

'I'll walk you out,' offered Bec's father. 'I always go for a final constitutional before retiring.'

Daniel didn't know whether he hid his disappointment. He'd been looking forward to coaxing a kiss from Bec. Ever since Sunday, he'd been anticipating when he could hold her in his arms again. Monday night had been fleeting. Tuesday night – he stopped a growl escaping from his throat – Bec had spent with Jim. And now her father was offering him his escort. He could hardly refuse.

Daniel wished Bec's mother goodnight, reminded Bec he would call for her at eight o'clock tomorrow evening, and then headed out with her father.

'No need to look so glum, my boy. Sounds like you'll have plenty of time to continue your acquaintance with my daughter this week.'

Daniel glanced quickly across at the other man. *Was he being warned off?*

As if reading his mind, Mr Cross said, 'Doing a good job of routing out the opposition, I hear.'

Not as good as he'd planned, but Daniel was thankful the observation didn't seem to require a response when the older man continued.

'I get concerned about my little girl. I'm all for independent women. After all, I married one. But Rebecca's independence rises from a sense of vulnerability, rather than one of strength, like her mother's. I've never been able to put my finger on the source.'

Daniel listened without comment, admiring his perceptiveness. He could hardly tell this man, Bec's father and protector – until she married – that the cause had stemmed from his inability to protect her in his shop, twelve years ago.

'Why are you telling me this?'

'I don't want you to get discouraged when you find her in full retreat. Despite how many gains you think you've made.'

'I'll add perseverance to my arsenal.' He hoped this conversation was Mr Cross's way of showing his support for Daniel's suit.

'Good man.'

'I have a question that you might help with,' said Daniel.

'Go on.'

'Do you know of a Williamstown businessman with a reputation for bullying?'

'That would be William Tailor, the patriarch of Tailor Bros., in Nelson Place. Do you know it?'

'Suiting?'

Mr Cross nodded. 'A bit of a curmudgeon. His son complains he frightens the clientele, insisting as he does on turning up in the shop every day. He comes in to me for a shave or cut and trim every week – has done for years. One of my first customers. Marches in, with the aid of a cane, still sprouting the same nonsense. I have to bite my tongue sometimes.'

'Why's that?'

'He insists women don't bring to marriage what a man does. Too busy fitting themselves for a career instead of learning the art of cookery and housewifery – as God ordained. It won't surprise you that his wife left him years ago. Pretty thing she was. He used to parade her in public, like a ribbon-winning horse.'

'Is he dangerous?'

'A pernicious tongue. Seems to have taken a personal exception to the poster advertising the debate. I got an earful this morning about Bec's participation.' Mr Cross pursed his lips. 'A year ago, I caught him swiping the backside of a horse with his cane – told him if he ever did it again, I'd have my wife castrate him!'

Daniel nodded.

'If there's anything I can help you with, let me know. I'll leave you here. Always enjoy our chats, Daniel. Goodnight.'

'Goodnight.'

As he walked home, Daniel wondered what to do with the information he'd gleaned. He didn't doubt that he had identified the right man. Was Bec at any risk? Perhaps it was time to get measured for a new suit and introduce himself.

CHAPTER 26

Bec pressed her handkerchief to the corner of each eye. She'd never been to a performance quite like this one. Milton Hayes was billed as an impromptu humourist. She hadn't known what that meant, and after forty-five minutes, she was none the wiser. The man's speech reminded her of a meandering stream. It bubbled along, bouncing over topics of the day – things that one might read in the newspaper, or overhear at a train station – sometimes changing course or stopping altogether. And yet his patter had the audience in gales of laughter. Her favourite was his cures for the bachelor blues.

Bec leaned towards Daniel as the artist bowed his way off stage to thunderous applause. 'Do you come here often?'

'A couple of times a month.'

'With Evelyn?' Bec could slap herself. Why did she have to bring up that woman's name? But Daniel seemed unperturbed.

'No. Vaudeville isn't Evelyn's idea of entertainment.'

Bec smirked. *No, it wouldn't be Evelyn's cup of tea. Too*

raucous! Bec loved the intimate atmosphere created between the performers and the audience. Seated in the dress circle, she felt as if she was experiencing the show from her family's living room – with twelve hundred guests.

'I never would have picked you for a vaudeville connoisseur. How did I not know that about you?'

'Maybe you haven't been paying attention,' murmured Daniel, his eyes appearing watchful.

Bec dropped her gaze to examine his mouth. A clean-shaven upper lip – asymmetrical with a redeeming cheeky quirk in the corner – and a full bottom lip. 'I'm paying attention now,' she whispered, pleased to see him swallow, as if a lump was stuck in his throat. He opened his mouth, but no words came out. The noise of the crowd receded and Bec breathed in the tantalising smell of fruit and spices – Daniel's signature scent.

'Ladies and gentlemen, please welcome all the way from Scotland, Will Fyffe.'

It took a moment for her to realise the next headline act was being introduced, although the accidental elbow to her ribs from the man beside her helped to break the trancelike state she'd fallen into. Curbing his effusive clapping, her neighbour apologised.

Daniel growled from her other side.

Bec returned her attention to him. 'Did you say something?' The look she received was smouldering. She gulped and presented him with her profile. *That would teach her to play games!*

So conscious was she of the tendrils of awareness weaving between them, it took over ten minutes to rein in her scattered thoughts. It didn't help that he'd not only captured her hand in both of his, but entwined their fingers, forcing her to acknowledge his undeniable attraction and the strength of their connection. She felt like a swimmer who, without warning, had been swept out of her depth. Her first instinct was to struggle, to regain control. But she knew, from her experience in the ocean, that would prove exhausting.

A chuckle from Daniel returned her attention to the stage and the actor comedian. His deep Scottish brogue washed over her. She surprised herself by laughing aloud at the antics of his characterisation of a Glasgow working man – muffler around his neck, bottle in his pocket, '... *jist a wee bit ...*'

Daniel was fun. She adored the physical aspects of getting to know him, replaying his kisses every spare moment. But she feared an emotional entanglement with him. Her fluency with words was no match for his, and she worried he would try to manipulate her to his way of thinking, to stifle her independence. Maybe not intentionally, but because of the role he saw himself serving: protector and provider. He was articulate, earnest and had become far too reasonable. She would be wise to remind her head to safeguard her heart at all costs. *What a muddle!*

Bec's words, *'I'm paying attention now'*, had scorched him. He'd lost the power of speech. Part of him was thankful for the crowd that surrounded them – their presence stopping him from kissing her witless. The other part of him wished they'd all leave so he could do just that! And they still had to travel home. She'd expect him to make conversation, not plunder her like a pirate.

As the last support act took to the stage, Daniel wondered what she was thinking. Her chin had risen a fraction, and he sensed, rather than saw in the muted light, a steely glint in her eye. He was becoming attuned to her moods. *Yep, he was in over his head!* But rather than filling him with fear, the thought energised him. He was a strong swimmer.

Had Alex felt this way when he'd first discovered Eliza was the one? They hadn't spoken about it. Men didn't rummage through one another's emotions.

Recent images of Bec – at the Icebreaker Challenge, surfacing from the water like a mermaid; dancing the tango, twined around him; and blushing, the hue depending on whether embarrassment or desire was the catalyst – had wiped the ones he'd had of the past four years. She was a constant in his thoughts. Only a shard of guilt brought Evelyn to mind at all. He needed to close out that chapter of his life, something he was avoiding. Evelyn would not take it well if her reaction to the end of Queenie's relationship with Alex was any indication.

As the last applause died and the full glare of the gas lights heralded the end of the show, Daniel murmured into her ear, 'Can I count you as a devotee of vaudeville now?'

She turned her head, their faces inches apart. 'I think so. Hayes and Fyffe were fabulous, and the support acts clever. We should come again sometime.'

Daniel liked that Bec was thinking of future dates, although the gunmetal grey of her eyes suggested that her previous flirtatious mood had passed. He gestured for her to precede him towards the exit and down the marble stairway. Palms, ferns and the water feature in the main foyer reminded him of the pond in the Williamstown Gardens, and the confidence Bec had displayed in him as she'd surrendered to their kiss.

'Will we stop into Birmingham's before making our way home?' Bec asked as they spilled out into Melbourne's East End Theatre district and turned right onto Bourke Street.

No! was Daniel's immediate reaction. However, he tempered his tone before speaking. 'I thought you might have had your fill of dancing, after last night.'

Bec grinned. 'A girl can never have enough dancing, but my feet were aching this morning.'

'All those progressives!'

'I met so many people.'

'Mmm. I would have liked to have met fewer.' *And danced more with you*, he added quietly. Although, he reminded himself, he had danced with her more times at Cledda's than would have been possible at Birmingham's. He'd even taught her a few steps of Argentine tango – requiring a closeness even greater than the French version.

'Watch out, you're turning into a killjoy,' Bec said, her dimple flashing.

Daniel kissed the back of her fingers and tucked her hand into the crook of his elbow.

'Is it wrong not to want to share you?' Daniel watched as Bec dropped her chin and moistened her lips with the tip of her tongue. He was glad he was wearing a heavy woollen overcoat that disguised his nether regions. His voice, though, sounded gravelly, even to his own ears. 'I don't want to end our evening at Birmingham's, Bec. But if that's your choice, then we'll go.'

He held his breath as she turned her head to look at him, her expression cautious.

'What's your preference?'

'Let's just walk,' he said, continuing eastward.

'If it's about Evelyn —'

'It's not about Evelyn.'

'Or Jim —'

'It's not about him, either.' Daniel sighed; he didn't usually struggle with words. 'Birmingham's is part of our old life. I feel like we're creating something new, just the two of us, so I guess it is about Jim ...'

'And Evelyn?'

'I haven't thought about Evelyn for weeks. I've been too preoccupied by a sharp-tongued minx who challenges me, teases me ... kisses me to distraction and ... refuses to leave my thoughts. Day or night,' he added softly.

'My goodness, you know how to ambush a girl, don't you?'

When they reached the end of Bourke Street, where the imposing footprint of Parliament House stood – the seat of Federal Government – Daniel turned right and headed for the gardens a short distance away. 'Hopefully, it's not unwelcome.'

They mingled with a small crowd, walking from the direction of the Princess Theatre – presumedly having attended the Friday-night performance of *No, No, Nanette*. Daniel slowed their steps to allow the group to move ahead.

'You confuse me. This attraction between us is unexpected.'

Not strictly true, Daniel argued silently, remembering back to their first introduction. 'Maybe it was always there ... simmering.'

'Perhaps.'

'Veiled behind our quarrels.'

Bec smiled. 'I am enjoying the opportunity to get to know you.'

'You make it sound like a business venture.'

'Hearts and minds, Daniel.'

'Well, I've given my mind the night off.'

Bec hooted.

'Is it possible that you can do the same?'

She hesitated. 'It's not that easy. I like to be in control.'

I know! 'How about you let your mind take control of the pace, and your heart to lead the direction?' Daniel didn't need to see Bec's face to hear her mind whirring – calculating risks and odds. This was a gamble, but he needed their relationship to keep moving forward, for Bec to understand that he was serious.

They'd reached Treasury Gardens, so named because they abutted the Treasury Building. In daylight, they would have trodden the sloping paths to the jewel at the centre – the Japanese garden – paused on a rustic arched bridge to admire the water-lily-covered lake, a carpet patterned with white and pink amidst dark, glossy green. But it was evening, and while quiet and restful, the gates were locked.

Bec turned to face him. 'The game of forfeit you proposed was part of a plan, wasn't it?'

Daniel searched the park over the top of her head, looking for the right answer, but the perimeter lighting only reached so far and beyond six feet, the gardens morphed into impenetrable darkness.

'It was a bit of ... fun,' he said. Bec didn't need to know the true state of his intentions at the time. Especially since they'd changed. 'It opened a window of opportunity. After all, I didn't initiate your outburst last Sunday. Your reaction to my *reasonableness* did that.'

When she went to protest, he leaned down and silenced her with a quick kiss. 'And the week has exceeded my expectations. We're suited, Bec, and not just physically. I'm convinced I want to date you ... exclusively.' *Marry you!*

He watched her worry her bottom lip and angled his head again to take possession of it, this time folding her into his arms, careless that they stood under the glow of a streetlight for all to see. Her familiar oriental scent wrapped around him.

Fweet! The sound of a whistle startled him into remembering where they were. There was no sign of the owner – probably a policeman on foot patrol.

'Have I made a convincing case?' he asked, caressing her cheek with his thumb.

'Are you sure you're not trying to seduce me into your way of thinking?'

Daniel lowered his head. 'Like this?' he whispered, before kissing her again.

'Digressing, Daniel?'

Daniel felt as if he was being peeled of all artifice as her eyes searched his. 'Seduce? Definitely. Manipulate? No. Influence? Yes. I'll keep challenging your views. If I can change your mind, then I will. But I'll do it openly and honestly.' *From this point on*, he promised himself.

'You are very articulate, Mr Sinclair. You'll make an imposing public figure one day,' Bec said with a smile in her voice.

When Daniel went to interrupt her, she laid a finger

against his lips. 'And you're extremely ... persuasive.'

Daniel's heartbeat was loud in his ears. *Say yes!*

'And a divine kisser.'

He caught hold of her finger and kissed the tip. 'Is that a yes? No Jim, just me.'

'No Jim. And no Evelyn.'

'No Evelyn.'

'Then ... yes.'

As Daniel moved to sweep her back into his arms, she braced a hand on his chest and held his gaze.

'But don't try to curb my independence, Daniel. My head has been ruling my heart all my life. It's not something that I'm willing to ignore. But where you're concerned, I'll allow it to consult my heart.'

Daniel picked her up and swung her around in a circle. It was a start. Kiss by kiss he would capture her heart, vanquish any fears, and make her his!

CHAPTER 27

Saturday 29 August 1925

'I'll fall,' grumbled Bec, clutching the handrail in a death grip.

'I won't let you,' cajoled Daniel, standing, perfectly poised in his rented ice skates, with his arms outstretched towards her.

'You tricked me. You said we were coming to watch the performances, not take part.'

'We will, after we skate one lap of the rink. I've never known you to be scared, Bec.'

'Give me unfrozen water any time. And I'm not in costume. Did you know this was fancy dress?'

Daniel smiled sheepishly. 'I admit, I didn't pay attention to the details.'

Bec shook her head. 'That's right, details aren't your forte, are they? You're more of a big-picture man.'

Daniel skated behind her, wrapping his arms around her waist. 'And yet, I remember every detail about you,' he murmured in her ear. 'Our tumultuous first kiss on the balcony of Birmingham's.' He nuzzled her ear. 'Our second at the sea baths ... the most money I've ever paid for a kiss.

Our third —'

'All right, all right, let's get this over and done with so I can return to dry land.'

'But I haven't finished.'

'You have less than thirty seconds to get me in a secure hold and skating, or else I'm leaving the ice. Crawling if I have to.'

'Grumpy. That's another thing I didn't know about you.'

'*Daniel!*'

'You'll have to let go of the rail and trust me.'

Bec prised both hands, finger by finger, from the railing, marvelling at how confidently Daniel manoeuvred them away from the edge towards the centre of the rink.

'Relax, I've got you. And unlike the ballroom, no one will cut in, I promise you.'

Bec giggled at the thought of exchanging partners. It would look more like a rescue attempt – they'd need ropes and harnesses. She noted other couples gave them a wide berth. Perhaps it was the look of fear on her face or Daniel's protective hold. Either way, she was thankful they didn't need to attempt too many changes of direction.

'Would you like to try a few steps on your own?'

Bec froze, and Daniel tightened the arm at her waist to maintain their balance. 'No! Do not let me go.'

He chuckled. 'I'm liking what I'm hearing. I think this is my new favourite pastime ... besides kissing, that is.'

'Daniel!' Bec felt the hairs on the back of her nape snap to attention.

'Keep your weight forward, don't lean back.'

'Bossy. How have I missed that character trait?' muttered Bec.

'How about *try* not to lean back.'

'Better.'

'Let's try a few steps – as we glide forward, pick up one foot and then set it back down, as if you're stoking the ice.'

Bec hated that this was something Daniel was at ease with and she wasn't. At least with swimming, they were more of an equal, although she'd never bested him in a race. He'd only ever made the mistake of allowing her to win once – she'd blistered his ears for five minutes afterwards.

Step ... glide ... step.

But it was more than the blow to her competitive streak. She hated being dependent on him to keep her upright. She hated being vulnerable. What if he skated off and left her? *Best not to think about that.* Her legs wobbled and she gritted her teeth. She could do this.

Step ... glide ... step.

With her confidence building, she risked a look around. A turquoise canopy enveloped the whole skating area, peppered with silver stars of varying sizes. It created the impression that they were skating at twilight. *Magical.* As was the warmth of being cocooned in Daniel's arms.

Bec sighed. Daniel had made no pretence of his intention to seduce her. That part of their relationship seemed to be blossoming. But what if she was only a temporary distraction for him? One of a bevy of conquests? Apart from being female, she was nothing like the women he usually dated. His choice of her wasn't logical. But every day that passed, any desire to return to a time when he didn't figure so significantly, dwindled. In less than a week, her heart was clamouring for a larger say in her affairs. But the courage needed to march forward and grasp what Daniel offered wavered, her heart unable to give her head the answers it sought. *What if she got hurt?*

'Can all skaters please return to their seats. Our gala performance will begin in fifteen minutes.'

She could see Daniel's quizzical expression as she clambered off the ice with a determination that wouldn't have been misplaced in the trenches of Europe's front line.

'Everything all right?'

'Why do you ask?' Bec tugged at the laces on her skates.

'Allow me.' He brushed her fingers away and took over, quickly untying the knotted fastenings. 'Your eyes have turned the colour of a battleship.'

'Nonsense,' Bec said, lifting one foot out of the leather boot.

'The colour is for camouflage, to hide from the enemy,' he continued conversationally. 'Are you thinking I'm the enemy, Bec?'

'Your sudden attention to detail is ill timed,' she retorted, abandoning the second boot and flexing her socked foot.

Instead of her reply deterring him, it seemed to make the dratted man more persistent. He stroked a finger under the arch of her foot. 'Is that another ticklish spot?'

'Are you trying to get us kicked out?' hissed Bec, glancing over her shoulder, relieved to see that no one was paying them any attention. She quickly slipped her feet into her black leather Oxfords.

'That's better. Storm clouds with a touch of smoke,' Daniel said, tilting his head.

'I'm feeling ... mixed up, that's all.'

'Ah, your head and heart are at odds in their advice.' His crooked smile appeared.

Bec sighed. *Yes, that was a good summary.* And he wasn't helping, with his enigmatic smiles and the occasional brush of his fingers, a hand at her waist or in the hollow just above her spine. She was saved from answering by the public address system. It seemed her heart no longer existed in a vacuum, but she had little control over the chemical experiment that had been unleashed.

'Can everyone please take their seats. The performance is about to begin.'

Daniel and Bec scrambled into the nearest vacant seat, beside a man dressed as a cowboy and a woman dressed as a shepherdess, complete with crook.

Daniel was unconcerned with Bec's admission. Her father had warned him not to be discouraged if she retreated. Mr Cross was a smart man. Daniel comforted himself with the thought that he must be making progress. She no longer objected to him holding her hand. Like now. Or drawing featherweight circles on the inside of her wrist, just above her pulse. If he concentrated, he could feel the moment it sped up. And a mixed-up feeling was a good sign, wasn't it? He wondered if he looked into her eyes at that instant, whether he'd see the allure of silver. He made a mental note to test his theory ... soon.

A piano glissando introduced a demonstration of pair skating by last year's European champions.

'That'll be us next time,' Daniel murmured as the couple completed a lift before dropping into a spin.

'Maybe without the aerial.'

'Agree. And no stunts or trick steps.'

'I think I can manage that,' Bec agreed. The corners of her lips tilted upwards, her eyes tracing the patterns of movement in front of them.

The program rolled on – a burlesque, an acrobatic routine and finally a performance based on the ballet *Harlequinade*. Created earlier in the century for the tsar and tsarina of Russia, Daniel dubbed it a romantic romp with a non-existent plot. Still, it was amusing, the costuming theatrical and the skating superb. The harlequin in a costume of red-and-blue diamonds was especially sprightly, his skating resembling someone perpetually skittering on hot coals.

The skirl of the bagpipes brought the evening's gala performance to a close. It was one of three sounds that brought the hairs on the back of Daniel's neck to attention. The howl of a south-westerly wind through pine groves being another, and recently ... the guttural moan which escaped Bec's throat when the intensity of his kisses overran her.

'This was a fantastic idea,' Bec said, clapping loudly as the performers took a final bow. 'I've loved every minute.'

'Even your skating lesson?'

Bec scrunched her nose. 'Surprisingly, yes. It gave me a better appreciation of the skill of the performers. If I hadn't been coerced into skating, I never would have known how difficult it really is. They make it look so easy.'

'Maybe our next date can be roller-skating.'

'I'm guessing you're good at that, too.'

He grinned. 'It's not my fault that I'm sure-footed on thin blades and wheels. It's genetic.'

'Hmm. Well, Mr Genetically Gifted, I think *I'll* choose the activity for our next date.'

Daniel pretended mock horror. But inside he was cheering – complete with balloons and streamers. Bec was offering to plan their next date.

They watched a woman attired as a Spanish lady and a man who it was announced was supposed to look like a naturalist – Daniel thought him overdressed – accept the prizes for best costumes, before making their way out of the venue.

As had become his habit, Daniel reached for her hand, entwining their fingers. Recent showers had left muddy puddles, causing them to zigzag their way along the footpath. They joined a steady stream of costumed couples.

'Would you really have wanted to ride the train home dressed as a duck?' Daniel asked as they passed an individual struggling to see, trapped as he was within a hood and beak arrangement. As a result, they'd watched him splash through two pools of water already.

Bec arched a brow. '*A duck?* I would have come as a warrior princess. And you?'

'Zorro.'

'Yes, I can see you in a mask and a flowing black cape.'

'Brandishing my sword, plucking you from the ice and skating to safety.'

Bec laughed. 'Scarring the rink with a "Z" in your midst. They would have awarded you first prize.'

'I already have first prize.' Daniel drew Bec off the main pedestrian walk of the bridge across which the yellowed hue of Flinders Street railway station awaited.

Leaning against the stone balustrade, he wrapped his arm around her waist. Positioned hip to hip, they watched the spears of light reflected in the inky blackness below, only a halo of light through the cloud hinting at the existence of the moon.

'Your reputation as a charmer seems well founded,' Bec said, nudging him in the ribs.

'Your opinion is the only one that matters. And you've been somewhat reticent.'

'What? Only yesterday I admitted you were a good kisser.'

'I hate to correct a lady, but the word you used was *divine*.'

Bec giggled. 'Are you going to catalogue my every word?'

'Perhaps. What else should I add?'

Pursing her lips, Bec began to list more accomplishments, counting with her fingers. 'On the positive side, you've been imaginative with our dates, attentive, entertaining – in a good way,' she hastened to add. 'That's three. You're easy on the eye —'

'And I have all my own teeth. That's five.'

'Daniel —'

'You know what I would have said if asked about you?'

Bec shook her head.

'You're gaining the reputation as my favourite book. Each day I turn a page, eager to discover more. Sometimes I'm discouraged, other times frustrated, but mostly I'm heartened by your responses. The expression in your eyes hints at your emotions, but I'm still scrambling to find the code to unlock them.' He pressed a kiss to her cheek. 'And your kisses ... leave me craving more.'

Daniel watched Bec close her eyes, open her lips and close them again. It was as if she was mustering up her courage to speak. When she finally opened her eyes, they were shimmering – the colour of mercury under water –

and fixed on him. 'The feelings you arouse scare me. My head tells me you're getting too close, but my heart keeps widening the door. I love that we're not just doing this under the glare of Birmingham's or the speculation of our friends and social circles. But I'm troubled that my views and opinions may no longer remain my own – independent of yours.'

It was a start. 'Is that so hard?'

'Uh-huh.'

'You just need more practice.' Daniel pressed a quick kiss to her parted lips, but conscious that they had probably already attracted curious glances from passers-by, he drew back. 'And for those words, you are less than an inch from being kissed soundly. I just wish I'd chosen a less public place for our tête-à-tête.'

'Me too.'

'You are not helping my equilibrium,' he murmured. 'Come on, let's go before we get moved on.'

They reached the stairs beneath the station's clocks. Daniel's hand settled possessively into the small of Bec's back as he glanced up to check the display of departure times. Ten minutes before the Williamstown train left.

He felt Bec tense as a familiar American drawl greeted her. 'Hello, Bec. Still furtherin' debate preparations?'

Jim had the look of a man who demanded answers. The quirk of his right eyebrow implied it. Daniel moved his hand so it was resting at Bec's waist. 'No, we took the night off. We've been ice skating.'

'I wasn't speakin' to you. Bec? I thought after Tuesday ...'

Daniel strode forward, but Bec was quicker, positioning herself between the two men.

'I meant to call you.'

Daniel didn't like where this conversation was going. 'Apologies, but we have to run. Our train is leaving in four minutes. Goodnight. Enjoy your evening.'

He tried to propel Bec up the steps, but Jim touched her hand.

'Are we still on for midday tomorrow?'

'Um ... yes, see you then.'

Daniel resisted his natural inclination to bombard Bec with questions as they hurried through the concourse. He hadn't organised anything for Sunday but had thought to invite himself for lunch. *Where was Bec going with that Yank? And why?* He felt a coldness invade him that had nothing to do with the winter air stealing into the carriage. He sat, glacial. Was Bec duping him? Was that the true reason for her reticence in talking of her feelings for him?

As if sensing his inner turmoil, she reached for his hand and gave it a squeeze. 'Dad suggested he wanted to acquaint himself with the American officer I'd been stepping out with,' she said, then quickly added, 'Before you.'

Daniel gave a tight smile, fearing his face would crack.

'I invited Jim to lunch more than a week ago. I'd forgotten about it, to be honest.'

Daniel faced forward, not trusting himself to speak.

Bec sighed. 'You're upset.'

He shrugged.

'It's lunch with my parents. It doesn't mean anything.'

'Like my lunch with your parents.'

At the sound of her sharply indrawn breath, Daniel knew he sounded churlish.

'I'm going to ignore you said that, and instead ask if you'll join us. We're dating. But that doesn't mean you can control who I speak to or who is invited to my father's table.'

Daniel counted to ten, reminding himself how much progress they'd made tonight. He was being irrational. The invitation had been issued before they'd agreed to date.

'I'll be there,' he managed, carefully avoiding her eyes. He didn't trust that his weren't burning green.

CHAPTER 28

Sunday 30 August 1925

The pharmacist's bell tinkled, and fingers of unease pricked Bec's spine. Turning her head, she met the fractious face of Tailor senior.

'Teddy's girl, isn't it?'

Bec nodded, automatically moving to clear a generous space for him and his cane at the counter. She wished her mother had been accepting of the pharmacist's offer to deliver the parcel of medications she'd ordered tomorrow. But no, she'd insisted it had to be this morning. She hoped the pharmacist's assistant, Mr Urban, would return soon.

William Tailor's eyes raked her up and down, settling on her breasts.

Bastard! Bec crossed her arms. She watched his slack, hanging mouth curl in amusement, before his gaze returned to her face.

'So expressive. Still learning your role in life, aren't you, lovey?'

She'd learned over the years it was best not to answer him. His diatribe worsened if challenged. What was it about her that brought out such forceful and bitter reproof? It was personal, but she'd never been able to figure out why.

'I'd be more than happy to teach you. Your father has been too lenient, as that poster proves. But your responses suggest you'd be an apt student.'

Bec's stomach roiled. There was no doubt William Tailor was an advocate for conjugal rights – did this extend to outside of marriage, too? For all his rantings, he'd only ever touched her with his gaze. Sometimes when they met he'd stare at her, other times his gaze would follow her, lingering on her breasts – like before – or on her hips. Once, in her father's shop, he'd sat facing her, legs spread apart. His behaviour was never overt, unless of course like today, he'd encountered her alone.

'A virtuous girl would excuse herself from such a public discussion of liberal ideas, and from displaying yourself so immodestly. You and your like have no business corrupting the thoughts and minds of the men of our city. You're wanton, exactly like your grandmother.'

By the look of his dress, he'd been to church. Even the power of a rousing sermon – she'd heard the Catholic priest was the fire-and-brimstone type – couldn't silence this man. Bec clenched her fists to stop her hand from reaching out and slapping the old man. However, tormenting the elderly, no matter how insufferable, was not the done thing. How dare he sully her grandmother's name!

'Not only will I not be withdrawing from the debate, Mr Tailor, but I'm the Tramways' newest employee.' Bec drew herself up to her full height, uncaring as to the truth of her statement. 'Melbourne's first female tram conductor.'

His colour went from dull to bright red. She hoped he

didn't collapse at her feet as nothing would compel her to touch this toad of a man. At best, she'd prod him with his cane or the heel of her boot.

'Good evening, Mr Tailor,' came the welcome voice of Mr Urban. 'I'll be with you in a moment. Here you go, Miss Cross. Give your mother our compliments.'

Bec hurriedly accepted the parcel he held out to her, turned and fled from the premises.

'Come, sit yourself down next to me, Jim,' Bec's father invited, patting the chair beside him. It didn't sound like a request. 'Daniel, you sit down yonder near Rachel. I like a balanced table – else it upsets my digestion.'

Bec watched as Jim eyed her father, his designated seat and its relationship to the rest of the table's occupants.

'Edward! You talk such nonsense,' Bec's mother scolded from the other end. 'Eliza, come sit next to Jim. Leave Bec the chair beside her father, to curb his talk.'

Eliza had been a late but welcome addition. Bec had updated her friend earlier that day on the progress of her relationship with Daniel, and his reaction to the lunch invitation extended to Jim. Eliza had danced her around in a circle and immediately offered to come along and help calm the waters, despite professing an understanding of her brother's reaction. *Would you be happy if Daniel invited Evelyn to lunch?* Eliza had asked. *Well, no,* Bec had admitted. *But I'm not, and never was enamoured with Jim – it was always a casual and temporary arrangement.* Eliza had patted her shoulder and smiled. *Mind reading has never been one of my brother's talents.*

Which had left Bec questioning whether she was being too guarded around Daniel.

Bec hovered, doing a quick check to ensure everything had made its way from the kitchen to the dining-room table.

'Come and sit, daughter,' her father coaxed. 'Everything looks lovely. And if there's anything missing, I'm sure one of the lads here would be only too happy to get it.'

Bec smiled. Her father enjoyed helping the next generation of men grow out of their superstition that involving themselves in domestic affairs was vaguely improper. He was an oddity amongst the men of his generation, but he insisted, to all who would listen, that it contributed a large part to his spousal success.

Jim seated her, having followed her around the table. He laid a hand on Daniel's shoulder as he went to rise. Bec choked down a giggle. *Men!* It was a moment rich with provocation and proprietary behaviour. The former, from Jim, the latter from Daniel, who looked ready to launch himself across the table as the officer took his seat.

'We don't stand on formality here, Jim. Please help yourself,' Bec's father said, breaking the tension.

'Although, maybe I'll do the honours with the first slice of pie. It can be a little tricky getting it out in one piece,' Bec's mother said, taking control of the pie server.

Tendrils of steam melted away as, slice by slice, the beef pie was sectioned and distributed. Boiled potatoes, pumpkin and green beans completed the plated ensembles.

'Are you disappointed you didn't sail with the fleet?' Eliza asked, reaching for her fork.

'The *Oklahoma* is my home away from home. So, on one level, I miss not being on board, despite the close confines and shared facilities. But Melbourne has been so hospitable ... and the girls,' Jim's pronunciation made it sound like 'gurls', 'so friendly and welcomin'.' He gave Bec a wink from across the table.

Daniel bristled beside her, back straight, eyes fierce, causing Bec to hide a smile. Maybe she should have supplied them both with jousting poles.

'How many of your mates are still at large?' Daniel asked.

'Just the one. And unless he hands himself in, the chances are he'll stay missin'. Not a bad result.' Jim shrugged. 'We lose a few in every port.'

'So, you'll be headed home soon, I guess. Job done,' Daniel probed.

Jim's grin encompassed everyone at the table, but his words were directed at Daniel. 'I'm here till the end of next month. And I'm plannin' on makin' the most of it – hopefully with a girl on my arm.'

Daniel's nostrils flared, and his right eye twitched. It appeared Bec wasn't the only one who could induce Daniel's tic.

'So, what have you found the most confusing since you've arrived, Jim?' Bec's mother asked, steering the conversation away from sailors, girls and activities that involved both.

'The language,' he answered without hesitation.

'Me too!' Bec's father laughed. 'I had a *loo-tenant* in my shop tell me he was off to *rubber-neck the 'orses*. Apparently, he was off to attend the races here at Williamstown. He asked about the direction as he was a little *buffaloed*, which I took to mean bamboozled.'

Jim nodded. 'It's got easier, but I still find it funny to hear Australians talk of petrol, not gasoline. Of motor cars, not automobiles. But one thing I do love are those little trams,' enthused Jim. 'They're the funniest. Especially when they have to be pushed over the intersection. It's like they just get tuckered out.'

'Bec and I had a group of sailors ask us, "What makes them go?" one evening on our way home. Remember that?' Eliza laughed. 'We told them it was a string under the road.'

'That's right. One got down on his belly and peered under the carriage. I thought he was going to get run over.'

'Is that the same type you're headed out on?' Eliza asked.

Bec turned to Daniel. 'I'm not sure, do you know?'

'I expect so, it's the most common in operation.'

'Your mother and I are still undecided about this ...' Bec's father waved his fork in the air, '... this escapade of yours.'

'Oh, Dad —'

'Don't *Oh Dad* me, young lady. And that imploring look hasn't worked since you were eighteen.'

'Unless you count earlier this morning,' quipped her mother. 'What your father is trying to say is that we're both concerned. Especially since your poster was vandalised. And you haven't been able to furnish many details.'

Daniel's head swung back and forth between her parents. 'What's that about Bec's poster?'

Her father snorted. 'Not just one. Three or four, ripped from the community noticeboards.'

'Teenagers with nothing better to do,' dismissed Bec.

Daniel's look suggested she'd been reading too many fairytales.

Bec injected her tone with a flinty resolve. 'Let's not talk about it. Now, in answer to your other question, tomorrow morning at seven or eight —'

'Seven o'clock,' interjected Daniel.

Bec suspected her mother was right. Her understanding of what the next two days involved was a little scant. She'd been so excited when Daniel had told her, she'd drummed her feet on the floor before wrapping her arms around him to express her gratitude. She smiled at the memory. She'd been effusive. Afterwards, he'd looked ... soundly kissed.

She shook her head. What had she been saying? 'I report to a Mr Banks at the training school at Hawthorn.'

'So, you're spending two days at the training school?' Her mother's tone was part question, part statement.

'No. After some ...'

'Training?' suggested Eliza.

She soldiered on. 'Yes, after some training, I'll head out on a tram for the day.'

'Half-day,' clarified Daniel.

'All right, half-day. And then I'll do the same thing on Tuesday.'

'You're not going out on your own, are you?' asked her father.

'No, Dad. I'll be buddied up with an experienced trammie.'

'And me,' said Daniel.

What? Daniel hadn't mentioned he was part of this. She'd imagined impressing her buddy with her aptitude. She'd be the talk of the tramways and the state would rethink the suitability of females in the role – one small leap forward for women. She had no need of Daniel's company or protection. 'Um ... I thought you were just joining me for the introduction tomorrow morning,' she said, trying for a tactful approach.

'And leave you on your own?'

Bec gritted her teeth. Even to her own ears, her '*Yes*,' was clipped.

'Not likely,' Daniel said, wiping the corners of his mouth with his serviette. 'I'm riding shotgun.'

Eliza giggled, and even Jim disguised a laugh with a discreet cough into the palm of his hand.

Was everyone against her? She didn't need Daniel babysitting. He'd stifle her, make her nervous, and then she'd become clumsy. She tried one last appeal. 'You said work was so busy you don't have time to eat a proper lunch. How can you spare two days?'

'Well, I do. I've made it a priority and cleared the next two mornings.'

'That makes us feel more comfortable, Daniel, knowing you'll be on hand,' said Bec's father, pushing his plate away.

'I can share the load if your schedule's too busy,' offered Jim. 'I've got time on my hands.'

Daniel laid his arm on the back of Bec's chair and leaned forward towards the American. 'Thank you, but no. Has to be someone that the Tramways Board knows and trusts.'

'Well, I'll look out for you. Should be easy. There'll be a queue of men linin' up to board the tram once they know there's a pretty conductress handing out tickets,' said Jim.

A frown darkened Daniel's face. 'I doubt Bec will be allowed to shoulder the cash bag.'

Bec gathered her fisted hands into her lap. This was another example of why she didn't want Daniel on the tram. He'd start dictating what she could and couldn't do. If he had his way, she'd spend the entire time sitting down, watching. She may as well be a passenger.

She needed to keep her wits about her, else she'd be

relegated as an extension of him – more like an additional limb than her own person. It wasn't a coincidence that he hadn't countered her concerns about maintaining her independence last night. She guessed he didn't want to be hypocritical!

'Well, I intend to immerse myself in the experience,' Bec announced to the table. 'Cash bags, tickets and all.'

Planting her feet firmly on the floor, she pushed her chair away from the table, dislodging Daniel's arm. It was a credit to his reflexes that he didn't topple over. But Bec was in an unforgiving mood. Standing, she hovered like a maturing thundercloud, glaring at him. 'You just concentrate on your shotgun. I can take care of myself.'

CHAPTER 29

Monday 31 August 1925

Daniel shoved his hands into the pockets of his coat and focused on the view out the window of the training facility.

Bec pushed his buttons. He didn't think she did it deliberately – actually, that wasn't true, he was sure she did it deliberately. The result? She left him feeling inadequate, unnecessary ... and embarrassed. Like yesterday at lunch.

She was just so ... *self-sufficient!* And her mantra of *I'll take care of myself* was beginning to grate. Even though he suspected what she really meant was she didn't want to be bridled, Bec needed to understand that he only had a limited amount of patience, and he was already digging deeper than he ever had.

Having peppered the initial introduction to Mr Banks with subtle hints about Daniel's workload, Bec had moved onto questioning the practicality of Daniel joining her on the tram. Daniel could have told her to save her breath. The Tramways Board could not afford any negative publicity, something Louis Chalmers had reiterated in a memo to the instructor and Daniel. So she was stuck with him.

Without arguing, Mr Banks had diverted her attention to the detail she'd need to be declared fit for tram duties. Once focused, Bec's thirst for information was unquenchable, and the next couple of hours passed studiously.

'And this here is Syd.' Mr Banks welcomed the trammie over their heads. 'Syd, this is Miss Bec Cross and of course you know Daniel.'

He and Syd exchanged nods. 'Yes, I've met the lassie before, Banksy. She bakes an excellent cake.'

Bec grinned at the instructor's puzzled look, but didn't enlighten him. 'I might bring some tomorrow,' she said.

Daniel watched a smile crease Syd's weather-beaten face.

'If you're good,' she added cheekily.

Syd lifted a bushy eyebrow before returning his attention back to Banksy. 'So, how's the training going? I hope you haven't taught her any of your bad habits.'

'No, I'm leaving that to you,' the instructor said, clapping Syd on the shoulder. 'I think she's ready for a couple of city-bound trips – understands the rudiments of a conductor's job, the fare structure, paperwork and how to punch a ticket.'

'I have my very own copy of the Services and Fares manual,' announced Bec, waving a blue bound book in Syd's direction.

The trammie nodded absently, frowning. 'What about her garb? Can't have her riding the trams in a skirt.'

'Valerie in the office has sorted something – pants, a jacket and a cap. We'll wander that way now. I've checked her shoes, good tread, and looks like the fine weather will hold.' Banksy motioned for Bec and Daniel to follow.

Daniel had turned his imagination to the sight of Bec in pants. He wondered if they would show off the length of her legs in the same way as the shorts of her swimsuit. He could think of worse ways to pass the day, although he'd have preferred to have been her only audience.

'For your first trip, lassie, I think we'll organise things so that I hold the cash bag, ticket blocks and running journal. You operate the ticket punch,' said Syd.

'Is that all?' asked Bec.

Daniel turned his head to disguise his smile. From the tone of Bec's voice, she sounded as if she'd expected to be running the tram, Syd's concession far from her expectations.

'It's an important job. Inspectors regularly board this route into the city. They'll check that the hole punched in the passenger's ticket corresponds with this here running journal and the location of the tram.'

'All right,' agreed Bec, pocketing the metal hand punch into the brown waisted serge jacket. 'Can I ring the bell?'

'What's the signal to start?'

'Two bells. Three, if you anticipate an accident,' Bec answered cheerfully.

'You can operate the bell.'

'And —'

'And I think that's enough for your first trip,' Syd interrupted firmly, examining his timepiece. 'Let's check these passengers over there before the tram arrives. Come on.'

Bec's gait was close to a skip as she followed the conductor over to where a group of three men stood chatting. *Maybe spring has arrived early*, thought Daniel as he leaned against a lamppost, enjoying the unseasonal warmth. He watched Bec's animated face and the reaction of the men to her. What was the term used for the young men who flirted with the conductresses in Chile? He'd made a point to read about them. Some insect. *Mosquito*, that was it. Because they were a nuisance and hung around. No doubt she'd attract her share. Even now, he wasn't the only one watching how her pert backside filled the trousers she wore as she bent down to show a young boy how the ticket punch worked.

Daniel heard the tram before it came into view around the bend, terminating just before the river.

'Well, lassie,' Syd explained as they joined Daniel. 'You're now about to travel the oldest cable-tram route in Melbourne. Remember, hold on. One hand should always be in connection with something. We don't have time to stop and collect you if you fall off.'

And with that, Syd turned and strode in the direction of the tram. After a bewildered look at Daniel, Bec hurried after him. Daniel followed at a more leisurely pace, although the thought of her falling and hurting herself or being abused quickened his pulses.

'This here is Alby.' Syd jerked his head towards a man twice as wide as Daniel and nearly as tall. 'He's the gripman. No one talks to the gripman when the tram is in operation. Alby, meet Bec and Daniel, who'll be riding with us today. Bec is here to experience life as a tram conductor.'

'Humph! Hope she doesn't fall asleep,' Alby guffawed, elbowing Syd in the ribs.

'I'll be ringing the bell,' said Bec.

Alby's eyebrows nearly reached his hairline. 'Well, make sure you ring it good and hard. And don't be changin' your mind like most females.'

At Bec's outraged expression, Alby shrugged his shoulders. 'Just sayin'.'

Daniel stepped forward before Bec could say anything and offered his hand, fearing for its safety, but fearing the effect of Bec's outspokenness even more. It surprised him that while firm, the man's handshake wasn't crushing. 'You'll only have us onboard until the Spencer Street terminus.'

'Well, let's get rollin', Syd. Best of luck, young Bec.' Alby nodded to Daniel before climbing aboard and taking charge of the grip.

Away from rush hour, the tram's passengers were few. The route would allow Bec to find her balance, which wasn't difficult as it was relatively straight, without many curves. Daniel found a seat at the front of the closed car, from which he could observe without being conspicuous, but could be on hand if needed.

The three men from the turnaround had chosen the open-air dummy, and while he couldn't hear what they were saying, he could see that they were trying to engage Bec in conversation. When one closed his hand over Bec's where she held onto a stanchion, Daniel braced himself to act. She wouldn't thank him for interfering, but there was no such thing as an innocent flirtation in his experience. He saw her raise her eyebrows, say something and the man removed his hand as if scalded. Daniel relaxed.

By the time the tram trundled past the Melbourne Cricket Ground, halfway in the three-and-a-half-mile journey, Daniel swore he'd worn a small depression in the floor at his feet. He was becoming a master at distinguishing between those passengers – all male – with genuine questions, and those with flirtatious intent. It was the body position, the shoulder turn that excluded others, and the incidental brush of fingers as a ticket was exchanged.

Daniel massaged his chest with the palm of his hand, trying to release the knot that had taken up residence. He'd lost count of the number of slips of paper she'd been passed with phone numbers and addresses – of course he couldn't know for sure, but he was a man, and that's what he'd have done given the chance. It surprised him that the advances by the male population were becoming his biggest objection to females in this role, or maybe just to Bec performing the role.

She'd shown herself to be deft in adapting her movements on the swaying carriage platform, and her long legs had negotiated the gap between the open and closed carriages with ease. *Why didn't more women wear trousers*, he mused, watching as Bec assisted an old lady onto the tram. *Probably because it would stop traffic.*

His mind wandered, thinking about what she'd look like wearing one of his white dress shirts. It would hover, teasing the length of her bare legs ... undone apart from one button at her navel ... taut nipples ... Daniel shifted in his seat to disguise the small tent pitched at the front of his trousers.

'Fares, please!'

Daniel started as Bec burst through the door of the carriage.

'You weren't sleeping, were you?' she asked as she passed him.

Syd winked as he followed her. 'Doin' real good, she is. Hang in there, Danny boy, not long to go.'

Not for the first time, Daniel wondered if Syd read minds.

The city was busy. The weak sunshine had encouraged people to walk or to linger, savouring the respite from battling the winter elements from beneath the shell of an umbrella. Did Bec need to return to work this afternoon, and if so, at what time. Could he convince her to take a long walk and maybe eat lunch with him? He'd resigned himself to a late night at the office to catch up, but it would be worth it if he could have her undivided attention for an hour or so. Sunday lunch with her parents had left him in a combative mood. The American had been too sure of himself. Did he still have designs on Bec? And what of her? She hadn't exactly dismissed Jim's winks and overtures. *And he was staying for another month!* Well, he wasn't spending it with Bec on his arm. Daniel would plan her days and nights to keep her to himself.

His nose announced they were approaching the fish market at the end of Flinders Street before his eyes registered the clock tower, turrets and copper spires of the building. The fanciful landmark sat on the corner of Spencer Street, which was the tram's destination. *Just a few more minutes.* Daniel rolled his shoulders as his gaze sought Bec. She and Syd had returned to the open carriage, and Syd seemed to be instructing her on negotiating the hard right-hand turn that the tram would navigate from Flinders to Spencer Street. Her head was darting between the conductor and the way ahead. He watched her widen her stance a fraction and tighten her grip on the strap she held.

'Mind the curve,' bellowed Syd, just before the gripman traversed the intersection, steering the ensemble up the hill towards the terminus.

It happened in a flash. Didn't most accidents? As the car

jerked to a stop, Bec was thrown off balance, flung sideways, her arms extended, her fingers waving wildly, trying to find purchase, something to grasp onto, and all the while fighting gravity.

Daniel was on his feet, but knew he'd never reach her in time. The only voice he heard was his own, loud in his ears. Bec didn't make a sound. Surprise, rather than fear, was etched on her face, eyes wide.

Only the quick action of Syd and one of the other passengers prevented her from being pitched to the ground. Daniel's memory charged into overdrive. It was his first project after graduating. An experienced trammie, over twenty years' service. It had been wet, the carriages overflowing. *God!* He could still hear the man's screams. He'd helped carry the stretcher ...

Syd's tone was harsh. 'What did I tell you, lassie. It's important to hang on. Always!'

Slumped on the step, head lowered, rubbing her shoulder where she'd hit an upright before being plucked to safety, she mumbled, 'I'm sorry.'

Daniel, knowing that Bec wouldn't appreciate the knot of interested bystanders gathered around her, thanked the young passenger for his timely intervention and hustled the small crowd on its way.

He crouched down in front of her, tilting her chin until he could see her eyes. 'Are you all right? Your shoulder?'

'No doubt I'll have a bruise the size of a dinner plate. I'm fine. Such a stupid mistake.'

'Lucky that's all, girlie,' said Alby. 'If not for Syd's reflexes, you coulda had worse.'

Bec nodded. 'I am so, so, sorry, Syd.'

'Took another year off my life you did, lass.'

'It won't happen again. I promise.'

Daniel exchanged a fierce glance with the trammie. Surely Syd wouldn't sanction Bec returning for another day.

'Humph! If you're feelin' up to it, let's do a last check of the paperwork and tickets, and then I'll release you into Daniel's care.'

For once, Bec didn't demur at the assumption she needed protecting, and bent her head over the figures on the tally sheet.

'What time tomorrow, Syd?' asked Bec, returning the ticket punch to him.

Syd pursed his lips and ran his fingers through his hair. 'I'm in two minds, lassie. My heart couldn't take another shock like today.'

'Please. I've learned my lesson.'

Syd sent Daniel an apologetic look before levelling Bec with a stern one. 'Make it seven o'clock. Flinders Street.'

'Thank you. You won't regret it,' said Bec.

Syd rubbed his chin. 'I hope not. Now, off with you. Danny's champing at the bit.'

Bec levered herself off the footboard, ignoring Daniel's hand. 'Thanks, Syd. See you tomorrow. Bye, Alby.'

They walked off in silence.

'I saw the look you exchanged with Syd.'

Daniel didn't trust himself to speak.

'I can take care of myself.'

Daniel steered her off the main footpath into the entrance of one of the city's many laneways. 'Like you did just before?'

She flinched at his tone. 'I made a mistake. Haven't you ever made a mistake?'

'We're not talking about me.'

'Daniel, when I was eight years old I fell off a horse. If my parents had adopted your attitude, I'd have never ridden again.'

'You were lucky today. You could have been seriously injured ... or worse ...'

'But I wasn't. And I learned a valuable lesson.'

Hands on his hips, Daniel gazed at the slither of blue sky visible between the tops of the overhanging buildings. *How could she be so cavalier?*

Bec tugged at his hands and offered a smile. 'How about lunch? I've worked up quite an appetite.'

Daniel's gut was roiling. He disengaged his hands. 'I'll pass, thanks. I've got a mountain of work to catch up on.'

'Daniel, I'm never going to be someone who enjoys being cosseted.'

'I'll see you tomorrow.' Turning on his heel, he joined the flow of pedestrians. He couldn't forget what he'd seen – Bec teetering – and he, unable to do anything. Completely useless.

CHAPTER 30

Tuesday 1 September 1925

'It's a disgrace,' the woman replied haughtily, shaking the offending ticket in Bec's face. 'The advertising of intoxicating liquor has no place on a ticket distributed to the public.'

Bec pasted a smile on her face. The public had come out in force to test her patience this morning. 'I understand that the matter is under review. They are part of an order of one hundred and twenty-four million placed last year. They'll be worked through in just a couple of months.'

'They should be immediately withdrawn and —'

'I'm sure madam wouldn't want her money wasted on the cost of replacement tickets. Your concerns have been heard. Good day, madam,' Bec politely but firmly responded, before continuing her way through the narrow corridor of the carriage.

'Well done, lassie.' Syd chuckled quietly. 'You're doing grand.'

Bec grimaced. She wasn't so sure that her response wouldn't see her accused of impudence and reported to headquarters. She'd already been threatened twice with this punishment – both times by females, both stylishly dressed. The first had argued her change, which Bec knew to be correct. She'd stood her ground, refusing to be swindled, since Syd would have to make up any losses from his wages. And the second had complained that Bec had rung the bell before allowing her to take a seat, causing her to collapse into the lap of another passenger. Bec had apologised but wondered how many seats it was reasonable to allow the woman to test before signalling the car to move on. Daniel, once again seated at the front of the closed carriage, had observed both altercations without expression.

His reserved greeting had surprised her this morning; she'd expected his qualms to have been extinguished by a good night's sleep.

She'd risen, prepared to acknowledge how powerless he must have felt yesterday, knowing he couldn't save her from injury. The shadows beneath her eyes were evidence of a restless night debating whether he'd overreacted or she'd been too defensive. She blamed Evelyn and women of her ilk for the overdevelopment of his protective instincts – expecting to be guarded from puddles, railway timetables, beetles and bulls. *Hell!* She didn't agree with cocooning people from life and its lessons. Everything involved risk – look how many people were injured crossing the street! But she couldn't ignore the tiny part of her that welcomed his concern.

'How are your feet?' Syd's voice brought her attention back from her musings.

'I won't pretend that they're not a little tired,' Bec confessed. 'It helps to keep moving though, not standing in the one spot.'

'We'll manage a short sit-down before returning to the depot,' Syd said. 'Time enough to sample that cake you brought me. Chocolate if my nose isn't mistaken.'

Bec winked at him, rolling her shoulders to relieve the weight of the cash bag. The bruising didn't help, but she was determined not to offer any excuses. Syd had agreed for her to take it for the return run to Toorak, but made sure he was on hand to supervise the tickets and cash handling. She'd quickly discovered it was too heavy to hang around her neck as he did and had fashioned the strap at an angle across her uninjured shoulder and back, resting it on her hip. The weight of the leather, pennies and tickets was greater than she'd imagined, and had already curbed the skip she'd perfected across the gap between the carriages.

'Hey there, little lady.'

Bec turned to see a man of about fifty years of age struggling to his feet, his eyes like his coat, half open. Grasping the back of the seat with one hand, he was brandishing a ticket in the other.

'Wanna have ...' he trailed off for a moment, his face twisting in concentration, '... my ticket punched.'

Concerned that the man would lose his balance and tumble off the carriage, Bec moved instinctively towards him.

Syd's hand on her shoulder stayed her. 'I'll handle Ronnie. Lost his wife recently and turned to the drink.' As he pushed past her, he added, 'One of our regulars, likes to get in just after opening. Harmless enough.'

Bec watched Syd greet the man and try to convince him to take his seat.

'Don't want you ...' the man said in a loud voice, slumping

back down, '... want that pretty lady.'

From the corner of her eye, Bec saw Daniel standing at the door of the trailing carriage. An unexpected shiver of pleasure ran down her spine. *God, there it was again.* She was a contradiction. One minute flaying him for being too protective and the next delighted with his attentiveness. But she had no time to ponder the implication, as Ronnie had started to sob like a child.

Bec approached cautiously, holding tightly to a pillar and ensuring her feet were firmly planted on the step. 'Have you got a ticket, sir?' she asked in a loud voice.

The man blinked up at her and smiled. His face as dry – and textured – as the sea sponges found washed onto the local beach during winter. She suspected crocodile tears but couldn't help returning his smile. He held out his ticket obediently.

'An angel ...' Ronnie rubbed his eyes.

'Who's got more to do than look after you. So, behave yourself and stay quiet,' ordered Syd in a gruff voice, although Bec could hear a hint of a smile as he levered himself to his feet.

Daniel had moved to a seat in the open car. 'Everything under control?' he asked as they moved past him.

'Men are suckers for the female touch,' said Syd, lifting his cap to rake his fingers through his hair.

Bec grinned triumphantly.

'At least this female,' she heard Daniel murmur as he pressed a piece of paper into her hand as countless others had done over the last two days.

She closed her fingers around it and raised an eyebrow.

'Call me.'

Her legs became as wobbly as her mum's lemon jellies at the intensity of his gaze, and it took all her strength to turn and navigate the gap between the two carriages.

Daniel's gaze roved over Bec when she reappeared, and if the pink tinge in her cheeks was any sign, she'd correctly interpreted his thoughts. Gone was the military-style neck-to-foot garb, replaced with an attractive display of ankle and a flash of knee. Unfortunately, skirts disguised the shape of her delightful derriere. He waited impatiently while she delivered an effusive farewell to Syd. The trammie playfully swatted her away as she delivered a noisy kiss to the side of his face and a swift hug.

'Thanks, Syd. Appreciate everything,' Daniel interrupted, securing Bec to his side.

Syd accepted Daniel's proffered hand and gave it a hearty shake. 'Happy to help. You got a good'n there. Keep hold of her.'

Daniel wondered at the heat of his own cheeks as he pulled Bec in the direction of the tram stop for their return trip to the city. The aloofness he'd engineered this morning had disappeared. He had deliberated long and hard on how strongly woven the protection of females was into the male psyche, and how much that would irritate a woman of Bec's independence. But the instinct was part and parcel of who he was, and Bec had already shown him it wasn't misplaced in all situations. Their date on the ice at the Glaciarium was a perfect example. He just needed to get better at reading the situations. After all, he didn't want a helpless wife.

'What's the hurry?'

'We have a lunch date, and ...' Daniel kissed the back of her hand, '... I'm tired of sharing you.'

Bec smiled, but when he glanced at her profile, she was looking straight ahead. Daniel sighed. He would have been happiest had she flung her arms around his neck and kissed him soundly. *That's what happened in his dreams.* He climbed up onto the tram behind her, glad she chose a seat that afforded some privacy.

'Bec?'

Glancing over her shoulder, she leaned towards him and kissed the corner of his mouth. Daniel was so surprised he was slow to react. She sat back, the tip of her tongue dancing briefly across her lips. 'Mmm ... peppermint,' she murmured. 'Thank you for today, by the way.'

'But I didn't do anything.'

'Exactly. Thank you.' And with that, Daniel found his fingers gathered and cradled in her lap.

God! Evelyn had never been this challenging to understand. Whereas with Bec, his mind was constantly performing mental gymnastics, and the other parts of his body ... well, they were engaged in their own acrobatics.

'Are you free for lunch?' he ventured, thinking, *Perhaps posing a question was a better approach.*

'Uh-huh, I've taken the rest of the afternoon off.'

Daniel immediately started calculating the potential possibilities of her statement and rearranging his schedule to accommodate them. Thankfully, he hadn't committed to any meetings this afternoon. Before he could think too hard, he leaned towards her and mimicked her kiss from before. 'Mmm ... liquorice.'

Bec giggled.

'Fares, please!'

Daniel groaned, untangled his hand from Bec's and hunted in his coat pocket for his travel card. Satisfied, the conductor moved away. But Daniel wasn't – satisfied, that was. Grabbing his hat as a shield in one hand and Bec's chin in the other, he placated the desire she'd ignited.

'Fares, *please*!'

Daniel gave Bec's mouth one more kiss before lowering his hat and scowling at the conductor. The man had the temerity to smile at him.

'Sorry, sir, didn't recognise you,' he said cheekily, before easing himself onto the seat across the narrow aisle from Daniel. 'Don't mind if I sit for a bit, do you? These bags get mighty heavy, they do, with all the paraphernalia we have to carry.'

'Do you think a female could do your job?' Bec blurted out beside Daniel. Clearly, her wits had recovered faster than his.

'Well, Miss, I've never really thought about it. Are you lookin' to become a trammie?'

'Maybe,' Bec hedged.

'Well, you look like you're the right height. What are you, five ten? Five eleven?'

'Five eleven. And before you ask, ten stone.'

The conductor nodded and drummed the fingers of one hand on his cash bag. 'A touch tall. But you look like you're a sweet-tempered lass.'

Daniel raised an eyebrow but refrained from commenting.

'And I'm guessin' you could do arithmetic quicker in that pretty little head of yours than I could ever do …

The dilemma becomes when you muddle the social and economic contract us males sign up to.' The man settled back against the seat. 'I can see that puzzled look on your face and I'm thinkin' that it's never been explained to you before.'

Daniel wasn't sure if *it*, whatever *it* was, had ever been explained to him before, either. Certainly, never like this.

'I have a social responsibility to take a wife ...'

Daniel's eyes widened. *Take her where?*

'... economically, marriage requires me to support one adult female and however many children we're blessed with ...'

'What about where women outnumber men?' Bec asked.

'Well, that ain't the case here. England maybe, but in Australia, it's important to let us men do our duty.'

'Humph! Sounds like —'

'An interesting perspective,' Daniel interjected. 'And we thank you for sharing it with us. Please don't let us hold you up further.'

The man lumbered to his feet and shuffled away.

Bec mumbled, 'I was going to say *claptrap*.'

'And here I'd understood you were such a *sweet-tempered lass*.'

Bec pulled a face. 'He meant I was a sweet lass with a temper.'

Daniel laughed.

'Which I'd have demonstrated had I listened to much more of that ... mindless drivel. When you speak of your role in providing and protecting, is that what you mean? What he said?'

Daniel sensed he was on dangerous ground. 'I don't agree

that men have a preordained social and economic contract. It all sounds very clinical. But if that works for his marriage, then who am I to criticise.'

'Humph!'

'But after yesterday, I won't deny a desire to protect those that I ... well, to protect you from unnecessary harm. Is that so hard to understand?'

Bec turned to face him, worrying her bottom lip. 'No ... actually it feels ... nice to have someone in my corner.'

'Nice?'

She nodded. 'With a capital N.'

As Daniel leaned forward to coax a more eloquent response from her, Bec held him at bay. 'But ...'

Daniel groaned. She looked as if a barrage of words was about to trip from her tongue. 'Oh no you don't,' he scolded. 'I will not be dragged into a discussion about how capable you are. I'm sure you could do anything you set your mind to. But sometimes we all need help.'

He watched the light fade from her eyes.

'I was serious before. We haven't spent any time together, any *meaningful* time, since Saturday night, and I plan to rectify that.'

Bec pouted. 'Am I to be consulted?'

Daniel grinned. 'Oh yes, sweetheart. You get to choose whether you want me to kiss you before or after lunch ...' Daniel dropped his voice and nuzzled her ear, '...where ... and for how long.'

CHAPTER 31

Wednesday 2 September 1925

'Stopped by your office yesterday afternoon,' Alex said in a voice, which, for all its casualness, intimated much.

Daniel ignored the undertone. 'Social or business?'

Alex shrugged. 'A bit of both.'

'I went for a walk.'

'Must have been a trek. Took you all afternoon.'

Daniel grinned. 'I had company.'

'Relations must be improving.'

'We're dating,' declared Daniel, taking a sip from his glass. The deep coppery colour reminded him of the highlights in Bec's hair. *How had he never noticed them before?* To be fair, it was usually confined within her cloche. But not yesterday. The sun had been shining, and he'd plucked it from her head, refusing all appeals for its return until she paid his – *very reasonable* – request for a kiss. She'd argued – unsuccessfully – that it was his place to pay a forfeit for his behaviour. Matters had been settled satisfactorily, very satisfactorily. He'd acted like a starving man, and Bec had met him kiss by kiss.

'The whisky not to your liking?' interrupted a voice threaded with amusement.

Daniel took another sip, realising he'd been staring into the liquid. 'Checking for sediment.'

'Is your Mr Chalmers pleased?'

'Pleased?'

'With your success.'

'He hasn't mentioned it. And just to set the record straight, Bec is not part of the path to my promotion.'

'Right.'

Daniel could feel the chords in his neck tightening. Alex's tone mirrored that of Theo Blake's earlier today, when he had the audacity to ask if Daniel had a wife in mind. He'd ignored him. Theo had smiled in a knowing way, hinting that the conditions for Chalmers' support were being speculated on around the office.

'You doubt my word?'

'I remember our conversation last Wednesday.'

Daniel massaged his neck. 'That was a whole week ago.'

'And in that time, you've fallen for Bec? In one week?'

'She's the one, Alex.'

'You're not answering my question. She could be the one because ...' Alex shrugged. 'Well, because she's the best of the alternatives. Or you're in lust with her.'

'That's disgusting.'

'Daniel, you've been obsessed with your promotion. Ranted and raved about the injustice of Chalmers' conditions. It's not an unreasonable question.'

'She's the one. I've changed. Become hyper-attentive to the smallest things.' Bec had once accused him that details weren't his forte. He'd argue that where she was concerned, he was on his way to becoming an expert. He smiled. *Or more a connoisseur ... learning the right pressure, speed ... and how to share control.* The electricity between them yesterday had sizzled. For a mechanical engineer, he wasn't doing too badly – electricity had always been more of Alex's thing.

'More willing to compromise?'

Daniel nodded. 'These days I hardly recognise myself.'

'Do you still argue?'

'Yes, but our skirmishes have a different quality to them. I'm making an effort to understand her point of view. Even when I don't agree with it. I can't believe I'm saying this, but I've fallen in love.' Prepared for another argument or a scoff, Daniel was surprised when Alex accepted his statement and moved on.

'What's the situation with Evelyn?'

'Tomorrow night. I'll speak to her at Birmingham's.'

'And Jim? Where does Bec's relationship stand with him?'

Daniel's fingers tightened around his glass as he raised it and threw the whisky down his throat. 'I have no idea.'

'So, your research is going well, then?' Elsie Timms pushed her tortoise-shell glasses to the tip of her nose and peered at Bec.

How did she answer that? What would be her boss's reaction if she told her that her initial body of research had expanded and now included an attractive, disconcerting model of masculinity who seemed bent on wearing down her defences? Who asked her opinion? Was willing to discuss the accountancy-training initiative so close to her heart?

That she feared he was making progress, as her views on equality, as they pertained to Daniel, changed day by day … kiss by kiss?

Daniel was a risk – a high risk – who, much to her annoyance, refused to be managed, and seemed to enjoy wresting the reins from her at regular intervals. Like yesterday.

He had suggested a picnic rather than lunch at the Federal or a tearoom. They'd caught the train from Flinders Street station to Williamstown. Like children, they'd snuck into his house, absconded with scones, fruit and homemade ginger beer, and continued to the beach. Bec had refused to share her lunch with the seagulls, distrusting their yellow eyes. Daniel had protested that she was stunting their self-esteem and crumbled pieces of scone for them, even stealing some of hers.

Hand in hand, they'd drifted to the Botanic Gardens. Under one of the old elm trees, he'd brushed a wayward curl from her forehead with his finger before trailing it down the side of her face, along her jaw, to her lips. She'd nipped it playfully, watching as his eyes had darkened. They'd roamed her face as if physically touching her eyebrows, skimming the length of her nose, dipping into her dimple, which she assumed was in evidence, as her smile stretched wide. He'd trailed the finger across her cheekbone before tucking her hair behind her ear and wrapping his hand around her nape. She'd been conscious of his other hand patrolling the area between her waist and the side of her breast.

Instinctively, she'd tilted her pelvis, closing the distance between them before taking the initiative and drawing his mouth down to hers. She wasn't sure who had groaned the loudest as their lips had met …

'Is it such a difficult question to answer, then?'

Bec took a moment to return to the room, and to Elsie, sitting patiently, head tilted to one side. She was glad to see her own hands demurely clasped in her lap and not roaming … where they shouldn't.

'It's … complicated.'

'Which part, dear? Is it the research? Are you finding it difficult to frame your arguments?'

Yes! The man mixes them all up. 'No, they're progressing well. The two days I spent with the tramways gave me a whole new appreciation for the work and its challenges, which I'll incorporate. There are changes that would need to be made to accommodate a female in the role, but I'm convinced that these would benefit the men, regardless. But there just isn't any reason to change as the men are used to current conditions.'

Elsie nodded. 'Is it your team members, then?'

Bec had lost the line of questioning, and it must have shown on her face.

'The complication. Is it arising from your team?'

Bec hesitated.

'I know Ida McAuley can monopolise things sometimes, but her heart's in the right place.'

'Ida seems … very experienced and we're lucky to have her. She's taken the first-speaker position.'

'And Daniel?'

'Is our biggest asset because he doesn't think the same as the rest of the team.'

'So, is the complication you?'

Bec opened her mouth to speak and then closed it again.

Was she the complication? 'I'm having to recalibrate ...' she trailed off, unsure of what else to say.

Elsie chuckled. 'Nothing wrong with that. Better to do it at your age than wait until you get to mine. It gets harder, and then ... well, you just refuse to try.'

'I'm —'

'*I'm* not telling you that for you to feel sorry for me. I'm happy with my choices ... mostly.' She grinned. 'Reconsidering your views and opinions can take a little time. And a lot of courage. If you're feeling adrift, that's natural, too.'

Bec smiled.

Elsie got to her feet. 'And best to do any of that deep thinking with a cuppa in hand.' She squeezed Bec's shoulder as she passed. 'Two sugars?'

Bec nodded, rubbing her eyes. It must be those dust mites.

Elsie's last comment, before she'd bustled through the door, courtesy of Columbus, hung suspended in the silent conclave. 'You can never cross the ocean unless you have the courage to lose sight of the shore.'

And that was at the heart of the complication. She wanted to set sail with Daniel – as an equal partner in life. But there was no way of calculating the cost to who she was as a person ... to her beliefs ... or to her heart? But the alternative would see her stuck, moored to cowardice. Perhaps it was time to weigh anchor.

CHAPTER 32

Thursday 3 September 1925

'This is a stupid game,' Bec grumbled to Jim as they danced down one side of the floor. Why had she let Eliza talk her into attending the Balloon Gala? Being trailed by a bright-pink balloon attached to her ankle was not Bec's idea of fun.

'Going right, hang on.'

Bec braced herself for whatever move Jim deemed appropriate to avoid their balloon being burst by other couples on the dancefloor. She saw Derek Fisher stomp on the inflatable – unsuccessfully – as Jim executed their course correction. His partner, Queenie Nolan, looked none too pleased with being thrust left then right.

'I thought I was the competitive one?' Bec said, settling back into the music's rhythm. 'Derek seems overzealous for a novelty event. And Queenie appears to have the balloon tied around her knee. No wonder no one's burst it. Where are the judges?' She craned her neck, looking for Mr and Mrs Birmingham.

'They won't beat us,' Jim asserted, eyes scouring the crowd over the top of Bec's head. 'Keep an eye on our flanks, would you?'

Bec briefly raised her eyes in the direction of the ceiling, but did as he asked. 'Incoming, right side.'

'And to our left. Hold on.'

Bec was amazed at Jim's reaction time. He stopped them for two full beats of music – enough time for the other couples to collide, and their balloons to pop.

Bec chortled. 'You are truly devious.'

'It reminds me of war games, but on a dancefloor.'

War games! Now that was something that she could take an interest in. Her job was to keep the balloon out of enemy hands and away from enemy feet. Peering around Jim, she guessed they were one of eight other couples on the floor. 'Can you lead me into a spin turn when we reach a corner so that we can assess our remaining competition?'

'Yes, ma'am.'

'Hmm, seven, counting us. I thought there were more.'

'Daniel and his girlfriend just retired.'

Bec could feel the weight of Jim's gaze. *Girlfriend?* The denial died on her lips. She'd forgotten that she hadn't explained Daniel to Jim. There hadn't been an opportunity. Tonight was their first appearance at Birmingham's in almost two weeks. She glanced in Daniel's direction, glad to see that he wasn't playing trellis to Evelyn's creeper. *Maybe the woman had a backbone, after all.* But the thought didn't lessen the hurt she'd felt when Daniel had chosen Evelyn and not her for the dance. She frowned. And now, he was escorting her out of the ballroom, her hand tucked possessively into the crook of his elbow. *What game was he playing?*

'Seen enough?'

Snapped back into the glare of the ballroom chandeliers, Bec nodded automatically. Her gaze focused on Jim's shirtfront, in case her eyes revealed too much. 'Do you have a strategy?'

'Well, it's too late to form an alliance.'

'Yes, I should have spoken to Eliza beforehand. And camouflage is out of the question – with me in pink.'

'I suggest a short skirmish. A test of nerves and ingenuity.'

She grinned. 'Good. My attention wouldn't span a marathon of endurance and persistence. Lead on.'

'All right, then, we'll make a quick and decisive attack on those two couples closest, and then retreat for a bit and reassess.'

In the end, it was easy. The two couples had been circling one another and were taken completely by surprise.

Bec was enjoying herself. 'Five ... make that three!' she said, watching two more couples exit the floor to the cheers of the crowd, who were becoming louder with each retirement.

'Quite a move by your friend's fiancé,' approved Jim. 'I'm goin' to add that to my arsenal.'

'As you tour the world? Officer by day, balloon-dancing competitor by night?'

'Hush. I'm plannin' our next move.'

'*Oh no!* Eliza has burst her own balloon. I think she must have caught it with her heel.'

'And then there were two. We're goin' to make a direct strike.'

'She's appealing, but Mrs B is shaking her head.'

'Bec, will you pay attention? A direct strike. I'm going to aim straight at Queenie ... and her partner.'

'Sounds personal,' Bec quipped, peering up at him.

'Just funnin',' he assured her. 'It's called a torpedo attack. We'll dance straight then into pivots, and whoever has the best shot takes it.'

Bec was thinking Jim had spent too long on dry land, but any chance to rob that dolt Derek of bragging rights was fine with her. 'I'm ready.'

The crowd anticipated Jim's manoeuvre. Bec could hear an array of comments as they stepped into the first of a series of spins.

'Watch out!'

'Go Bec!'

'Smart move!'

She was focused on making sure she avoided dizziness, so that she had the best chance of spotting Queenie's balloon. Suddenly, it was beside her – a floating orb of gold, to match Queenie's starburst heels. With split-second timing, she bayoneted it with her small pin.

Jim brought them to an abrupt halt and Bec found herself squeezed into a tight hug. 'You did it!'

'*We* did it,' Bec corrected, laughing.

'Congratulations to you both.'

They turned as one to face Derek and Queenie, the former sporting a rueful grin. The latter's moue was more wistful, her eyes directed towards Jim from beneath her darkened lashes, as if in accusation. Not for the first time, Bec wondered whether Queenie had set her sights on Jim, and he was refusing to follow the rules – *her rules*.

'Thanks. Well played,' Jim said, shaking Derek's hand. 'You too, Queenie.'

Mr B bustled up to them. 'Well done, all of you. Quite a contest.' He looked around. 'And here is my lovely wife with the winner's prizes. A new felt hat for you, young man. Let me know if it doesn't fit and we'll fix that.'

'And, Bec, your colour, I think,' beamed Mrs B. She held a cinnamon felt with a gorgeous hydrangea-blue band, which Bec fell in love with.

'Derek, Queenie, better luck next time. I think they outgunned you.' Mr B chuckled, delighted by his turn of phrase.

'Yes, dear, very witty.' Mrs B patted his arm as she tucked her hand into the crook of his elbow. 'Time to announce the next dance. Once again, congratulations all.'

Jim led Bec from the floor towards Eliza, who embraced her warmly. 'Well done. What a beautiful colour.'

'But what about you? What went wrong?'

'Silly of me. I stepped onto my balloon,' grumbled Eliza. 'Maybe I should have worn it higher up my leg, like Queenie,' she whispered into Bec's ear. 'That wasn't in the spirit of the game.'

Bec chuckled. 'Lucky for me, she did. In the end, it made for an easier target.'

'Please take your partners for a spotlight dance,' Mr B announced.

Bec casually surveyed those in the vicinity of her friend. No sign of Daniel ... or Evelyn. *Was this the night she'd lose a boyfriend and gain a hat?* Nothing had been amiss earlier – he'd greeted her warmly, they'd danced ... and then *Evelyn* had arrived.

'Come on,' Eliza said, grabbing Alex's hand. 'Maybe we'll be luckier this time.'

'Bec?'

'Thanks, Jim, but I'm going to sit this one out. Let me stow our winnings with the cloakroom attendant,' she said, reaching for his hat.

Queenie's reaction to her statement provided at least some entertainment – the woman tilted her head towards Jim, one eyebrow arched, her Cupid's-bow lips parted as if in invitation. Derek, standing to her right, was forgotten.

'Mind if I take Queenie for a spin around the dancefloor?' Jim asked politely of Derek.

Bec suppressed a smile. Derek was clearly flummoxed. He had no claim on Queenie. He knew it. Jim knew it. Bec knew it. And as for Queenie ... well, she looked as if she was warring between giving Jim a set-down for his impertinence and having him to herself.

Bec turned on her heel. Time would tell if Jim fell under Queenie's spell or Queenie at Jim's feet. She paused mid-stride, realising her interest levels were closer to a curious bystander than a wronged sweetheart.

Her mind returned to Daniel and his disappearance. He didn't need to be obvious in his attentions to her, but she didn't expect that he would show such a discernible preference for Evelyn. *Where did that leave her?* Perhaps he wanted to renegotiate the exclusive terms of their relationship. Maybe he was bored. Bec blinked, straightening her spine. *No man was worth tears.*

Smiling brightly, she chatted to the cloakroom attendant – Harry – Birmingham's oldest employee. A breath tickled her nape.

'Leaving?'

Bec smiled at Harry in farewell before turning to face Daniel. 'Stowing spoils,' she responded. At his puzzled look, she added, 'The prizes Jim and I won.'

'I saw him dancing with Queenie.'

'Yes. I told him I'd sit this one out.'

Bec watched Daniel's jaw tighten. 'I came looking for you.'

'Don't feel that you have to divide your time,' quipped Bec, moving purposely towards the ballroom. 'I'm not short of partners.'

'But I am,' said Daniel, intercepting her march and wrapping her hand through his elbow.

Bec scoffed. She cast him a quick look out of the corner of her eye. *Were his lips swollen?* Impossible to tell without being obvious. 'We must be talking of a different Daniel.'

'How many do you know?' he countered softly, shepherding her up the stairs to the gallery above the dancefloor.

'Just one.' She sighed in exasperation. 'Daniel, where are we going? And why?'

He glanced around and proceeded to the farthermost side without answering her question. The lights had been muted to enhance the atmosphere on the dancefloor below, and the wall sconces did little to dispel the impression of intimacy. Bec noted the silhouettes of other couples dotted in seats in the different rows, no doubt escaping the scrutiny of Birmingham's patriarch and matriarch. Daniel chose the middle row of tiered seats, and she found herself nestled into padded brushed velvet.

'Why? Because I fear your thoughts have taken you in the wrong direction.'

'I'm listening,' she said, turning to face him.

'Bec, do you trust me?'

She considered the question. 'It depends.'

Daniel frowned. 'Physically? Do you trust me with your physical wellbeing?'

'You can be overprotective, but yes.'

'With your opinions and other matters of importance?'

What was this – a quiz? 'You infuriate me at times, but again, yes.'

'With your heart?'

Bec's breath hitched. *She wanted to …*

'I broke up with Evelyn. I wanted to do it in person, in private, without giving her the chance to make a scene. I should have done it at least a week ago, after we made our commitment to one another.' He shrugged. 'But I've been … busy.'

'Oh.' Bec swallowed and looked out over the railing to where the shaft of the spotlight was picking out a lucky couple. 'I thought …'

'That I was what? Planning on two-timing you? Jilting you for Evelyn?'

Bec's gaze returned to his face. 'I thought you might be reconsidering.'

'*God, Bec!* What type of man do you think I am?'

How did she answer that? It's not you, it's me …

'What more can I do, or say, to make you realise I'm serious about you? *About us!*'

He sounded … vulnerable. And her heart was doing that sloppy, ice-cream thing.

'Nothing,' she whispered.

'Is it all one-sided? Do you not feel the same way?' Daniel raked his hands through his hair.

Bec leaned forward, placing her lips a fraction of an inch from his. 'It's not one-sided.'

Daniel's hands cupped the sides of her face, raising his chin to kiss the tip of her nose. 'Sometimes, you are the most infuriating —'

'I prefer the word intoxicating.'

'Maddening —'

'Invigorating.'

Daniel dropped his voice. 'Desirable female, I have ever known.'

'I try my best!' His possessive tone sent tingles through her.

As the band's tempo changed, the lights blazed into full illumination. Bec blinked, shielding her eyes for a moment until they became accustomed to the glare.

'Let's get out of here. I'll see you home,' said Daniel.

'A little early, isn't it?' Bec joked.

'It means we have time to walk the long way,' he said, pulling her to her feet. 'Come on, before we're discovered.'

'Jim —'

'Can find his own way home,' came the curt reply, his jaw taking on a stubborn demeanour.

She was glad Daniel hadn't asked where matters stood with the American. Would Daniel jump to the same conclusions she had if given the opportunity? *And why hadn't she ended things?* Lack of opportunity? Or had she been keeping Jim in the wings as insurance, in case things didn't work out with Daniel? She cringed. She was guilty of adopting one rule for her and another for Daniel. A situation she wouldn't tolerate if the shoe was on the other foot!

CHAPTER 33

Friday 4 September 1925

'You left early last night,' remarked Eliza as she took her place opposite Daniel at the breakfast table.

'Did I?'

'Bec disappeared about the same time.'

'Did she?'

'She forgot to collect the prize she won. With Jim.'

Daniel looked up from his study of the newspaper spread before him and speared his sister with a look. 'And your point?'

Eliza shrugged her shoulders, finishing her mouthful of toast before replying. 'Just making conversation.'

And pigs might fly. Daniel sipped his coffee before returning to his reading.

'Alex and I won a prize in the spotlight dance ... as did Queenie and Jim.'

Daniel turned a page.

'And Evelyn looked like she'd been crying.'

Daniel counted to ten before looking up and raising an eyebrow.

'Argh! Why won't you tell me what's going on?' exclaimed Eliza.

'You seem to be up to date.' He rose to his feet. 'Now, if you'll excuse me, I'm late for work.'

A volley of words erupted from behind him as he headed out the door. The loudest complaint seemed to be, *'But I'm your sister and she's my best friend.'*

If Bec wanted to enlighten Eliza, that was her business. Daniel grinned. But he doubted that she'd share how she'd clung to him in the shadows last night as he'd kissed her senseless. He'd started slowly. Like a cartographer, he'd mapped out her lips, followed by her mouth. Their tongues had tangoed, touching and tangling. And the tension had built slowly, undertones of suggestion, promise and longing. Daniel adjusted his winter coat.

He'd once thought Bec opinionated. He was learning to love her confidence. She knew what she liked and didn't like but was open-minded to his ... *ideas.* Her speed of adoption astonished him regularly. Last evening, her exploring fingers had discovered his nipples, and she'd laid siege to them with her tongue through the fabric of his shirt. He'd almost lost his —

'Daniel.'

'Alex!'

'Are you all right? You look ... disorientated.'

Daniel shook his head. He'd arrived in the city without realising how he'd got there, his mind consumed with Bec. 'Um, just running through some ... calculations.'

Alex grinned. 'Anything to do with the theory of electrical attraction?'

Daniel offered his mate a wry smile. 'Something of that

nature.'

'Coming to the meeting?'

'Yes, Chalmers wants to be kept across progress. And I, for my sins, seem to be the resident expert on female labour relations, thanks to the damn *debate*.'

'The debate has had its positives.'

'I'm not denying that. But I have projects to oversee. I have no desire to be involved every time Trades Hall gets antsy. What is it this time? Something about the employment of female bus conductors?'

'Yes. The private companies.'

'Why is that our problem? Last time I checked, we worked for the state.'

Alex stopped on the pavement outside the Tramway Board's building. Turning to face Daniel, he folded his arms. 'I'm sure I don't need to explain to you that it boils down to money. The men want to make sure they're competing fairly for jobs. That means they don't want the females being paid less. And the state wants to make sure that we're not being forced to compete against the privates, who have a lower wage cost.'

'You know, I think all sides want the same thing – to compete on equal terms. But every time one side acts, the other side reacts.'

'That's quite profound for a Friday morning. Maybe your true vocation lies in arbitration.'

'Newton's third law – for every action, there's an equal and opposite reaction.' He could as easily have been talking about Bec.

Alex clapped him on the back as they headed through the door and up to the third floor. 'And that, my friend, is why you're here.'

'If we removed all the legal and formal barriers that prevented women from competing with men, and allowed people's strengths and skills – irrespective of their sex – to determine who did what, we could get on with more important things, such as electrifying the tram network.'

'Does that mean you're happy for Bec to take a role as a tram conductor?'

'No!'

Alex laughed. 'I thought not.'

Daniel grinned. 'But that's only because her talents lie in a different direction.'

Bec threw down her pencil. 'It makes my blood boil, it does.'

'What's that, dear?' Elsie Timms peered at her over the rim of her teacup.

Bec tapped the file she was reading. 'This young woman, Merle Cooper. Recently sacked from the public service because she got married. She tried to keep it a secret, but a caller to her office asked for her by her married name and she was discovered.'

'What are her circumstances?'

'Her husband is on the basic wage, which we know wouldn't support a *boy scout*.' Bec snapped her fingers for effect. 'And they have Merle's widowed mother living with them, whose health has deteriorated since she caught influenza a couple of years ago.'

'It makes you angry. But there's nothing we can do in the short term to fix the rules. What are her prospects?'

'Slim. She doesn't have any of the skills for work regarded as *unsuitable for men*.' Bec stood up to dissipate her frustration. '*Grrrr!* I can't even believe I used that term.'

'What about a bus conductor? Marney Motorbus Line is recruiting.'

'How do you know that?'

'The owner is a friend of mine.'

Bec gave the older woman a calculating look. Elsie had a friend – a male friend. But her countenance didn't invite confidences. She gave her a quick hug. 'Elsie, you're a treasure. I'll get onto it right away. Hopefully, Merle is interested.'

'Bec, you've got a visitor. He's in the lounge. And this was just dropped off for you.'

'Thanks, Hannah.' Taking the envelope, Bec absently noted her name written in bold, legible ink.

'And I can't guarantee he won't be spirited away if you don't attend to him,' the receptionist said with a wink, before turning on her heel and disappearing the way she'd come.

Bec checked the clock. Eleven-thirty. Too early for lunch. And she'd already had her tea break.

'Take half an hour,' said Elsie, as if sensing her dilemma. 'You'll make it up. You always do.'

Bec dropped the envelope on her desk and hurried out to reception. Maybe Daniel had stopped by to surprise her. She felt her stomach tighten as she remembered her sassiness from last night. He'd assured her he was delighted with her initiative, just not in words ...

'Jim!'

A bevy of females scattered like dandelion balls in a strong wind. Jim emerged from the centre, unhurt and with a wide grin. 'Hello, how's my girl?'

Bec quirked an eyebrow at him. *My girl, indeed!*

'I was just introducin' myself.'

'I'm sure you were. What brings you here?'

He held up her prize from the balloon dance. 'You left in such a hurry last night, you forgot this.'

'Hand delivered to my door. Thank you.'

'And I thought you might fancy some lunch.'

'Aw, that's sweet of you, but I can't today.' It wasn't strictly true, and she felt guilty when she saw the corners of his mouth droop. 'But I have half an hour to go for a walk if you'd like, maybe up to the gardens and back,' she offered. After all, she needed to explain the situation with Daniel, and she'd prefer to do it without an audience. Although, Jim would have to be blind not to have guessed.

'That would be swell.'

'Give me a minute. I'll grab my coat.'

This time, when she returned to reception, Jim's smart blue uniform and gold braid had attracted two more admirers.

'Everyone's so friendly,' he drawled, his brown eyes teasing as he passed Bec her hat. 'Well, maybe not everybody ...' Bec heard him amend.

She turned, intuitively knowing who had walked into reception. The rush of cold air had carried with it the smell of citrus and spices – her favourite new aroma. But its familiarity was not matched by the expression on its owner's face.

'Daniel!' Bec took a step forward and then stopped. His demeanour held no invitation.

'Going out?'

'For a walk,' said Jim.

Bec groaned. She couldn't believe that the waves of anger rolling off Daniel were lost on Jim; he sounded so affable.

Daniel tilted his head and looked at her, his eyes blazing, the warm hazel tones replaced by a darker shade and streaks of green. She'd never seen a shade quite like that before.

It wasn't in her nature to babble, but she fought an urge to do exactly that. To explain what Jim was doing here, why they were going for a walk, and that it meant nothing. 'Jim stopped by with the hat we won at Birmingham's last night.'

'Was that all?' His voice sounded as if it had been squeezed through a vice.

'And an invitation to lunch,' said Jim.

Daniel growled.

'Which Bec refused.'

'Ahem.'

Bec swung round towards Hannah, who, with minimal cues, suggested they take their discussion someplace else. Bec's quick glance around the waiting area confirmed they were gathering a discreet but attentive audience – fans of Jim's.

Bec moved between the two men, turning to face Daniel. 'I'm glad you stopped by. Give me a moment.'

Grabbing Jim's hand, she towed him out the door to the front. 'Daniel and I are dating,' she began without preamble. 'This was not how I wanted to tell you ...'

'Honey, I understand. He's been wound up tighter than an antique watch for weeks.'

Bec gave him a lopsided smile. 'Thanks.'

'If you were my girl, I'd be actin' up a storm, too. You better go.'

Bec followed Jim's gaze to where Daniel stood, hands in pockets, just inside the front door to the building.

'But I won't be denied a dance ... or two,' he said with a wink, before kissing her lightly on the cheek.

Bec took a deep breath as she watched him walk along the street. She pulled her hat down to prevent the south-westerly from snatching it from her head. She may as well take that stroll. Daniel needed to cool off, and they needed to discuss ground rules. It was easier when she was occupying his mind and mouth with other things – things that didn't need words, just actions and reactions.

CHAPTER 34

Saturday 5 September 1925

'He's an old windbag,' declared Ida McAuley with a decisive sweep of her arm. 'And his supporters are about the size of a wedding party. *A small wedding.* But he gets me madder than anyone else I know.'

Bec studied the pamphlet. 'It says the object of the League is *to voice the social aspirations of the normal womanhood of Great Britain.* What would a man know about that?'

'Apparently quite a lot. Wifehood and maternity,' said Daniel, stabbing the passage with his finger. 'Look, it says it right there. He's summed it up beautifully.'

As Bec opened her mouth to give him a most certain set-down, he kissed her full on the lips. He'd calculated the risk of being caught as next to none. Ida was on her high horse and seemed in no hurry to dismount. Jenny was yet to make an appearance. He was feeling confident, although with Bec, nothing was certain. Jim had been dismissed, and he and Bec were getting along well. *Very well.* He'd even added a couple of ground rules of his own to Bec's short, succinct list, during their walk yesterday. Trust and individual interests were all well and good, he'd told her, but having a regular dose of kisses was essential.

'It's his plumy Pommy voice I object to the most,' continued Ida. 'And the thought of him here. In this city. On the same stage as us. It makes my blood boil.'

'I used the same words yesterday,' said Bec.

'Were you remembering our time together Thursday evening?' murmured Daniel, leaning forward.

Bec shook her head and rolled her eyes. 'To Miss Timms.'

He pretended to be shocked. 'I haven't shared those moments with anyone.'

'Daniel! I was at work.'

'I think of you when I'm at work. I think of you all the time.' He dropped his gaze to her lips and felt his cock harden as the tip of her tongue slipped out to moisten the corner.

'Please be serious.'

'I am —'

'But I've faced stronger opposition,' interrupted Ida. 'A loss to him is unthinkable!'

'Who? Sorry I'm late,' apologised Jenny, bustling into the room and smelling of freshly baked scones.

'That English double-barrel-named captain. The head of the Women's Protection League,' said Ida stiffly.

'Ah … Captain Davis-Jones,' said Jenny, nodding her understanding.

'Is he dangerous?' asked Bec, turning to Ida.

'Captain Double-barrel?'

Bec nodded.

'Sends my blood pressure up the scale, but I haven't heard of any physical altercations. Why?'

'This note was delivered yesterday.' Bec slipped a single

sheet of paper from the envelope she'd been tapping against her fingers, then unfolded it and began reading. '*You have all the rights and privileges you need in marriage and motherhood. Desist or burn in hell.* It's unsigned.'

Ida shook her head, as if clearing cobwebs. 'Stuff and nonsense.'

'It sounds personal,' said Jenny.

'Yes, it was addressed to me.'

Daniel studied the sprawling script dominating the envelope. 'Looks like a man's hand. Why do you suspect the captain?'

Bec hesitated. 'I don't. It's just the timing, the debate, his appearance and now this ... it reads as a warning.'

'May I?' Bec passed him the note. The script was upright, smudged in places, the i's meticulously dotted. 'And you have no idea who sent it?' Daniel asked.

'No. Hannah said a young boy raced into reception, stepped around those in line, thrust the envelope at her and raced out as if pursued.'

'Do you think it's connected to the vandalisation of your posters?' Daniel persisted. He wouldn't put it past Bec to omit details, believing she could handle things herself.

'I don't know.'

'We've had criticism about the poster to our office, and a letter to the editor of *The Argus* suggesting the debate would encourage feminism to grow like mushrooms,' said Jenny.

'The usual behaviour from small-minded individuals,' dismissed Ida.

Daniel refolded the paper and slid it into the envelope. 'Can I keep this?'

Bec shrugged. He took that as a yes.

'I'll alert Hannah in case anything else is delivered,' said Jenny. 'And I'd suggest not working back on your own, at least until after the debate next week.'

It surprised Daniel that Bec didn't launch a protest. Why was it all right for Jenny to make suggestions for her safety and not him? He had no doubt Bec's reaction would have been different had he made the proposal. *Infuriating!*

Jenny started moving three chairs into line on one side of the room. 'I'll request a couple of constables for the night of the debate. As insurance. Now, help yourselves to scones, and then let's have a run-through of your arguments.'

Daniel advanced towards Jenny, following his nose.

Ida seated herself in the first of the chairs, her spine straight, obviating the need for the chair's support, and began perusing her notes.

'A reminder that the opening speaker has fifteen minutes, and the other two, eight minutes,' said Jenny. 'And the adjudicator, Councillor Lister, is a stickler for time.'

'Shall I start, then?' asked Ida.

Purely a rhetorical question, Daniel concluded, as Ida launched into her opening. 'Our team will argue that women can equally meet the demands of the role of a tram conductor, and that emotionally, intellectually and physically, females are up to the challenge.'

Daniel, seated in the mock-audience area, turned his chair sideways to focus his attention on Ida's presentation. Bec, seated to his left, was too distracting, licking melted butter from her fingers and excess jam from the corners of her mouth. *Unladylike! And arousing as hell!*

Ida's arguments, in proving the emotional and intellectual strength of females, referenced examples from around the world – some as far back as the last century. She anticipated the affirmative's disparagement of the female temperament – its inconsistency, random tendency to sheer obstinacy and sway by sentiment – agreeing that not every female, or male, was suited to a role serving the public. She cited countries where women already held conductor and supervisory roles, and hinted that perhaps Australia was not looking forward but clinging to the auspices of an earlier era.

Her voice grew in intensity as she moved into her final argument. Cheekily, she contended that a female tram conductor would not herald the end of mankind. Marriage rates wouldn't decline, nor birth-rates, and traditionalists would be glad to know that despite performing a full day's work, females could still perform their biological duty – since they did it already.

Daniel chuckled at the barb, intended no doubt for Captain Double-barrel. 'Well done, Ida. Some very persuasive points.'

She didn't preen. Ida McAuley was a mature campaigner, it would seem, not easily swayed by praise. He knew half-a-dozen men who could benefit from taking a leaf from her book.

'It needs further refinement,' she countered. 'Not my best … *yet.*'

'Do you think it would be helpful to narrow the definition of "female" as it pertains to the debate?' asked Bec. 'We're not suggesting that all females could do the role.'

Ida nodded. 'They would need to meet the requirements.'

'But if they did, they could apply,' said Bec.

'I'll strengthen the points around suitability,' said Ida.

Jenny patted the back of the chair beside Ida. 'Bec, you're next.'

Daniel was well acquainted with Bec's arguments, having helped her formulate the points to be made about the physicality of the role and the rebuttals of the anticipated affirmative's arguments, over the past couple of weeks. Their time together hadn't been all pleasure. He focused on her style. He'd learned the hard way that this was as important as a sound argument. Her passion was clear. It showed in the strength of her voice, and she remembered to vary her speed and tone. But she was too reliant on her notes. *Perhaps there had been too much pleasure ...* They'd have to work on that before Thursday.

'Bravo! I especially liked the fact that you brought in your own experience from the two days,' Ida said as she clapped. 'I'd suggest practising without your notes, Rebecca, for the remainder of the week to come.'

'And don't be afraid to make eye contact with the audience,' added Jenny. 'You didn't look at me once.'

Bec nodded. 'Thanks. I feel better having had a proper run-through. I'll work on your suggestions.'

'Daniel, your turn,' invited Jenny. 'Although, I realise that besides summarising the team's arguments, whatever you prepare will need to be adapted to negate the other team's points.'

'I'm still working on the closing. I'd like to incorporate a rebuttal that ties in the financial sustainability of the tramways with the enterprise or daring to recruit females into the role —'

'Isn't that demeaning?' Bec challenged. 'It suggests the value of conductresses is as a magnet for men.'

'But it is quite ... playful,' insisted Ida. 'I like it!'

'And a strong debate is entertaining – a marriage of fact

and emotion, with good old-fashioned humour,' said Daniel. He didn't allow his gaze to linger on Bec, but realised his words, although not orchestrated, described the future he was looking to create with her. Time would tell, of course. But how patient was he expected to be? He couldn't be the only one in their relationship making concessions.

Ida returned his thoughts to the present. 'But it requires a hook in either mine or Rebecca's points. You can't introduce anything new.'

Daniel nodded. 'That's right.'

'I think it would be best to incorporate it in Bec's,' offered Jenny. 'That way, it will be front of mind for their third speaker.'

'The trick will be to bait the hook ...' Daniel trailed off.

'What about if I include suggestions to invest in technological and process innovations? Or upgrades that would reduce the physicality of the job?'

'Such as the electrification,' suggested Daniel.

'Or a different design for the cash bag and ticketing. They might pick on the associated costs,' said Bec.

'That's clever,' enthused Jenny. 'But is it too subtle?'

'Not if we choose the right language.' Daniel rested his chin on his hand. 'It might be just the thing.'

'You work on that, and we'll meet up again ... Tuesday? Hopefully, Daniel will have finished his closing,' said Jenny, coming to her feet. 'Thanks, everyone, good work.'

Daniel was pleased. He was enjoying the collaboration. The women weren't as competitive as his colleagues in the Public Works. No, that wasn't true. Ida, Bec and Jenny sorely wanted to win. Maybe it was just that their ambition was targeted towards the opposition and not each other. It struck him as an interesting observation. Of course, he was also impatient for the debate to be over so that he and Bec could pursue a collaboration on more intimate initiatives.

CHAPTER 35

Sunday 6 September 1925

'I feel ridiculous!' Bec groused, sweeping her arm wide to take in the surrounding gardens. 'I'm practising making eye contact with trees. Oh God, saying it out loud makes it sound even worse.'

'You have to admit they're an attentive audience,' Daniel argued from his position on a bench a few yards away. 'Apart from the palm rustling and the pine-tree whispering, there've been no disapproving looks or outcries.'

Bec shook her head. 'I'm not sure this is helping.'

'One more time. And remember to look at me, too.'

'It would help if you wore an academic expression on your face, instead of ... whatever that is.'

Daniel gave her a wolfish grin, before schooling it into a professional demeanour.

'Better.'

'And don't forget your reward at the end,' Daniel reminded her.

Bec's heart gave a thump. Daniel had described in whispered confidences what she could expect if she was diligent in her debate preparations. He hadn't even touched her, and she'd become warm and restless. She even had to press the tops of her thighs together. 'You may have hit on the problem.'

'It's proving too much of a distraction?'

'Not motivational enough.'

He lunged towards her, but she'd anticipated his move and held out an arm to stop him, palm facing up. 'Please return to your seat. We can negotiate terms following my rehearsal.'

Daniel stood his ground.

She stretched to her full height and pointed behind him. 'Your seat.'

He moved back to the bench, crossing one leg over his knee and stretching his arms along the back rail.

Bec took a deep breath, pushed the sleeves of her knitted sweater to her elbows, threw her notes onto the grass and addressed the nearest elm tree, remembering to make eye contact. Before the halfway mark of her arguments, rain touched her cheeks. So light, she felt as if she was being blessed by a butterfly – the moisture evaporating almost on contact.

Her eyes roved the back row of shrubbery before settling on Daniel. Gone was his relaxed position. He was leaning forward, forearms resting on his knees, appearing to focus on every word ... or her ... or both. Difficult to tell, as his face was a study of neutrality. Spearing the Moreton Bay Fig with a stern look, Bec delivered her concluding remarks.

A slow clap heralded the progress of Daniel from his seat towards her. 'That was a one-hundred-and-fifty-percent improvement on last time. Well done.'

Bec was pleased. Her confidence was growing with each run-through. Bending to pick up her notes, she straightened and raised her face to him. 'And my reward?'

He tapped the tip of her nose. 'Lunch.'

Bec dropped her chin, feeling foolish. It seemed her mother's cooking was a more attractive option than she was. *What about his promises of never-ending kisses and ...?*

'Come on.'

Straightening her shoulders, she fell into step beside him. They passed beneath the spreading boughs of the fig tree, zigzagging to avoid those reaching for the ground, weighed down by glossy green foliage. He hadn't even reached for her hand. Maybe he was growing tired of their relationship. She didn't think she'd been a pushover. Should she have held out for longer? After all, the chase was where the excitement was, not the catch.

'Maybe we could start with a snack.'

She marched on. 'You don't want to ruin your appetite.'

His arm snaked around her waist, and he gathered her to him – her back to his front. 'Maybe a morsel, then.'

Cool air kissed the back of her neck as Daniel brushed the weight of her hair to the side. A warm breath hovered, as if scouting the contours of her skin.

'We'll be late.'

'What for?'

Bec rolled her eyes. Of course, the effect was lost on Daniel. 'Lunch. You said —'

'That was your reward. My diligence to your preparation needs rewarding, too.'

When his lips finally landed, a sigh escaped her. He was greedy, nuzzling the top of her spine before trailing kisses down the side of her neck. Her notes fell to the ground, and she squirmed against the arm anchoring her to him, eager to turn around.

In response, he crisscrossed the other across her abdomen, a thumb circling her belly button through the ribbing of her cable knit.

His attentions multiplied the restlessness that the first touch of his lips had initiated. Bec slipped a hand behind her, between them, and stroked the insistent surge in the small of her back. His hips bucked, but the symphony of lips and tongue continued.

Another rush of cold air, this time lower, was followed by the warmth of Daniel's hands skimming her ribcage to cradle her breasts in his palms. A deep moan escaped her. She arched her neck and let her head rest against his shoulder. His hands felt ... wonderful. It wasn't all about the chase ... it seemed capture brought its own rewards.

Daniel was in trouble. He didn't want to stop. The bite-sized pieces of Bec he'd stolen up to now were no longer enough. He circled her nipples, wishing he could reward the salute they gave him with his lips and tongue. She was so responsive, even more so after having worked herself into a high dudgeon.

He trailed his palms back down her ribcage and rested them at the indent of her waist. Someone had to regain control. This was a public garden, and he didn't want them discovered by a curious local or tourist. And what if her father came looking for them ...

'Easy, sweetheart,' he crooned against her ear.

He gave her a moment before spinning her around to face him. He wanted ... needed to see her eyes. They were smoky-grey whirlpools, drawing him in. *Maybe not such a good idea.*

. Daniel steeled himself, taking a deep breath, and smoothed her sweater back into place. He'd almost blurted out the *L* word. But something had stopped him from diving over the precipice. It was too soon. Not for him; he sensed Bec needed more time. He wasn't sure how much he could afford her, but her father's advice about perseverance seemed wise.

Bec's trust in him was growing, her vulnerability dissolving. For his part, he no longer wanted to turn her into the type of woman who would be satisfied with marriage and motherhood. The sentiment in the letter she'd received had disgusted him. *Had he been at risk of turning into such a man before Bec?* He needed to find an opportunity to convey his changed thinking. It wasn't something he could just blurt out as a 'by the way ...'.

'Still hungry?'

Daniel's gaze followed the path of his hands earlier before returning to her face. 'More than ever.' He was inordinately pleased to see her pupils dilate. Hopefully, she was in no doubt that his appetite was for her alone.

'So, how are things, Daniel?'

It was mid-afternoon, and Bec's father had accompanied him on his walk home. Daniel realised that the man's strategy was as much about offering advice as keeping his finger on the progression of Daniel's romance with his daughter. Although if pressed, it was part of his daily constitutional.

'I'm dating your daughter.'

'I figured that must have been what brought the colour to her cheeks.'

'I'm serious about marrying her.'

Nodding, his future father-in-law laid a hand on his shoulder. 'I don't doubt your intentions, Daniel. What about Bec?'

'We haven't talked about it.'

'Give her time ... but not too much,' came the sage advice. 'I love my daughter, but like her mother – another intelligent woman – she can accumulate a store full of excuses as to why she can't move forward.'

Daniel nodded. He wondered what Bec's reaction would be to his latest task – to open talks with the owner of the Marney Motorbus Line about their plans to employ additional female bus conductors. The state was trying to head off a major confrontation with Trades Hall and the sacrifice of a few female jobs was considered justifiable collateral. Who was he kidding, he knew what her reaction would be. Knew she would count his involvement against him.

'Well, son, looks like, as usual, you have a lot of thinking to do. I'll leave you to it. You have my support.'

Daniel shook the man's hand in farewell and returned to his musings.

He was still evolving his strategy, but he had a half-baked idea around convincing all parties that if the females were employed under the same arrangements as the men

– including pay – there wasn't any concern to be had. He realised it was a vastly different strategy than he would have employed a month ago.

His life – his views and opinions, his everything – was quickly dividing itself into 'before Bec' and 'after Bec'. And if pressed, he preferred the model of himself after Bec.

The *new* Daniel would make the opportunity to have a discussion with Bec, both about what he'd been tasked with, and more importantly, how he felt about it. The *old* Daniel hesitated.

Their relationship was still too new, their emotions unseasoned. Was now the right time to test their strength? Eventually, Bec would grow to understand that in his career, he couldn't always choose his battles. That didn't mean he would abandon the fight, but that it would take longer.

He couldn't risk opening up the discussion now. They had a debate to win. He'd talk to her after they'd won.

CHAPTER 36

Tuesday 8 September 1925

'This arrived for you today.'

Bec's father dropped an envelope addressed in a familiar bold, flourishing script onto the table beside her plate, and continued to his chair.

'Well, aren't you going to open it?'

Bec continued buttering her bread. She didn't want to even touch it, let alone open it. 'Maybe later.'

Her father continued. 'There's no stamp, so it's been hand delivered.'

Bec was aware of the glance that passed between her parents and then settled on her, but she refused to look up.

Then it was her mother's turn. 'Bad news, love?'

She swallowed before meeting her mother's concerned gaze. 'Why would you think that?'

'You're as pale as the tablecloth.'

'Oh.' Bec reached up to pinch her right cheek. 'Better?'

Her father carefully placed his cutlery on either side of his plate and leaned towards her – never a good sign. 'Enough. Either you open it, or *I will.*'

Bec sighed. 'From the writing, I suspect it's another letter bullying me to withdraw from the debate.'

Her father snatched up the envelope and ripped it open. '*Another* letter?'

'I received the first on Friday.'

Pushing back her chair, her mother moved to stand beside her husband. 'Why didn't you say something?'

'We agreed it was nonsense.'

'*We?*' chorused her parents.

'Daniel, Ida, Jenny and I. It was delivered to work by a message boy.'

'*Freedom, like fire, is a good servant, but a poor master. Populate or perish,*' her father read aloud then proceeded to examine both the envelope and letter. 'It's unsigned.'

Bec nodded. 'Like the first one. It suggested I desist or burn in hell.'

'A man's hand,' declared her father.

'Yes, that's what Daniel guessed.'

Her mother returned to her seat. 'This man is no better than a coward.'

'Maybe, Rachel. But I don't like it. Not one bit. First the posters and now this.'

Bec crossed her arms. 'I'm not giving whoever it is the satisfaction of withdrawing.'

'Of course not,' agreed her mother. 'We wouldn't expect you to.'

'Grandma always used to say that such behaviour was a sad commentary on the morals and mental processes of the man, not the woman.'

Bec's father raised his eyes to the heavens. 'God save me from generations of independent women. Have any of the other participants received a letter?'

'Not Daniel. And Ida didn't mention anything.'

Her father drummed his fingers on the table. 'So, it's personal. And they know where you live. That suggests they're local.'

Bec's stomach – in fact, her whole insides – spasmed. Her suspicions were crystallising.

'Sherlock Holmes has got nothing on you, Edward. Now, the question is who?'

Her father levelled his gaze on her. 'You know who I'm thinking of, don't you?'

Bec nodded.

'When did you suspect?'

Her mouth firmed. 'Just now, as you made sense of things.'

'*Who?*' her mother's exasperated voice increased in volume a notch.

Bec and her father spoke as one. 'William Tailor.'

'He baled me up at the pharmacist last Sunday. Ranting and raving about the evils of liberal ideas and a lot more.'

'He's been in my ear at the shop at every opportunity. That poster of Bec has really set him off. I slapped a hot towel across his mouth last week to give me some peace.'

'And he accused me of being as wanton as my grandmother. I wanted to slap him. How could he say such a thing, Mum?'

Her parents exchanged a look.

'They had a fling when you were about five years of age.'

Bec shuddered. 'No!'

'He wasn't the curmudgeon that you know today. He was dashing. A confirmed bachelor – fortyish – with a business that bankrolled a lavish lifestyle.' Her mother shook her head as if she too found it difficult to marry the man he'd become with what he had been. 'Adelaide was flirtatious, attractive and six years widowed. She wanted some fun. To make up for lost time.'

'She would have been ... *old*.'

Bec's mother frowned. 'Fifty-four. My age.'

Bec was reeling. Her grandma and William Tailor? She scrunched up her face in distaste. She couldn't even imagine them being seen together, let alone flirting, or ... *Urgh ... in the act.* It was worse than the image of her parents, and yet she knew they'd done it at least once. But her grandma?

'It gets better as you get older.'

'*Mum!* Not at the dinner table.'

'Well, it's not like you've eaten anything. At least finish the piece of bread you buttered.'

Bec obliged, even though it tasted of sawdust. Anything to change the subject. A mouthful of water washed the last of the bread down her throat. 'What happened.'

Her father's matter-of-fact tone cut in. 'She got bored. He wouldn't accept it was over. She found someone else ...'

Bec's eyes widened. Her grandmother was ahead of her time.

'... Tailor was humiliated.'

Her mother sighed. 'They never would have made a suitable match anyway, even if Adelaide had been looking for a new husband. *Which she wasn't.* Both were stubborn.'

'Rejection turned to bitterness and to ... well, whatever this is.' Her father slapped his hand over the note where it lay on the table.

'But he got married,' said Bec.

'Yes, but he was never the same,' said her mother. 'And

when his wife left with the youngest ... well, he was served with another helping of humiliation.'

'Back to this note.' Bec's father tapped the offending envelope. 'Tomorrow, I'll talk to the local senior constable about our suspicions. He's only new, transferred from Hamilton, but I've heard he's a stickler for old-fashioned policing.'

'I still don't understand why he'd target me. I was only, what age did you say five, when all this happened?' Her mother nodded.

Her father pursed his lips. 'I don't know, love. It seems he's declared war against what he calls "the corruption of women's morals" and this debate, and by extension you are in his sights. Until this is over, you're not to take unnecessary risks. I can't ground you, but I would if I thought I could.'

Bec nodded. 'I'll be careful.'

CHAPTER 37

Wednesday 9 September 1925

Bec stopped a passer-by and asked him for the time. One o'clock. She was half an hour early for her appointment with Mr Marney, owner of the motorbus company.

She looked around her with interest. The terminus and main office were situated on a busy intersection, and although the frontage seemed small, she noted the land behind the brick building looked extensive. She must remember to ask how many buses they ran.

The smell of petrol permeated the air and she wrinkled her nose. She doubted bus conductors were required to spend a lot of time here, so the odour was hopefully only a small irritant. Thankfully, Miss Cooper – Merle – didn't strike her as a missish female, so she didn't expect it would pose a problem. The woman had welcomed the suggestion of the potential role, adding it would be a pleasant change to be out on the road. Bec hoped she felt the same way after a shift in Melbourne's changeable weather.

But there wasn't much of that today. Spring had opened its arms and Bec welcomed the mild sunshine. A fresh northerly wind whipped at the accordion pleats of her skirt, where they peered from the bottom of her coat.

Noting it was twenty minutes past the hour, she approached the door to what she assumed was the office just as it was flung open, and two men headed out onto the footpath.

'Daniel?'

'Bec! What are you doing here?'

'Ah ... I have an interview.' Bec inclined her head towards the gentleman beside Daniel. 'Mr Chalmers.'

'Hello again, Miss Cross.' Whipping off his hat, he stroked the ends of his snowy-white moustache with the fingers of his other hand. 'It seems congratulations are in order.'

Bec's head whipped back to Daniel. *Was that colour staining his cheeks?*

'Um ... thank you, sir,' she said.

'Daniel, I'll give you a few moments and meet you in the car. Miss Cross, I hope to see you again soon.'

Bec smiled at the older man before turning her attention to Daniel. 'What are you doing here?'

'Some ... business. Ongoing discussions, that sort of thing.'

Bec frowned at Daniel's guarded explanation. 'And why is he congratulating me?'

'Um ... I told him we were dating.'

'You did? Why?'

Daniel pushed his hand through his hair. 'You said you had an interview?'

So he was trying to side-track her, was he? Two could play that game. 'Yes. For the role of bus conductor.'

'What? When were you going to —'

'It seems Mr Chalmers is growing impatient.' Bec smiled,

interrupting the likely barrage of questions Daniel looked like he was about to deliver. 'You don't want to keep him waiting. And I don't want to make a poor first impression on Mr Marney.' And with that, she kissed his cheek, opened the door and sailed through, the sight of Daniel's dumbfounded expression etched in her mind.

Bec walked up the steps of the Russell Street headquarters in a state of emotional ambivalence. She was not unused to experiencing an excess of opinion, but facing an inability to take a position was new.

Mr Marney had been down to earth with a dry sense of humour. He'd seen first-hand the capability of women during his time fighting in Europe, and was not, unlike many of his counterparts, unwilling to expand their involvement in paid work.

She'd left with a cautious agreement for Miss Cooper to attend an interview on Friday. The owner, with a few judiciously chosen words, had intimated that he was facing challenges on several fronts – government policy on routes and licences, and Trades Hall on the employment of women – which, if left unresolved, would have adverse financial implications. Bec interpreted that to mean Merle's application, even if successful, could be short-lived. Daniel's appearance at the bus company's premises was not coincidental. She'd bet money on it.

Bec drifted into the office she shared with Elsie. It was empty, and she remembered she was accompanying the Industrial Officer on factory visits as a follow-up to recent placements. Grateful not to have to display a cheerfulness that she didn't feel, Bec closed the door, threw her coat and hat on a nearby chair and paced. She did her best thinking while moving.

What was Daniel's involvement? Was it on routes and licences or the more damning issue of restricting women's work choices? He'd been so eloquent on Monday afternoon in delivering the third speaker's arguments that Ida had petitioned him to join her organisation. At the time, Bec had been entertained at how he'd circumvented her offer, claiming to be able to do more for women's causes if not tied to any one in particular. Was his apparent endorsement for equality just a charade? She reminded herself that it was a debate, after all. There was no rule demanding a speaker's rhetoric equate to their actual views.

Her confusion, though, ran deeper than the sincerity of Daniel's oratory. On Monday night as he'd walked her home after dining with his parents, Eliza and Alex, he'd spoken of the changes she'd wrought in him. He'd teased that he was no longer satisfied with a girlfriend he couldn't match wits with ... a partner without the courage of her convictions ... or a wife who restricted herself to matters of the home.

Her hopes had blazed as if struck by lightning. But she'd batted back his observation, joking that an alliance with a doting female would have many mutual advantages that perhaps one with a sassier outlook would not.

Daniel had turned, gathered her in his arms and kissed her soundly. 'That hasn't been ... and isn't my experience,' he'd murmured when they'd both come up for breath. 'I'm a recent convert for strong-minded, bold and pert.'

Bec shook her head. Had she interpreted his words to

mean what she'd wanted to hear? *Did he really want her — opinions and all?* She threw herself into her chair in a most unladylike pose and gazed up as if the answers she sought were written on the ceiling.

A knock at the door had her sitting upright and crossing one knee over the other. 'Yes?'

A familiar pair of green eyes under a straight fringe peered around the door. 'Are you hiding?' asked her best friend.

'No ... yes. Just come in, will you, and shut the door.'

Head cocked, Eliza did as asked, before advancing into the room and perching on the edge of Bec's desk. 'What's up?'

'I think ... I may ... like your brother. A lot.'

'And that's a problem?'

'And I think he's acting for the state and maybe the unions, to displace female bus conductors with men.'

'*That's* a problem.'

Bec was relieved at the conviction she heard in Eliza's voice. She had been concerned that her and Daniel's budding romance would spoil the strength of her friendship with Eliza. 'Thank you.'

'We'll always be friends first, Bec,' Eliza said, giving Bec's hand a quick squeeze. 'How do you know this?' She waved her hand in the air. 'The business about the conductors, I mean, although my true interest lies in your first declaration.'

Bec told her about the visit to the bus line, Daniel's appearance, Mr Marney's intimations and her subsequent suspicions. 'Daniel's presence doesn't sound accidental, does it?' Bec urged. 'And Minister Chalmers was there, too.'

Eliza worried her bottom lip. 'You're right to have

misgivings. But one thing I've learned from growing up around a father in local politics is that things aren't always as they seem.' Eliza slid back onto the top of the desk and let her feet dangle. 'I remember one time our letterbox was blown up with a firecracker because the local newspaper reported incorrectly that Dad had voted against ...' She shrugged. 'Some resolution.' At Bec's raised eyebrows, Eliza defended her inability to recall the details. 'I was only six at the time and more concerned that the postman wouldn't know where to deliver my birthday cards.'

'Your point being? Not that it's not a delightful, if incomplete, story.'

'Ask Daniel directly what's going on. There will be more to this.'

'I did. Business and ongoing discussions was his explanation.'

'Maybe he couldn't say any more because his boss was present.'

Bec shook her finger. 'And that's the other thing. Mr Chalmers congratulated me, looking very pleased about something. Daniel said he'd told him we were dating. Who does that? I haven't rushed to tell Elsie.'

'Well, you're just going to tie yourself up in knots, speculating. You'll have to ask him.'

'He'll think I don't trust him,' Bec groaned. 'And it's one of our ground rules.'

It was Eliza's turn to raise her eyebrows.

'You know, relationship ground rules. Don't pretend you don't have them. One of ours is trust. It seemed a good idea when the shoe was on the other foot ... when Daniel was getting worked up over Jim.'

'What's the alternative? I refuse to lose a prospective sister-in-law because it might offend my brother that you're challenging his loyalties. It's not as if *you've* done anything wrong.'

Bec grinned.

'Have you?'

'I may have led him to believe I was applying for the role of a bus conductor.'

CHAPTER 38

Thursday 10 September 1925

Daniel was beyond frustrated. Bec was avoiding him.

Yesterday, he'd worked late into the evening to prepare a proposed response for Chalmers, to the employment of female bus conductors, making it impossible to catch Bec – either at work or home. And he'd spent much of today talking through the other matter on the table, that of bus licences. At times like this, he longed to be a humble engineer rather than being groomed for the complexities of political service.

On arrival at the YWCA, he'd sought her out. After a perfunctory kiss to his cheek, she'd stepped around him to continue with the set-up of the hall for the debate. And now, standing opposite him as they chatted to her parents, she was conversing with his chin.

When Jenny joined the small party, Daniel muttered an apology, careless of what anyone might think, and compelled Bec down the corridor.

'Where are we ...?'

He checked the room beyond the first doorway and pulled her in behind him. The distinct smell of leather mixed with paper, ink and glue – not dissimilar to the aroma of unwashed socks – filled his nose. Nostalgia for the simplicity of his university days swept over him.

'You're avoiding me,' he said without preamble, closing the library door and leaning back against it for good measure.

'It hasn't been hard. We've both been busy.'

Daniel was glad Bec wasn't the kind of woman inclined towards evasiveness. Although, he hadn't always considered this to be one of her attributes.

'Why?'

'What's your involvement with Mr Marney?'

'I can't talk about that. Discussions are delicately poised.'

'Humph! I bet they are. And how many women will lose their jobs?'

'Bec, things aren't always what they seem —'

She held up her hand. 'And who tells their boss who they're dating?'

'Chalmers is a devoted husband and takes a personal interest in his employees.' Even to his own ears, his explanation sounded lame.

'I don't believe you, he —'

'My turn. What's this about becoming a bus conductor?'

Crossing her arms, Bec raised her chin. 'I've organised an interview.'

Scowling, Daniel pushed himself off the door and stepped towards her. 'Without talking it over with me?'

Bec's grey eyes held his steadily. 'You don't decide what I do or don't do. And as my mother would say, *people in glass houses shouldn't throw stones.*'

Daniel swore under his breath at a knock on the door.

'Daniel? Bec? Are you in there? We're starting in ten minutes.'

Bec recovered first, striding forward and opening the door to reveal Jenny's concerned face.

'Everything all right? No, don't answer that – I can see it isn't. Just promise me you won't fight it out on stage.'

'I promise,' said Bec, walking out into the corridor. 'Daniel has given me a timely reminder that winning is what matters. It'll guarantee my funding and his promotion. Anything else is incidental.'

Daniel sucked in a breath as Bec headed back the way they'd come. *What did she mean?* The debate wasn't more important than their relationship. But they'd all worked so hard. Bec needed to be reasonable.

'Daniel?'

'Give me a minute and I'll be there,' he said, giving Jenny a tight smile. He was relieved when she nodded, turned and followed Bec.

Daniel closed his eyes and took more deep breaths. *Damn his boss.* It was a hell of a time for him to turn garrulous. Normally, he was hard pressed to offer more than a civil greeting. The stupid thing was, Chalmers hadn't even pried. Daniel had volunteered the information, buoyed by Bec's reaction to his confidences on Monday evening. He'd been as surprised as Chalmers to hear the words escaping from his lips. He couldn't ever remember revealing the state of his personal relationships to a colleague before, let alone his boss.

Daniel looked at his watch. Time to take the stage – he had a debate to win and then a heart to secure.

Bec paused next to the front row of seats, behind Ida, waiting to be introduced by the chairwoman, the YWCA's very own Jenny Sherman. She was inviting the affirmative team to make their way to the stage – Messer's T. Blake, S. Clerke and Captain Davis-Jones.

She scanned the crowd, looking for a friendly face amongst those seated and those still arriving. The event had been a sellout. Many of the staff had stayed on in support, and she returned their smiles of encouragement. Her eyes locked onto Jim's handsome face. Seated behind Eliza and Alex, towards the front, he gave her a cheery salute. She winked at him. *Had he forged a new relationship since their split?* There was no sign of Queenie, but a woman about her own age, with a loose bob of cinnamon-brown curls, appeared to be more than a chance seating.

The skin at her nape prickled, and she turned her head. Daniel. He'd evidently seen the exchange if the stare he sent Jim was any indication. Bec decided she was a mass of contradictions and wondered if she knew herself at all. Daniel's show of possessiveness, rather than infuriating her, had warmed her core. Yet she resented his almost proprietorial expectation to be consulted about her non-existent interview for the role as a bus conductor. She ignored the fact that his interpretation was because of her fabrication. *It was the principle that mattered!*

'You look gorgeous,' Eliza whispered from her vantage point in the audience two seats in.

Bec smiled. She knew she looked good – the drop-waisted dress, accented by a decorative buckle of paste diamante stones at her hip, emphasised her slim silhouette. And the pink silk-velvet fabric caressed her skin.

Alex's eyes flicked over her from where he sat beside Eliza and Bec heard a low growl. Evidently, even best friends were not immune to Daniel's proprietorial affliction.

At Jenny's introduction, Bec climbed the short flight of steps onto the stage – glad that her legs functioned as required – and took her seat at the table designated for their team.

Daniel's leg brushed hers as he slid into the chair on her right. Bec gazed out at the audience, avoiding the possibility of locking eyes with him. It was a mistake. From up here, the rows of people seemed to stretch endlessly, and still more chairs were being hastily sought for those ticket holders who remained standing. She swallowed.

'It always helps me to think of the audience wearing nothing but their undergarments,' Ida murmured.

Bec disguised her laugh under a discreet cough as the adjudicator, Councillor T. Lister, was introduced.

'Welcome. It is fantastic to see so many faces here tonight. No doubt the mild weather has helped,' Jenny greeted those gathered. 'You are in for a treat. The topic for debate? That women cannot meet the emotional, intellectual and physical demands required for employment as tram conductors.'

Above the applause, a voice boomed, 'They can't!'

Heads turned. Bec scoured the rows for the heckler, to no avail. The voice had sounded familiar.

'There's always one,' Ida muttered. 'Remember, you have the stage. They don't.'

Bec nodded.

'I'll now call the first speaker for the affirmative to the rostrum, Mr Theo Blake.'

Bec found little in the man's grey-striped worsted suit to distinguish him from many of those seated in the audience.

That was until he spoke, his deep voice immediately commanding her attention.

'Focus on what he says, not how,' whispered Daniel, placing a pencil in her fingers where they rested on the table. 'He's a skilled storyteller, but so were The Brothers Grimm.'

Bec nodded.

'... and so, each of the demands ... emotional, intellectual and physical are best examined both in their own context, but also from an economic and social perspective ...'

Clever. Introducing additional elements to support their case. Bec noted Ida was scribbling furiously, no doubt already planning either an opposition to the expansion of the topic or a firm rebuttal.

'...our team won't dwell on the potential that the role of tram conductor has for the masculinisation of women ...'

Snap!

Bec handed Ida another pencil.

'... nor the threat to gender norms.' The speaker paused. 'That is for a different debate.'

'Well, maybe he can now get back to *this* debate,' Ida muttered.

Daniel grinned.

'Relax, Ida,' Bec whispered. 'Don't get caught up in his theatrics. We knew they'd be a tough opposition.'

Ida gave her a brief smile. Noticeably, her shoulders dropped from around her ears and Bec could hear her take a calming breath.

The rest of the speaker's arguments were of little surprise, apart from the ending, where he once again referred to a woman's distinctive set of skills being best suited for domestic life.

Jenny rose. 'Thank you, Speaker Blake. I'd now like to call Miss Ida McAuley, as first speaker for the negative.'

A round of applause, punctuated by a loud '*Boo*', preceded Ida to the rostrum. 'Thank you, Madam Chair.' She faced the audience, warrior like, but with a smile. 'I hope that you,' she began with a wide arm gesture encompassing the total environs of the hall, 'were not as perplexed as I by the affirmative speaker's tangential train of thought. While my colleagues and I would happily speak to the broader role of women in society, that is not the topic under debate. Rather, we are here to argue that the role of tram conductor is not too emotionally demanding ... not too intellectually challenging ... nor too physically exacting for women.'

After each slight pause, Ida's voice rose. *Bravo*, thought Bec, hoping that she could also channel her passion to great effect. She wasn't as experienced as Ida, but Daniel had been generous with his time tutoring her efforts. He'd been generous in other areas also, but they were less pertinent to her performance tonight.

Unbidden, the question arose as to how authentic his attraction to her was. *Was that something else engineered?* To her, Daniel was a magnet. But what if his responses were part of an act? It happened. Usually, however, there was an advantage to be had. And Bec was neither wealthy nor titled. She pushed her doubts away; she needed to concentrate.

Ida was rebutting the affirmative's suggestion that the heavier weight of the male brain equated to a higher intellectual capability. Citing medical evidence from the last century, she noted that the brain weight of some lunatics had been found to be considerably heavier than those of sane people.

'Is the affirmative suggesting they possessed keener minds?' Ida asked. 'Perhaps a higher arithmetical agility?'

Bec watched what appeared to be genuine smiles cross the audience's faces at Ida's rhetoric.

'The opposing team has argued that women are irrational, unpredictable, unfathomable and therefore emotionally unsuited to a role that serves the public. Again, I turn to science, which has observed just as many men displaying the same capacities. Further, reports suggest such capacities are distributed equally over mankind.'

Responding to the murmurs that her statement generated, Ida paused before continuing. 'Perhaps, this is best illustrated by a story of a woman with a squint who came to live in a new community. Unfamiliar to such an infliction, the townsfolk interpreted the defect in her vision as a suspicious way of looking at people, and she was therefore considered dishonest and unable to be trusted. Ignorance can be cruel.' Ida once again paused. 'Perhaps, the emotional characteristics attributed solely to women are born of the same vice. That of ignorance. Thank you.'

Ida returned to her seat amidst loud applause – and a persistent dissent – receiving Bec and Daniel's congratulations with apparent equanimity, although the light of battle in her eyes suggested she was pleased with her effort.

The second speaker for the affirmative, Mr Stewart Clerke, had a loud and unattractive voice. Perhaps it came from having to battle within the union ranks. He was, however, persuasive, once Bec tuned into his arguments, his choice of language driving a strong emotional response.

She made copious notes, assisted on one side by Ida and

on the other by Daniel. At one point, he enveloped her, one arm across the back of her chair, the other leaning on the table, his head inches from her own, as he perused her notes. She breathed in his scent – warmed citrus – resisting the impulse to turn her head and touch her lips to his. It irked her that the pull of attraction for her was strong, yet Daniel's demeanour suggested he was oblivious to his effect on her. *How the tables had turned.* She was glad when he sat upright and her focus returned to the rostrum.

'Thank you, Speaker Clerke.'

And then it was her turn. Walking to the lectern, she remembered Ida's words from before. Facing the audience, she smiled as an image of Elsie Timms in red-coloured silk flashed into her mind. Her gaze passed quickly over her parents, not wanting to even entertain their choice or colour of undergarment, and took a deep breath.

'Physicality, the opposing team would argue, is the greater reason for women's unsuitability for the role as a tram conductor. Of course, already there are men, many men, who do not meet the exacting standards required by the tramways. That is a matter of public record. Our team are not asking – not even suggesting – that these same stringent requirements do not apply equally to women.'

A short wave of applause echoed across the audience, from which Bec drew confidence and her voice strengthened.

'Physicality is not, as many would suggest, solely about strength. It is about those elements that cannot be classified as mental, emotional or spiritual. By its very definition, it ranges from agility and immunity, to appearance and everything in between. Women live longer than men and contract disease less readily. So says the Bureau of Census and Statistics. And nature has ensured we are better equipped to handle wear and tear. As you all know, women play a far more active part in the business of reproduction.'

Bec let her glance rest briefly on Jim, imagining boxers with red ship anchors, before launching her next point.

'Women's superiority in enduring pain, and in the rapidity of convalescence, are matters of common knowledge. And the women of today are stronger, the outcome of exercise and sport. Ask any jeweller. Apparently, the size of our fingers and arms have become larger and more toned.'

Bec was enjoying herself. Her arguments were drawing quiet laughter – and not just from her family and best friend. She'd taken Daniel's advice to focus on her points and key rebuttals rather than speed through a shopping list of items.

Before closing, she cheekily added, 'Most women, if attendances at the recent Fleet week events can be believed, love dancing and are relatively good at it. The best floor for dancing is that of a cable car. What woman would not enjoy the daily opportunity to do this for a living – to jazz, glide or aerial waltz as the tram rounds a curve. A woman is hardened to experiencing the odd elbow, bumped nose and trodden toes – these do not deter us. Women are used to soothing tempers and moody outbursts, all while calculating the cost to our shoes, stockings and dresses. Thank you.'

A pernicious voice rang out, 'Utter claptrap,' before being drowned out by the loud clapping from the contingent of YWCA staff and the general audience.

Raising her chin, Bec walked back across the stage and resumed her seat.

'Good job, Rebecca,' applauded Ida.

'Just as we practised,' murmured Daniel in her ear.

Bec busied herself with straightening her notes, wondering if her cheeks were as pink as her dress.

'They're probably a shade darker.'

At her indrawn breath, he chuckled and leaned back in his chair.

Bec's attention was diverted to Ida's stiffened posture. Captain Davis-Jones had moved purposefully to the lectern and was now holding it captive, his hands gripping either side. She put his presence and booming voice down to his military training. His summary of his team's arguments was clear and concise, if somewhat dry. His rebuttals carried the tone of his antipathy towards women occupying any role other than matrimony and motherhood. Bec gritted her teeth.

As he delivered his final point, wild cheering broke out, and ten or so men and women rose to their feet to applaud. Two women, sitting at the back, waved placards. 'THE HOME – A WOMAN'S TRUE CALLING' and 'FEMINISM – ALIENATING TO REAL WOMEN'.

Bec laid a hand over Ida's white knuckles, and for the first time wondered if William Tailor was seated somewhere out there. Her father had briefed the local constabulary, and they'd undertaken to make enquiries. No other letters had followed, and Bec had pushed the warning to the back of her mind – until now.

'Thank you. Please resume your seats,' directed Jenny from the podium.

The two women stood defiantly, holding their banners higher. And *him*, William Tailor. That's why the voice was familiar.

'What is it?' Daniel asked.

Bec shook her head. 'Nothing.'

'Ladies. Your seats.'

Bec had never become used to associating Jenny's commanding voice with her diminutive stature. Her intonation implied consequences, and all three huffily resumed their seats. The sight of two constables striding into the hall couldn't have hurt, either.

'Our final speaker for this evening is Mr Daniel Sinclair.'

Standing, Daniel gathered his notes, pushed back his chair and buttoned his suit coat. 'Time to have some fun.'

'Good luck,' Bec and Ida called in unison, but he was already halfway to centrestage.

Bec leaned her elbow on the table, rested her chin on her hand and drank in the sight of him. Not for Daniel the popular pinstripes of his contemporaries. He wore grey wool, with the new wide leg style of pant – the Oxford bags – which hid the strength and tone of his legs. *I know that ... how?* She smiled, her eyes already on an upward trajectory to his face in profile. A prominent forehead she'd read recently showed intelligence, combined with a firm, well-cut, *stubborn* chin, suggested a dependable and desirable character. *It's not the desirable I'm having difficulty with.*

The laughter of the audience interrupted her contemplation.

'... and it has been well documented that those workplaces that women have entered have benefited from their perspectives and approaches. Technology and innovation are mitigating physical constraints. We see this in Melbourne, with the replacement of the cable trams with electric and continuing evolution of the W-Class trams. We see this in other countries – in Mexico, where a tram ticket now represents an entry into a monthly lottery where valuable prizes can be won ...'

Daniel was emphasising his points with firm hand and arm gestures. His zeal was hypnotic. *But was it real?*

'Education means that women have the formal qualifications to prove that their arithmetic agilities are the equal of any man, if there was any doubt. And empathy and intuition have been a stalwart of women's characters for centuries. I have been the beneficiary of female comfort on many occasions, and I can say unequivocally that I prefer it to any male.'

More laughter.

'Finally, an attractive conductress in a piquant uniform would do much to reverse the financial fortunes of the Tramways Board and the state. It is the opinion of our team that the battle between bus, train and tram patronage will be won by whichever organisation has the enterprise or daring to employ women into the role. Thank you.'

Laughter and loud applause. Daniel had clearly left an impression.

'What an excellent close, Mr Sinclair ... Daniel,' Ida gushed. 'Hopefully, it put that pompous Brit in his place.'

'Shhhh ... we don't want the adjudicator deducting points for poor team spirit, Ida,' Daniel admonished tactfully as he resumed his place beside Bec.

Under cover of the sound of shuffling feet and heightened conversation as people responded to Jenny's announcement of a short tea break, Daniel asked, 'No congratulations for me?'

Turning, Bec met his eyes. 'You were very engaging.'

'But ...'

'No buts. You did a great job,' Bec replied honestly. 'You have a way with words.'

'But —'

Whatever Daniel was about to say was lost as Eliza stormed the stage, followed by Alex. 'I'm so proud of both of you. And I loved your closing, brother dear.' Hugs and handshakes followed.

Bec's parents strolled across to where they stood.

'Well, if that Lister bloke doesn't award your team the points, it's rigged,' announced Bec's father.

'Dad!'

'And what a fetching dress. Do they award points for best dressed? Perhaps we can organise a popular vote?'

'Edward, you're embarrassing her.' Bec's mother laughed. 'Well done, love. You too, Daniel.'

Bec reached out and drew Ida to stand between Daniel and her. 'And don't forget Ida. Our wonderful first speaker. Ida, these are my parents, best friend, Eliza and her fiancé, Alex.'

She still doesn't trust me. Daniel observed the way Bec – now on the opposite side of their small circle – once again had distanced herself from him. Had she not heard him speak? He'd poured a lot into those short eight minutes, but most importantly, he'd scripted the words, not just to win the debate, but as a message to Bec that he was on her side. Although ... if she accepted a role as a bus conductor, it would surely test that support. He sighed. *But if that's what it took ...*

An American drawl snapped him out of his contemplations to find Bec wrapped in a hug. Only Alex's hand on his arm, and his insistence to step away, stopped him from storming over and extricating her.

'Not a smart move.'

Daniel glared at his best friend.

'It was an entirely platonic gesture of congratulation.'

'No such thing,' grumbled Daniel. 'The feelings Bec rouses go well beyond friendly.'

'In you!'

'Says the man who remains ready to skewer any man that looks sideways at Eliza.'

Alex laughed. 'Point taken. But acting on those impulses is an entirely different matter. Anyway, our Jim has brought a friend – of the female variety.' Alex nodded to a serious young woman hovering at Jim's side. 'What you need is a stiff drink.'

Turning his back on the assembly, Alex pushed a small silver flask into Daniel's hands.

Pocketing it, Daniel nodded his thanks. 'Once the adjudicator's decision is in.'

Jenny's voice rang out as if on cue. 'Can everyone please take their seats?'

Alex clapped him on the shoulder. 'Good luck ... with the debate, too.'

Jenny was chivvying everyone good-naturedly to make haste, as Daniel, chuckling, returned to Bec's side.

She was speaking with Ida and didn't acknowledge his return. Daniel pulled his chair in beside her and pressed his thigh firmly against hers. Bracing his arm across the back of her chair, he leaned in. 'Team tactics?'

Bec glared at him, but he pretended not to notice, addressing Ida instead. 'Who do you think will win?'

'Too hard to call. But I have my fingers and toes crossed.'

From Bec's flushed cheeks, he knew she wasn't unaffected by his nearness. He allowed his thumb to connect with her back and lightly trace the raised velvet pattern on her dress. She was trapped, and they both knew it.

Unfortunately, Bec wasn't the only one aroused by his ministrations. It would be embarrassing if he was asked to stand.

'Perhaps you could pour a glass of water for us?'

Daniel grinned at the breathless note in Bec's voice, but acceded to her request.

The adjudicator, Mr Lister, had made her way to the lectern. 'A very entertaining debate and congratulations to all the speakers.'

What followed was a short summary of matter, method and manner.

'Just get on with it,' muttered Bec, tapping her pencil.

'And now to the results ...'

Finally! Daniel was surprised at his impatience. He usually enjoyed listening to the helpful critiques offered. He blamed Bec and her restlessness.

'For the affirmative, Mr Blake seventy-seven points, Mr Clerke seventy-four points and Captain Davis-Jones seventy-two points. Team work seventeen points for a total of two hundred and forty points.'

This was greeted with polite applause. Daniel gripped his glass.

'The negative, Miss McAuley seventy-four points, Miss Cross seventy-one points, Mr Sinclair seventy-seven points. Team work nineteen points for a total of two hundred and forty-one points.'

'We won!' All three of them spoke together. Ida triumphantly, Bec wonderingly, and Daniel with relief and a hint of chagrin. He and Theo had scored identical points, so not a personal triumph. *But they'd won!*

Daniel wrapped his arms around Bec and pulled her into an embrace, kissing her full on the mouth. Even in celebration, he wasn't feeling platonic. He remembered to let her go, reach across, grasp Ida's hands and kiss the backs of them. 'We did it!'

The sight of two constables striding down the centre aisle gave Daniel pause. Their target soon became apparent. A man of undisputed taste, at least in his attire, stood, cane thumping the floor, and wiped spittle from his mouth with a spotted handkerchief. And one look at Bec confirmed his identity – a ghost would have more colour. *William Tailor.*

Rants of 'ungodly', 'the destruction of society' and 'rigged', spewed forth. Daniel thought him a tragic comic, but there was nothing comical about Bec's reaction.

Under cover of the table, he grasped her hand. 'You're safe.' He wished he'd found time to be measured for that suit. Perhaps this would have been avoided.

She nodded as the old man was led politely but insistently towards the exit, the impact of his cane striking the floor echoing around the shocked hall.

The audience took some time to quieten, even under Jenny's insistent command. Daniel and Bec propelled Ida towards the rostrum to acknowledge their opposition, thank the adjudicator, madam chair, and those who came out to support the debate.

And then it was over – all those weeks of preparation, confusion and consternation.

At the back of the hall, Daniel's eye was drawn to the figure of his boss, standing ... assessing. He'd known he was here somewhere but hadn't sighted him until now. Louis Chalmers would be pleased with the result. He was a man who liked to win. *As did Daniel.* Did this secure his support for Daniel's promotion? *Had he done enough?* Strictly, he and Theo had tied.

Daniel fingered the silver flask resting in his coat pocket. He needed that drink. But it seemed that it would have to wait. Louis Chalmers and Theo Blake were converging on him – on their team. It was too late to alter their paths. Daniel hoped to avert another conversation that would involve awkward explanations. The stubborn set of Bec's chin suggested the progress they'd made over the last month may have already come to naught.

CHAPTER 39

'Well done!' said Louis Chalmers. A hearty clap to Daniel's shoulder and a firm handshake were followed by a broad smile encompassing Bec and Ida. 'To all of you.'

'Thank you. You remember my girlfriend, Bec Cross?'

'I do.'

'And our first speaker, Miss Ida McAuley.'

'Miss McAuley.'

'Ladies, Victoria's Public Works Minister and co-sponsor of the debate, Louis Chalmers. And, my colleague and first speaker for the opposition, Theo Blake.'

'Mr Chalmers, it's a pleasure,' gushed Ida. 'We hope you found the exchange of arguments entertaining.'

'It was just what I needed to wind down after a long day at the office, Miss McAuley.'

His sincerity surprised Bec. She'd expected a hint of tokenism, although she couldn't explain why.

Mr Chalmers now turned his attention to the man beside him. Bec's immediate impression was of exaggerated masculinity – prominent cheekbones and an imposing jawline. 'What say you, Theo? Did you find the experience entertaining?'

'Our opponents injected a lot of humour, sir. Of course, I'm disappointed with the outcome.' Seeing the frown that had materialised on the older man's face, he conceded, 'But let me offer my congratulations ... ladies, Daniel. It was a close contest.'

Ida nodded. 'Thank you, Mr Blake. Daniel, of course, was instrumental to our win.'

'Really ...' Theo crossed his arms. 'Is he a convert to feminist aspirations, then?'

Ida patted her curls. 'I'd like to think his time with us preparing for the debate has engendered more than a modicum level of support for our cause.'

'A wily servant of the state, our Daniel. Perhaps he was simply inspired to meet the brief he'd been assigned.'

Could a man appear charming and insincere in the same breath? Theo Blake seemed to have perfected the art. Bec didn't know what to make of him.

'Brief?' Ida's tone was sharp.

'He means the brief to win the debate,' said Daniel, spearing Theo with a flinty gaze.

'No need to talk shop. I'm sure no one is interested. If you'll excuse me, ladies, I have a patient and understanding wife awaiting me at home. Goodnight. Daniel, Theo, don't forget, eight o'clock sharp tomorrow.'

Bec watched him weave a path to the exit, stopping to exchange a few words here and there, extending his hand to some, while to others merely inclining his head. That he was in demand was not in doubt. Louis Chalmers was a man who understood his consequence. He oversaw an enormous portfolio and there were discussions underway, if the papers were to be believed, to expand his responsibilities further. He was a man worth knowing, and whose support was worth securing.

Ida added a hasty farewell. She'd caught sight of a colleague in conversation with Captain Double-barrel and had to hear what was being said.

'Do you think ol' Chalmers has made up his mind?'

Daniel's attempt at a nonchalant shrug did not deceive Bec. Nor, it appeared, to quell Theo from continuing. She wondered if he remembered she was even there, his gaze fixed on Daniel's face.

'Don't pretend you don't care. You'd die in a ditch for that promotion.'

'Let's not discuss —'

'Why not? I'm just recalculating the odds. You won the debate, although we scored the same points.'

'No sense speculating,' said Daniel.

'Did you get *the talk*? The one about a successful man always *pulls in double harness*?'

Bec frowned. '*The talk?*'

Daniel's eyes met hers and then shied away. 'That's enough, Theo.'

'We've set the date, y'know. I'll be telling him that tomorrow when we meet. I asked Nell's father last Sunday after church.'

'Congratulations!' Bec and Daniel chorused.

'But will it be enough?'

Bec sensed Theo was talking more to himself. Past his shoulder, she caught sight of Eliza and Alex, moving to join them, when Theo spoke again. This time, directly to her.

'I take it you haven't accepted his proposal?'

Daniel's tone was guttural. '*Theo.*'

A smile split Theo's rugged features. 'No? So, the odds are equal again.'

'*Odds?*' Bec's mind was working in slow motion, as if mired. She glanced at Daniel; his colour was high. 'Are you intimating that this promotion is tied to your marital status?' She kept the full weight of her gaze trained on Theo.

Theo's lips transformed from a smile into a round 'oh'. His eyes darted to Daniel's face before returning to hers. He swallowed. 'Um ... it's not one of the formal criteria.'

'Bec, I know that this sounds —'

She turned to face Daniel. 'Calculated? Contrived?'

He nodded slowly. 'All of those things. But that's not —'

Bec wondered if this was how a pugilist felt just before a fight – controlled and detached. '*What? Not* a stipulation of your promotion? *Not* something you'd considered until, let me guess, your boss mentioned how important it was.'

Daniel stood there without speaking. Bec felt cheated. She couldn't argue with silence. His gaze, unable to hold hers, spoke volumes. *God, she'd been so gullible.* Hearts were so naïve, and hers had proven to be unreliable.

'Let's hope Evelyn has a forgiving heart, or else the odds tip back in Theo's favour.'

'What about us?'

The gall of the man. '*Us?* There is no longer any *us*.'

'Don't —'

Bec spun on her heel, Daniel's anguished tone ringing in her ears, before her gaze collided with her best friend's. Eliza's shocked face confirmed she hadn't misinterpreted what she'd heard. Even Alex, standing beside her, looked grim. *The betrayal.* Bec would never have thought Daniel was a man who judged a woman's capability on how she could serve him and his ambitions. It just proved what she'd always known. The heart had no place in life's decisions.

Eliza linked arms with her. 'Your father's ready to leave. I said I'd find you. Come on.'

Bec nodded, glad of her friend's support.

Without a backward glance, she allowed Eliza to lead her out of the hall to where her father was helping her mother into her coat.

'Here she is. Ready, love?' her mother asked, tugging her cloche into place. 'Thanks, Eliza.'

Her father squeezed her shoulder. 'What's with the long face?'

How did she explain the depths of Daniel's deception to her parents? They'd really liked him, had teased her on more than one occasion that her lips had resembled the colour and plumpness of raspberries. That had been embarrassing – her parents noticing that *and* commenting on it.

Bec squared her shoulders. 'I'm just tired.'

'Not surprising, given the verbal jousting you entertained us with. Your mother and I are immensely proud of you.'

Tears pricked the corners of Bec's eyes. At least her parents' love and support were unconditional. Her anger dissipated, leaving her drained.

'Thank you,' she mumbled as she pressed her face into her father's coat front and wrapped her arms around him.

'Hey! What's this, then?' her father's voice rumbled above her as he returned her gesture and rested his chin atop her head. 'I could get used to these.'

Bec offered a wavy smile as she stepped back.

'Let's get you home. There's nothing that a good night's sleep won't fix.'

Dad's answer to everything. She doubted one night would be enough. Maybe like the fairytale, she could fall asleep for one hundred years. She sighed. In her current state, she doubted even that would be enough time to recover from Daniel's duplicity.

CHAPTER 40

Friday 11 September 1925

'Bec Cross, you are one lucky girl,' exclaimed a body struggling through the door to Bec's shared office.

It sounded like Hannah, but all Bec could see was a pair of arms cradling the biggest arrangement of flowers and foliage she'd ever seen, atop a pair of trousered legs.

'*Oomph!*'

Bec rushed forward to save the receptionist from colliding with any more furniture and helped her place the arrangement on Elsie's desk – the only empty space.

'So beautiful,' said Bec, admiring the coral-and-pink hues of the star-shaped flowers.

'And here's the card,' said Hannah. Crossing her arms, she scowled as Bec made to tuck it into the pocket of her skirt. 'Don't even think of not revealing who sent these after my herculean effort.'

'All right.' Scanning the note, she burst out laughing and read aloud, '*Great job! You can conduct my tram any time! Jim.*'

'The American Casanova?'

Bec nodded. 'The same.' Hannah had nicknamed Jim this

after his one and only visit. *'You should have seen all the girls giving him the glad eye,'* she'd complained to Bec.

'Humph!' Hannah turned on her heel, narrowly missing a collision with Eliza as she slipped through the doorway.

'What? ... Oh, how gorgeous, I can smell the eucalyptus tips from here. Are they from —'

'Jim.'

'Oh. I thought ...'

'Your brother? *Truly*, after last night?' Bec had also entertained the briefest of hopes when Hannah had appeared, but she couldn't admit that, not even to her best friend. It was too humiliating. Instead, she concentrated on wrestling her misery back into the box labelled *'Stupidity'* and slammed the lid.

Eliza drew out a chair and sat down. 'I just thought ... maybe ... it was an apology.'

'I don't think there are enough flowers in Melbourne.'

'You didn't see the look on his face.'

'The one as if he'd swallowed a snail?'

'No. The one after you left. I've never seen Daniel look like that – not even when his pet goldfish died when he was eight. He was gutted.'

'You are on my side, aren't you?'

'Why?'

'*A goldfish?* You're comparing our relationship to the bonds Daniel had with a goldfish?'

Eliza crossed her arms. 'Well, he loved that stupid fish.'

Bec shut her eyes tight.

'I admit it's not the best comparison.'

They lapsed into silence.

'I know that other man ...'

'Theo Blake,' she supplied automatically.

'Yes, him. He intimated Daniel's promotion required him to marry.'

'Oh, I don't think there's any question, do you? And Daniel didn't deny it.'

'But I think there's more to it. I tried talking to Alex, but he buttoned up. Said this was a matter between you and Daniel and that he wouldn't interfere. He knows more than he's letting on ... I just don't know what.'

Tears threatened, but Bec forced them back and tried for a businesslike tone. 'I feel so stupid. My head kept telling my heart to slow down, but it wouldn't listen. And I don't understand. If all he needed was a wife, why didn't he just ask Evelyn? She'd have jumped at the chance.'

Eliza continued to sit quietly, listening.

Bec slumped in her chair and contemplated the scuff on the toe of her shoe. 'We didn't agree on everything, but his views had ... softened. As have mine. We had more common ground. I'd started to believe that marriage to him could be more of a partnership. Even grown to enjoy the way he looks out for me – takes care of me. And his kisses ... they seemed real.'

'Oh, Bec!'

Eliza wrapped her arms about her, and Bec gave into her tears. Daniel had got under her skin and into her heart. She didn't want to admit it, not now, after last night, but she'd fallen in love.

'God, I hate this,' she sobbed. 'I've been so naïve.'

Eliza didn't distract her with platitudes, for which she was grateful. Her best friend simply held her, and as Bec's tears subsided from a torrent to a trickle, she pushed a handkerchief into Bec's fingers.

'Better?'

Bec managed a wobbly smile.

'You love him, don't you?'

Bec nodded. 'Yes.'

'I'm glad.'

'What?'

'I feared you might keep your heart locked up forever. That it might become impenetrable ... unbreakable.'

Bec squeezed her eyes shut, annoyed that they were still shedding moisture. 'Instead, it's been wrung out and broken.'

'You're giving up?' Eliza quirked an eyebrow, and Bec was instantly reminded of Daniel's expression when he challenged her. 'You don't fall in love by building walls or restraining the distance your heart is allowed to wander.'

But it was safer. Bec didn't have the energy to do anything more than simply stare at her friend.

Eliza jumped up from her seat. 'Your heart is a muscle, just like your ... well, your other muscles. It needs use!'

'I think it's had all the exercise it can take for the foreseeable future.'

'Bec, you are one of the strongest people I know. It would take more than Daniel to break you.'

Bec wasn't sure, at this precise moment, that she could agree.

Eliza began to pace. 'As I said before, there's more to this. I think you're onto something. It is odd that he didn't ask Evelyn if all he needed was a willing wife. He went to a lot of trouble.'

Choking back a sob, Bec said, 'You're saying I wasn't the easiest option.'

Her friend drew in an impatient breath. 'I'm saying I've never seen Daniel so persistent or single minded. He's never pursued a woman beyond a week. With you, he organised a whole campaign.'

Bec stared at Eliza. Daniel had gone to a lot of trouble, she realised.

'And he's shared parts of himself with you even I didn't know existed – his love of vaudeville for one.'

'You think I should talk to him.' It wasn't a question. Bec already knew the answer.

Eliza shook her head. 'I think ... no, I know you'll be miserable if you don't go after the answers to the questions running around in your head. Even if you don't like everything you hear.'

Bec hesitated, before whispering, 'I think I'm lucky to have a best friend like you.'

'But we need a plan.'

Her shoulders lifted. 'That's usually my forte. When did you become adept at planning?'

'Since I got myself a fiancé.' Eliza grinned. 'Nothing too elaborate. Daniel will join the dots.'

It was time to understand how far her heart had been led astray. It might be out of shape, but it wasn't irrevocably broken, and it wasn't dead. 'Time to flex my muscle.'

'That's more like the Bec I know,' teased Eliza.

'As I was just explaining to your American friend, she's not here.'

'He's not my friend,' growled Daniel to the YWCA's

receptionist.

'Did she get my flowers?'

'Yes, sir, she —'

'You sent Bec flowers?' Daniel took a step towards Jim. *Why hadn't he thought of that?*

'I can report Bec was delighted with the flowers ... and the card.'

Daniel wanted to punch something ... or someone. He'd send her a lorry full of flowers if he thought it would help.

'Hello, Hannah.'

Daniel swung around to find his best mate standing behind him.

Hannah nodded in greeting. 'Alex.'

'So, where did you say she was?' Jim drawled.

'I didn't. It may surprise you, gentlemen, but we are not running a dating service. Now, neither Bec nor Eliza are here. And won't be returning until Monday.'

'Is she all right?' asked Daniel.

Hannah gave him a long, suffering look over the top of her glasses. 'She'd stopped crying by the time she left. Now I'd thank you all to move on.'

'What do you mean ...?' Both Daniel and Jim spoke at once, but Hannah was busying herself with another enquiry. They'd been dismissed.

'Gentlemen,' Alex commanded, steering both men back out the way they'd come. 'I speak from experience when I say Hannah is as closed as an oyster about the movements of the women here. You're wasting your breath.'

'What are you doing here?' Daniel stabbed a finger in Jim's direction.

'Checkin' on my girl.'

'She's not your anything!'

'Well, I wouldn't be too sure after last night. Shopping for a wife, are you?'

Daniel lunged for the man's mocking face. Only Alex's quick reaction held him in place.

Jim stood his ground. 'And Hannah in there said she'd been crying.'

Daniel sobered. *Bec never cried.* 'I've got to find her. I need to explain ...'

'Too late for that. I doubt she'd give you the time of day.'

'Thank you, Jim,' said Alex, maintaining his hold on Daniel. 'That's not helpful.'

'Why are you still here?' spat Daniel.

'Believe it or not, I'm actually on your side.'

'Well, you've got a strange way of showing it.'

'I don't know why I'm tellin' you this. You don't deserve it after the way you treated her.' Jim hesitated. 'But Bec lights up when she's with you.'

Daniel speared Jim with a look. *Did she? Was the American being honest or messing with him? And if so, for what purpose?*

Jim shrugged. 'But, if she's finished with you, well ... I'm here. Ready, willin' and available.'

Daniel growled, 'Let's get one thing straight. Bec is *not* some ornament to further my career. I love her.'

'You have a strange way of showin' it.'

'What would you know?'

Jim folded his arms. 'I'm guessin' you haven't told her you love her, have you?'

'I was waiting ...'

The American shook his head.

'I love her, I'm telling you.'

'It ain't me you need to convince.'

Alex nodded. 'You need a strategy.'

Jim rubbed his chin. 'Your mate's right – best to have a plan. And it better be water tight, because Bec's as smart as all get out.'

Turning his back on the American, Daniel faced Alex. 'Any need for another engineer at the Tramways Board?'

'Ol' Strickland would have you back in a heartbeat. But don't throw away your dreams too quickly. Politics needs you.'

'And I need Bec.' It wasn't logical, but it didn't change the fact. That was how he felt.

'Well, we won't sort anything out standing here. Let's move this discussion to the bar,' said Alex. 'You better come too, Jim – you've shown yourself to be adept at planning campaigns.'

Alex – and Jim, Daniel conceded grudgingly – were right. He needed a plan – a bloody good one. It wasn't enough to resign as a way to right the hurt he'd caused Bec. He needed to regain her trust, to have her believe in him. He needed her – head, heart, body and soul.

CHAPTER 41

Saturday 12 September 1925

Bec drifted from the dining room to the lounge room and back again. She never drifted – she moved purposefully through life. *Argh!* It was all Daniel's fault.

Eliza had left her last night with a plan to casually disclose that Bec's mum and dad had left for the Holbrook Agricultural Show – Bec's mum was judging the livestock. They'd taken the Austin and wouldn't be back until Monday. If she knew her brother at all, Eliza said, she expected he'd be knocking at Bec's front door within the hour.

It was now lunchtime. Eliza had misjudged Daniel's enthusiasm and the depth of his feelings. Bec had served her purpose. She didn't doubt Evelyn would welcome his return with open arms. *That hurt.* Was she so interchangeable?

Maybe she'd start planning for her meeting with the owner of the accountancy firm next Wednesday to initiate her pet project. It had been the driving force behind her participation in the debate, after all. Daniel's deception had robbed her from celebrating her success in securing the necessary funding.

Bec sat down at the dining-room table, pen in hand, the sun through the glass warming her back. Her mind was blank. She wrote '*Agenda*' at the top of the page, and after a few more minutes added the date, '*Wednesday 16th September*'. She underlined both in bold strokes. Next, she wrote the number one and circled it.

After ten more minutes, she threw her pen down in frustration. It was no use. Nothing about the initiative could capture her attention – not even thinking of it as a runway to the extension of female aspirations.

Well, she couldn't remain here, mooning. She'd walk down and check on her father's shop – do some cleaning. She grimaced. *Things were bad if she was seeking comfort in housework!* But it might help to dislodge the boulder that had taken up residence where her heart used to be.

Nelson Place was its usual hustling corridor of Saturday activity. Bec opened the shop's door and coughed at the stuffiness that greeted her after twenty-four hours of closure. Preceded by a north-easterly, she wedged open the door to allow the wind full access, hoping it would sweep the stale air away.

Toeing off her brogues, Bec skated across the polished timber floor, stained with years of oil, soap and cologne, in her socks. It reminded her of childhood antics.

Someone had pushed the three oak barber chairs together into a tight circle. Bec fancied she'd caught them chin-wagging. She giggled. Men might argue that it was a special peculiarity of women, but from the anecdotes told by her father, men were notorious gossips.

As expected, the mirrors – in front of which the fate of men, countries and the world's problems had been discussed and decided over the years – could do with a clean. Setting the keys on the small counter beside the till and a container of peppermints, Bec set to work, glad for an excuse to burn off her pent-up energy.

With her hands occupied, her thoughts roamed. At what point had she allowed her heart to silence her head where Daniel was concerned? Was it after her conversation with Elsie? When she'd imagined herself alone, a spinster, being smiled at with condescension and pity? Unlike other single women – spinster aunts like Elsie – Bec hadn't been brought up to sacrifice herself for her younger brothers and sisters, willingly and unselfishly. Was that where her future was headed, sans the nieces and nephews?

Was it when she realised her fear of being vulnerable had compelled her need to be always in control? A habit she now acknowledged, thanks to Daniel, that had influenced her thoughts, feelings, behaviours and reactions. It was nice, more than nice, not to always be in the driving seat. Daniel had shown her that. And she hadn't turned into a lesser version of herself – less capable, relevant or ... fierce.

But try as she might, Bec couldn't identify any one word, expression, conversation or event that had set her on a new path. It reminded her of the fable of the boiling frog. With the frog being heated slowly, the poor animal didn't realise it was being cooked alive until it was too late. Bec shuddered. *What a horrible analogy. She was no frog!* And she'd survive this episode in her life. The mirror reflected her scowl. In fact, it probably should have happened earlier in her life – then her heart wouldn't have been such easy pickings.

Lost in thought, it was some moments before she registered a staccato tapping filling the quiet space. Switching her focus from the smudge she'd been polishing to the room reflected behind her, she discovered William Tailor's sturdy physique filling her field of vision.

His mouth twisted into a half-smile as she turned to face him. 'If it isn't Teddy's girl. Fresh from her debate triumph.'

'Can I help you?' Her hands had automatically found her hips, but when she noticed that this drew his attention to her breasts, she quickly dropped them to her sides.

'Where's your father?'

Bec hesitated, reluctant to tell him the truth, but eager to be rid of him. 'He's running an errand. Would you like to make an appointment? Or leave a message?'

The man took a step forward. 'Rebecca, isn't it?'

Bec picked up the rag she'd been using for polishing and the bottle of methylated spirits. 'Yes.' What game was he playing?

'*Servant of God.* Did you know that was the meaning of your name?'

'No. Now if there's nothing else ...'

His expression morphed into a sneer. 'But you're not dutiful, are you?'

She gripped the bottle. 'Get out.'

He took another step towards her, and another, raising his cane. 'Your duties don't include playing on trams, dressed in sexually explicit uniforms, serving the great unwashed.'

Bec rapidly calculated her options. Her socks did not support a quick dash for the door, nor a feint charge as she'd seen on the football field. Dousing his person in spirits would probably just make him angry. Could she defend her attack on an elderly gentleman? Elderly anything? As this man was no gentleman.

'I tried to warn you.'

'The letters?'

'Yes.' He moved forward again.

Bec realised that only the three chairs separated them.

'Your grandmother's behaviour set a poor example for you. I understand that now. Although at the time ...'

Bec's skin crawled at the unfinished memory.

'Our excessive indulgences led her to prostitute herself at the altar of free love. You shouldn't have witnessed that.'

'You're delusional.'

'Your father and mother have done nothing to discourage your dangerous feminist ideals, or to protect you from sexual exploitation. I have secured a special licence; all I need is your signature ...'

Should she scream? The position of her father's shop meant there was little passing foot traffic. Customers were either attracted by the large red-and-white sign or knew their purpose in approaching. Perhaps the florist next door might hear her. What was the time? She closed promptly at two. But Bec daren't take her eyes off this man.

'I swore on your grandmother's grave I'd protect you.'

'Get away from her.'

Bec had never seen Daniel so angry. The single shop light she'd turned on caught the sheen of moisture coating his forehead and the crimson painting his cheeks as he advanced through the doorway.

Eyes wide, William Tailor turned. 'Now see here,' he blustered.

'Away. Now.'

The older man would be stupid to invite the attention of the fists balled at Daniel's side, thought Bec, *or ignore the power emanating from his stance.*

'There's been a misunderstanding.'

Daniel grabbed the man's arm and shoved him towards the door. 'I know what I heard. Now get out.'

The old man stumbled before regaining his balance with the help of his cane. 'You have no right —'

'*You* have no right. She will never marry you. Now get out, you miserable excuse of a man.'

Their raised voices had attracted a smallish crowd – the florist and three women with shopping baskets. William Tailor raised his cane to make a path for his exit, demanding that they move out of his way.

Bec was saved from the embarrassment of making any explanation when Daniel, uncaring of appearances, shut the door firmly in the faces of the curious onlookers and drew the blind.

Bec stood like a sapling, unsure of its roots. Now that the threat had been dispensed with, her legs didn't feel quite her own. She moved towards the couch at the rear of the narrow shop premise and the cheery sight of the bright scatter cushions.

She'd taken less than half-a-dozen steps when she was swept into the air. Daniel ignored her half-hearted protest, sinking onto the couch with his arms wrapped around her. Fumbling in his coat pocket, he flourished a handkerchief and pushed it into Bec's palm.

'I won't waste tears on that man,' she muttered, blinking furiously at the moisture that had accumulated at the corners of her eyes.

Daniel tucked her head under his chin and asked her how things had unfolded.

Her voice grew in strength as she related the events. '... And then you appeared ... I should thank you ...'

Daniel shook his head. At least that's how she interpreted his chin scraping the top of hers.

'A time and a place for that.'

'I thought after Dad spoke to the police ...'

Beneath her, she felt Daniel tense. His heart rate reminded her of a clockwork train she'd owned as a child, which, when let loose, would race furiously along its tracks.

'The posters, the letters, it was him, wasn't it?'

'Yes. And he was at the debate.'

Daniel eased her away from his chest and waited until her eyes met his. 'Bec, how do you feel about making a police statement?'

'He's just full of hot air,' she said, dropping her chin and tracing the pattern on his sweater with her finger.

Daniel hesitated, suggesting he was choosing his words carefully. 'Staying silent won't stop him.'

Her head snapped up. 'Do you think he's capable of more?'

'He's had his sights set on you since you were thirteen. His behaviour today demonstrates he's fanatical and desperate. What if he abducted you?'

She scoffed. 'He's an old man.'

'Or arranged to have you abducted?'

Bec's gaze drifted over his shoulder and swallowed. 'I'll think about it.'

'I —'

'I said I'd think about it. That'll have to be enough for now.'

Daniel looked like he would have liked to argue, but after gazing at her for what seemed ages, he nodded. 'All right. In the meantime, let's get you home.'

CHAPTER 42

Sunday 13 September 1925

Bec smoothed her palms down her skirt and tugged her cream fair-isle sweater over her hips as she approached the front door.

On the doorstep, the object of her thoughts stood, drooping flowers in hand and a lopsided smile on his face.

Bec pulled him into the hallway. 'Don't just stand there, the neighbour's curtains are twitching already.'

His smile reached his eyes.

Exasperated, Bec turned and strode purposefully back towards the dining room and her best friend. Daniel had insisted that Eliza stay the night and Bec had been too tired to argue. They'd talked before Bec had fallen into an exhausted sleep. She was grateful Eliza hadn't judged or berated her for keeping secrets.

'Good morning, brother dearest.'

'Sister. Anything to report?'

'The patient slept soundly. Her appetite has returned.'

'Hello, I can speak for myself,' said Bec, giving her friend a mock scowl.

'Are you always this grumpy of a morning?' Daniel asked.

'No, not normally.' But she was feeling off balance. Despite his actions yesterday, she was not ready to trust this man. Already, her body was bracing for an argument, her brain on the lookout for manipulative or persuasive ploys.

'Argumentative?'

He must be a mind reader. 'Sometimes.'

'Time to make my escape,' said Eliza, rising and clutching the crossword she and Bec had been contemplating in her hand. 'Mind if I take this?'

Bec shook her head. 'Thanks for giving up your Saturday evening with Alex for me.'

'Any time.' Eliza gave her a quick hug. 'It's said absence makes the heart grow fonder. I'm about to put it to the test. I'll see myself out.' And with a wave and wink, she was gone.

Bec studied the man opposite her. He was looking far too sure of himself. Anger and embarrassment competed within her for attention. *How or where to begin?* 'Tea? Coffee?'

Daniel shook his head and advanced around the table, thrusting the flowers that looked as if they'd been plucked haphazardly from his mother's garden towards her.

'For you.'

'Um ... thank you.'

'I've missed you.'

Bec didn't know what she'd expected, but not that. She straightened. 'The feeling's not mutual.'

'No?'

'No. Thank you for yesterday ... and for organising Eliza to stay. Your help was ... well ... I appreciated it.'

'Still playing safe, Bec?'

'Safe? Wouldn't you?'

Daniel touched the flowers she was strangling in her hand. 'Aren't you going to read the message?'

Bec turned the bouquet over. 'The card must have slipped out.'

'There's no card.'

Did he enjoy setting her at a disadvantage? 'I've never learned the language of flowers.'

'Allow me. The pansies are to tell you that you occupy my every thought.'

She rolled her eyes. 'I bet.'

'The bluebells are for constancy.'

'That must have been a new word for you.'

'The ivy to tell you I've found my one true heart.'

Bec firmly planted her feet as he reached for her. *She would not be distracted. They still had things to sort out ... important things.* His hands settled on the tops of her shoulders.

'Pretty words, Daniel. Did you think I'd fall into your arms after hearing those? I am not, and will never be, some by-line that you can use to progress your career.'

'That's not how it is.'

'Really? You've got fifteen minutes to tell me your version before I ask you and your flowers to leave. But be warned, Theo's version was convincing. As was the look on your face.'

She tensed as he skated his hands down her arms to tangle their fingers around the bouquet.

'I was jockeying for promotion. Competing not just against Theo, but against the archaic years-of-service program that exists in the public service.'

Bec stood tall, steeling herself for the worst.

'Chalmers assigned us to the debate, on opposite teams. I felt I'd drawn the short straw, and yet I still needed to win if

I wanted the promotion.'

Daniel lifted his gaze to the ceiling before resting it back on her face.

'He also suggested a wife was an essential asset to the career of a public servant and future politician. I didn't want to hear that. Initially, I thought about a pretend engagement – anything to appear as if I was considering marriage, while still continuing my bachelor ways.'

Bec wrenched her fingers from his. She crossed her arms, flowers crushed in one hand. 'And that's where I came in.'

'Yes and no. It was Alex who first suggested that my life's partner might be right under my nose. Meaning you.'

'*Wonderful.*'

'The more I thought about it, the more I knew that marriage to you would be no hardship.'

'Music to my ears. Just what every woman wants to hear.'

Raking both hands through his hair, Daniel implored her, 'You wanted me to be honest. Warts and all.'

'Go on.'

'Physically ...' Daniel shrugged. 'Well, I think you know I can't keep my hands off you. And when we kiss, all coherent thought disappears. I dream of you ... of us, together ...' He blushed. 'And the attraction is not one-sided, so don't suggest it is.'

Bec refused to admit anything aloud. Stomping down traitorous tendrils unfurling in her stomach, she glared at him. 'It's not enough.'

Daniel swallowed. 'Long before we got to the debate, I knew I wanted to marry you. I even told your father —'

'You spoke to my father? I can't believe you did that!' Bec spun away from him, paced towards the windows overlooking the fernery, then turned back to face him. 'Before you spoke to me?'

'He wanted to know my intentions. I told him I was serious but that you and I hadn't talked about it.'

Bec closed her eyes. 'Right. Well, now we have. This is where I thank you for your candour and you shuffle off. Time's up. I'm sure you can find your way out.'

'I still haven't told you the most important thing.'

Closing her eyes didn't block out his voice. She opened them. 'There's more? This just keeps getting better.'

'I love you. And the honeysuckle, we never did get to that, is for devoted love.'

Bec's breath hitched as she inhaled in the scent of honey and ripe citrus. Despite her sweater, goosebumps broke out on her arms.

'Bec, did you hear what I said?'

'Yes —'

Without waiting for her to finish her response, Daniel had closed the distance between them and kissed her. More than that, he'd delved into her open mouth like an ardent hummingbird – supping. *He loved her.* Her heart was capering, her body melting against his. Her head reminded her that she still had questions. *'Mmmpptthh.'*

Daniel delivered a last kiss to her lips and withdrew. 'You said something?'

Bec speared him with a look, but it did nothing to quell his smile. 'You're doing it again.' At his raised eyebrow, she exploded, *'Kissing me!* As I said before, it's not enough.'

'You want more kisses?'

'No!' *Why wasn't he taking her seriously?*

'I don't believe you.'

'I have questions.'

His smile lines deepened, and his eyebrows did a jig. 'And I have answers.'

'I'm serious. Normal questions. With words.'

'Ah!' He nodded, still smiling. 'Let me continue with a few more answers.'

She arched a brow.

'I'll support your decision if you wish to become a bus conductor.'

She moistened her lips. 'Um, about that ...'

His expression turned fierce. 'But next time, can we talk about it before you run off to an interview?'

'Um, I'm not accepting a role as a bus conductor. I love my job – my current job – and have no intentions of leaving. Not for anything!'

Bec felt the brush of Daniel's thumb across her cheek before he tucked a strand of hair behind her ear then nodded.

'My boss is not on a mission to drive women from the workforce. He's not a champion of their entry, either, although he understands my views that they're more capable than their current representation suggests.'

'What about the women bus conductors?'

'It's complicated, Bec. I've outlined a way forward, but I won't lie to you. It has less than a fifty-fifty chance of being accepted.'

'You could have told me you were involved.'

'I wasn't confident you'd understand.'

'You didn't trust me.'

'We didn't trust each other.'

She smiled ruefully. 'Yes, I can see that. But any conversation is better than letting me jump to my own conclusions.'

'Agreed.'

He was taking the wind from her sails. She'd been all set for a debate – an argument, if she were truthful. He just didn't play fair.

But he wasn't finished. His eyes, now the colour of dark amber, locked with hers. 'I want to marry you. Not because it's an expectation of my career.' His thumb caressed the underside of her jaw. 'I'll resign if you don't believe me. Alex has confirmed there's a job at the Tramways Board if I want it. No promotion is worth losing you.'

Did she believe him? Was this another attempt to manipulate her?

Daniel reached into the pocket of his coat. 'My resignation.' He held it out to her. 'It's yours. You hold the fate of my future in your hands – and I'm not just talking about my career.'

Bec placed the crushed bouquet on the table, took the letter, unfolded it and scanned the contents. It was dated today. Her mind was whirring. He'd anticipated all her objections. She shook her head. 'That won't be necessary. I ... I've been naïve. Politics is messy and you'll need someone strong at your side.'

Daniel's gaze seemed to search her very soul before he appeared satisfied that she meant what she said.

'I won't always agree with what you say and do, and I won't hold back in letting you know. I trust you'll do the same with my opinions.'

He nodded. 'I wouldn't have it any other way.'

Bec slipped Daniel's resignation into the pocket of her skirt.

'And I would like children ... with you ...'

She swallowed. 'Right.' So inadequate as responses went, but that was all she could manage. The thought of a small, rambunctious Daniel ... *Breathe, Bec.*

'And for you to return to work as soon as practicable, if that's what you want.'

She watched his face. His eyes, the amber now tinged with green, his pupils wide. And then there was the tic, only slight, but apparent. *Daniel was nervous.*

'Daniel —'

'Did I tell you I love you?'

Bec ran her hands up the sides of his body, from his waist to his chest, loving the feel of his muscular torso. 'You may have mentioned it ... once or twice.'

'Do you have any other concerns or questions?'

Bec hesitated. *Could she fall any deeper under this man's spell?* With each admission, each concession, she felt herself succumbing. But instead of feeling weak, she felt strong – stronger.

'Bec? Is there anything ...?'

'Um ... just one.' *She couldn't allow him the last word.*

His tic intensified. 'Ask me.'

Did she dare? Bec swallowed. 'Will you marry me?'

It took Daniel a moment to process Bec's question, having steeled himself for a more rigorous challenge. And then he couldn't decide what to do first – kiss her, answer her or have her repeat the question.

Pulling Bec against him, he possessed her lips and danced them in a slow circle. *God, he loved this woman.* The thought of losing her had shown him what was truly important in life. He'd hoped she'd felt the same way, hoped that there was nothing brief or casual about their relationship. After the events of yesterday, he'd wanted to wrap himself around her and never let her out of his sight. But he'd forced himself to leave her to Eliza's ministrations, and to return home to gather his courage.

It wasn't until she'd answered the door, and he'd seen her agitation, that he was convinced she cared, although her initial responses had had him doubting himself all over again. He'd wondered if he'd been ambitious to think he'd secretly secured her heart. *And now she'd proposed.* The thought reminded him that he still hadn't given her his answer.

Determined to incorporate one traditional element, he dropped to his knees and tilted his head up. *Well, somewhat traditional.* 'Ask me again.'

Bec giggled. 'Will you, Daniel Sinclair, take me, Bec Cross, to wed?'

'Oh yes.'

He watched her worry her bottom lip before whispering, 'And to bed?'

Daniel wondered if his ears were tricking him. His cock, however, was in no doubt what it had heard, more than ready to consummate the tension that had been building.

Her fingers sifted restlessly through his hair. 'Please ...'

Daniel moved his hands to her hips and set out on an exploration. Lifting the ribbing at the bottom of her jumper, he discovered bare skin. Using his thumb, he painted her belly button with slow circles before replacing his thumb with his tongue. She moaned, leaning into him.

Daniel moved his palm, skimming her ribcage until he

reached his destination – her breast. Puzzled, he scouted its contour, before murmuring, 'No shirt ... and no brassiere. You realise there will be consequences ...'

He felt a shiver rack her frame. 'I hope so.'

Daniel chuckled, using his breath to dry the moisture he'd sketched on her belly. Pleased with his discovery, he cupped her, massaging one taut globe – a perfect handful. He passed a thumb over her nipple before circling it with thumb and forefinger. She cried out, and he wished he could absorb it into his mouth. She was so sensitive!

Deciding hard floors were not conducive to romance – or bedding – he rose, allowing his other hand to join the first, and watched the play of emotions across her face. Bec's fingers closed around his wrists. He feared she was intending to push him away, but she surprised him by encouraging him to increase the pressure. He was incapable of arguing.

Daniel became conscious of heat. A shaft of sunlight warmed his back. Thoughts led to where they were and how to proceed. He was not enthusiastic for Bec to experience her first sexual escapade against a wall or doorjamb. Of course, he could – would – call a halt to things. He had in the past. Was prepared to wait if she wasn't ready ...

'Don't even think of stopping,' she whispered in his ear. Nipping the bottom of his lobe, Bec again closed her fingers around his wrists and led him down a short corridor and through the door at the end. 'The fire has been on all morning.'

Daniel's gaze was drawn to the double mattress. It was difficult not to, since it dominated the small room.

'A present for my twenty-first.'

Not for Bec florals in various shades of baby hues. Silk –

like his ties – in a sea of blue, and as he advanced into the room, the flickering light from the fire suggested tinges of green.

Daniel looked up to find Bec hovering, as if her courage, which had brought her this far, had dissipated. He crossed to her side and wound his arms about her. 'Nervous?'

'As you know, I hate not being in control.' She leaned back in the circle of his arms. 'And I will not lie there and think of England.' A mutinous expression crossed her face. 'Like the girls in those penny romances.'

'I should hope not,' replied Daniel in bemusement.

'Don't you laugh at me, Daniel Sinclair. I plan to be an active participant.'

'No argument from me, honey.'

But his love was on a roll. 'And Eliza has been extremely reticent in providing any useful information on the whole bedding process,' she grumbled. 'So, how should we go about this?'

Daniel placed a finger over her lips. 'Shhhh. First, I don't need any pointers from my little sister … or tips from her fiancé,' he said sternly.

'But —'

He gently pressed her lips together to stop her from continuing. 'Second, I don't know where you got this idea that your part is simply to lie there and think of England – or any other damned thing. I can promise you, your wits will be so addled that you'll be fortunate to remember your own name.'

He watched her eyes widen in what he hoped was anticipation, not fear.

'And third, this isn't a process that you plan in that mixed-up head of yours. We don't perform step one, followed by step two, and so on. Making love isn't a project.'

She smiled, or at least as much as she could with her lips pressed together.

'Now I'm going to remove my fingers and I'm going to kiss you. I'm not telling you so that you can agree or disagree or even make a sound. In fact, I don't know why I'm telling you at all ...'

Despite initiating it, the intensity of the kiss surprised Daniel. Bec had opened her mouth without prompting, her tongue eager to dance with his. To rise and fall, sway and swing. They fell into a languid rhythm. He would be happy to stay locked like this for hours.

He bit her lip softly, reminding her, 'No thinking.'

She returned the favour, and Daniel heard a growl of approval emanate from his throat. He hoped Bec wasn't thinking of bloody England. *He hadn't felt this much pressure since he was nineteen.*

Reluctantly, he abandoned her mouth and lifted her sweater in search of her nipples. His tongue followed the path of his fingers, and when he arrived the areolas were standing to attention as if at a military parade. She groaned at his touch, her restlessness increasing.

'Easy, sweetheart.'

'Easy for you to say,' she muttered, as if to herself.

He smiled, massaging both breasts and taking turns to lavish her nipples with his mouth, enjoying her sighs of pleasure.

His equilibrium, though, was challenged when her fingers successfully sought his manhood, stroking the length of him through the fabric of his trousers. He cursed his unprecedented response. It wasn't just the hardness of his erection, or the quickening of his pulses as if he'd arrived at the end of a hundred-yard dash. It was the ferocity of his response and the emotional tidal wave that was engulfing him.

'Too many clothes,' he heard her moan. And then she was reaching for the waistband of his Oxford bags and ripping at the buttons in her haste to unwrap him. The drawstring of his undergarments slowed her, which only fired his anticipation, and then she was caressing him, from the tip of his penis to its base.

'Ahh ...'

She immediately stopped. 'What? Am I hurting you?'

'Don't stop!' gasped Daniel, reaching down to guide her hand.

'You feel so alive!' She giggled. 'But I feel restricted. I need you naked.'

'All of me?' he teased.

'Is that a problem?'

'No,' he said, gently untangling her fingers and their bodies. 'But since you're all about equality, you'd better strip too ... you've got thirty seconds.'

Bec's breath hitched as he revealed a flat stomach, abdominals, chest ...

'Twenty seconds.'

The look in his eyes appeared to galvanise her into action.

Unprepared to miss the unveiling of the body that had taken over his dreams, Daniel had stripped quickly ... faster than any time before.

'Do you know how beautiful you look?' he said from where he knelt in the middle of the bed.

Wide shoulders topped Bec's long legs, and a toned, boyish figure. But it was her eyes that had him transfixed. He watched the colour change from steel to silver. Mercurial. She surveyed him silently. He reached for her, and their eyes locked.

'Stop thinking,' he reminded her as she hesitated, resisting his pull, remaining steadfast beside the mattress.

He bent and kissed her navel, circling it with his tongue and dipping into the small slit. She squirmed, and he held her body in place, capturing the orbs of her butt.

His tongue travelled upwards to lavish attention on her breasts, her collarbone, the side of her neck, and finally her mouth. He kept their bodies a hair's breadth apart, building tension.

With a cry, Bec closed the distance. He'd unleashed a bearcat. Her hands and mouth were everywhere.

Lifting her, he fell backwards and rolled, straddling her body. He wrested back control, kiss by kiss, caress by caress. The fingers that had captured his cock had set up a rhythm that would have him erupting like a volcano, molten seed flying, if he didn't distract her.

'Soon,' he whispered as he brought Bec's hands to his shoulders, kissing the frown lines that had appeared between her eyes, before possessing her mouth.

Skating his hand down the length of her, he cupped her mound, and with the heel of his hand set up a cadence that quickly had her writhing. His fingers sought her entrance, and he plunged them into wet heat.

'Daniel, I need ...'

'Soon.'

'Now!' she insisted.

Bec was pulsing, her body on the verge of igniting. She opened her legs to allow him more access. His fingers had lit a fire, gliding in and out, massaging her with a devilishly flexible thumb. He was the conductor of her orchestra, and as the music reached a crescendo, she arched her body, hovered and then crashed. Her cry, like the sonic effect from a pair of cymbals, accentuated the moment.

She watched Daniel position himself between her legs. He seemed to take things slowly, as if she were made of fine bone china. She knew this was their first time, but she wanted him *now*! Snatching back control, she locked her legs around him, heels pressed into his buttocks and rode him. Daniel plunged into her. Any pain was fleeting – she barely flinched – so intent was she to move things along.

She was following her instincts. Any plans she'd hoped to deploy, any guises she'd thought to adopt, were beyond her ability to remember, let alone implement. She'd become a being without thought, driven by touch, by smell and impulse.

Daniel levered his body weight onto his elbows, wanting to watch the myriad expressions crossing Bec's face, to get lost in the allure of her eyes. This was new for him. While he'd always worked to pleasure his partners before, he'd never wanted to encourage the connection that he craved with Bec.

'Are you all right?'

'Uh-huh,' she said shyly, closing the distance to kiss him.

Daniel moved, slowly at first, his tongue matching the leisurely tempo of his thrusts, his fingers massaging her nipples, tweaking them. Bec's body orgasmed again, her cry not as loud this time, but throatier.

'Beautiful,' he groaned, increasing his pace, his body absorbed in meeting her demand for completion and his for release.

He pumped into her, spending as if he was a randy youth before collapsing on top of her, their bodies still joined, humming and in harmony.

'That was incredible,' Bec whispered.

'For me, too,' said Daniel, brushing the hair from her eyes. 'You were incredible.'

'And you were right,' she murmured, reaching up to draw his lips to hers.

'About?'

'I didn't think of England once!'

CHAPTER 43

Bec rested her chin on one hand and waved her fork in the air with the other. 'So, how should one feel if they'd been ... what was the word? *Debauched?*'

Daniel eyed his fiancée's pert mouth across the table, pretending to give her question some thought. He was reliving their afternoon together. After making love, they'd fallen asleep. Daniel had woken mid-afternoon to the feel of one of Bec's legs hitched around him, and an arm thrown across his waist. *Trapped.* He could get used to that.

He'd lain, drinking in the sight of her rumpled curls waving upwards and outwards, framing a set of lips that looked as if they'd been well exercised. Smoky lashes disguised her expressive eyes, and Daniel could almost forget he'd chosen a jaunty whirlpool – *his sister's phrase* – to love and to hold ... until death do us part. He would suggest they omit the word *obey* from their vows. There wasn't any point in being hypocritical.

He'd warred with himself whether to stay, or get dressed and go home, but when Bec had mumbled and snuggled closer, he'd treated it as a sign and stayed.

It was six o'clock in the evening before Bec had awoken. She'd been playful. Conscious she'd be sore, he'd distracted her – and his cock stand – with a game of truth and dare. She'd lost, and he'd demanded dinner. Her pout had suggested eating had been the furthest thing from her mind. That was when he'd explained that he'd already debauched her, and he didn't want to face her father with more transgressions on his mind.

'Well?'

'They'd be feeling well loved and … ready to make coffee.'

Bec snorted. 'You're the debauchee, you should make my coffee.'

'I —'

The sound of a key in the front door halted further debate.

'We're home.'

'Dad!' Bec mouthed, pushing back her chair.

Daniel was glad he'd insisted they dress, intending to head out for a walk after dinner.

'Anyone?'

Bec moved towards the hallway. 'In here, Dad. You're home a day early.'

'Hello, sweetheart, your mum finished up quicker than expected.' Her father placed an arm around her shoulders. '*Daniel*. What a surprise.'

Daniel had risen to his feet and stepped forward to shake hands, all the while trying to decide the best conversational route to take.

Bec's mother appeared, patting her curls in a move reminiscent of Bec. Her greeting was half statement, half question. 'Daniel ...'

'I was just about to make coffee —'

Daniel interrupted Bec as she made a dash for the kitchen, looping his hand around her waist. 'We have some news. Bec has agreed to marry me. We wanted you both to be the first to know.'

The announcement acted as a salve to what Daniel expected would have been a very awkward conversation. Although Bec's parents didn't let him off, thinking he and Bec had fooled them.

As Bec's father congratulated Daniel, he muttered, 'And here I was worried about my little girl all alone ...'

Her mother pulled him in for a hug. 'Congratulations,' she said warmly, before whispering, 'Tuck your shirt in.'

When Bec disappeared with her mother under the pretences of helping her to unpack, her father gestured for Daniel to take a seat.

'I'm glad it's you. I get seasick and didn't fancy a voyage to the States.'

Daniel nodded, figuring that was the safest response.

'Was it patience or persistence that won the day?'

'Um ... a bit of both, and lots of conversations.'

'You can never do enough talking.'

Daniel grinned, thoughts of his and Bec's recent *conversation* fresh in his mind.

'Is it safe to return?' Bec's head appeared around the doorjamb.

'Yes, love. I speak for both your mother and me when I say we're incredibly happy to welcome Daniel to the family.'

Bec's mother nodded, sliding a chair out from the table and taking a seat.

'It's a pity you've got your eye set on politics, though, as I would have liked someone to take over the shop, eventually.'

Daniel sobered at the mention of the barbershop. He met Bec's eyes.

'What? I was joking!' her father said.

'Dad, there's something else you need to know.'

Daniel held out his hand, and Bec sank into the chair beside him.

'You sound serious.'

Bec outlined the incident succinctly and unemotionally, her eyes steady on her father's face. Daniel was so proud of her. His stomach roiled as he relived the words he'd overheard.

'The bastard!' His future father-in-law's gaze was glacial.

'I'm going to castrate the old goat,' said her mother.

'I'm sorry,' said Bec.

'What do you have to be sorry for?' asked her mother. 'You didn't encourage him.'

'No ...'

Daniel squeezed Bec's hand.

'But I should have said something a long time ago,' said Bec, speaking to the tablecloth.

'What are you talking about?' asked her father.

'It first happened when I was thirteen. I was studying in the shop.'

Bec's father wiped a hand across his face. 'In my shop? Where was I? Why didn't I protect you?'

'You didn't know.'

Her father shook his head. 'But I knew something had happened. You retreated into yourself for a while. And then when you re-emerged, you kept people at a distance. Not your mother and me, but other people. If a boy got too close, you dispatched him. We thought it was puberty – you know, all those hormones flying around.'

'How could I explain that words ... that a look ... could make me feel so violated? I thought I could take care of myself. I just made sure I was never alone with him. Of course, I couldn't avoid running into him around town, in the pharmacy, the grocer, but I always kept him at arm's length.'

Bec's mother's hand found hers. 'Did he ever ... touch you?'

'No, Mum.'

'Have you been to the police?' asked Bec's father.

'Tomorrow. I ... wanted to talk to you first,' said Bec.

'We'll go together,' said Daniel, squeezing Bec's fingers. 'The man needs to be restrained. And on top of the information you shared, they should have enough to act.'

Bec's father nodded. 'After his wife left him, he found religion. But not in a good way.'

Bec's mother was blinking back tears. 'We're so glad you were there, Daniel. Who knows what might have happened?' In a fierce voice she continued, 'Never keep anything like this from us again, you hear?'

In answer, Bec pushed back her chair and knelt at her mother's feet like a small child, wrapping her arms around her waist. 'I promise.'

Daniel exchanged a look with Bec's father, assuring him as best he could without words that he would take care of her.

'Now, if you'll excuse us, I'm going to steal my fiancée away for a walk. It's been a tumultuous few days.'

Bec breathed in the sea air and pulled up the collar of her coat – the wind had changed direction. Wet weather was expected. She and Daniel had retreated to their favourite place, the Botanic Gardens. At this time of night, they had the ornamental pond and its surrounds to themselves – although the occasional throaty growl suggested possums.

'What a weekend!'

Daniel nodded. 'Yes. I'm looking forward to returning to work for a rest.'

'No stamina,' teased Bec, swinging their joined hands.

'I wouldn't go that far.'

'I wasn't the one that retired from our ... exertions, earlier.'

Daniel stopped in the middle of the path, halting her momentum and tugging her into his arms. 'Unfair! You should thank me. As it is, your parents suspect something.'

Bec kissed the underside of his jaw. 'Mmm! I'm sure you'll parry away any improper suggestions.'

Daniel speared his fingers into the locks of her hair, tilting her face up to his. 'I thought I'd leave that to you. After all, I remember being told, on several occasions, that you could take care of yourself. That you were not my responsibility.'

'That was before.'

Daniel quirked an eyebrow.

'Before I realised that refusing to ask for help and locking my heart away aren't signs of strength and independence, they're expressions of weakness.'

Daniel kissed the tip of her nose. 'I'm loving the liberated woman more and more.'

'Me too. Thank you for your perseverance.'

'And patience.'

'And our endless conversations.'

'The ones without words?'

'Especially those,' Bec whispered before sealing his lips with hers.

HISTORICAL NOTE

It wasn't until August 1941 that women filled the role of tram conductor. Preference was given to wives of the Tramways Board employees serving abroad with Australian forces, followed by wives of other servicemen.

Opposition raged, including disgust that the war was being used as an excuse for introducing cheap labour, since women were paid less than men, and that the role would prove too physically demanding. But by November 1943, over 1000 tram conductresses were in the employ of the Tramways Board.

As part of their contract, these women signed statements that they would make way for the return of servicemen. WWII ended in September 1945, and by April 1946 only 400 women remained in the job. By August of the same year, there were only 138.

1920s
LANGUAGE

Alarm clock	The last person you want around when you're trying to have fun.
All get out	A Southern American saying. Often tacked on the end of a variety of expressions, it means 'extremely'. As in, 'She's as smart as all get out' or 'It was as loud as all get out.'
'Bama	Short for Alabama, a state in the south-eastern region of the United States.
Bearcat	A lively, spirited woman, possibly with a fiery streak.
Beef	An outstanding or unsettled disagreement with someone.
Claptrap	Absurd or nonsensical talk or ideas.
Collation	A light, informal meal.
Die in a ditch	Desperately resisting to the end.
Direction	Address.
Fire extinguisher	A chaperone who's killing the party vibe.
Glad eye	To look at someone in a way that shows you are sexually attracted to them.

Grip	The moving cable that started or stopped the tramcar.
Gripman	The cable-tram driver who operated the grip.
Handcuffed	Another 1920s slang term, meaning engagement ring.
High horse	An attitude of moral superiority.
M&mtb	Melbourne & Metropolitan Tramways Board.
Making sport	To ridicule, mock or tease someone.
Pulls in double harness	Marriage
Push his buttons	To do something that creates a strong emotional reaction in someone.
Put the wind up him	To make someone anxious, upset or frightened.
Speak with a forked tongue	To speak duplicitously or beguilingly.
Stanchion	An upright post.
Three sheets to the wind	To be drunk.

ABOUT VICKI MILLIKEN

Vicki Milliken is an Australian author who writes stories invested with humour and heart.

Her historical romances are told through 1920s heroines as they waltz, foxtrot and tango through life's storms during the period between the two world wars.

Vicki grew up living in many parts of Australia but calls Melbourne home.

When not writing, you can find her chaperoning her golden retriever on the local beach, cycling or drinking chai lattes. Most times in that order.

She's looking forward to the day her writing keeps her in champagne.

vicki@vickimilliken.com

www.vickimilliken.com

ACKNOWLEDGMENTS

Unsurprisingly, books don't spring from the fingers of an author to bookshelves and devices.

Editor Alexandra Nahlous and designers Pascal Han-Kwan and Sophie White are my talented and patient creative team. And then there's a host of family and friends who channel their support either in person or across the miles; and Courtney and Odhette, without whom characters and plots might never see the light of day.

Thank you!

PLEASE LEAVE A REVIEW

Reviews help authors to keep writing
and readers to find books.

If you enjoyed *Kiss by Kiss*,
please pop over to Goodreads

https://www.goodreads.com/vickimilliken

and leave a review.